DEAD MEN DON'T SKI

THE HENRY TIBBETT MYSTERIES
BY PATRICIA MOYES

A Six-Letter Word for Death
Angel Death
Who Is Simon Warwick?
The Coconut Killings
Black Widower
The Curious Affair of the Third Dog
Season of Snows and Sins
Many Deadly Returns
Death and the Dutch Uncle
Murder Fantastical
Johnny Underground
Murder by 3's (including *Down Among the Dead Men*,
Dead Men Don't Ski, and *Falling Star*)
Falling Star
Murder à la Mode
Death on the Agenda
Down Among the Dead Men
Dead Men Don't Ski

DEAD MEN DON'T SKI

by **PATRICIA MOYES**

An Owl Book

HOLT, RINEHART and WINSTON
New York

Copyright © 1959 by Patricia Moyes
All rights reserved, including the right to reproduce
this book or portions thereof in any form.
Published by Holt, Rinehart and Winston,
383 Madison Avenue, New York, New York 10017.

Library of Congress Cataloging in Publication Data
Moyes, Patricia.
Dead men don't ski.
"An Owl book."
I. Title.
PR6063.O9D38   1984   823'.914   84-6732
ISBN 0-03-000092-0 (pbk.)

First published in hardcover by
Holt, Rinehart and Winston in 1960.
First Owl Book Edition—1984

Printed in the United States of America
1 3 5 7 9 10 8 6 4 2

ISBN 0-03-000092-0

CHAPTER ONE

IT WAS JUST nine o'clock on a cold and clammy January morning when Chief Inspector Henry Tibbett's taxi drew up outside the uninviting cavern of Victoria Station. From the suburban lines the Saturday morning hordes of office-bound workers streamed anxiously through the barriers to bus and underground—pale, strained faces, perpetually in a hurry, perpetually late : but here, at this side-entrance that led into a sort of warehouse fitted with an imposing array of weighing-platforms, were assembled a group of people who looked as paradoxical at that hour and place as a troupe of Nautch girls at the Athenæum. They were not all young, Henry noted with relief, though the average age was certainly under thirty : but young or middle-aged, male or female, all were unanimous in their defiant sartorial abandon—the tightest trousers, the gaudiest sweaters, the heaviest boots, the silliest knitted hats that ever burst from the over-charged imagination of a Winter Sports Department. The faces were pale, true, but—Henry noted with a sinking heart—quite aggressively merry and free from any sign of stress : the voices were unnaturally loud and friendly. The whole, dingy place had the air of a monstrous end-of-term party.

" Will you pay the taxi, darling, while I cope with the luggage ? " Emmy's amused voice recalled Henry from his fascinated appraisal of the dog beneath the Englishman's skin.

" Yes, yes, of course. No, don't try to lift it . . . I'll get a porter . . ."

The taxi grumbled on its way, and Henry was gratified to see that a small porter with the face of a malevolent monkey, who had been lounging by the wall rolling a cigar-ette with maddening deliberation, now came forward to offer his services.

5

"Santa Chiara, sir? 'Ave you got skis to register through?" The porter almost smiled.

"No," said Henry. "We're hiring them out there. We've just got——"

But the porter had abruptly lost interest, and transferred his attentions to a taxi which had just drawn up, and which most evidently had skis to register through. A man with a smooth red face and unmistakably military bearing was getting out, followed by a bristling forest of skis and sticks, and a large woman with a bad-tempered expression. As the wizened porter swept the skis and sticks expertly on to his trolley, Henry caught sight of a boldly-written label —"Col. Buckfast, Albergo Bella Vista, Santa Chiara, Italy. Via Innsbruck."

"They're at our hotel," he muttered miserably to Emmy. She grinned. "Never mind. So are those nice youngsters over there."

Henry turned to see a group of three young people, who were certainly outstanding as far as good looks were concerned. The girl was about twenty years old, Henry judged, with short-cropped hair and brilliantly candid blue eyes. One of the young men was quite remarkably handsome, fair and grey-eyed, with very beautiful hands—at once strong and sensitive (" I've seen his picture somewhere," whispered Emmy). The other youth did not quite achieve the standard of physical perfection set by the rest of the party—he was tall and thin, with a beak of a nose and dark hair that was rather too long—but he made up for it by the dazzling appearance of his clothes. His trousers, skin-tight, were pale blue, like a Ruritanian officer's in a musical comedy: his sweater was the yellow of egg-yolks, with geranium-red reindeer circumnavigating it just below the armpits: his woollen cap, in shape like the ultimate decoration of a cream-cake, was royal blue. At the moment, he was laughing uproariously, slapping a spindly blue leg with a bamboo ski-stick.

"Good heavens," said Henry. "That's Jimmy Passendell

—old Raven's youngest son. He's . . ." He hesitated, because the idea seemed ludicrous—" . . . he's a member of Lloyd's."

At that moment a burly porter, evidently deciding that the time had come to clear the pavement for newcomers, seized Henry's luggage unceremoniously, tucking a suitcase under each arm and picking up the other two with effortless ease ; and with a bellow of "Where to, sir ?" he disappeared into the station without waiting for an answer.

Henry and Emmy trotted dutifully after him, and found themselves beside a giant weighing machine, which at the moment was laden with skis.

"Which registered ?" asked the porter laconically, twirling Emmy's dressing-case playfully in his huge hand.

" I'm afraid I don't quite understand about . . ." Henry began, feeling almost unbearably foolish. Everybody else obviously understood.

" Registered goes straight through—Customs here— don't see it again till Innsbruck," said the porter, pityingly.

" We'll register the two big ones," said Emmy firmly.

For the next few minutes Henry trotted between luggage, porter, and ticket office like a flustered but conscientious mother bird intent on satisfying her brood's craving for worms—the worms in this case being those cryptic bits of paper which railway officials delight to stamp, perforate, clip, and shake their heads over. Eventually all was done, the Customs cleared, and Henry and Emmy were safely installed, with the two smaller cases, in the corner seats reserved for their journey to Dover.

Henry sank back with a sigh in which relief was not unmingled with apprehension. For the moment they had the carriage to themselves, and the screaming chaos of the luggage shed had given way to the sounds of muted excitement which precede the departure of a long-distance train.

" I suppose the Yard know what they're doing," said Henry. " Because I don't. I wish we'd decided to do our skiing somewhere else."

"Nonsense," said Emmy. "I'm enjoying myself. And I haven't seen anybody in the least suspicious yet, except the taxi-driver and that screwed-up porter."

Henry gave her a reproving, walls-have-ears glance, and opened his *Times*, turning gratefully to the civilised solace of the crossword puzzle.

Henry Tibbet was not a man who looked like a great detective. In fact, as he would be the first to point out, he was not a great detective, but a conscientious and observant policeman, with an occasional flair for intuitive detection which he called " my nose". There were very few of his superiors who were not prepared to listen, and to take appropriate action, when Henry said, suddenly, " My nose tells me we're on the wrong lines. Why not tackle it this way ?" The actual nose in question was as pleasant—and as unremarkable—as the rest of Henry Tibbett. A small man, sandy-haired and with pale eyebrows and lashes which emphasised his general air of timidity, he had spent most of his forty-eight years trying to avoid trouble—with a conspicuous lack of success.

"It's not my fault," he once remarked plaintively to Emmy, " that things always seem to blow up at my feet." The consequence was that he had a wide and quite undeserved reputation as a desperado, an adventurer who hid his bravura under a mask of meekness : and his repeated assertions that he only wanted to lead a quiet life naturally fed the flames of this rumour.

Emmy, of course, knew Henry as he really was—and knew that the truth about him lay somewhere between the swashbuckling figure of his subordinates' imagination, and the mild and mousy character he protested himself to be. She knew, too—and it reassured and comforted her—that Henry needed her placid strength and good humour as much as he needed food and drink. She was forty now—not as slim as she had been, but with a pleasantly curving figure and a pleasantly intelligent face. Her most striking feature was her skin, which was wonderfully white and fair, a piquant contrast to her curly black hair.

She looked at her watch. " We'll be off soon," she said. " I wonder who else is in our carriage."

They very soon found out. Mrs. Buckfast's voice could be heard raised in complaint a full corridor away, before she finally entered the carriage like a man-o'-war under full sail. Her seat, naturally, was the wrong one. She had definitely been given to understand that she would have a corner seat, facing the engine.

" I can only say, Arthur," she said, her eyes fixed on Henry, " that reservations seem to mean absolutely nothing to *some people*." Unhappily, Henry offered her his seat. Mrs. Buckfast started, as though seeing him for the first time ; then accepted the seat with a bad grace.

Soon a cheerful commotion in the corridor heralded the arrival of Jimmy Passendell and his party. (" Seven in a carriage is *far too many*," Mrs. Buckfast announced to nobody in particular.) The girl became engrossed in the latest copy of *The Tatler*. Colonel Buckfast nodded briefly at the handsome young man, and said, " Back again this year, eh ? Had a feeling you might be." The young man remarked that he hoped the snow would be as good as it had been the year before, and proceeded to cope expertly with the baggage, even coaxing a sour smile from Mrs. Buckfast by lifting a large number of small cases up to the rack for her. Jimmy Passendell immediately counteracted this momentary lightening of the atmosphere by producing a mouth organ and inviting the company to join him in the chorus of " Dear Old Pals ".

" After all," he remarked brightly, " we soon shall be— we're all going to Santa Chiara, aren't we—to the Bella Vista." After a pause, he added, " Yippee ! " The pretty blonde giggled ; the handsome youth looked uncomfortable; the Colonel and Henry retreated still further behind their respective *Times* ; Emmy laughed outright, and produced a tin of digestive biscuits, which she offered to all and sundry.

The young people fell on them with whoops of delight, and for a time conversation was mercifully replaced by a contented munching. The train moved slowly out of Victoria into the mist.

The channel was grey and cold, but calm. The skiers clumped cheerfully up the gangplank in their resounding boots, and made a concerted dash for the warmth and solace of the saloon, dining-room or bar according to temperament. As the steamer moved slowly away from the dockside and out of the narrow harbour entrance, Henry and Emmy had the deck to themselves. They leant over the rail, savouring the peace, the absence of strident human voices, and watching the familiar outline of the cliffs grow dim in the haze.

" There's nobody else going to Santa Chiara," said Emmy, at last. " And none of that lot look like dope-peddlers to me, whatever other failings they may have."

" The whole thing's probably a wild goose chase," said Henry. " I hope it is. Heaven knows I don't want any trouble. I want to learn to ski. After all, we are on holiday."

" Are we ? " Emmy gave him a rueful smile. " Just pure coincidence that we're going to the hotel which Interpol thinks is a smugglers' den?"

" It was just my luck to pick that particular place," said Henry, ruefully. " And when Sir John heard we were going there, I couldn't very well refuse to keep my eyes open."

" Interpol know you're going to be there, though, don't they ? "

" Yes—unofficially. They've no evidence against the place as yet—only suspicions. They were thinking of sending one of their own chaps to the Bella Vista as an ordinary holiday-maker, but when Sir John told them I was going anyway——"

Behind them, a familiar voice boomed. " It was *clearly* understood that we would travel first-class on the boat . . ."

" Let's have a drink," said Henry, hastily, and piloted Emmy down the companionway to the bar.

It was crowded, smoky and cheerful. Henry battled his way between young giants to the counter, and secured two Scotches and two hundred cigarettes for a laughable sum. By the time he had fought his way back to Emmy, she had already installed herself in the last remaining chair in the bar, and was chatting amicably to the fair girl, whose escorts were storming the bar in search of duty-free cognac.

" Oh, well done, Henry. Come and meet Miss Whittaker." Emmy seemed for some reason to stress the surname as she said it. Heavens, thought Henry. Somebody I ought to know. The girl beamed at him.

" Miss Whittaker sounds too silly," she said. " Please call me Caro."

Henry said he would be delighted to, and gave Emmy her drink. A moment later the handsome, fair-haired young man emerged from the scrum at the bar, laden with glasses and bottles. Caro fluttered into a whirl of introductions. This was darling Roger—Roger Staines, actually—who was a *frightfully* good skier and was going to shame them all— but *shame* them—and this was Henry and Emmy Tibbett and they were going to the Bella Vista—actually to the same hotel—wasn't that too extraordinary and blissful, Roger darling ? Then darling Jimmy arrived with his ration of duty-free, and the party made merry, while the grey sea-miles slipped away under the keel, and the seagulls wheeled purposefully over the writhing white wake of the ship.

Calais was a scramble of porters, a perfunctory interlude with the Customs, a trek along seeming miles of platform— and eventually all five travellers were installed in Compartment E6 of a gleaming train, which had a showy plaque reading " Skisports Special " screwed to its smoking flanks. The hand-luggage was stowed away neatly above the door, and the first bottle of brandy opened (by Jimmy). The great train heaved a spluttering sigh, and pulled smoothly out of the station, heading south.

" And here we are," said Jimmy, " until to-morrow. Have some brandy."

France rolled away behind them in the already deepening dusk. Henry did his crossword ; Emmy dozed ; Jimmy took another swig of brandy ; Caro read her magazine, and Roger stared moodily out of the window, a sulky look of bad temper ruining his impeccable profile. A small man in a leather jerkin, wearing a red armband embroidered with the words " Skisports Ltd." in yellow, put his head into the carriage.

" I'm Edward, your courier on the train," he announced brightly, blinking through thick-lensed spectacles. " Anything you want, just ask me."

" Have some brandy," said Jimmy.

Edward tittered nervously, refused, and withdrew. They heard him open the door of the next compartment.

" I'm Edward, your courier on the train. If there's anything——"

" There most certainly is, my man." Mrs. Buckfast's voice rose easily above the rhythmic pulse of the wheels. They could hear it rumbling on in discontent even when the unfortunate Edward had been lured into the carriage, and the door firmly shut behind him.

A few minutes later, Caro got up and went into the corridor, where she stood leaning on the window rail, looking out at the darkening fields, the lighted farmhouse windows, the tiny country stations, as they flashed past, tossed relentlessly from future to past by the insatiable, mile-hungry monster of which they were now a part.

Emmy glanced after Caro, suddenly awake, then settled herself to sleep again. Roger Staines got up from his corner seat, and went out into the corridor, slamming the door behind him. He stood beside Caro, two backviews, inexpressive, lurching with the movement of the train, Henry could see that he was talking earnestly ; that she was replying hardly at all. He could not hear what they were saying.

At five o'clock the lights of the train came on suddenly, and at six-thirty the bell sounded merrily down the corridor for First Dinner. Jimmy consulted his ticket and found that he was, indeed, due to dine at the first sitting : so, collecting Roger and Caro who were now leaning relaxedly against the carriage door, smoking and chatting idly, they went off with considerable clatter down the corridor towards the dining-car.

It seemed very quiet and empty when they had gone. Henry got up and shut the door carefully. Then he said, " Roger Staines . . . I wish I could place him. . . ."

" I've remembered where I've seen his picture—in the *Tatler*," said Emmy. " He's what they call a deb's delight. Look——"

She picked up the magazine that was lying on the seat where Caro had left it. It was open at one of the familiar pages which report so tirelessly on the night-life of London, and there was a photograph of Roger and Caro toasting each other in champagne. " Miss Caroline Whittaker, Sir Charles and Lady Whittaker's lovely daughter, shares a drink and a jest at the Four Hundred with her favourite escort, Mr. Roger Staines," said the caption, coyly. Henry looked at the picture for a full minute, thoughtfully. He said again, " I wish I could place him— further back. Quite a bit further back."

" Goodness, I'm hungry," said Emmy. " Have a biscuit."

The train sped on towards the frontiers of Switzerland.

Henry and Emmy shared their table at Third Dinner with Colonel and Mrs. Buckfast. The latter, having obviously had the time of her life making mincemeat of poor Edward, was in a comparatively good humour, and agreed to take a glass of Sauternes with her fish ; she even pronounced the food eatable. Her husband, evidently cheered by this unaccustomed serenity, became conversational over the coffee.

"Your first time on skis?" he asked Henry, his smooth red face aglow with affability.

"Yes, I'm a complete rabbit, I'm afraid," Henry replied. "My wife's done it before."

"Only twice," said Emmy. "I'm no good at all."

"Finest sport in the world," said the Colonel. He glanced round belligerently, as if expecting instant contradiction. Mrs. Buckfast sniffed, but said nothing. "My wife doesn't ski," he added, confidentially. "Jolly sporting of her to come out with me, year after year. I appreciate it. Of course, I'd absolutely understand if she wanted to stay behind and let me go alone . . ." His voice took on a wistful note.

"The mountain air is good for me," said Mrs. Buckfast, flatly. "I find ways of passing the time. It really wouldn't be fair to let poor Arthur do this trip all by himself."

"I've often told you—" he began, but she cut him short with a "Pass the sugar please, Arthur," that brooked no further discussion. There was a short silence, and then the Colonel tried again.

"Been to Santa Chiara before?" he asked.

"No."

"Interested to know what attracted you, if you're not a keen skier. Not everybody's cup of tea—hotel stuck up all by itself at the top of a chair-lift. Can't get down to the village at all after dark, you know."

"They told us the skiing was excellent," said Emmy, "and we wanted peace and quiet more than anything."

"Then you certainly picked the right spot," said Mrs. Buckfast, sourly. "I dare say," she went on, with ill-concealed curiosity, "that your husband has been working very hard. Perhaps his job is a very exhausting one."

"No more so than any other business man's," said Henry. "It's just a question of temperament, I suppose. We always like quiet holidays, off the beaten track."

" So you're a business man are you ? How very interesting. In the City ? "

" Not exactly," said Henry. " I work in Westminster."

Mrs. Buckfast, foiled in her attempt to extract more information about Henry's profession, went on. " Quite a distinguished party going to Santa Chiara this year. Caroline Whittaker, who had that huge ball at Claridges last year, and the Honourable Jimmy Passendell—" her voice sank to a whisper—" Lord Raven's son you know. A bit *wild*, I understand, but charming . . . so charming . . ."

" The other lad seems pleasant, too," said Henry. " Roger Staines. I seem to know his face."

" I know nothing about him," said Mrs. Buckfast, with great firmness. " *Nothing*," she added, " whatsoever."

When Henry and Emmy got back to E6, the triple tiers of bunks had been set up, but the party showed no signs of going to bed. Jimmy had opened another bottle of brandy, and was leading the company in a variety of more or less bawdy songs. Henry and Emmy accepted a nightcap gratefully, and then suggested that they should retire to bed on the two top bunks, out of everyone's way. " Don't mind us old drears," said Emmy. " Sing as loud as you like. We enjoy it."

" Jolly decent of you," said Jimmy. " Have another drink before you embark on the perilous ascent." He said the last two words twice to make sure of getting them right. Caro was smiling now, sitting in the corner and holding hands with Roger.

In fact, the singing only went on for half an hour or so, before the whole party decided to get some rest. Caro took one of the two middle bunks, Roger and Jimmy the two lowest. Soon all was dark and quiet, except for the tiny blue bulb that burned in the ceiling, the soft breathing of the sleepers, and the thrumming wheels on the ribbon-stretch of rails. In his tiny compartment at the rear of the last coach, Edward cursed Mrs. Buckfast steadily, and with satisfaction, as he compiled his passenger list: between him and the engine driver, the sinuous length of train was all asleep.

At breakfast time next morning they were miraculously among mountains. True, the railway itself ran through wide, flat green valleys, like the beds of dried-up lakes, but all around the mountains reared proudly, fresh green giving way to grey rock, to evergreen, and finally, high above, to glistening white snow. All along the train, voices and spirits rose. The sun shone, and the snow, suddenly real, suddenly remembered, was a lure, a liberator, a potent magic. Soon, soon. . . .

The Austrian border was left behind at half-past nine: by eleven the train was winding along the broad green valley of the River Inn, ringed by lofty mountains: at eleven-twenty precisely, the engine drew to a hissing, panting halt, and a guttural voice outside on the platform was shouting "Innsbruck! Innsbruck!" into the crisp, sunny air.

CHAPTER TWO

At Innsbruck, the compact phalanx of skiers who had travelled *en masse* from Victoria dispersed abruptly : hotel buses or small, energetic mountain trains bore them off to their respective Austrian resorts. Only the Santa Chiara party remained, suddenly rather desolate, suddenly rather out of place in their aggressive sweaters. Edward, who had come in for some uncomplimentary remarks from E6 on the train, now seemed like their last—and faithless—friend, as he hurriedly compiled his reports, and headed for his overnight lodgings in Innsbruck.

Inevitably the cameraderie of isolation manifested itself. Jimmy fetched a cup of coffee for Mrs. Buckfast, the Colonel carried Emmy's overnight case up the subway for her, Roger (with a superior command of German) collected the registered baggage, and Emmy and Caro ventured together in search of the Ladies'. Henry, feeling rather out of things, contented himself with buying enough English magazines at the bookstall to keep the whole party happy until teatime, when they were due at their destination. Eventually all seven travellers, complete with luggage, were assembled on the correct platform to catch the Munich-Rome express, which was to carry them on the penultimate stage of their journey.

Evidently not many people wanted to exchange the exhilarating sunshine of Innsbruck for the uncertain joys of Rome in January, for nobody else was waiting for the train except an elderly couple who, Henry guessed, had been marketing in Innsbruck and were probably going no farther than Brenner, the frontier town. A few minutes before the train was due, however, a flurry of porters and expensive luggage appeared from the subway, followed by a tall and very thin man, dressed in a sort of Norfolk jacket made of bright green tweed, with a fur collar, and dark grey trousers

17

of extreme narrowness. His face was long, and creased with deep lines of intolerance, and his lean, vulpine features were crowned incongruously by a green Tyrolean hat. With him was a girl of striking beauty : she had the face of a Florentine Madonna, with deep golden hair swept smoothly back from a broad brow and coiled on the nape of her neck. She wore pale grey ski trousers cut by a master, and a little grey jacket with a collar of snow leopard that framed her face like a cloud. Her make-up—in the Italian manner—emphasised her magnificent dark eyes, and her honey-coloured skin, while her full, lovely mouth was brushed lightly with a wild-rose pink. "Very, very expensive," Emmy whispered to Henry, as the procession of porters swept past.

Mrs. Buckfast gazed after the newcomers with uninhibited curiosity : Caro looked sheepish, suddenly conscious of her crumpled, slept-in trousers : the men, involuntarily, turned to admire, and were rewarded by a scowl from under the Tyrolean hat.

When the train pulled in, dead on time, and they had secured an empty carriage for the party without difficulty, Henry and Emmy went to the window to take a last look at Innsbruck. To their surprise, Tyrolean Hat was on the platform alone, obviously saying good-bye to the Madonna, who stood, cool and beautiful, at the window of a first-class compartment. There were kisses, protestations of affection, fussings over baggage—all of which the girl received with what looked more like dutiful resignation than enthusiasm. At one point, when the man was engaged in some sort of altercation with the porter, Henry caught her looking at him with an expression of mingled contempt and dislike which was chilling in its intensity. At last the whistle blew, and the train started. The last view of Innsbruck was of a Tyrolean hat waving, somehow pathetically, on the end of a long, thin arm.

At Brenner, after a short and amicable interlude with the

Italian Customs, the whole party filed down the corridor to the dining-car. The young people secured a table for four, and the Buckfasts a table for two : Henry and Emmy, arriving last, were ushered by a smiling waiter to the last table in the car—a four-seater at present occupied by one person only, the Madonna from Innsbruck. She was ordering her meal in fluent Italian, completely relaxed, spontaneous and excited—a very different person from the cool beauty of Innsbruck station. "Like a little girl out of school," Henry thought.

Throughout a delectable meal that started with *fettucini* and meandered through *fritto misto con fagiolini* to a creamy *bel paese* cheese, there was more concentration on food than on conversation. With the coffee, however, a pleasantly replete and relaxed mood took over ; the beauty made the first move by inquiring in excellent English whether Henry and Emmy were from London, and were they holidaying in Italy ? They said they were.

"So am I," she said, with a ravishing smile of pure happiness. "I am Italian, you see. But my husband is Austrian, and there we must live, in Innsbruck."

"I envy you," said Henry. "It must be a beautiful city."

"Yes," said the girl, shortly. Then, smiling again— "But where do you go ? Rome ? Venezia ? Firenze ? "

"As a matter of fact, we're going to ski," said Emmy.

"Oh ! I, too."

"Perhaps we might even be headed for the same place," Henry suggested.

"I am sure we are not," said the beauty. "You go to Cortina, of course. All English and Americans go to Cortina."

"No," said Henry. "We're going to a little place called Santa Chiara. The Albergo Bella Vista."

To his surprise, the girl's smile faded abruptly, and for an instant a look of sheer panic crossed her face.

"Santa Chiara," she said, almost in a whisper. "I . . . I go there, too."

"Well, how nice," said Emmy, quickly. "We must introduce ourselves. We are Henry and Emmy Tibbett."

"And I . . ." There was an unmistakable hesitation. Then the girl seemed to shake herself, like a puppy coming out of the sea, and her smile flashed again. "I am the Baroness von Wurtberg. But you must call me Maria-Pia. When I am in Italy, I forget that I have become an Austrian."

There was a tiny pause.

"My children are already at the Bella Vista, with the fraulein," the Baroness went on. "Hansi is eight, and Lotte six. You will meet them."

"I'll look forward to that," said Emmy, suppressing her instinct to remark that the Baroness looked ridiculously young to have an eight-year-old son. "What a pity," she added, daringly, "that your husband can't be with you, too."

Once again the panic flickered in the huge, brown eyes. "He is very busy, he cannot get away. He lets me—I mean, he likes me to return to my country each year, but he does not love Italy."

"I bet he doesn't," thought Henry, remembering the harsh features under the Tyrolean hat. He felt very sorry for the Baroness and did not know how to convey his sympathy without seeming impertinent : so he quickly paid his bill and, with friendly assurances that they would meet again soon, ushered Emmy down the dining-car. As they went, Henry felt, curiously, those magnificent eyes following him. At the door he turned, to meet the Baroness's quiet, quizzical gaze. She looked him full in the eyes, and raised her head very slightly, as if in defiance. Henry, somewhat embarrassed, smiled and stepped into the swaying corridor.

At Chiusa, they made their last change. The great express rushed on southwards towards Verona, leaving the nine travellers standing in the sunshine on the little country station. All round them, the Dolomites broke the skyline with their warm, pink summits—flat rocks, pinnacled rocks, shapes whittled by wind and snow into primeval patterns of frightening strength and durability ; the strength of the very old, the very tough, that has endured and will endure, for time beyond thinking.

From the majesty of the mountains, a shrill tooting brought the party back to reality. There, on the opposite line, stood the most endearing train in the world. The engine—tiny, of 1870's vintage, with a tall, slender chimney and gleaming brasswork—headed just two coaches made of pale, fretted woodwork, with elaborate iron-railed observation platforms at each end. The Gothic windows of one carriage were chintz-curtained, marking them as First Class. The seats throughout were of slatted wood, with overhead racks for skis.

The young English exclaimed with delight, and made a concerted scramble for the train with their cases, closely followed by Henry and Emmy. Mrs. Buckfast remarked that it was high time they put new coaches on this line—the wooden seats were a disgrace. The Baroness, with every porter in the place at her heels, walked slowly across the flat railway track with an expression of pure love on her face. The luggage was loaded, the train shrilled its whistle, and the last lap of the journey began.

As the crow flies, it is about twenty miles from Chiusa to Santa Chiara : as the railway line winds, it is over thirty —thirty miles of tortuous, twisting track, of hairpin bends on the edge of precipices, of Stygian, smoky tunnels, of one-in-five gradients, and of some of the most breathtaking views in the world. Almost at once, they crossed the snow-line, among pine trees. Soon Chiusa was just a huddle of pink and ochre houses far below. Valleys opened out gloriously, houses lost their Italianate look and became steadily more and more Alpine, with wooden balconies and eyebrows of snow on their steep, overhanging eaves. Up and up the engine puffed and snorted, nearer and nearer to the snowfields and the pink peaks. At village halts, white-aproned peasant women clambered on and off the train with baskets of eggs and precious green vegetables. Then they saw the first of the skiers. Round a steep bend, a glistening nursery slope opened up alongside the railway line, peopled with tiny, speeding figures. Excitement rose, like yeast. Up and up the train climbed, through three small resort villages, until at last a pink, onion-domed church came into view, clustered about with little houses.

"Santa Chiara," said the Baroness.

They all craned to look. The village was set at the head of a long valley—a valley of which the floor itself was over 5,000 feet above sea-level. All round, the mountains stood in a semi-circle, at once protective and menacing. The village seemed very small and very brave, up there in the white heights.

There was not, strictly speaking, a station. The train, showing signs of exhaustion, clanked and rumbled to a halt in the middle of a snowfield near the church : here, by a small green-painted shed, several hotel porters waited with their big luggage sledges, while skiers returning to the village for tea zoomed in an uninhibited manner across the railway line.

As the Baroness got out of the train, there was a sudden flurry as two diminutive skiers hurtled down the slope, crossed the railway tracks, and swung round in perfect parallel cristiania turns to stop dead in a spray-shower of snow beside the train.

"Mamma ! Mamma !" they yelled, and the Baroness dropped her white pigskin dressing-case in the snow and rushed to embrace them. The reunion was noisy, sentimental and rather moving : it was not for several moments that Henry noticed a slender, dark girl in black who had skied quietly but extremely competently down to the train behind the children, and now stood a few paces away, silently watching the out-pourings of affection. She was very pale, in sharp contrast to the bronzed faces all round her, and she wore no make-up. She might have been beautiful, Henry thought, had she taken even the most elementary steps to make herself so : as it was, she seemed to concentrate on self-effacement, on anonymity.

The first greetings over, the Baroness—one arm round

each of her children—beamed at the dark girl and spoke to her in German. Then she said to Emmy, " I go now with Gerda and the children for tea. The porter will take you up to the Bella Vista, so I shall see you at dinner."

She gave instructions in rapid Italian to a burly porter who had " Bella Vista " embroidered in gold on his black cap, and then, as the children skied slowly down the hill to the village street, she ran after them, laughing and teasing, trying to keep up with them. The dark-haired Gerda let them get near the bottom of the slope, then launched herself forward with a lovely, fluid movement, and took the gentle hillside in a series of superbly-executed turns, gathering speed all the way, so that she was waiting for the others at the bottom, as still and silent as before.

As the porter loaded the baggage on to his sledge, Colonel Buckfast spoke for the first time that Henry could remember since Innsbruck.

" Look," he said, pointing upwards.

They all looked. Behind the railway line, the mountains reared in white splendour : by now, the sun had left the village, but lingered on the rosy peaks and on the high snow-fields. Far up the mountain, where the trees thinned out, just on the dividing line between sunshine and shadow, was a single, isolated building, as dwarfed by its surroundings as a fly drowning in a churn of milk.

" The Bella Vista," said the Colonel, almost reverently.

There was a silence.

" I didn't realise it was so far up," said Emmy at last, in a small voice. " How do we get there ? "

" We get there," said Mrs. Buckfast, " in a diabolical contraption known as a chair-lift. Every year I say I'll never do it again, and every year Arthur talks me into it. The very thought of it makes me feel sick. This way."

The Monte Caccia chair-lift, as all the brochures emphasise, is one of the longest in Europe. The ascent takes twenty-five minutes, during which time the chairs, on their stout overhead cable, travel smoothly and safely upwards, sometimes over steep slopes between pine trees, a mere twenty feet from the ground, more frequently over gorges and ravines which twist and tumble several hundred feet below. About once a minute, the strong metal arm which connects the chair to the cable clatters and bumps as it passes between the platforms of a massive steel pylon, set on four great concrete bases and equipped with a fire-broom and a sturdy snowshovel in case of emergencies. For parts of the trip, the lift travels above the *pistes*, or ski runs, giving the passengers a bird's-eye view of the expertise or otherwise of the skiers below. It is one of the coldest forms of travelling known to man.

Henry was amused to see the varying reactions of the party (including himself) when faced with this ascent—especially when the first-timers grasped the fact that the chairs did not stop at any point, but continued up and down on an endless belt, so that one had to " hop " a moving chair as it passed.

The Colonel slid expertly into his chair, and waved his hand from sheer exhilaration as he soared skywards: Mrs. Buckfast took her seat competently, but with resignation, having grudgingly accepted the bright red blanket proffered by the attendant. Caro, glancing at the seemingly endless cables stretching up the mountainside, turned rather pale and remarked that she hadn't imagined it would be quite like this, and that heights made her dizzy.

" Don't worry, you'll get used to it in no time," said Roger, briskly. " There's absolutely nothing to be frightened of. I'll be in the chair right behind you. Just put down the safety-bar, and then relax and enjoy the view."

Caro showed no signs of enjoying herself, but she got on to the next seat without further demur, clutching a little desperately at the vertical metal arm, like a nervous child on a roundabout, as the chair sped upwards. Roger exchanged a joke in Italian with the attendant, and had time to discover that his name was Carlo and that the lift stopped working at seven o'clock each evening, before he slipped casu-

ally into his chair, leaving the safety arm flapping. Jimmy
made a loudly facetious remark about dicing with death,
which made Henry suspect that he was genuinely appre-
hensive, but he hopped his chair gamely enough, the neck
of a brandy bottle protruding from his hip pocket. It seemed
to Henry that he had had to wait an eternity for his turn,
but in fact the chairs came round so rapidly that it was less
than a minute after the Colonel had boarded the lift that
Henry—only partly reassured by Emmy's encouraging
smile—found himself waiting in the appointed spot for the
next down-travelling chair to complete its circuit by clank-
ing round the huge wheel in the shed ; a couple of seconds
later it came up and hit him in the back of the knees. He
sat down, and the ascent began.

The ride up to the Bella Vista was certainly cold : and
over some of the more precipitous ravines Henry found it
advisable to keep his eyes focused stubbornly on the
heights to come, rather than glancing down to the huddled,
snowy rocks below. But there was a magic, too, in the slow,
steady, silent ascent—silent, that is, apart from the clatter
and rattle each time the chair passed a pylon : and yet the
unnerving effect of this noise was counteracted by a momentary sense of security, for the inspection platform of the
pylon passed a mere eighteen inches below his dangling
feet, and, noticing that a steel ladder led down from the
platform to the ground below, Henry hoped fervently that
if the lift did decide to break down, it would do so when
he was passing a pylon, rather than at a moment when he
was suspended over a precipitous gorge.

To the right, about ten feet away, was the downward
cable of the lift, on which a procession of empty seats followed each other towards the valley with the stately melancholy of a deserted merry-go-round. Just occasionally,
however, a down-going chair was occupied—generally by
a booted and be-furred lady of uncertain years. It was very
much, Henry reflected, like being on an escalator in the
London underground, watching the faces that glided down-

wards as one ascended, to come face to face and level for a
fleeting moment before the inexorable machinery churned
on. When it came to scenery, however, all resemblance
disappeared. Instead of the garish rectangles of advertisement which London Transport provides for the entertainment of its passengers, there were vistas of snow, cloud and
mountain, of pine trees and pink rock, of misty valleys and
sun-touched peaks. At last, a tiny hut came into view at the
top of an open snowfield—the trees were all but left behind.
As the chair approached, a little wizened man with a walnut-
brown face stood ready to take Henry's arm and help him
as he slid maladroitly out of the chair before it clattered on
round the wheel to begin its descent.

Emmy came sailing up serenely on the next chair, slipped
gracefully out of it, and came over to stand beside Henry.

" Well," she said, " here we are. And isn't it wonderful ? "

Far, far below them, Santa Chiara looked like a toy
village laid out on a nursery floor, the miniscule houses
dotted haphazardly round the apricot-pink church. Ahead,
over the ridge where the ski-lift ended, a shallow, saucer-
shaped sweep of snowfields stretched away to still more
mountain peaks ; and to the right, round the bend of a snow-
banked path, was the Albergo Bella Vista. The rest of the
party were already walking up the path to the hotel, stopping
every few yards to draw each other's attention to some fresh
beauty. Henry and Emmy followed them slowly, hand in
hand and very much at peace.

CHAPTER THREE

ONE OF THE charms of mountain architecture is its consistency. The deep eaves and steep roof-tops, the wooden balconies and shuttered windows, have been universal above a certain altitude for centuries—simply because they are functional, providing the greatest comfort and security for men living among the snows. So the Albergo Bella Vista looked exactly like any other mountain chalet, with its neat mosaic of stacked firewood nudging one wall, its balcony-veranda and pale wooden shutters pierced with heart-shaped holes.

In the hall—floors and walls of honey-coloured waxed pine—a man in a light blue suit, plump as a capon and with sparse grey hair trained carefully to hide his pink baldness, was oozing welcome.

"Allow me to present myself . . . Rossati, Alberto . . . welcome to the Bella Vista, *meine Herrschaften* . . . ah, welcome back Colonel Buckfast . . . Herr Staines . . . if you would kindly sign the register . . . this way, *bitteschoen* . . . may I have your passports, please . . ."

One by one the travellers signed in, surrendered passports, were allotted keys. By this time the luggage had arrived, having made the ascent on one of the two tray-shaped luggage-carriers attached to the chair-lift. At last all was sorted out, and Henry and Emmy found themselves alone in their bedroom. It was of light wood, like the rest of the building—the floor bare of carpets, yet warm to the touch, for an enormous radiator shimmered heat from below the window. The big intricately-carved bed had, in place of blankets, two vast white downy quilts, a foot thick and light as thistledown. A very large wardrobe, a plain deal dressing-table, a wash-basin and two upright chairs completed the furniture.

An exchange in Italian with the chambermaid elicited the information that a bath was certainly available, at the price of 500 lire.

"That's more than five shillings," said Henry, outraged.

"Baths are always a terrible price in the mountains," said Emmy, cheerfully. "I never reckon on having more than one a week. But just at the moment I think it would be cheap at a pound."

So they bathed luxuriously, and changed into clean clothes, and by a quarter to seven were ready to face the world and an apéritif.

The bar ran the whole length of the building, one side of it being composed entirely of windows, which gave on to the veranda. It was dark outside, for the moon was not yet up, but still the snow glimmered faintly white below the ink-black sky. The furniture consisted of little tables covered in red gingham table-cloths, milk-white wooden chairs, and a long chromium bar with stools upholstered in deep red leather. On the bar, inevitably, an Espresso machine hissed and wheezed like a cauldron of snakes. Henry and Emmy perched themselves on stools, and a dark, smiling girl served them with Campari-sodas. There was only one other customer in the bar—a man who sat at a table in the farthest corner and toyed with a glass of tomato-juice.

Indicating the stranger with the tiniest nod of her head, Emmy whispered, "Doesn't look like a skiing type to me."

Henry half-turned to look. He saw a small, smooth man in his fifties : everything about him was chubby, from his fat little fingers caressing the stem of his glass to his short, stumpy feet, whose outline could not be disguised by his tapering suède shoes. His face was pink, round and benevolent, with small eyes that twinkled obscurely behind thick-lensed spectacles.

After a minute or so Signor Rossati, the proprietor, came into the bar. He went quickly over to the man in the corner, and spoke to him quietly in German. The man nodded amiably, finished his drink, and the two went out together, deep in conversation. They crossed the hall, and Henry heard the door of Rossati's private office click shut, cutting off the voices.

" Our host seems to be bilingual," Emmy remarked.

" Nearly everyone is, in these parts," Henry replied. " We're only just over the Austrian border, you know, and this province was part of Austria until 1919. Italian is the official language now, but German comes far more naturally to a lot of the people—especially in the smaller villages."

" Does it rankle at all, I wonder—being handed over arbitrarily to Italy ? " asked Emmy.

" Officially, no. Unofficially—yes, of course. But strictly under the surface. Nothing must upset the tourist trade." Henry turned to the barmaid. " Do you speak English—*parla Inglese* ? " he asked.

She giggled, shook her head, and said she didn't.

" *Tedeschi* ? "

Her face lit up. " *Ja, ja.*" A quick stream of German followed, but Henry just smiled and shook his head negatively. To Emmy, he said, " You see ? I'm not letting on I understand her, because I don't want our English chums to know I speak German or Italian. But you heard what she said ? "

" She went too fast for me," said Emmy. " My German isn't all that good, you know. The best that can be said for it is that it's better than my Italian."

" Well," said Henry, " she was saying that German was her mother-tongue, and she'd be delighted to speak it with us since we don't know Italian. It would be quite a relief, she said."

Suddenly the hall outside became shrill with a babble of Italian voices and a cheerful stamping of boots.

" The *sci*-lift . . . finish . . ." said the barmaid.

Through the open door, Henry saw the Baroness following Gerda and the children upstairs. A man's voice said, " Maria-Pia . . ." and she stopped, letting the others go on ahead of her. A dark young Italian, in extremely elegant royal blue ski-trousers, moved into Henry's line of vision. He stood at the foot of the staircase, and placed a hand on the Baroness's arm, restraining her, and talking urgently but softly. Gently, she freed her arm, shaking her head, but he caught her hand in his, pulling her down the stairs towards him. At that moment, Gerda reappeared round the bend of the staircase, her pale face impassive. Abruptly, the young man released the Baroness's hand, made some laughing remark, and ran upstairs past the two women, taking the steps two at a time. Gerda said something to the Baroness and they walked upstairs together. Meanwhile, Henry was amazed to see Colonel Buckfast and Roger Staines come in, dressed in full skiing regalia, their boots caked in snow.

" *Signori Inglesi* . . . very much *sci* . . . already to-day . . ." said the barmaid, trying hard. " Co-lon-el Back-fist, he *sci molto* . . . you not *sci* ? "

" Not yet," said Henry.

" There's a nasty, icy side-slip halfway down Run Three," the Colonel was saying, in the hall. " Sensible of you to stick to Number One."

" I'm taking Run Three first thing in the morning," said Roger, defensively. " I just thought the light was a bit tricky for it this evening."

" Very wise. Never run before you can walk," said the Colonel, maddeningly. Then, in a lower tone, he added, " That cove Fritz Hauser is here again. Remember him ? I saw him in Rossati's office as I went out. Don't like the fellow."

" Hauser ? Oh yes, the fat little German . . . was here last year . . . can't think why he comes when he doesn't ski . . ."

They went upstairs.

Dinner started gaily enough. The Baroness, ravishing in black velvet trousers and a white silk shirt, sat alone—but talked merrily and loudly to the dark young Italian, who also had a table to himself. Gerda, presumably, took her dinner upstairs with the children, for there was no sign of her. The Buckfasts (Mrs. Buckfast resplendent in lilac crêpe) made quite a thing about their "usual" table, which was no different from any other, but somehow established seniority. Henry and Emmy, at Jimmy's expansive invitation, joined up with the three young English at a large table in the middle of the room. The other diners were an unmistakably German family—a comfortably plump, blonde woman in her forties, an upright, sallow-faced man with a deep scar on his cheek, and a buxom girl, presumably their daughter, who wore no make-up, had her hair twisted into unbecoming ear-phone plaits, and never spoke a word. At a table in the corner, Fritz Hauser ate alone, rapidly and with serious concentration.

Roger was full of his first run of the season.

"The snow's still difficult," he announced, pontifically. "Not quite enough of it, unfortunately—it was far better this time last year. Still, it's quite simple if you know how to manage it."

"I for one certainly don't," said Henry. "I intend to enrol in the ski school first thing to-morrow morning."

There was a chime of agreement from Jimmy and Caro.

"I'll come along with you," boomed Colonel Buckfast from his table, not to be outdone by Roger. "Just to introduce you, of course. I know them all down there. Splendid lot of chaps. You want to get Giulio, if you can. Best instructor in the place. Failing him, his brother Pietro. They're the sons of old Mario, you know—man who works the top end of the chair-lift. Used to be the star instructor himself until he crocked himself up."

The Colonel settled back in his chair with a comfortable affability, delighted at having established his claim to local knowledge.

Before anybody else could speak, the Baroness said quietly, "Giulio is dead."

"What!" Roger dropped his spoon into his soup plate with a clatter, swinging round to look at the Baroness. Then,

conscious that his own party were staring at him, he muttered, " I mean, I knew him quite well. He taught me when
I was here last year."

" I say—I'm damned sorry to hear that," said the Colonel,
who had turned a deep raspberry red. He looked genuinely
distressed, but whether on account of Giulio's death, or
because somebody else had found out about it before he
had, Henry could not be certain.

" How did it happen, eh ? " the Colonel went on. " He
was only a lad."

" It was a skiing accident, so they told me in the village,"
said the Baroness. After a pause, she added : " Last week."

" He was a young man of great . . . great foolishness."
The dark young Italian joined in, speaking very earnestly,
partly from deep sincerity and partly because he found
English difficult. " This was not surprise. If not ski . . .
then that so-rapid automobile he drive . . . no chains . . . he
must die."

" He was on the Immenfeld run, just over the Austrian
border," the Baroness went on. " It's very dangerous terrain
there, and the run was definitely prohibited because of the
snow conditions. But just because it was forbidden, Giulio
must attempt it. He was like that. They found him at the
bottom of a crevasse. One ski was still on his foot. The
other ski and his sticks they never found."

There was an awkward pause.

" Poor old Mario," said the Colonel at last, wiping his
moustache with his napkin.

There was a clatter of wood on wood as Fritz Hauser got
up and replaced his chair neatly at his table. Only he and
the German family seemed quite unmoved by the conversation. " They probably don't understand English," thought
Emmy.

Hauser stopped at the Germans' table, said something in
a low voice to the girl, and crossed the room to the door.
There he paused, as if taking a decision. Then he turned,
and said in good English to the room in general : " This

idiot Giulio is dead. So—it is his own fault. He disobeyed orders. Let it not be a discouragement to other skiers." He gave a curious little bow, and walked out.

"What a vile little man," said Caro.

"Yet it is true what he was saying," said the Baroness. "There is nothing to fear if one is sensible. Only the foolish come to grief."

"That's what I always say." Mrs. Buckfast spoke firmly and surprisingly. "You just have to be a little careful." All at once, Henry had an extraordinary impression of tension, as if each remark had more than its surface meaning, as if purposeful streams of innuendo were being directed by the speakers towards—whom? Everybody? One other person? He glanced round. Caro was looking uncomfortable, her eyes on her plate. Roger had pushed his food away, and seemed really distressed. The Colonel brooded, chin on chest. As quickly as it had come, the impression faded, became ridiculous. The Baroness remarked that it was a great tragedy, but that these things happened, and they mustn't let it spoil their holiday. She added that since the ice had now been broken, she'd like to introduce them all to Franco di Santi—the dark young Italian—who was a sculptor from Rome, whom she had met here on a previous visit. "So we are old friends," she added, with a dazzling smile.

This restored the conversation to normal, and when they had all professed themselves delighted to know Franco, Roger asked the Colonel pointedly if he intended to try the Gully—which was, as he explained to the others, the most direct but also the most precipitous route from the hotel to the village. The Colonel answered tartly that he had made enquiries about it, and that the *piste* was closed until further notice, owing to the extremely dangerous state of the run. Fearing that this might lead the conversation back to Giulio's foolhardiness, Emmy asked Roger how the residents of the Bella Vista generally spent their evenings, isolated as they were. Roger brightened up and said there was a damn good radiogram in the bar, and why didn't they all go and dance ?

"What about that poor little German wretch," said Jimmy *sotto voce*, indicating the other table. "Let's ask her to join us."

"Yes, let's," said Caro, in a stage whisper. "The poor thing looks too bullied for words."

Henry hoped for politeness' sake that the German family did not understand English : certainly they gave no sign of knowing that they were being talked about, but continued to plough stolidly through monoliths of cheese and dishes of gherkins.

"You ask her, Roger old dear," said Jimmy. "You're the expert in Hun-talk."

"Yes, go on, Roger darling," said Caro.

With some reluctance, Roger got up and went over to the other table. They saw him exerting his not inconsiderable charm as he proffered the invitation : his reception, however, was quite brutally abrupt. Before the girl could say a word, her father rasped out a curt refusal, and all three got to their feet and stumped out of the dining-room. Roger returned to the table looking crestfallen and angry.

"Charming, I must say," he remarked, dropping into his chair again.

"What did he say, the old pig ? " asked Caro, solicitously.

"Just bellowed that it was out of the question, and dragged the poor kid off before she could open her mouth," Roger answered.

"A maiden in distress . . . how splendid." Jimmy was enjoying himself, and his conspiratorial glee was infectious. "We must rescue her from the dragon's clutches. Who knows where her room is ? "

Caro volunteered that she had seen the girl coming out of the room opposite hers on the top floor. " And my room's at the back," she added, " so hers must be over the front door."

"All right then," said Jimmy. "We'll wait until they've

all gone to bed, and then Roger and I will climb up to her balcony and serenade her——"

"Don't be silly, everyone would hear you," objected Caro.

"We'll serenade her very quietly," said Jimmy, a little severely. "Then she can leave a bolster in her bed and creep downstairs . . ."

Still plotting delightedly, they all adjourned to the bar. ". . . and if that old bastard comes down and makes a scene," Jimmy was saying, "I promise you I'll——"

He stopped abruptly. From the bar came the strains of a sentimental Neapolitan love song, recorded by a lush tenor to an accompaniment of dreamy guitars: and through the open door they could see the persecuted damsel waltzing sedately with Fritz Hauser, while her parents sipped coffee and Italian brandy at a table.

Emmy burst out laughing. "So much for your maiden in distress," she said.

Poor Jimmy came in for a lot of good-natured teasing, which he took with his usual equanimity. Soon they were all dancing. The Baroness danced once with Roger and several times with Franco, and then said she was exhausted and wanted to be up early next morning to ski. Soon after she had gone, Henry and Emmy decided that they, too, were ready for bed, and Franco agreed with them. When they left, Roger and Caro were demonstrating the cha-cha-cha to Jimmy, while Colonel Buckfast ordered just one more brandy, positively the last to-night, and Mrs. Buckfast complained that the Italians would never learn to make good English coffee.

Lying in bed, Emmy reached out a hand to put out the light, and said, "Poor Jimmy. His Sir Galahad act fell a little flat."

"Yes." Henry's voice was heavy with sleep. "Still, who knows . . . he may need it again one of these days . . ."

Emmy raised herself on one elbow. "You mean she wasn't enjoying herself with Hauser?"

" Well, would you ? "

" I don't know. He seems quite a reasonable little fellow. Henry——"

" Mm." Henry was almost asleep.

" Henry, do you think the Baroness came here for a secret assignation with Franco di Santi ? He's terribly good-looking, and I'm certain he's in love with her . . ."

" Oh, go to sleep," muttered Henry into his pillow.

In the silence that followed, the sound of the gramophone drifted up faintly to them, rhythmic and cloying. Emmy's last waking thought was of the unknown young man, Giulio, lying frozen and alone at the bottom of the ravine, with one ski still strapped to his foot.

CHAPTER FOUR

THE NEXT MORNING, Colonel Buckfast made it clear that he intended to be as good as his word and accompany the beginners to ski school.

"It's in Santa Chiara," he explained, "but once you've enrolled and got the whole thing organised, I'll try to persuade them to send an instructor up here for you each day. For this morning, you'd better go down on the lift, and I'll meet you at the bottom."

Roger announced his intention of trying some of the new ski-hoists which had been installed only that season in the other valley, on the far side of the hotel from the village.

"Ah, yes, the nursery slopes," said Colonel Buckfast. "Sensible chap to change your mind about Run Three."

Roger glared, but said merely that he would see them for lunch. Mrs. Buckfast installed herself in the sunshine on the veranda, her comfortable wicker chair ranged alongside those of the German couple and Fritz Hauser, who appeared in dark glasses the size of saucers and natty leopardskin boots.

The Colonel strapped on his skis, and, calling out that he'd see them at the bottom and what a glorious morning, by Jove, set off down a narrow track which was signposted with an arrow and a bold numeral 1. The others trooped off down the path to the chair-lift.

Already skiers were coming up: not every chair was occupied, but there were enough arrivals to keep Mario busy. Henry watched the little man as he bustled good-naturedly about his work, and wondered why he had failed to notice the previous evening that he had a pronounced limp —presumably the result of the "crocking up" to which the Colonel had referred. Mario certainly seemed to be a popular figure. Every skier who came up knew him, and he greeted nearly all of them by name, remarking on the

dismal lack of snow in the merriest possible manner. If he
was heart-broken at his recent bereavement, he did not show
it : but Henry sensed that as a life-long skier the old man
would accept the risks involved with philosophic fatalism
—and he knew, too, the code of honour observed in districts
which depended on tourism for their prosperity. Never must
personal distress be displayed in public : the show must go on.

Henry had expected the ride down to be, if anything, even
dizzier than the ride up—but he was wrong. It was, in
fact, a delightful, Olympian sensation to glide silently
earthwards between the tree-tops towards the village below
—as Apollo or Mercury might descend to intervene in the
small affairs of mortal men. It was also much warmer, in
the growing heat of the sun. As they went down, chair
after chair passed them going up—there were no empty
seats now—and Henry noticed that everybody coming up
had removed their skis for the ride, and placed them across
their laps instead of using the safety-bar.

Carlo helped them off at the bottom, and took their ticket
money: and there, by the turnstile, was the Colonel, skis
on shoulder, beaming welcome and breathing in great
draughts of clear mountain air.

"Come along, then," he boomed, cheerfully. "All
present and correct ? Right. First stop, the ski shop."

As it turned out, he was extremely efficient and helpful.
First he escorted the English party to a small, dark, raftered
shop smelling of hot wax and pinewood, where they were
fitted up with hired skis and sticks, and—in the case of
Henry and Emmy—with boots as well.

Next, they all trooped off to a small, blue-painted building
in the village street, where they enrolled for ski school and
paid for a week's instruction in advance. Emmy, with her
superior experience, was allotted to Class Two (she modestly
refused to attempt a higher class until she had had some
practice, which earned a nod of approval from the man at
the desk). This meant that she would have to ski or take
the lift down to the village every morning to join her class,

unless they proposed to start their day's runs from the Bella
Vista : but since there were four beginners at the Bella
Vista (including, they discovered, the German girl, who
was referred to by everybody at the ski school as " poor
Fraulein Knipfer ") and as it was early in the season and
therefore quiet, it was agreed that a special beginners' class
should be formed there, and that an instructor should come
up each morning to them. The Colonel put in a strong
plea—in execrable Italian—for Pietro Vespi, old Mario's
second son : and since he was apparently one of the few
instructors who spoke any English, this too was arranged.

" Pietro will meet you at two-thirty for your first lesson,"
said the man at the desk, handing them their ski-school cards.

This business satisfactorily concluded, the Colonel went
off to the ski-lift again for a few more runs before lunch, and
the others decided to explore the village and do some shopping. " You won't get English cigarettes, I warn you," called
the Colonel from the ski-lift queue. " And the only shop
that sells American is the *generi misti* opposite the Hotel
Stella. Rosa Vespi runs it . . . Mario's wife . . . nice woman
. . . tell her I sent you . . ." He disappeared through the
turnstile.

Santa Chiara is much like any other Alpine resort. A
long, straggling village street runs from the massive white
bulk of the Hotel Stella at one end to the architecturally
weightless apricot-pink church at the other. The food
shops, the wine shops, the hardware shop and the chemist's
are small and dark, for they cater for the villagers. In
contrast, two gleamingly modern sports shops display
tempting windows-full of the beautiful sweaters, silk
scarves and anoraks which the Italians design so supremely
well, flanking this delectable merchandise with ranks of
shiningly colourful skis and sticks. Every shop, no matter
what its stock-in-trade, has racks of picture postcards—
glossy and sepia-tinted for 20 lire, or in crudely unjust
colours for 30 lire.

The English party roved happily, window-shopped,

bought postcards. They soon realised that at that hour—it was half-past eleven—the life of the village was centred in the bars and cafés. These were numerous, and at varying levels. A décor of advanced colours—purple and orange —and modern ebony furniture from Milan characterised the smart Bar Olympia : red plush and candles in birdcages breathed Old Vienna into Alfredo's : chromium and shabby *art nouveau* set the Café Paloma firmly in its lower position in the hierarchy : while not only the scrubbed wooden tables and benches, but also the very name of the Bar Schmidt put it virtually out-of-bounds to visitors. Here it was that the locals drank their beer and vermouth, and said what they thought of the tourists : only when a visiting skier had achieved really good terms with the villagers was he ever invited into this *sanctum sanctorum*, which was the real heart of Santa Chiara, from which circulated the life-blood of the village—gossip. Finally, the English tourists settled for coffee at the Olympia.

" It's sure to be fiendishly expensive," Jimmy complained. It was. It was also charming, and the coffee was excellent.

As they had all realised in their loneliness on Innsbruck station, the English and Americans have not yet discovered Italy as a winter sports' country. No other English voices greeted them. The Olympia was full of beautifully-dressed Italian and French women, who had elected to spend the morning in leisured chatter while their husbands skied : there was a sprinkling, too, of more homely Germans and Austrians. Many heads turned in interest at the sound of English voices : here was fresh grist for the mill of conversation.

At the next table sat two Italian girls, darkly lovely and expensively pampered. As she drank her coffee, Emmy caught the words " Maria-Pia von Wurtburg " from the spate of Italian behind her. Her foot touched Henry's under the table, and he nodded almost imperceptibly. When the two girls had gone, Emmy said she really must get some cigarettes, and Henry agreed to walk with her to Rosa

Vespi's shop, while the others had a second cup of coffee.

Outside, she grabbed his arm. " Come on, spill the dirt. What were they saying ? I'm dying to know."

" I always thought you didn't listen to gossip," said Henry, reprovingly.

" Oh, don't be beastly. Do tell me."

He grinned. " Very well then. You aren't the only one who thinks Maria-Pia is up to no good," he said. " They talked as if they used to know her pretty well in Rome before she married. They also know Franco di Santi. Apparently he hasn't a penny to his name, and they seem to think the Baroness is sailing pretty close to the wind. I gather her husband is in no mood to be trifled with."

" I could have told you that. You only had to look at him . . ." Emmy shuddered slightly. " Poor Maria-Pia."

" I wonder why she married him when she hates him so much," said Henry.

" She may not actually hate him——"

" Oh, yes, she does. Did you watch her face at Innsbruck ? "

" Yes, but——"

" Here we are," said Henry. They had stopped outside a small, crowded shop which displayed a sign reading *Generi Misti.* The stock was certainly both general and mixed. Great barrels of spaghetti and macaroni of every shape and colour jostled festoons of children's shoes strung up like Breton onions ; picture postcards (of course) shared a counter with sugared almonds and cheese ; Parma ham glowed pinkly delicious beside disorganised heaps of sunglasses ; graceful flasks of Chianti dangled from hooks alternately with salami and mortadella and snow-boots. The shop had a mingled smell of garlic, dust, cheese and liquorice which was quite irresistible. There was no sign of any cigarettes whatsoever.

Behind the counter, a stout woman in black, wearing a spotless white apron, was engaged in weighing out juicy black olives on a pair of bright brass scales. Her strong brown face was creased with lines of laughter, and she chattered incessantly to her customer—a tiny boy in a ragged cloth cap.

" *Eccoli !* " Rosa Vespi threw another couple of olives on to the already tipping scales, and deftly made up a paper cone, through which the black juice oozed as the boy clutched the package in his small fingers.

" Signora Vespi ? " Henry asked.

" *Si, Signore.* "

" *Non parlamo Italiano,* " said Emmy firmly.

" *Ah, Inglese ?* " Signora Vespi beamed. " *Sigarette Americano, no ?* "

" Yes, please, " said Henry.

There was a flurry of black petticoats as Rosa Vespi lowered her considerable bulk to rummage in the dark depths under the counter. Flushed and triumphant, she rose again like Aphrodite from the waves, with four packages of Camels.

Henry proffered a 5,000-lire note, newly-cashed at the hotel. Rosa clucked over it, scraping for change in the battered drawer which served as a till, like a hen scraping for worms in the dust. Eventually, not being able to raise enough grubby notes or bright tin coins, she beamed at them reassuringly, said, " *Momento, signore* " several times, and disappeared through a door behind the counter which led to the family's living quarters.

Through this open door, Henry had a good view of the parlour—a small room ponderously furnished with large, shabby pieces of mahogany and horsehair, and liberally decorated with plaster statuettes of some six or seven assorted saints. Two items in particular, however, caught the eye. The first was a very new and obviously expensive radiogram, which stood incongruously under the drably-curtained window. The second was an elaborate sort of shrine made out of black crêpe and black paper laurel leaves, which occupied the centre of the mantelpiece : a small candle flickered at either side of it, and in the centre a sepia-tinted photograph of an excessively handsome young man with jet-black hair stared arrogantly from behind looped rosaries. This could be none other than Giulio, the young ski instructor who had died so tragically—Rosas' son. Henry could not help wondering whether this ostentation of mourning—so at odds with Signora Vespi's apparently cheerful mood—was no more than pious window-dressing, a mere gesture towards parental grief, or whether it represented the true, deeply-hidden sorrow of a family which could not afford any public appearance of heart-break.

Within a minute or two, Rosa re-appeared with the change, and shut the door carefully behind her. Henry and Emmy thanked her, promised to call again soon, and stepped out of the darkness of the shop into the blinding sunshine of the village street.

They found Jimmy waiting for them outside the Olympia. Caro, he told them, had finally been unable to resist the lure of Italian sweaters, and had disappeared with her Travellers' Cheques into the glossier of the two sports shops. "Which means, old man," said Jimmy, with gloomy earnestness, "that the blasted girl won't have a bean from now on, and guess who'll have to pay for every ruddy thing."

With that, he stalked off to retrieve the errant Caro, his blue knitted cap bobbing ludicrously above his gaunt, lanky figure.

As they walked up the hill towards the chair-lift, Emmy said, "I'm somehow surprised at Jimmy being worried about money—he must be terribly rich."

"He only has the same currency allowance as the rest of us," Henry reminded her.

"I know, but——"

"Hey, there!" yelled a voice from above them. They looked up the mountain, where the ski-run emerged from the trees to cross the last field to the foot of the chair-lift. A ski-stick waved energetically, and they recognised the Colonel—recognised him, that is to say, by his clothes, for otherwise there seemed nothing whatsoever in common between the weighty, cumbersome Colonel as they knew

him, and this avian figure speeding downwards towards
them with all the grace of a swift in flight. This was a
totally unsuspected Colonel Buckfast—a Colonel who had, as
it were, not only found but actually become the blue-bird.
As they watched him, fanaticism became reasonable. For a
few brief weeks each year, they realised, the Colonel
entered his own element : became a man liberated from his
life, his wife, his environment, his own limitations . . .

The graceful figure swung in a snow-scattering arc to
stop beside them, and instantly became familiar—an over-
hearty, portly, cliché-ridden, middle-aged man, making
maddeningly predictable little jokes as he stamped the snow
off his skis.

They all went up on the chair-lift to lunch.

Roger had evidently returned early from his morning's
skiing, for when the others came into the hall they saw him
in the bar, chatting with Fritz Hauser, the only other
occupant. While everybody else headed for their rooms,
Henry saw that Caro had walked over to the open door of
the bar, and was standing there, as if hesitating whether or
not to go in.

When the others came down again, Hauser had disappeared. Caro and Roger sat at the bar drinking Cinzano,
and the Knipfers had established themselves at a corner
table with *steins* of beer. There was no sign of Maria-Pia
or Franco, who had left early in the morning with packed
lunches ; but the children were playing a noisy and complicated game in the lounge-hall, where Fraulein Gerda sat
quietly reading—only looking up at intervals to say " Hansi
. . . Lotte . . ." with such unemphatic authority that there
would be silence for at least half a minute afterwards.

At lunch, the Colonel suggested to Roger that they
might try a few runs in company : he seemed anxious, in
his present mood of exuberant bonhomie, to make amends
for his unkind remarks about Run Three. Roger agreed,
and the two of them went off together to the ski store, dis-

cussing the merits of various grades of ski-wax for the prevailing conditions. Henry noticed that they both carried little boxes of different-coloured waxes in their pockets, and they spent much time and care anointing the backs of their skis before they finally set out.

Mrs. Buckfast announced that she positively could *not* spend another three hours in the Knipfers' company.

"They did nothing," she confided to Henry, in a stage whisper, "but *eat*. Disgusting. Mr. Hauser is quite pleasant but he's had to go to Chiusa on business. So I shall just lie down for a little while, and then take the lift down to the village for tea."

Emmy went down on the chair-lift to join her class, and Henry, Jimmy, Caro, and Fraulein Knipfer were left on the terrace, their skis lined up neatly against the wall, waiting for Pietro and their first lesson. At precisely half-past two, they saw the brilliant red of an instructor's anorak coming round the bend of the path that led to the lift.

It is, of course, traditional for ski instructors to be handsome. But Pietro was outstanding even among ski instructors. He was tall and spare, with a classically perfect face burnt nut-brown by the sun : his eyes were as dark and blue as sapphires : when he smiled, his teeth glistened whitely —and he smiled a great deal. Henry could detect at once a family likeness to the ill-fated Giulio—but whereas the latter's hair had been black, Pietro was as blond as a Botticelli angel, his hair burnished and glinting in the sunshine.

"Good afternoon," said this vision, in excellent English. "I am Pietro, your instructor. May I have your ski school cards, please, so I may learn your names ? "

So the first lesson began. To start with, Pietro made them climb laboriously up a small mound on their skis, standing sideways to the slope, and tramping up, ski above ski, until their leg muscles ached. Then he showed them how to balance on their skis, how to bend their knees and throw their weight forward. After this, he invited them to follow him down the gentle incline. One by one they

launched themselves, gathered speed, flailed the air wildly
with their sticks, and sat down—all except Jimmy, that is,
who remained upright not so much from a natural aptitude
at skiing as from an extreme sense of caution which prevented
him from moving at all. This was in sharp contrast to Caro,
who launched out fiercely, and maintained a fairly good
position at speed for some three seconds before she came
gallantly to grief, head-first. Fraulein Knipfer, who had
been having lessons for nearly a week, was obviously a
ragged mass of nerves and hated every minute of it.

"Courage, Fraulein! Faster! Faster!" shouted Pietro
encouragingly, in German. The poor girl made a stab at
the snow with her sticks in a half-hearted effort to increase
her speed, and promptly fell over. Henry began to feel
sorry for Pietro, whose patience seemed inexhaustible.
They were all pretty bad, he reflected, but after all it was
only their first day. He could see already that by to-morrow
they would have left the fraulein behind, simply because she
was too pathetically frightened even to try to learn.

After a few more runs, it became clear that Caro, with her
blithe abandon, was going to be the star pupil of the class.

"Bravo, Miss Caro!" Pietro called, as she took the little
hill far too fast, and then attempted a turn at the bottom.
Caro somersaulted into soft snow. "You are impatient,
Miss Caro. That we learn to-morrow." Clearly, Pietro
was delighted.

Jimmy remained caution personified.

"You too need courage, Mister Jimmy," said Pietro,
which made Jimmy furious.

"I'm not nearly as bad as the Knipfer girl," he whispered
crossly to Henry. Jimmy had been utterly confident that
there was really nothing difficult about skiing, that one only
needed enthusiasm and the rest would come easily. It was
not working out like that.

"Bend ze knees," shouted Pietro. "Lean *forward*,
Mister Jimmy . . . no, no, not to stick out behind . . ."

"I'll get it right if it kills me," remarked Jimmy, emerging like a snowman from a soft bank which he had just entered headfirst. He went on doggedly practising while the others were having their turns.

Henry turned out to have the makings of a good, steady, average skier. "A little more *coraggio*, a little more to concentrate, and we will make you ski good, Mister Henry," said Pietro—more kindly, Henry felt, than he deserved. Then they all climbed the tiny hill to try it again.

So, during the first afternoon, the commonplace miracle occurred. Three pairs of feet (it is impossible, alas, to include Fraulein Knipfer's) had started the lesson convinced that never, *never* would these great, unwieldy planks be anything but sharp, skiddy death-traps : and by four o'clock, these same feet had learned to accept and use their skis, as practical and delightful extensions of their own function : and each of the beginners had experienced, even if only for a brief moment, the quiet glory of a smooth, swift, silent descent.

The lesson over, they returned to the hotel in high spirits, feeling like veterans already.

"I," announced Caro, her mouth full of cream cake, "am *madly* in love with Pietro."

"Don't be so conventional. It doesn't suit you," said Jimmy, a little acidly. "It's frightfully suburban to fall for your ski instructor. And anyway, I think he's conceited."

Caro was up in arms at once. "Why must you always pick on anyone I like" she said, warmly. "You'd be conceited if you were as beautiful as that and skied like an angel and—" She stopped suddenly in mid-sentence, and said in quite a different tone, "Wherever can Roger be ?"

"He went off with Colonel Buckfast," said Henry. "I daresay they'll be back soon."

"The Colonel's back already," said Caro. She got up and went over to the window. Sure enough, there was the Colonel, skis on shoulder, heading for the little lean-to ski-store at the back of the hotel.

"Oh, for heaven's sake, don't panic, Caro," said Jimmy, easily. "Roger can look after himself."

Caro said nothing, but stood looking out of the window at the Colonel's backview as it retreated through the dusk.

A moment later, Emmy and Mrs. Buckfast arrived, having come up on the lift together.

"Wonderful, wonderful," said Emmy, throwing herself into a chair. Her cheeks were glowing, and her short black hair glistened with still-unmelted snow. "Darling, I'm a bit better than I thought I was. I'm to be promoted to Class Three to-morrow. We did Run One twice, and the second time I only fell once. How did you get on?"

"I fell twenty-five times," said Henry, with a touch of pride. "I counted."

"Damn it, I forgot to count," said Jimmy. "I bet I beat you, though."

"Caro's the prodigy of our class," said Henry. "She's going to be really good."

"And guess what," added Jimmy, "She's fallen in love with——"

"Don't tell me—the ski instructor." Emmy laughed. "Caro, how could you?"

Caro wheeled round from the window. "I wish you'd all shut up," she said. Abruptly, she walked over to the door, and almost collided with Colonel Buckfast. To everybody's surprise, she grabbed his arm.

"Colonel Buckfast," she said, "where's Roger?"

"Young Staines? Not a bad skier. Not bad at all. Could have used him in the Team in the old days, with a spot of training. Mad about speed, of course, like all the youngsters. We ended up with a shot at Run Three, and we did it . . . not very well, but we did it."

"But where is he?" Caro persisted.

"I can tell you where he is," said Emmy. "He's having tea at the Olympia."

"By himself?" asked Caro, rather too loudly.

Emmy glanced at Henry. "No," she said. "He's with Fritz Hauser. They must have met in the village. I saw

them going in there together while I was waiting for the
lift up."

"So there you are, silly," said Jimmy. "The precious
boy friend's safe and sound, if in dubious company."

Caro had gone rather white, but she managed a smile,
and said, "I'm sorry. I'll go and have a bath, I think."
And she ran upstairs.

"What a fidget that girl is," remarked Mrs. Buckfast.
"I only hope she doesn't take all the hot water." She
produced a sheaf of picture postcards from her enormous
handbag, and began to write energetically.

Half an hour later, Roger came up on the lift, greeted the
others shortly, and went up to his room to change. It was
not until after seven that Henry saw Hauser picking his
way, delicately as a cat, up the path, having presumably
come up at the last possible moment, before the lift stopped
for the night.

Dinner that evening was an uneasy meal, owing to the fact
that Roger and Caro were obviously quarrelling. Not all
Jimmy's breeziness or Emmy's determined good humour
could gloss over the fact that Roger's handsome face was
set in lines of stubborn bad temper, or that Caro was
ominously silent. The Baroness and Franco di Santi were
now sharing a table and a degree of warm intimacy which
was in itself enough to cause a pang of disquiet to anyone
who remembered the harsh face under the Tyrolean hat at
Innsbruck. Only the Knipfers, the Buckfasts and Hauser
appeared quite at ease. Mrs. Buckfast was well in her stride,
complaining successively of cold soup, tough veal and a
draught, while the Colonel withdrew into his own cocoon
of silence, happily re-living the day's sport : Hauser ate
with rapid, finicky movements, like a bird, speaking to no-
one, and again claimed Fraulein Knipfer as a dancing partner
in the bar afterwards.

Roger and Caro both disappeared after dinner. At nine
o'clock, Jimmy said, "What on earth are those two doing ?
I'm going to look for them."

He went out of the bar, and returned in a few minutes with both of them in tow. To Henry's relief, they seemed to be on better terms than they had been at dinner.

"What have you been up to?" asked Emmy, smilingly. "Secret skiing practice? Or something more sinister?"

"Of course not," said Roger, shortly.

"I'll vouch for them," said Jimmy. "All very innocent. I found them playing pencil and paper games, of all things."

Caro only stayed long enough to have a cup of coffee, and then went off to bed. Jimmy drank brandy and tried to flirt, in excruciating Italian, with Anna, the barmaid. Roger talked skiing to the Colonel, while Mrs. Buckfast did her knitting. Maria-Pia and Franco sat at a table in the corner, speaking very little. Even when Gerda, the children's fraulein, came downstairs in a severely simple black dress, and Roger persuaded her to dance, the Baroness apparently did not even notice. Henry and Emmy, alone at the table, grinned at each other.

"Any clues, Mr. Holmes?" said Emmy.

"Too easy," said Henry. "I'm just waiting for something to happen. Meanwhile let's forget it and enjoy ourselves." They did.

Life at the Bella Vista soon fell into a pleasant pattern. Breakfast at nine, ski school from ten till twelve, lunch and ski-talk until two-thirty, more skiing until half-past four. Then came tea at the Olympia—after a few days even the beginners were tumbling and slithering down Run One to the village—and the final ride up to the Bella Vista for drinks, dinner and dancing.

On the fourth night, the snow fell: and over the new, light, powdery surface, even Class One began to feel well on the way to becoming expert. They had learnt, now, to snow-plough—putting the tips of their skis together to slow down or stop: and to do stem turns by transferring the weight to one foot or the other in the snow-plough position. They had experienced the fascinating, muscle-aching sensation of traversing diagonally across and down a steep slope (" Lean *out* from the mountain . . . out into the valley, Mister Henry . . . watch as Miss Caro does it . . . and BEND ZE KNEES . . ."). Now they were tackling the sideslip—skidding sideways down icy slopes, their skis flat against the mountain-side—defying, as it seemed to them, all the laws of nature and gravity by leaning outwards over the valley to maintain their balance. This proved the most difficult manœuvre they had yet encountered, and they all fell many times (" That is not side-slip, Mister Jimmy . . . that is back-slide . . ." Pietro laughed hugely at his small standard repertoire of English witticisms).

Fraulein Knipfer, following a long and earnest talk with Pietro after ski school one day, had left the class and embarked on private lessons with a middle-aged and lugubrious instructor called Giovanni—much to the relief of the others. Every day, the two incongruous figures could be seen on the gentle slopes near the hotel, Giovanni proceeding downhill at tortoise-pace, with the facial expression of a bored bloodhound, while the girl—rigid with nerves and misery—came tumbling clumsily after him.

On Friday evening, after their fifth day of skiing, the English party were surprised and pleased to find Pietro in the bar of the Bella Vista when they came out from dinner. He was chatting over a drink with Fritz Hauser, who had dined early : but on the arrival of the English, the little German moved away to join the Knipfers. Pietro beamed.

" I eat at home, and come up before the ski lift finish," he explained. " To-night is full moon, so I may ski down when I wish."

After waltzing politely with Emmy, Pietro proceeded to monopolise Caro for the rest of the evening. She was in high spirits, and obviously revelled in the flattering attentions of the handsome young instructor. Roger, apparently in no way put out, disappeared upstairs and came back about ten minutes later with a protesting Gerda, whom he insisted must make up the party.

As usual, Maria-Pia and Franco went up to bed early. They had made no attempt to join in the dancing, but had been sitting at a remote table, talking earnestly. Henry thought that they both looked extremely worried, and even frightened, and he noticed that they both glanced frequently in Hauser's direction.

Everybody else, however, succumbed to the general air of gaiety, and stayed up late. Fritz Hauser danced energetically with Fraulein Knipfer, and the two elder Knipfers surprised everybody by taking the floor and giving an extremely competent demonstration of the Viennese waltz. Roger danced with Gerda, only once or twice glancing sharply at Caro and Pietro, who were swaying cheek to cheek, oblivious to everyone else in the room. Hauser and the Knipfers finally went up to bed soon after one o'clock, but the party went on. Henry, like everyone else, drank rather too much *grappa*, and he was glad that it was Pietro and not he who was setting out on the moonlight run to Santa Chiara at half-past two in the morning. They all turned out in the bitter cold to speed him on his way.

There was something ghostly but breathtakingly beautiful about the mountains glimmering in the icy moonlight, and it was good to see the lights of the village twinkling reassuringly from the valley. Joining the village and the hotel, the ski-lift made a slender rope of light—for after dark a single lamp was switched on at each pylon, throwing out a warm, yellow circle of illumination on to the blue-white snow. Pietro snapped on his skis and set off. They strained to watch his graceful, rapid figure as it disappeared into the trees, appeared again briefly where the *piste* crossed underneath the chair-lift, and finally plunged out of sight into the woods below.

The next morning, they all woke up with slight hangovers, and skied rather worse than usual in consequence: otherwise, there was no intimation of impending disaster. Which was strange.

CHAPTER FIVE

THE DAY PASSED like any other, marked only by small incidents which took on a significance—merited or otherwise—in the light of what followed.

At breakfast, Hauser called for Signor Rossati and asked for his bill. He would leave, he said, by the last train that evening, but was going down into Santa Chiara during the morning and did not expect to return to the hotel. The Baroness, as usual, breakfasted in her room; but on his way to fetch his skis, Henry noticed her with Hauser in the deserted bar, talking rapidly and with much emotional gesture. She looked up as Henry passed the door, and he caught again the same expression of panic that he had seen on the train. A moment later, Franco di Santi came out of the kitchen with two packed lunches under his arm, and called her away. Henry was still waxing his skis when the two of them came into the shed. They collected their skis, and went off together without a word.

Pietro was talking to Mario at the top of the lift when the class assembled. He saw them, put his arm round his father's shoulders for a moment in a curiously protective gesture, and then came over with his usual greeting— "*Bon giorno . . . comé sta?* All very good to-day, I think. Not too much *grappa* last night, Mister Henry?"

"Far too much," said Henry, miserably.

"Then we start with easy thing . . . first we side-slip."

"Oh, no," groaned the class.

"Miss Caro will show us first if she side-slip as well as she dance," said Pietro, with a flashing smile. "We go this way." And off they went.

Roger and Colonel Buckfast waved them good-bye as they passed. They were taking advantage of the excellent snow conditions, and tackling the Immenfeld run, which had just been officially declared open. This long and difficult run took them over the Austrian border into the little resort village of Immenfeld, whence they would return by train.

Gerda and the children set off down Run Three. Emmy took the lift down to join her class, which was headed for a day's skiing on the Alpe Rosa run, on the other side of the village. On the terrace of the Bella Vista, Mrs. Buckfast sat knitting with dedicated concentration, as far away as possible from the Knipfers, who were munching milk chocolate in unsmiling unison. Their daughter, wobbling unhappily on her expensive hickory skis, contrived to fall down twice on the path from the hotel to the lift, where Giovanni was waiting for her. The sun sparkled on the snow. It was a perfectly ordinary morning.

At lunch-time, Henry announced that he really must do some shopping. "I'll lunch down here in Santa Chiara," he said, "and join you afterwards. If I'm late, don't wait for me. I'll find you somewhere."

He bought cigarettes, razor blades and postcards from Signora Vespi's shop, and then, feeling rather daring, he lunched in the Bar Schmidt, where he was received with cold and curious glances from the villagers. Afterwards, he took the bus to Montelunga, the little town farther down the valley. At half-past four, when the rest of the class assembled in the Olympia for tea, they found him waiting for them, munching éclairs and apologising for his laziness.

"You missed a perfectly heavenly afternoon," said Caro. "We did Run One twice, and it was divine."

"All make good progress now," said Pietro, who had come in with them, as he usually did. "A very good class."

"Pietro says we can start on stem cristies to-morrow," Caro added.

"Not to-morrow—Monday," said Jimmy. "It's Sunday to-morrow, no ski school. Thanks, I'd love another cake. More coffee, Caro my beauty?"

"In a minute," said Caro. "I'm going to powder my nose."

She went off to the cloakroom, and Pietro made his way to the bar to buy cigarettes.

Left alone with Henry, Jimmy said: "What do you think of young Caro's behaviour?"

"How do you mean?" Henry asked.

Jimmy nodded slightly towards the bar. "Pietro," he said. "She's making an absolute ass of herself, if you ask me."

"I don't think it's anything too serious," said Henry. "After all, she's very young."

Jimmy was silent for a moment. Then he said, "She certainly has an infallible instinct for getting herself involved with the wrong people."

Before he could elaborate on this statement, Caro and Pietro came back to the table. Fresh supplies of coffee and cakes were ordered, and the conversation turned to Fraulein Knipfer.

"We saw her this morning with Giovanni," said Jimmy. "Honestly, the girl's a wash-out. I ask you—nearly two weeks of lessons, and she still can't stand up on her skis. She ought to pack it in, and take up bird-watching."

Pietro smiled, wryly. "It is sad, but I agree with you," he said.

"I feel terribly sorry for her," said Caro. "Her room's just opposite mine, and I often bump into her going to the bathroom. She always looks utterly miserable. Mind you," she added, "I'm not surprised, so would I if I had to spend all my evenings with Fritz Hauser."

"I don't know why you've got such a down on the poor little man," said Jimmy. "He's not all that bad. I daresay the Knipfer girl dotes on his company."

"Don't be silly. Nobody could," said Caro, shortly.

"Anyway," Henry put in, "she's free of him now. He's gone."

At a quarter to five, Emmy joined them. She was in high spirits, and her hair was glistening with snow.

"We had a gorgeous day on the Alpe Rosa," she announced. "We had lunch at the restaurant at the top—the view is fantastic from there. And afterwards we came down the difficult way. I fell umpteen times, but it was wonderful. Heavens," she added, as she caught sight of herself in a mirror, " I'd better do something about my hair. Order me a lemon tea, will you, Henry? I won't be a moment."

By five o'clock, Roger and the Colonel had stamped the snow off their boots, hung their anoraks in the cloakroom, and were relaxing over steaming cups of hot chocolate.

"Tricky run, that one to Immenfeld," said the Colonel. "Hidden crevasses in the last snowfield—where young Giulio came to grief, you know." He suddenly realised that Pietro was at the table, and turned bright purple : but the instructor was talking animatedly to Jimmy, and apparently had not noticed the reference to his brother.

"It sounds terribly dangerous," said Caro.

"Rubbish," said Roger. "No trouble at all if you stick to the piste. And anyway we took it very slowly. The Colonel doesn't approve of speed."

"Nonsense," said Colonel Buckfast, rather brusquely. "Just don't believe in breaking my neck, that's all."

"Roger always takes risks," said Caro. "He adores danger."

"That's quite untrue," Roger remarked. "I always know exactly what I'm doing."

"But after all," Pietro put in, "what is the fun of life without risks ? "

"I suppose it's a good thing you feel that way," said Jimmy. "I mean . . . skiing as a profession. God, how I envy you," he added. "Living here, skiing all the time—must be a wonderful life."

"You think so ? " Pietro's face grew suddenly grave and determined. "You would not say that if you lived here.

This little village . . . there is no opportunity for a young man. It's the same for all of us. We teach ski, we teach climbing, we make a little money . . . then we grow old, and work the ski-lift, like my father. I do not mean to end like that. One day, I shall be rich. And do you know what I shall do then ? "

" What, Pietro ? " asked Caro.

Pietro flashed her a smile. " I shall go to America," he said. " That is the country to make money. I shall go to New York and ride in a big Cadillac, and ski only for fun, at the weekends."

" I don't know anything about New York," said Jimmy, " but I'm prepared to bet they don't have cream cakes like these. Anyone else join me in another couple of dozen ? "

At twenty-past five, when they were talking about leaving, the Baroness and the children came in on a wave of chattering voices—the children proudly clutching new sweaters which their mother had just bought them. A few moments later Gerda joined them : she had taken off her anorak, and wore a white sweater with her black *vorlagers*, which had the effect of making her look paler than ever. She ordered a cup of coffee, refused anything to eat, and sat listening silently to the excited volubility of her two small charges. Henry noticed that Maria-Pia glanced nervously and expectantly at the door every few seconds, and sure enough it was not many minutes before Franco di Santi came in.

He went straight over to the Baroness, and said something to her in Italian. Her face lit up with a brilliant smile, and Henry heard her say, " How wonderful. Oh, how wonderful. I can't believe it."

Pietro asked Maria-Pia if she had had a good day's skiing, and, as the conversation became general, Roger and Franco pushed the two tables together, and yet more coffee, chocolate and tea were consumed. Maria-Pia and Franco both seemed filled with an infectious gaiety, which communicated itself to the others, and Henry, remembering their sombre faces in the bar the previous evening, marvelled at the volatility of the Italian character.

It was five past six by the clock over the bar when Gerda, cutting Pietro short in the middle of a story about how he had once been the sole survivor of an avalanche, remarked quietly that it was getting near the children's bed-time : this effectively broke up the party, and they all decided it was time to go back to the hotel.

They all said good-bye warmly to Pietro.

"*Arrivederce*," he said. "I shall see you on Monday."

"Why don't you come up to the Bella Vista again to-night, Pietro ? " said Caro. "It's still full moon."

"No moon to-night, Miss Caro," Pietro answered, with a smile. "Look, the snow."

Sure enough, snow was falling in big, soft flakes when they came out of the café, turning the village street into a carpet of ermine. They had almost reached the turnstile of the lift, when Emmy gave an exclamation of annoyance.

"My goggles," she said. "I've left them at the Olympia. Blast it, I'd better go back."

"I'll come with you," said Henry.

Pietro was still there when they got back. He was drinking *grappa* at the bar, and invited Henry and Emmy to join him. They took a leisurely rum grog each, and then strolled back through the dark village, and bought their tickets for the lift. The chairs were clattering past, empty and forlorn, and Carlo stamped his feet and blew on his fingers in the freezing air.

It was eighteen minutes to seven by the big, white-faced clock in Carlo's cabin, and Henry was just getting into position to hop a chair, when he noticed to his surprise that someone was coming down on the lift—a huddled figure, silhouetted against the light from the first pylon. The man's coat-collar was turned up against the snow, and his head was sunk into the folds of his fur-collared coat : but the natty leopardskin boots were unmistakable.

" Hauser's cutting it a bit fine for the last train," Henry remarked to Emmy.

As the chair approached, Carlo stepped forward to help Hauser off—although Henry had noticed that long practice had made the little German adept at coping with the lift. This time, however, he seemed more awkward than usual. As Carlo took his arm, he lurched clumsily sideways, and then suddenly tipped forward and fell on his face in the snow, where he lay still. Carlo cried out in German, and fell on his knees—a gaunt, elemental figure under the single harsh light that burned in the little shed. Henry and Emmy ran to his side.

" Herr Hauser," said Carlo, uncertainly. " Herr Hauser . . . *er ist krank . . .*"

Henry, kneeling in the snow, rolled Hauser gently on to his back. Then he looked up. " He's not ill, Carlo," he said, in German. " He's dead."

Emmy always remembered the scene that followed as a sort of El Greco tableau. The lean, cadaverous figure of Carlo, his long face creased into vertical lines of distress, lit sharply by the stark glare of the single bulb in the cabin : the skeletal shapes of the empty chairs as they clattered on their way : the huddled figure lying motionless in the yellowing, trodden snow : and the whole scene veiled in a white mist of falling snowflakes.

Henry got to his feet. " Stop the lift," he said.

As though thankful for something definite to do, Carlo scrambled up and threw the switch which disconnected the electricity supply. There was a sudden, unearthly quiet as the machinery stopped. In the silence, the telephone rang shrilly from the cabin.

" Mario," said Carlo. " He's wondering why the lift has stopped."

" I'll talk to him," said Henry.

He picked up the telephone and spoke briefly. Then he said to Carlo, " Mario will stay up at the Bella Vista for the time being. Everybody else from the hotel is already up. Now, ring the police station at Montelunga. I want to speak to Capitano Spezzi." To Emmy, he said, " Go back to the Olympia, darling, and have a drink or some coffee. Carlo and I can cope here."

" I'd rather stay with you," said Emmy.

Very quietly, Henry said, " Hauser was shot. I want you to see who you recognise in the Olympia. I'll join you as soon as I can."

He gave her hand an encouraging squeeze, and then propelled her gently down the slope towards the street.

Emmy walked in a sick daze. The shock of Hauser's sudden death had been bad enough, but now to have to face the implications of suicide or murder, the agonising web of suspicion that loomed ahead . . . she had an insane desire to take to her heels and run . . . anywhere, so long as it was away from the smell of death.

" Pull yourself together, girl," she told herself, severely : and found some comfort in the thought that at least by going back to the Olympia she could clear the menace of suspicion from everyone she saw there.

She pushed open the swing doors, walked over to a purple and orange alcove, and sat down at a wrought-iron table. She could see Pietro at the bar : he had been joined by several other instructors, and was standing a round of drinks, flourishing a thick wallet crammed with bank notes. Looking round for other familiar faces, Emmy saw to her surprise that a corner table was occupied by Signor Rossati. He had chosen a table tucked away discreetly behind a complicated modern mobile made of tin and string, and he seemed even more ill at ease than the contemplation of this object would suggest. He kept on glancing at his watch, and then stirring his coffee with quite unnecessary vigour.

" Waiting for someone," Emmy noted to herself. The hands of the clock over the bar stood at five minutes to seven. Emmy had ordered a black coffee and a brandy, and the waitress had just brought them, when two things happened. First, Pietro noticed her and came running over.

"Signora Tibbett, is time the lift stop . . . you must go up . . ."

He leant across the table, his beautiful face darkened by real concern. At the same moment, the door of the café swung open with an imperious flurry, and an exceedingly bad-tempered voice rasped out, in German, "It is only five minutes to seven. Why has the ski-lift stopped?"

Emmy looked up over Pietro's shoulder, straight into a pair of black eyes that glowered from under a green Tyrolean hat.

There was a sudden silence. The Baron strode across the room and banged his fist on the bar. "I have to go to the Bella Vista to-night. Why has the ski-lift stopped?"

A pandemonium of voices and gesticulations broke out. Emmy got up and pushed her way through the crowd until she stood face to face with Baron von Wurtberg. In English, she said: "I think I can explain. There has been an accident."

"An accident?" Pietro was at her side. "What accident is this, signora?"

Emmy took a deep breath, prayed for guidance, and said, "Herr Hauser."

The instructors crowded round her, gabbling in Italian and German. Pietro said, nervously, "They wish to know what has happened. Is it that the lift is broken?"

"No," said Emmy. "Herr Hauser was—taken ill, I think."

The instructors relaxed visibly as Pietro translated this to them. A serious accident on the ski-lift could bring the resort into disrepute, and endanger their livelihood: so long as the lift was not to blame, they had little pity to spare for the misfortunes of an individual. Only Pietro continued to show concern.

"Herr Hauser," he repeated. He took Emmy's arm. "You must tell me," he said.

"So the lift will work again to-night. That is very

fortunate." The Baron spoke icily, in impeccable English. He gave a little bow. "Thank you, madame." Then he turned to the bar, coldly, and ordered a drink. As Pietro guided Emmy back to her table, she glanced over to the corner where Signor Rossati was sitting. He was quite still now, staring in front of him with a tiny, curious smile creasing his plump features.

Pietro sat down at the table opposite Emmy. "What is this—illness or accident?" he asked, intently. Before Emmy could reply, she saw, with a great surge of relief, that Henry had come in and was making his way to the table.

"Let's go," he said.

Emmy stood up. "I'm sorry, Pietro," she said. "I have to go. You'll hear all about it to-morrow, I'm sure."

Henry took her arm, and they went out through the swing doors into the flurrying snow. As soon as they were outside, Emmy said, "The Baron's here. Maria-Pia's husband."

"I saw him," said Henry. "I was expecting him. When did he arrive?"

"I don't know when he got to Santa Chiara, but he came into the Olympia soon after I got back, terribly angry because the lift wasn't working. And Signor Rossati was there too, lurking in a corner, waiting for somebody."

They walked in silence for a moment, and then Emmy said, "Was it suicide?"

Henry shook his head. "Almost impossible. We'll know for certain when the doctor's report comes in, but it didn't look like a close-range wound to me."

At the ski-lift cabin, there was great activity. A photographer with a flash-lamp was photographing the body, and a posse of *carabinieri* chattered and smoked and shooed away the curious villagers and tourists who were already gathering, scenting sensation.

A tall, fair man in uniform detached himself from the group as Henry and Emmy approached.

"This is my wife," said Henry. "Capitano Spezzi."

The capitano bowed, and kissed Emmy's hand. "Enchanted, Signora," he said, in halting English. " I wish we might to meet at a happier time. This—" he shrugged, eloquently—" this is a bad business."

" I'd like to get up to the Bella Vista as soon as I can," said Henry. " And there are a couple of other people stranded down here. When can we get the lift started ? "

At that moment, there was a small commotion as a stretcher was unfolded, and the inert body loaded on to it.

" Now, as soon as he is away," said the Capitano. Emmy shivered as the sad little procession stumbled down the slope to the waiting ambulance. A *carabiniere* was sent off to the Olympia to tell the Baron and Signor Rossati that the lift was about to work again. Carlo, white-faced and with trembling hands, set the machinery in motion, and the chairs creaked into action.

It was a cold, eerie ride up, and Emmy was thankful to see the light twinkling in Mario's cabin at the top. Helping them off their chairs, the old man looked like a puzzled, ill-treated monkey. He questioned Henry in earnest Italian, and Henry spoke reassuringly. As they walked up the snow-path to the hotel, Henry said, " Poor Mario. He's very shaken. It's a nasty thing to happen, and I think he feels somehow responsible."

" Does he know—that Hauser's dead, I mean ? " asked Emmy.

" I told him," said Henry. " Everybody in the village knows by now."

They went into the hotel.

The bar was crowded. Caro, Roger and Jimmy were chattering animatedly over Martinis. The Buckfasts sat at a small table next to the Knipfers, with whom Mrs. Buckfast seemed to have achieved speaking terms. Maria-Pia and Franco sat at the bar, a little apart, drinking brandy and talking quietly.

" I'm going to make an entrance," Henry whispered to Emmy. " Watch their faces."

He walked in, his face grave. As the others turned to greet him, he said in what sounded to his own ears a ridiculously melodramatic voice, " I have very serious news. There has been an accident. Fritz Hauser is dead."

For a moment there was absolute silence. Then, suddenly, Frau Knipfer broke into a frenzy of high-pitched, hysterical laughter.

" *Danke Gott ! Danke Gott !* " she screamed. Before anyone else could move, her husband stood up and slapped her hard across the face. She subsided into a soft, shapeless bundle of sobs. Herr Knipfer looked round at the circle of faces, defiantly.

" My wife has been under a great strain," he said, in English. " I must ask you to forgive. She must rest now. Trudi—" Fraulein Knipfer, expressionless as ever, had already put her arm round her mother's quivering shoulders, and now helped her to her feet. Herr Knipfer took his wife's other arm, and between them they led the weeping woman through the silent, wary bar. The door banged behind them.

" Well, that was a curious exhibition," said Jimmy. " Will somebody please tell me if the old girl was heart-broken or pleased ? "

" She was saying 'Thank God'," said Roger soberly.

" And so do I ! " It was Caro who spoke, in a strangely strident voice.

" Shut up, Caro," said Roger, dangerously.

" I won't ! None of you knew . . . none of you——"

" Caro ! "

" Shut up yourself, Roger. I'm not going to tell tales. All I say is—thank God he's dead. That's all."

" Take it easy, old girl," said Jimmy, in a worried voice. " I admit Hauser wasn't the answer to a maiden's prayer, but——"

" He was vile . . ." Caro turned suddenly to Henry. " You knew, didn't you ? " she demanded. " You knew all the time—but you didn't do anything about it. And now someone has done something, and I'm delighted."

"What do you mean, someone has done something?" Roger's voice was like a whiplash. "Henry said it was an accident, didn't he?"

"An accident? Accidents don't happen to men like Hauser." Caro looked Henry straight in the eyes. "He was murdered, wasn't he?"

"Yes," said Henry. "I'm afraid he was."

There was a shocked silence. Then Jimmy said, uncertainly, "Now you've gone and put your foot in it properly, old sport. Suspect Number One, Miss Caroline Whittaker. Can you explain to the jury, Miss Whittaker, just how you came to know that the deceased was murdered, before anyone had——"

"Oh, be quiet, you fool!" Caro jumped up and ran towards the door. Jimmy was after her in a flash.

"Caro, come back . . . I want to talk to you . . ." He grabbed Caro's arm, but she shook his hand off angrily, and ran out into the hall. Jimmy followed, still protesting, and both of them disappeared upstairs.

Meanwhile, the Buckfasts had risen and joined the group at the bar. Maria-Pia and Franco had not moved, but were sitting listening tensely, white-faced, and holding hands. There was a commotion in the hall as the outer door opened, and Henry said quickly, "Baroness—I'm afraid all this excitement put it out of my head—I meant to tell you that your husband is here. That must be him now."

Maria-Pia inclined her head gravely. "Thank you," she said. "I have been expecting him."

She slid off her stool, and walked into the hall, head high, like a martyr entering the arena. For a moment Franco made as if to follow her—then thought better of it, and edged his stool closer to the English party, as if anxious to lose himself in the anonymity of a crowd.

"Did you say murdered?" The Colonel's voice was

unusually tremulous. "Bad business. Very bad indeed. What happened?"

"He was shot," said Henry. "On the ski-lift."

"I don't believe it," said Mrs. Buckfast, flatly.

"I'm afraid it's true," replied Henry. "He was coming down—the only passenger, and easily identifiable even in the snowstorm with those fur boots of his. The doctor's report isn't in yet, but I saw the wound, and I'm prepared to bet that the bullet was fired from a point about level with his body, or maybe slightly below it, and roughly ten feet to his right."

"From one of the up-going chairs, in fact," said Roger. There was an endless pause.

"I saw the fellow coming down as I went up," the Colonel said, at last. "Who else was on the lift then? All of us, I suppose."

Henry looked round the bar. "Yes," he said. "Everybody here except Mrs. Buckfast. Plus Miss Whittaker, Mr. Passendell, the Baroness, Gerda and the children."

"And you, Mr. Tibbett?" asked Roger, acidly.

"No," said Henry. "My wife left her goggles at the Olympia, so we went back for them, and had another drink with Pietro. We got to the lift just as poor Hauser reached the bottom."

"How singularly fortunate for you," Roger gave Henry a cold, hard look. "That means that you two, Mrs. Buckfast and the Knipfers are the only people at the Bella Vista who are in the clear? Am I right?"

"Yes," said Henry, levelly. "You are."

Roger stood up. "I see," he said. "Well, even a condemned murderer is allowed a meal, I understand. I'm going to eat. Coming, Franco?"

"I'm not hungry," said Franco, who had gone surprisingly pale.

"Please yourself," said Roger, and strode out of the bar towards the dining-room.

"I must say you asked for that, Tibbett," said Colonel

Buckfast. "Could have been more tactfully put, y'know."

"I'm sorry," said Henry. "I just thought you'd all like to know how things stand before the police arrive and start asking questions."

"But they can't seriously believe that any of *us* . . . ?" Mrs. Buckfast's unfinished question hovered like smoke between the three men.

"I'm afraid they may," said Henry. "After all, they know nothing about any of us, and we know precious little about each other. Still, I dare say we shall find out a great deal more very soon. Shall we eat ?" he added, to Emmy.

She nodded, and the two of them walked silently out through the almost tangible emanation of fear that eddied like mist through the home-spun Alpine cosiness of the bar.

CHAPTER SIX

At HALF-PAST eight, Capitano Spezzi arrived with half a dozen *carabinieri*, the ski-lift having been put into operation for a short time for the express purpose of conveying the majesty of the law to the Bella Vista. The bulk of the policemen started at once on a fruitless search for the missing gun, while Spezzi arranged with Signor Rossati to use his office for interviews. When he had established himself there, he dismissed his shorthand writer—a tall, gangling youth who seldom opened his mouth, but recorded conversations in his neat notebook with the precision of a well-oiled machine. Then the Capitano asked to see Henry.

"I see that you were right in what you said this afternoon, Inspector," he began in Italian, with a rueful smile. "Things have moved even faster than you anticipated."

"I blame myself," said Henry. "I should have come to see you sooner, but I had so little to go on. It never occurred to me that this might happen."

"You are not in the least to blame, my friend," protested the Capitano, warmly. "On the contrary, these unfortunate events are my responsibility, for they happened on my territory." He sighed, a touch melodramatically, and offered Henry a black, coarse-textured cigarette from a very bright orange package. Henry declined politely. There was a short silence.

"Well, at least there's no doubt now that Hauser was our man," said Henry, at last.

Spezzi shrugged. "In life, my dear Inspector, there is always doubt . . ."

"Perhaps," said Henry. "But not in death. To my mind, Hauser's murder clinches the matter."

"He was a bad man." The Capitano sighed again, and sat down with careless elegance at Rossati's desk, his long legs asprawl. " He was deeply concerned in dope-running, I agree. In other things, also, I suspect. Blackmail of many kinds. But the pattern is still far from clear."

" It seems to me," said Henry, " that we have two problems here. The first—and in many ways the less important —is to discover who killed Fritz Hauser, a man who is undoubtedly better dead. The second is to round up the organisation which is smuggling cocaine from Tangiers to Europe. Hauser may have been only a link in the chain, or he may have been the boss of the whole outfit. The two problems may be connected, or they may not."

" After you left this afternoon," said Spezzi, " I made a complete report for you of what is already known about this dope-ring. Would you like to hear it ? "

" Very much," said Henry.

Spezzi drew a sheaf of papers out of his brief-case, glanced at them, and said, " I think I can summarise it for you. The police in Rome know all about the private yacht which carries the contraband from Tangiers to Sicily . . . they could arrest the boat any day, but the gang would find another. I agree with you that the cocaine almost certainly travelled from Rome to Santa Chiara in Hauser's briefcase —and from here it crosses to Austria by ski in the winter, and in the rucksacks of mountain climbers in the summer : that is the obvious way. But we have not been able to discover who is taking it, or the method used, even though we have checked up carefully on all skiers. Then it is known to your people that the stuff also reaches London : and here again we are completely in the dark as to the gang's operations, although I have a few ideas of my own on the subject. However, all this explains why we have not acted sooner. We wished to smash the whole organisation, to identify the leader. Hauser's death is a great misfortune."

" Then you don't think the dope traffic will stop, now that he is out of the way ? " Henry asked.

" Frankly, Inspector, I do not know. If he was only a hireling, it certainly won't stop, but the plan of operation will be changed and we shall have to start all over again. If he was the leader—" The quick, brown hands gesticulated meaningfully. " I would rather have a live dope-peddler in prison than a dead one in his grave—and some poor wretch sentenced for an act of public benefaction. However—let us get to work."

" You have the doctor's report ? " Henry asked.

Spezzi pushed a sheet of closely-typed foolscap paper across the table. From a thicket of medical terminology, the simple facts emerged clearly enough. Hauser had been killed by a bullet from a .32 pistol, fired from a distance of about ten feet to the right of the victim, and slightly below him. The bullet had entered the heart, and death—which was instantaneous—had taken place less than an hour before the doctor's examination. There were no other injuries.

" No sign of the gun, of course," Henry remarked, rubbing the back of his sandy head in an abstracted way which always indicated impatience.

" Of course not. My men are searching the hotel now, and they will search below the ski-lift to-morrow. But it is a waste of time. A revolver tossed from the ski-lift into a ravine, and covered at once with falling snow . . . it may be summertime before we find it."

Henry nodded. " What I'd really like to know," he said, " is Hauser's background—his history, all you know about him."

Spezzi inhaled deeply. " It's all here," he said, tapping the bundle of papers, " but I can tell you quite simply. Our knowledge is still not complete. Inquiries were started as soon as he came under suspicion, naturally—but that was not long ago. I am still waiting for final reports from Rome. You know, of course, that he was Italian ? "

" Italian ? "

" He was born in 1901, in Santa Chiara."

" Here—in this valley ? "

Spezzi smiled. " Yes. He was, of course, born Austrian —but like everybody else, his nationality changed to Italian in 1919. His family were simple village people, but he was clever—you might say brilliant. From the village school, he won a scholarship to a university in Vienna, where he qualified as a doctor of medicine in 1927. He obtained permission to work in Austria, and set up a practice in a poor quarter of Vienna, where he became prosperous—almost suspiciously so. With all that has happened since "—Spezzi dismissed the cataclysms of history with a wave of the hand—" it is difficult to trace records exactly, but it is certain that he came under suspicion for illegal traffic in drugs. The case never came to court—one imagines that there was not sufficient evidence. In any case, Hauser apparently got worried, for he sold his practice in 1924, and left Vienna. Here there is a gap in his history which we have not yet filled—we may never do so. He turns up next in 1936, in Munich."

" His politics ? " Henry asked.

" That is the interesting thing. He was apparently a man without politics."

" Was that possible—in Germany just before the war ? "

" One would say—no. Let us say that he could not have been actively anti-Nazi, or he would never have survived, let alone been allowed to work—even though relations between our two countries were undoubtedly . . . cordial . . . at that time." Spezzi paused, in some embarrassment, and then went on quickly. " Anyway, Hauser steered carefully clear of politics in public. He practised in Munich until late 1938, when he moved to Berlin. By now he was a rich man. He had become a fashionable doctor . . . a big house, two cars . . ."

" And no connections with the party ? "

" None that could be proved. Some of his patients were Nazis, of course—that goes without saying. But a doctor can hardly be held responsible for the politics of his patients. He never treated any of the hierarchy. His practice was divided between old aristocratic and army families, and the entertainment world—actors and actresses, musicians, film producers. His fees were high, and he lived well."

" What happened to him when war broke out ? " Henry asked.

" He returned to Italy. In all those years, he had never changed his Italian nationality. He came to live in Rome, and started up a practice there."

" And was he equally successful ? "

" My friend—our two countries were closely-knit. The world of entertainment is international. With his recommendations from Berlin, he soon acquired clients in Rome. When Italy entered the war, he joined the staff of a large hospital, and so escaped military service."

" Was he a Fascist ? " Henry asked, somewhat diffidently.

Spezzi shrugged his shoulders. " Who wasn't ? " he replied. " I can assure you, Inspector, that to talk to us Italians now, you would think that Mussolini had not one single supporter—and yet, it is evident that he had many. A certain party was in power—very well. Most of us wanted nothing more than to live our lives in peace . . . and for that, one did not make demonstrations against Fascism. As I told you, Hauser had no interest in politics . . . like a great number of us."

" I see," said Henry.

Spezzi went on, hastily. " Until four years ago, we have no record of his activities—our men in Rome are working on it now. He left the hospital after the war, and was to all intents and purposes a successful, law-abiding doctor. Only when the Caroni case broke did a breath . . . the merest breath . . . of suspicion come his way.   You remember the affair ? "

" I certainly do," said Henry, " and I remember what a meal the press made of it, all over the world . . . a drug-scandal involving prominent social personalities in Rome. The girl who died was an actress, wasn't she ? Sofia Caroni . . . Wait a minute. An actress. You mean she was one of Hauser's patients ? "

" She was," said Spezzi. " So, inevitably, suspicious eyes

were turned on Hauser—as they would have been on any doctor who attended her, innocent or not. There was no proof—no proof of any kind. But Hauser was the soul of discretion. Before the case ever came to court, he announced his intention of retiring and devoting himself to research. He set up a small laboratory, where he worked on perfectly legitimate experiments connected with virus diseases. Occasionally he published an undistinguished article in a medical journal. He travelled widely. He declared that his income came from investments."

"What I don't understand," said Henry, "is that he spoke nothing but German, and was always referred to as Herr Hauser—not even Doctor Hauser. If he was Italian, and lived and worked in Rome——"

With a smile, Spezzi said, "My dear Inspector, do you not have in England the snobbism of the foreign doctor? Hauser had worked in Austria and Germany—it was part of his stock-in-trade to pass as a great Viennese doctor. His patients did not ask to see his passport. As for being known as Herr Hauser—that was only in Santa Chiara, where he never laid stress on being a doctor. In Rome, he was always Doctor Hauser."

"Was it his real name?"

"Oh, yes. Many families in this district had Austrian names, and still have. Some of them changed to Italian names when the region changed hands—just as the towns and villages were re-christened. Montelunga, for instance, used to be Langenberg—to some people, it still is."

"What about the rest of Hauser's family—the ones who stayed here?"

"None of them are left now," said Spezzi. "His parents died many years ago, and his only brother was killed in the war."

"I see," said Henry. "What was it, then, that first aroused suspicions against Hauser in Rome—apart from the Caroni case?"

"There were no suspicions," said Spezzi, "until a few

weeks ago. That was when he made his first mistake—or rather, somebody made it for him."

" What was that ? "

Spezzi paused. " There are," he said, " there always will be certain young men of an adventurous turn of mind who find smuggling irresistibly attractive. After a war, in particular, they turn up, these young pirates. They have been in the Navy . . . they have learned to live dangerously and to handle boats. So they get hold of a ship of some sort, and run contraband in it. For many of them Tangiers is a convenient jumping-off ground."

" Henry nodded. " Don't I know it," he said. " It starts as a great lark, with cigarettes and brandy, and then—" He suddenly stopped dead. Spezzi looked up at him, and grinned.

" Aha, you have it now, Inspector ? "

" Roger Staines," said Henry, slowly. " The *Nancy Maud*. Three years ago. It was his boat . . ."

" Your memory is very good."

" My memory's rotten," said Henry, annoyed. " I should have placed him at once. Let me see how much I can remember now. The *Nancy Maud* was arrested landing a cargo of contraband cigarettes in Sicily, with two young Italians aboard. Staines had sailed her out singlehanded from the Solent to Tangiers, and was staying with friends there. He insisted that the boat had been stolen—he had not been near her for ten days, he said, and so he knew nothing about her disappearance. The Italians, on the other hand, maintained that Staines had hired them to do the trip for him. They went much too far, however, and denied that they knew what the cargo was—which was pretty thin, considering that they were caught rowing it ashore to a lonely creek at two o'clock in the morning. The police believed Staines, and the Italian lads went to prison. Am I right ? "

" Absolutely. I don't suppose you remember the boy's name—the ringleader ? "

Henry shook his head. "You have me there," he admitted.

"It is not important. He was called Donati—known to his friends by the endearing nickname of Lupo—the wolf. He was—he still is—a criminal type. A bad criminal type."

"But that was only cigarettes," said Henry. "That wasn't——"

"Certainly, it was only cigarettes—that time. Lupo Donati came out of prison two years ago. He went back to sea, on a merchant ship, but that was much too much like hard work, and he quit. Then, last year, he bought a boat of his own—a nice little motor craft called *Carissima*. You can imagine that she was closely watched, especially since she made frequent trips to Tangiers. It was obvious that Lupo could not have had the money to buy her himself— somebody was financing him. A few weeks ago, we got definite proof that the *Carissima* was running dope—but what was the use of arresting Lupo again? We wanted to find the people behind him. So, when he came to Rome, he was called in for questioning. At first, he was very frightened. Then, the police appeared to believe his stories, and he thought he had bluffed them. He is a very conceited young man. He left police headquarters very pleased with himself indeed. He was careless. He took a taxi straight to Hauser's laboratory."

"Did he indeed?" said Henry.

"Hauser himself answered the door. He was very angry. He pretended not to know Lupo, and sent him away. But it was enough. Inquiries were started. The Rome police became interested in Hauser's frequent visits to Santa Chiara. Perhaps it is natural that he should visit his birth-place—but again, perhaps it is not. And why should he stay at the Bella Vista when he does not ski? That is the pattern that begins to take shape. And now some fool kills him."

"You said something about blackmail—" Henry began.

"That is a suspicion only. In Rome, they investigated his sources of income. True, he has many investments.

But also, much money is paid into his bank account, always in cash, regular sums at regular intervals. That can mean blackmail—no ? "

" No—I mean yes," said Henry.

" So—now you know all that I know."

" Thank you, Capitano." Henry was thoughtful. " Rome, Vienna, Berlin . . . but not London. And yet, there must be a connection with London, because we know the stuff has been getting through—from somewhere. Maybe not from here. The whole thing is very vague at our end. In any case, it's difficult to associate any of the English people here with such goings-on—with the possible exception of Roger Staines. And somehow I don't think . . . Oh, well, there's no use guessing. By the way," he added, " what about Hauser's luggage ? "

" It was at the Olympia," said Spezzi. " I examined it myself. There was nothing of interest in it, apart from the fact that the lock on his briefcase was broken—it could have happened long ago, or to-day, who can tell ? There were no fingerprints on the luggage, apart from those of the barman at the Olympia, who took it in."

" What was in the briefcase ? "

" A half-written medical treatise on virus diseases and some pornographic magazines," said Spezzi, with delicate distaste.

" Not a very promising haul," Henry smiled. " Anything useful in Hauser's pockets ? "

" No," said Spezzi, shortly. " The keys of his apartment, money, a cheque book, a handkerchief. Just what you would expect to find."

" Oh, well," said Henry, " I suppose it was too much to hope for." He glanced at his watch. " It's getting late. I'd better leave you to get on with your interviews."

Spezzi looked slightly sheepish. " There is a favour I would ask of you," he said. " You understand it is necessary to question all the people concerned. Now—" he smiled, diffidently—" my English is not good. I would be deeply grateful if you would undertake to interview the English guests. I will be present, of course, just as I hope you will be present when I speak to the others."

Henry looked profoundly unhappy.

" I understand, my friend," said the Capitano kindly, " These fellow-skiers have become your friends——"

" And they don't know who I am or why I'm here," said Henry. " Oh, well, I suppose being disliked is all part of the job. All right, I'll do it. Incidentally, can your chap take shorthand in English ? "

" I fear not."

" Then perhaps you wouldn't mind if my wife sat in with us and took notes for me ? "

" I should be charmed," said the gallant Capitano, looking round automatically for a hand to kiss.

So Emmy and the young *carabiniere* were summoned, and installed in opposite corners of the room on small, hard chairs, each with a notebook poised. The Capitano relaxed in the swivel chair behind Rossati's desk, while Henry perched on the window-sill and wished himself a thousand miles away.

" Where shall we start ? " he asked.

" First, we need facts." Spezzi drew a snow-white writing-pad towards him. On it he wrote, neatly, " Time sequence of events." Henry, who tended to conduct his investigations mainly on instinct, was much impressed.

" I suggest," said the Capitano, " that we start with Signor Rossati."

CHAPTER SEVEN

ANY MAN, Henry reflected, might be forgiven for appearing agitated and unhappy in Signor Rossati's position. A death in the hotel is never a comfortable thing for the proprietor to cope with at the best of times, let alone a murder in which a large percentage of his guests are obvious suspects : add to that the humiliation of being interrogated in his own office, perched miserably on a small upright chair while an arrogant policeman lounged at the desk, and almost any degree of anxiety and exasperation would be only too understandable.

Signor Rossati, however, appeared to be standing up well under the strain. He sat watching the Capitano, rubbing his fat pink hands together, with an expression at once respectful and alert on his circular countenance.

Spezzi spoke slowly and quietly. " First, we wish to establish the movements of everyone concerned as precisely as possible, Signor Rossati," he said. " Suppose we start with Herr Hauser. When did you first see him to-day ? "

" To-day—it was at nine o'clock, near enough——"

" He had breakfasted ? "

" He was eating breakfast. I myself take breakfast in my private suite, and come down to the office afterwards. But to-day he sent Anna, the waitress, to fetch me to the dining-room——"

" Do you usually allow yourself to be disturbed at that hour ? "

Rossati looked slightly uncomfortable. " Herr Hauser was a valued client of the hotel. One is prepared to make small concessions."

" And what did he want with you ? "

" He asked me to prepare his bill. He was planning to leave Santa Chiara by the evening train, he said, and would probably be out for the rest of the day."

" Did anyone overhear him saying that ? "

" Anyone ? " Rossati made an expansive gesture. " Everybody, *caro Capitano*. All the guests were there—isn't that so ? " He appealed to Henry, whose presence he seemed to accept without question. Henry nodded briefly.

" In what language did he speak ? " asked the Capitano, suddenly.

" In German, of course. "

" Of course. They tell me in the village that you prefer to speak German, Signor Rossati. Is that so ? "

" I—" Rossati was clearly rattled now. " I speak both languages, as you know, Capitano. I have no political views —none whatsoever . . ."

" Yet you prefer to speak German ? "

" Well, I . . . for us people of this region, Capitano, both languages are equally——"

" But you have not spent your whole life in these parts, have you, Signor Rossati ? " The Capitano's voice was quiet and easy. " From your accent, I would say you are a Roman."

There was a tiny pause. " I was born in Rome, Capitano."

" No connection with Austria or Germany at all ? "

" Since I have been here, it is inevitable that——"

Spezzi smiled. " You misunderstand me, Signor. I do not suggest that you have connections with those countries. On the contrary. I merely ask myself why a Roman, speaking no German, should become so proficient in the language after a few years . . . how long is it, exactly, that you have been here ? "

" Three years in March . . ." Rossati's voice was almost a whisper.

" So proficient in three years," Spezzi went on, " that he should actually prefer to use it. But perhaps you would rather not discuss that just now. There is plenty of time. For the moment, we want facts."

In the silence that followed, Rossati, as red as a beetroot, loosened his collar with a plump forefinger.

The Capitano went on, as softly as before. " So, Hauser asked for his bill at nine o'clock, in full hearing of all the guests, and speaking in German. What did he do then ? "

" He finished his meal, and we came in here together," said Rossati. His voice shook slightly. " I prepared the bill, and he paid it."

" By cheque ? "

" No . . . as it happens . . . in cash . . ."

" May one ask what it amounted to ? "

This innocent question seemed to upset Rossati quite immoderately. After an agonised moment of doubt, he said, " He paid a large part of it last week."

" What do you mean by that ? "

" Just what I say, Capitano. He had been here for just three weeks—three weeks to-day—but last weekend he prepared to leave and he paid his bill. Then he changed his mind and stayed longer——"

" Have you any idea why ? "

" None. None, I assure you. He is a man—I should say, he was a man of means, Capitano, and he enjoyed being at my little hotel. So he decided to stay on a further week."

" So he paid one week's bill in cash this morning. And after that——? "

Signor Rossati relaxed visibly : clearly, in his view, the worst was over. " He went upstairs—to pack, I imagine. I noticed the porter bringing his luggage down at . . at about half-past ten, I suppose it must have been. It was just after Anna had taken Mrs. Buckfast's coffee to the terrace, and she always——"

" His luggage was at the Olympia cafè," said Spezzi. " When did it go down ? "

" That I cannot say. Before lunch, I imagine. The porter will be able to tell you."

" And when did you next see Herr Hauser ? "

" He made a telephone call from my office at about eleven o'clock."

Spezzi leant forward, interested. " Where to ? " he asked.

" It was to Innsbruck, Capitano. More than that I cannot tell you. I left him alone, naturally, while he was on the line."

" I see. And did you see him again ? "

" Not until this evening." Rossati was speaking easily and fluently now, without hesitation. " I presume he must have gone down to the village for lunch, for he was not here. Indeed, I thought that he had left for good. But when I went into the bar just before five o'clock, to see all was in order before the skiers returned, he was there."

" Did you speak to him ? "

" A word, no more. I think I said I was surprised to see him, and he reminded me that he was not leaving until the last train. I myself was hurrying, for I had an appointment in the village."

" May one ask what it was ? "

" But of course, Capitano. It was with the bank manager. And after that, I had arranged to meet a friend in the Olympia, but unfortunately he did not arrive. I was still waiting there when—when Signora Tibbett brought the news . . ."

Spezzi, who had been jotting notes on his pad, looked up. " Before we go any further," he said, " I'd like to have a clear idea of your own movements throughout the day. We have got as far as nine o'clock, when Hauser paid his bill in here. What did you do then ? "

" My day is a routine, Capitano. All the staff will tell you. Every day is the same—or very nearly so. When Herr Hauser had paid his bill, I returned to my room to finish my coffee. Then, as always, I came in here to make up the account books of the hotel."

" Did you notice the skiers going out ? "

" Frankly, no, Capitano. There was plenty of coming and going in the hall—there always is at that hour : and since I need to concentrate, I pay no attention unless I am actually disturbed by somebody who wishes to speak to me."

" And were you, to-day ? "

" No, Capitano."

" I see. And after that——? "

" The skiers were all away by ten o'clock. Then I went to the kitchen, as I always do, to arrange to-morrow's menus with the cook, and to check that all was well with to-day's meals. It was as I came out to return to my office that I saw Anna taking out Mrs. Buckfast's coffee, and Beppi —that's the porter—carrying Herr Hauser's luggage downstairs. In the office, I typed the menus for to-day's lunch and dinner, and made out my marketing lists. It was while I was doing this that Herr Hauser came in and made his telephone call."

" I see. And these duties took you until lunchtime ? "

" Yes. I also dealt with my mail—Mario brings the letters up from the village when he comes to start the ski-lift. This morning there was not much post—the usual bills and receipts, and a couple of requests for rooms."

" At what time do the skiers return ? "

" At about half-past twelve—those who are lunching here. To-day, it was only the beginners' class—except for Signor Tibbett, who was not with the others."

" That's right," said Henry. " I lunched in the village."

" And of course poor Fraulein Knipfer was here," added Rossati.

" Did you speak to any of them? "

" I always go into the bar at lunchtime for a word with the guests, Capitano—just to make sure they are all happy. To-day there were only Mr. Passendell and the young English lady."

" And were they happy ? "

" I think so. How can I say ? They made no complaints."

" What were they talking about ? "

" What does every skier talk about ? " asked Rossati, beaming. " The snow. The morning's sport. The progress they have made. The instructor."

" Nothing else at all ? "

" No, Capitano."

" And what did you do then ? "

" I took lunch in my sitting-room, as always."

" Then how can you be sure who came in to lunch ? Someone else might have come later."

" I am sure because Anna brings me the lunch-chits to enter on the bills."

" Were there any non-residents lunching here to-day ? "

" No, Capitano. Sometimes we have other skiers, or visitors who come up to see the view—but it is early in the season for them. No—to-day there was nobody."

" And after lunch ? "

" Nothing, Capitano. I had a little rest in my room, and read the newspaper. Soon after four, Beppi called me to see one of the attic rooms, where there is a little dampness on the ceiling. A hotel is like that—always something to be fixed, always more expenditure. Then I went to the kitchens again, to be sure that all was in order for dinner, and to fetch a fresh bottle of brandy for the bar. It was while I was taking it in that I saw Herr Hauser, as I told you. Then I took the lift down to the village."

Spezzi made a note, and then said, " Thank you, Signor. You have been most helpful. Just one or two more questions. Herr Hauser had been here often before ? "

" Oh, many times. Several times each year, since I have been here."

" Did he generally stay as long as three weeks at a time ? "

" He . . . no, it was usually one or two weeks . . ."

" I see. Signor Rossati, do you own a gun ? "

" A gun ? " Rossati beamed indulgently, as at an idiot child. " Whatever would I want with a gun, Capitano ? "

" Hauser was shot. Somebody must have had a gun."

Rossati's smile grew wider. " That is simple, Capitano. There was only one person in this hotel with a gun, and that was Herr Hauser himself. I saw it many times."

" He showed it to you ? "

A tiny pause. " I . . . saw it. It was a small black automatic pistol. He kept it in his briefcase."

" Have you any idea why he carried it ? "

Rossati shrugged. " How can I know? He travelled much. Perhaps he had enemies . . . clearly he had enemies, for he is dead."

Spezzi was leaning forward now, intent. " Who else besides yourself knew about this gun ? "

" You ask impossibilities, *caro Capitano*. How can I say ? It is not the custom in an hotel such as this for the guests to lock their bedroom doors——"

" Not even Herr Hauser ? "

" No. I cannot remember that he ever did so."

Spezzi looked at Henry, and raised his eyebrows. " You are sure of that, Signor Rossati ? "

" I cannot say that he never locked it. Only that I never recollect him doing so. Why should he ? Nobody else did." Rossati's smile ran down his chin like warm olive oil.

" So anybody could have known about the gun, and anybody could have stolen it ? "

" Si, Capitano."

" Did you steal it ? " The question came out like a bullet, but Rossati was completely unperturbed.

" I ? But why should I ? Herr Hauser was a valuable client . . ."

" When did you last see this gun ? "

Rossati hesitated. " I really cannot remember, Capitano. This week, last week . . . I cannot say. I knew Herr Hauser always had it with him."

Spezzi looked annoyed, but it was impossible to get a more precise answer out of the proprietor, so he contented himself with a scowl, and said, " One last question. What was your personal impression of Herr Hauser as a man? Did you like him ? "

" He was a valuable client."

" And therefore you liked him ? "

" Of course. It would be bad for business to do otherwise."

Spezzi looked at Henry. " Do you wish to ask Signor

Rossati any questions ? " he said. Then, turning to Rossati, he explained, " Signor Tibbett is connected with the English police. He is helping me in my investigations."

If this was news to Rossati, he didn't show it. He merely nodded, and transferred his bland gaze from Spezzi to Henry.

" Just one question," said Henry. " When you go to the village to see your friends, Signor Rossati, which bar do you normally use ? "

" I go very seldom, *signor*. I——"

" But to which bar ? "

" The . . . the Bar Schmidt, as a rule, *signor*. It is . . . it is for the villagers rather than for the tourists, you understand . . ."

" But last night you were meeting your friend, who didn't arrive, at the Olympia ? "

" My friend was one of the ski instructors, *signor*," said Rossati, very quickly. " They prefer the Olympia."

" I see," said Henry. " That's all."

" Thank you, Signor Rossati, you may go now." Spezzi glanced at the bell-push on the side of the desk. " When I ring, please ask——" he turned to Henry. " Which of the English party will you see first ? "

" Look here," said Henry, " I don't want to interfere with your plans, but it's nearly ten o'clock, and if I start on the English people now, we'll be here all night. Can't we leave it until the morning ? "

" If you wish." Spezzi didn't sound pleased. " Very well, Signor Rossati. Tell the guests they may go to bed when they wish, but they are not to leave the hotel, to-night or in the morning. We will start at nine-thirty. Now, have you prepared rooms for my assistant and myself ? "

" But of course, *caro Capitano*. I will show you myself . . ."

Rossati leapt up with surprising agility and selected two keys from the board on the office wall. " This way, if you please . . ."

When the two policemen had been shown their rooms, Spezzi returned to the office, accompanied by the Sergeant who had been in charge of the search for the gun. The latter reported gloomily on his lack of success.

"Never mind," said Spezzi, consolingly. "It was only what we expected." He made arrangements for the terrain below the ski-lift to be searched in the morning, and then a sleepy Mario was called and ordered to start up the lift in order to convey the *carabinieri* back to the village.

"There's just one thing," said Henry. "If I were you, I'd definitely prohibit the Immenfeld run for a few days. We don't want anyone making a getaway."

"I have already done so," said Spezzi, somewhat coldly.

When he and his aide had retired to their rooms, Henry and Emmy looked at each other, and grinned.

"Come on," said Henry. "I need a drink."

The bar was deserted except for Jimmy, Roger and Franco, who were standing together at the far end of the room, elbows on the bar, heads close together, talking earnestly. Behind the bar, Anna yawned and polished an already gleaming glass. Everything was very quiet. All three men looked up as Henry and Emmy came in.

"Hallo, there," said Jimmy. "Come and have a drink. You've been in there long enough, I must say. What was it, third degree? Are you the chief suspects?"

"I've told you what they are," said Roger sourly, gulping down a brandy in one.

Jimmy laughed, a trifle self-consciously. "Don't mind old Roger," he said. "He gets the most extraordinary ideas sometimes, and he's pretty pickled, anyhow. For some obscure reason, he thinks——"

"I don't think—I know damn well," said Roger. He left the bar and walked rather unsteadily up to Henry. "You're a bloody copper, aren't you?"

"Yes," said Henry. He added, "I'm sorry."

"What are you doing here, then?" asked Jimmy, in a voice thin with strain.

"Taking a holiday—or I was."

"Bloody liar." Roger lurched back to the bar and slammed down his glass. "Another brandy, Anna. He's snooping, of course . . . after someone . . . going to get some poor devil hung . . ."

"Pull yourself together, old dear," said Jimmy, a little uncertainly. "After all, somebody did kill our lamented friend Hauser, and personally I'll sleep better when he's caught. It's not very pleasant to think of a murderer running around loose in a small hotel like this."

"Please . . . what is this ? . . . I do not understand." Franco had been switching his anxious gaze from face to face, trying vainly to keep up with the conversation. Roger turned to him.

"This man's an English policeman," he said, in Italian.

"*Carabiniere ?* " Franco's face relaxed into a smile. "Ah, welcome, *signor*. This is fortunate, no ? "

"No," said Roger.

"I'm very glad you think so," said Henry gravely, to Franco. "May we have two brandies please, Anna ? "

Emmy said, "I had no idea you spoke Italian so well, Roger."

"I only fought the bloody Huns all round the coast of Italy. Any objection ? "

"Of course not."

There was a silence as Anna poured the drinks, and then Franco excused himself politely, in laboured English, and went to bed. Jimmy finished his drink quickly.

"I'm off, too," he said. "I suppose the fun will start to-morrow."

"I'm afraid so," said Henry. "We'll try to make it as painless as possible."

"Decent of you, I'm sure," said Jimmy, dryly. "It'll be fascinating to see a sleuth at work. Any clues yet ? "

"It's rather early for that," said Henry. "Besides, this isn't my affair at all—it's a matter for the local police. But they insist that I should interview the English people, because of the language difficulty."

Jimmy looked straight at Henry for a moment. Then he grinned. "You poor fish," he said. "You have my sympathy." And with that he walked out of the bar.

Roger sat down on a stool and contemplated Henry with an expression of concentrated dislike.

"Holiday," he said, at last. "Holiday, my Aunt Fanny. Curious coincidence having a murder here the very moment a cop chooses to take his holiday. Or don't you think so?"

"I admit I was mixing pleasure with a little business," said Henry. "But my business wasn't murder."

"What's all this in aid of, anyway?" Roger demanded, suddenly flaring into anger. "You're going to grill us to-morrow. All right then. Save it for the morning. Don't think you can come in here drinking with us and swinging the old pals act. I've seen your lot on the job before now, and there's one thing I know . . . everything they say . . . everything they do . . . all for one purpose. Get you to slip up. Get you to give yourself away. Well, in this case, it won't work. I'm going to bed."

"I'm sorry you feel like that," said Henry, "because I came in here specially hoping to have a word with you."

"You bet your sweet life you did."

"When I question you to-morrow, the Italian police will be there—and the Capitano understands English pretty well. In any case, it's an official interview, and Emmy will be taking everything down in shorthand."

"So you're in it, too, are you?" said Roger, rudely, to Emmy. "Pity, I rather liked you."

"So I thought," Henry went on, imperturbably, "that this might be my last opportunity to talk to you alone."

"O.K. Go ahead and talk. Don't expect me to answer. I give you two minutes."

"I shan't need as much as that. I just want to warn you to give yourself a chance to-morrow. Just because you're in a blue funk——"

"How dare you say that?"

"—there's no need to lose your head and land yourself

in real trouble. For instance, Capitano Spezzi knows all about the *Nancy Maud*."

There was dead silence for a moment. Then Roger said, very quietly, "Thank you."

"Don't mention it. You surely didn't think that it wouldn't come to light ?"

"It was a long time ago. I didn't think there'd be any need to drag it up now . . ."

"Well, there is. So for God's sake tell the truth, that's all. Come on, Emmy. Let's go to bed."

"I'm coming too," said Roger.

They all left the bar together, and climbed the steep wooden staircase. At his door, Roger paused.

"No need to shout your mouth off about this to . . . to the others," he said.

"Of course not," said Henry. "But surely . . . some of them know already, don't they ?"

"No, they don't." Roger was emphatic. "Nobody knows."

He went into his room and shut the door. They heard the key turning in the lock.

CHAPTER EIGHT

HENRY'S FIRST action the following morning was to compose a lengthy telegram to the Assistant Commissioner at Scotland Yard. Realising that it would be more than flesh and blood could stand for the village post-mistress not to circulate the contents of such a document—he could not be certain that she understood no English—he asked Capitano Spezzi if the other Italians and the Germans could be interrogated first, so that Emmy could take the cable into Montelunga and send it from there.

So the English party sat on the terrace in uneasy silence, sipping coffee, while Beppi, the hotel porter, was sent to take over the ski-lift: a few minutes later, Mario was ushered into Rossati's office. Spezzi had intended to start the morning by questioning the Baroness, of whom he stood in considerable awe: but Gerda had informed him shortly that her mistress was unwell and would not be getting up before lunchtime. Spezzi did not argue.

Mario sat perched unhappily on the edge of a chair, like a bedraggled sparrow on a telegraph wire, twisting his woollen cap nervously in his gnarled hands and darting frightened and bewildered looks at Henry, Spezzi and the shorthand writer in turn. Spezzi was gentle with him.

" You must understand that we are not blaming you in any way," he said, " but we must question you to reach the truth of this sad affair. Now—your name ? "

" Vespi, Mario," the old man admitted, uneasily.

" Now, Mario, you were on duty at the top of the ski-lift last night ? "

" *Si, Capitano*. I am always there."

" What can you tell us about Herr Hauser's last trip down to the village ? "

It was more than Mario could cope with to volunteer an unprompted account. He looked piteously from Spezzi to Henry, tongue-tied.

"Well, tell us what time he went down," said Spezzi, with a trace of irritation.

"It was . . . it must have been about ten minutes past six, Capitano."

"Was anybody else using the lift at the time?"

"Nobody. No more skiers were coming up, for it was already dark."

"But the Bella Vista party had not come up?"

"No, Capitano. I was wondering what had become of them."

"Why do you say that?"

"Well . . . forgive me, Capitano, it's none of my business, I know . . . the ladies and gentlemen come up at whatever time they please, naturally . . ."

"I think," said Henry, "that Mario means that we usually come up before half-past five. But last night we all met by chance at the Olympia, and lingered over our tea."

Mario shot a glance of pathetic gratitude at Henry.

"I see," said Spezzi. "Ten-past six approximately: the ski-lift deserted: the Bella Vista guests still in the village. What happened then?"

"Then I saw Herr Hauser."

"Where?"

"He was coming down the path from the hotel."

"How could you be sure it was him? It was dark, and snowing hard."

Mario looked scared stiff, and was understood to mumble something about boots.

"What boots?"

"Herr Hauser's boots." The old man grew a little bolder. "Fur," he said, "with black spots. I knew them well: and there is a light on the path. In any case," he added, with a little burst of confidence, "I was expecting him."

"Expecting him?"

Mario suddenly looked scared again, and explained very rapidly, " His luggage had already gone down—before lunch, I sent it . . . Beppi brought it from the hotel; and he told me there was no hurry, as Herr Hauser was not leaving until the last train. So I knew he must go down on the lift."

" I see. Did he say anything to you ? "

" He said good evening, as he always did. He was a very polite gentleman." Mario gazed hopefully at Spezzi to see if this answer pleased him.

" Nothing more ? "

" No, Capitano. I helped him on to the chair, and wished him a good journey."

" Did he seem quite normal—in good spirits ? "

" He was just as usual, Capitano."

" And that was the last you saw of him ? "

" *Si, Capitano.*"

Spezzi studied the notes he had made, frowningly. Then he said, " You can't be any more precise about the time Herr Hauser got on to the lift ? "

Mario's monkey-face broke up into crevasses of distress. " I am sorry, Capitano . . . forgive me . . . I didn't know it would be important . . ." The old man seemed on the verge of tears.

" Don't worry," said Henry. " I can tell you exactly. It takes just twenty-five minutes to come up or go down, as I know only too well. It was precisely seventeen minutes to seven when Hauser reached the bottom. So if you want stop-watch accuracy, he must have got on at exactly . . . six-eighteen."

" Thank you." Spezzi entered the figure on his neat chart with some satisfaction.

" But Capitano . . ." Mario, desperately eager to help, was bursting with information. " That is not quite right, even so. It must have been sixteen minutes past."

" Why ? "

" Because the lift stopped for two minutes soon after

Herr Hauser got on to it," said Mario, with the triumphant air of a conjurer producing a hard-boiled egg from behind a spectator's ear. "A fuse blew," he added.

"At your end, or at Carlo's?"

"At my end, Capitano. Poor Herr Hauser—he had just started his descent—I could see him in his chair. I fixed the fuse as quickly as I could, but it always takes two minutes. You can see it entered in the book I keep. And I know the time is right, for I noted it from the clock in my cabin. It is electric, and cannot go wrong," he added, with some pride.

"Thank you," said Spezzi.

"Of course," Mario went on, warming to his subject, "It might have taken me a little more than two minutes. Then Herr Hauser would have got on to the lift at . . . at fifteen and a half minutes past six——"

"All right, all right, we have it near enough," said Spezzi testily, aware of Henry's amused scrutiny. He underlined a figure on his chart. Some people, his expression implied, might sneer at accuracy of detail—but they would learn.

"Right," he said, at length. "What happened then?"

"Nothing, Capitano . . . nothing until the ladies and gentlemen from the Bella Vista came up."

"And what time was that?"

"I . . . I'm afraid I cannot be sure, Capitano . . ."

Again, Henry came to the rescue. "I think I can pinpoint it for you," he said, "if you really want to know."

"It is very necessary, please understand," said Spezzi acidly, in English.

"Of course," said Henry. "Well, we were all in the Olympia when Gerda pointed out that it was five-past six. So we all paid our bills and left. We walked down the street—that doesn't take more than two minutes. Say ten minutes at the outside between leaving the Olympia and boarding the lift. That would mean that the first of the party got on to the lift at a quarter past six, and arrived at the top at twenty minutes to seven ... I'm sorry, eighteen minutes to seven, allowing for the breakdown."

" I see," said Spezzi. He entered the figures on his chart.

" In fact," Henry went on, " they must have reached the top just about as Hauser got to the bottom—and since it took us a little while to grasp the fact that he was dead, and to stop the lift, I imagine that the last of the party had only just got off the lift when it stopped, on my instructions. Is that so ? " he asked Mario.

" *Si, si, signor*. The last was Fraulein Gerda, I remember. She was walking up the path when the lift stopped."

" Can you remember the order in which the people came up ? " asked Spezzi.

Mario smiled miserably, ingratiatingly. " It is very difficult, Capitano. So many people every day ..."

" Do your best."

" Well ... Signor Jimmy was the first, that I do remember. Then after him, all the English. I think Signor Roger was the last of them. Then Signor di Santi, then the Baroness, then the two children and Fraulein Gerda," he finished at a gallop, in evident relief.

" Thank you, that is very helpful. What happened then ? "

" Then the lift stopped."

" And what did you do ? " prompted Spezzi, seeing that the trickle of narrative was once more drying up.

" I rang Carlo. It wasn't time for the lift to stop and I thought it must be another fuse. Signor Tibbett answered the telephone." He glanced at Henry for confirmation. " He told me there had been an accident, and I should wait in my cabin until the lift started again. He asked if all the skiers from the hotel had arrived, and I told him they had."

" Now, Mario." Spezzi finished writing his notes and leant back in his chair. " I want you to try to remember some of the people who used the lift earlier in the day."

Mario's face fell. " But Capitano ... they come up all day long ... hundreds of them ..."

" I am more interested in those who went down. For instance, did Herr Hauser use the lift earlier in the day ? "

" Yes, Capitano. He went down just before twelve o'clock."

" Before or after his luggage ? "

" Before, Capitano. The luggage had been in my cabin since about half-past ten," Mario explained, " but I was too busy with the lift to attend to it. Beppi had told me there was no hurry . . ."

" All right, all right. Go on."

" At twelve, the ski school finishes for lunch, and things are quiet. It was then that I sent the luggage down. Herr Hauser told me to tell Carlo to take it to the Olympia for him when the lift stopped for lunch."

" Just a moment," said Spezzi. " I'd like to be clear about the times when the lift works. When does it start in the morning ? "

" At a quarter to nine, Capitano—that is when I come up. But no skiers are allowed on to it until nine, so that I shall be at the top when they arrive. Then it continues until half-past twelve, when it stops for lunch."

" You go home for lunch ? "

" *Si, Capitano.*"

" How do you get down to the village ? "

" On skis, Capitano," Mario answered. " My leg is not so bad that I cannot do a simple run."

" I see. And when does the lift start again ? "

" It is the same as in the morning, Capitano. I go up at a quarter to two, and at two o'clock the lift is open to the public. It continues until some time after seven."

" What do you mean—some time after seven ? "

Mario looked nervous. " Nobody may board the lift at either end after seven o'clock, Capitano," he said. " Sometimes people get on just before seven, and then the lift must continue until they have all completed their journeys. But always Carlo and I speak on the telephone. If nobody has started the trip after half-past six—which is often the case

—then we stop at seven. I ride down in the evening, as it is dark, and then when I arrive at the bottom, we stop the lift."

" Right," said Spezzi, making a note. " Now, let's get back to Herr Hauser. At what time did he return to the Bella Vista ? "

" It was during the afternoon, Capitano. I can't say exactly when . . . it was at the busiest time." Mario looked hopefully at Henry, but the latter shook his head.

" Can't help you this time, I'm afraid," he said.

" A pity. Perhaps Carlo will remember. Presumably," added Spezzi, " you noticed him coming up, because you said you were expecting him to go down again."

" Yes, Capitano. But the time . . ." Mario shrugged hopelessly.

" And Signor Rossati ? Did he go down ? "

" Yes, Capitano. At about five, it must have been, for it was beginning to get dark." Mario ventured a smile, obviously proud of his irrefutable logic.

" Can you remember if anyone else from the hotel went down ? "

" I don't think so, Capitano . . ."

" All right, Mario, you can go now. And don't," added Spezzi, " go gossiping in the Bar Schmidt about the questions you've been asked."

Mario looked shocked. " Of course not, Capitano."

" By the way, is there anything you want to ask him ? " As an afterthought, Spezzi turned to Henry.

There was, in fact, a lot more that Henry wanted to know : but, having decided to keep his questions for a less formal interview, he merely shook his head. Mario limped hurriedly out of the room, and his place was taken by Beppi, the porter—a large and cheerful character with the physique of an ox.

Beppi confirmed that Signor Rossati had told him in the morning to take Herr Hauser's luggage to the lift, and that he had done so at about half-past ten.

" What did his luggage consist of ? " Henry asked.

" We have the luggage," Spezzi put in. " Two coach-hide cases, a small canvas overnight bag, and a briefcase."

" That's right," said Beppi, beamingly. " Always the same luggage, Herr Hauser had. I knew it well."

" Was he in his room when you collected the cases ? "

" *Si, Capitano.* He was standing by the window, looking out, with his hands in his pockets—so. He was very happy."

" Why do you say that ? "

" He was whistling," said Beppi. " I wished him a good journey, and hoped he had had a pleasant stay, and he said to me, ' Not only pleasant, Beppi. Also beneficial.' I told him there is no place like the Bella Vista for a healthy climate, and he said, ' Yes, indeed. It has done me a great deal of good.' "

" Is that all he said ? "

" He told me he was catching the seven o'clock train to Montelunga, and that Carlo should take his baggage to the Olympia. Nothing else."

" And then you took the cases to the lift ? "

" Yes. Poor old Mario was very busy—he wasn't pleased to see me, I can tell you. But I told him there was no hurry."

" And did you see Herr Hauser again ? "

" I saw him in the afternoon. About half-past four, it must have been. I went into the bar to put back a chair I had been mending, and he was there with Signora Buckfast."

" Did you overhear what they were saying ? "

Beppi looked hurt. " I do not listen to the guests' private conversations," he said. Then he grinned, widely. " In any case, they were speaking in English. I couldn't understand a word. Later on, I saw Herr Hauser leaving the hotel."

" At what time ? "

" Soon after six, Capitano. I cannot be exactly sure. I was passing through the hall, and he said good-bye to me as he went out of the door."

Beppi was followed by Carlo, who gave a faithful if

uninspired account of the scene at the foot of the chair-lift.
He also confirmed Mario's recollections of the times when
the various residents of the Bella Vista had used the lift,
but he could not be precise about the time when Hauser
had gone up again in the afternoon.

After Carlo's departure, Spezzi called Gerda. Henry
noticed again her curiously disturbing air of watchful repose.
She was dressed entirely in black—black *vorlagres* and a
high-necked black sweater—and her face had its customary
pallor. She sat down gracefully and waited, motionless, for
Spezzi's questions. Every movement she made seemed
pared down to a minimum—a deliberate economy which
suggested to Henry deep, untapped reserves of energy and
strength. Spezzi looked at her with undisguised admiration,
apologised for having to bother her, and began the interview
somewhat tentatively, in German.

" Would you mind telling us your full name, Fraulein ? "

" Gerda Augusta Braun."

" And you are employed by the Baron and Baroness von
Wurtburg ? "

" Yes."

" In what capacity ? "

Gerda raised her eyebrow a fraction. By this millimetre
of movement she indicated precisely that everybody's time
was being wasted by asking questions to which they all knew
the answers. Spezzi, ruling out a fresh page of his dossier,
did not notice.

" I look after the children," she said.

" Have you any other duties ? "

" How could I ? I have plenty to do as it is."

Spezzi glanced up, and went slightly pink, but there was
no trace of insolence on the calm face. He went on, " Please
tell us exactly what you did yesterday."

There was a short pause. Then Gerda said : " Is it the
custom in Italy that one is questioned in front of other mem-
bers of the public ? "

She turned her quietly intent gaze to Henry.

Spezzi was by now becoming agitated. "I conduct my investigations as and how I please," he said. He threw his pencil down on to the table, and the point broke with a delicate, snapping sound. "It is no business of yours, but it so happens that Herr Tibbett is connected with the British police——"

"Ah." Gerda looked at Henry with an expression that might have been satisfaction. "In that case, I am delighted that he is here."

The needle-fine insult did not escape Spezzi. He flushed, and looked very crestfallen, but said nothing. Gerda went on. "Yesterday, I awoke at seven o'clock, as usual, and got the children dressed. We breakfasted at half-past eight, and were ready to start skiing by nine-thirty. I took the children down to the village first, on Run Three, and then we went up the cable railway to Alpe Rosa. We did the run three times—once in the morning and twice in the afternoon. We ate our packed lunches on the terrace of the Albergo Rosa, at the top of the mountain. It was very beautiful," Gerda added, unexpectedly, "in the sunshine."

"And then?"

"At five o'clock we finished our last run, and met the Baroness by appointment at the sports shop—she wished to buy new sweaters for the children. When that was done, we all went to the Café Olympia, where we joined Signor di Santi and the English party."

Spezzi listened to the meticulous, gentle voice with an expression of mingled admiration and exasperation. As Gerda paused, he said, "Did you see Herr Hauser at all during the day?"

"At breakfast. I heard him call for Signor Rossati and ask for his bill, as he was leaving by the last train."

"And you did not see him again?"

"Not until the evening."

Spezzi leant forward. "What do you mean by that?"

Again Gerda's eyebrow lifted slightly. "Going up on the

lift, of course. When he was coming down. I presume he was dead by then." She spoke with no emotion at all.

" Tell us about it."

" What is there to tell ? I was the last on to the lift. The English had gone up first, then Signor di Santi, then the Baroness, Lotte and Hansi. I must have been about half-way up when I saw Hauser coming down."

" You recognised him without difficulty ? "

" Of course. It was dark and snowing, but there was a good light from a pylon lamp, and he was wearing his leopardskin boots."

" You said just now that you presumed he was dead already. Did anything of the sort occur to you at the time ? "

" That he was dead ? No. He was huddled up, sheltering from the snow, with his chin on his chest and his hat over his eyes. I did notice that he swayed in his chair as it bumped past the pylon—I thought perhaps he was asleep." Gerda paused, and then said very deliberately, " I hoped for a moment that he might fall off the lift and break his neck. But of course the safety-bar prevented that."

If Gerda had produced a hand-grenade from her pocket and laid it on the desk, she could not have caused a greater sensation. She watched calmly as Spezzi jumped to his feet, invoked the Deity, implored her to repeat what she had said—which she did—and finally subsided, mopping his brow.

" Do you realise the danger you put yourself in by saying such a thing, Fraulein ? " he cried, in a sort of anguish. " Why should you say it ? Why ? "

Gerda gave him a short, withering look, and addressed herself to Henry. " You would find out in any case," she said. " It is better for me to tell you. I hated Fritz Hauser. He killed my parents."

Once again, Spezzi was galvanized into a frenzy of Latin excitement. " Let us keep calm ! " he shouted.

Gerda paid no attention to him. " My father's name was Braun," she explained carefully to Henry, " but my mother's was Rosenberg. She was Jewish. You may have heard of my father—Gottfried Braun."

"The actor," said Henry.

"Yes."

"He was brilliant. I've seen all his films. He worked with Jannings and Reinhardt——"

"Yes."

"And didn't he——?" Henry stopped, embarrassed.

"He committed suicide," said Gerda, evenly, "after the Gestapo had arrested my mother. She died in Ravensbruck."

"What did Hauser have to do with all this?" Spezzi was trying desperately to regain his grip on the interview. Gerda looked at him coldly.

"I don't suppose you know anything about my father," she said. "He was a great actor and a good man, but he was weak. He hated the Nazi régime without having the courage to oppose it openly. He had a bad nervous breakdown, and he consulted Hauser, who was practising in Berlin at that time. I think that was when he first started to take drugs."

There was an uncomfortable silence.

"Life in Berlin between the wars was . . . difficult," Gerda went on. "Or so they tell me. I was very young at the time, and my mother took good care that I knew nothing of . . ." She paused. "To me, life seemed very good."

Henry had a vivid mental picture of a solemn, dark little girl, secure in her mother's love, sheltered from violence and corruption by the frail pink and blue walls of a pretty nursery: and of what must have happened when those walls crumbled.

"I knew Hauser, of course. He was our doctor. My mother never liked him, but my father would have nobody else. I suspect now what I am sure my mother suspected then—that he supplied my father with cocaine."

"Go on," said Henry, quietly.

"When things got too bad for . . . for the Jews . . . and my father's position was no longer a safeguard, my mother and I went away to my uncle and aunt in the country. I suppose we were hiding—but I didn't know it at the time. To me, it seemed like a holiday that went on and on. My father used to visit us from time to time. I was only seven, but even I could see how ill he was becoming . . . and how desperate. One day, when I was playing in the garden, I heard my father weeping. My father . . . weeping." The only emotion in Gerda's voice was a mild astonishment at the recollection. " I listened. I heard him say, ' They won't give me work . . . they are all too frightened . . .' And my mother said, ' It's all because of me.' And then she said, ' Why can't we get away—all three of us ? It would be a risk, but it would be worth it. We could go to America— you are well known there . . .'

" So the talk went on." Gerda glanced at Spezzi. " One day, soon after that, my father arrived, very excited, with bright eyes. He told my mother to pack quickly, for we were going to America. ' But how ? ' she said : and my father said, ' Hauser has fixed it.' Then my mother said, ' Oh, you fool. What have you done ? '—but my father didn't listen. ' It is expensive, of course,' he said, ' but it's worth it, just as you said. I've sold everything—the house—the car. His friends will pick us up here to-night . . .' "

Gerda paused. " I remember that my mother started to cry. I ran to her, and she kissed me. It was then that we heard the car outside and the knock on the door. It was the Gestapo, of course. They arrested my mother, and they would have taken me, but my aunt told them I was her child. I don't know why they believed her. They were very stupid sometimes. Then they complimented my father on his loyalty to the Fatherland in divulging his wife's address to ' the proper quarters'. That night, my uncle and aunt took me away in their car. My father refused to come with us. He waited until we had gone, and then he blew his brains out."

There was a silence. Spezzi, deeply moved, blew his nose loudly.

" And you ? " Henry asked.

"We went into hiding for a while, but they had lost interest in us. We came back to the farm, and I lived as their daughter. After the war, I trained as a children's nurse, and three years ago I went to work for the Baroness."

"When did you meet Hauser again?"

"The first time I came here with the children—three years ago. I recognised him at once. I have a very good memory," she added.

"Did he know who you were?"

"No, I am sure he didn't. Braun is a very common name in Germany."

"Why did you not go to the authorities with your story after the war?" Spezzi put in.

Gerda smiled faintly. "My story?" she said. "A conversation overheard by a child of seven? What proof is that of anything?"

"And so you planned your revenge." Spezzi spoke quietly now, in a flat, hopeless voice.

"How could I? I hated him. That was all."

Spezzi seemed to steel himself to a deeply distasteful task. He leant forward over the desk. "When did you take the gun?" he asked.

For the first time, Gerda appeared really surprised and disconcerted. "The gun? What gun?"

"You knew that Hauser carried a gun?"

"No. I did not."

"And that is all you have to say?"

"Yes, Capitano. I have saved you a lot of tedious work—but I cannot help you any more." Gerda stood up. "I did not kill him," she said. "I wish I had, but I did not."

Spezzi gave her a despairing look. "You may go now," he said, "but do not attempt to leave the hotel."

"Thank you, Capitano." For a brief moment, Gerda's eyes rested on the Capitano's handsome brown face, and Henry thought there was a sort of wistfulness in her look: then she turned on her heel, and went out as silently and swiftly as a black shadow.

" Well," said Henry, when the door had shut behind her. " There's nothing like being frank. She was perfectly right in assuming that you'd find out anyway. The question is— was she being disarmingly honest or very clever indeed ? "

" She is like an angel of death," said Spezzi, gloomily. " I think—I fear—we need not bother with the reports from Rome. There is your motive. There is your opportunity. There is your murderess." He sighed deeply.

" I wouldn't jump to conclusions, if I were you," said Henry, sympathetically. " You may be wrong."

There was a firm but gentle knock on the door.

" Come in," called Spezzi, sharply. He was not a little disconcerted to see Gerda standing there once again, as self-possessed as ever.

Spezzi got to his feet. " You have decided to tell us something more, then ? " he asked, quietly.

Gerda lowered her eyes, and shook her head. " I have told you all I know, Capitano," she said. " I have only come to give you a message from my mistress. She is up now, and will be pleased to talk to you. She would prefer the interview to take place in her room."

With that, she turned and went out.

Henry raised his eyebrows slightly. " Do we go up, or do we summon the lady down here? " he asked.

Spezzi shrugged his shoulders glumly. " Her father is Count Pontemaggiore," he said, " and her husband is the Baron von Wurtburg. We go up."

CHAPTER NINE

GERDA WAS WAITING in the hall when they came out. She preceded them up the wooden staircase, with its faint, delicious tang of polish and pinewood, and stopped outside a door on the first floor. It was the Baron's voice that answered her knock with permission to enter. Gerda opened the door.

"The police," she said, shortly, and stood back to let the three men go in.

Signor Rossati had evidently done his utmost to provide accommodation worthy of his important guests. The two best bedrooms in the hotel—which were linked by a connecting door—had been mobilised to form a suite. The room into which Henry and Spezzi now stepped was the sitting-room—that is to say, the bed had been replaced by a sofa and two arm-chairs, and a small table struggled manfully to impersonate a writing-desk, under the thin disguise of a blotter, an inkwell, and a potted cyclamen. A chintz screen in one corner evidently concealed the wash-basin. Through the open door leading to the other room, Henry got a glimpse of tousled bed-clothes and a dressing-table burdened with expensive glass bottles of scent and cosmetics. The balcony which encircled the building at first-floor level ran past both rooms, and sunshine was streaming in through the long windows, which stood open. Beyond them, the pink summits of the mountains soared to pierce the ink-blue sky, and the dazzle of the snow threw into sharp relief the rich darkness of the pinewoods. Far below, Santa Chiara looked like a settlement of dolls' houses, and the chairs of the ski-lift sailing placidly between the trees could have been a clockwork toy.

At first sight, the room appeared empty. Then Henry saw the Baron. He was on the balcony, his back towards the room, leaning on the honey-coloured wooden rail and gazing down into the valley. He straightened slowly, turned, and came into the room.

Without the hat, his face seemed longer and craggier than ever. He was smoking a Turkish cigarette, the aroma of which eddied and lingered in the crisp air, and he looked exceedingly angry and at the same time uneasy. Spezzi clicked his heels politely, and gave a little bow.

"Capitano Spezzi, Carabinieri di Montelunga," he introduced himself, formally. The Baron inclined his head slightly in acknowledgment. Then he turned his pale blue eyes to Henry for a second, and said to Spezzi, in German, "Who is this man?"

Spezzi quavered noticeably. "He is a high-ranking officer of the British police, Herr Baron, who is concerned in these investigations – " he began, timorously.

The Baron frowned. Henry, who was beginning to get cross, said, "My name is Tibbett. I come from Scotland Yard. You must be Baron von Wurtburg." He produced a card from his case, and held it out.

The Baron did not even glance at it. Still addressing Spezzi, he said : "I fail to see what interest this case can hold for the British police."

"It is a matter of some complication, Herr Baron——" began Spezzi, sweating a little. "There are certain aspects of the deceased's activities which——"

Henry cut him short. "I am afraid I am concerned in the case, Herr Baron," he said. "I dislike the fact as much as you do. However, fortunately we need not trouble you. It is your wife who can help us by answering a few questions."

The blue eyes grew dangerously cold. "Nobody interviews my wife except in my presence," he said.

Simultaneously, Henry said, "I am afraid that is out of the question," and Spezzi said, "Naturally, Herr Baron. Just as you wish."

There was an awkward pause. Then Henry said, "Forgive me, Capitano. This is your interview, and of course you must conduct it as you see fit."

The Baron merely looked at Henry with icy dislike. Then he went to the bedroom door, and called, " Are you ready, my dear ? "

Maria-Pia, who had obviously overheard every word, came in at once. She was very pale, and Henry thought she had been crying. Her fragility was enhanced by her huge, loose sweater of pure white wool, worn over sky-blue *vorlagers*. She smiled at Henry—a desperate little smile that mutely apologised for her husband's behaviour and begged him not to think hardly of her. Henry grinned back reassuringly.

She walked gracefully across the room, and sat down in an arm-chair. Instantly, the Baron perched himself on the arm, in an attitude at once protective and minatory. Henry took the other armchair, Spezzi plumped for the sofa, and spread his notes out on the seat beside him. The shorthand writer sidled thankfully out of the Baron's range of vision, and established himself at the pseudo-writing-desk.

Spezzi began on an ingratiating note. " I am desolated to have to put you to this inconvenience, Baroness——"

The Baron interrupted. " Kindly speak in German," he said.

Red-faced, Spezzi began again. " I would gladly have spared you this unpleasant interview, Baroness, but the fact that you were on the chair-lift at the crucial time makes it——"

" I know, I know. Let's have the questions," said Maria-Pia, in Italian. Spezzi mopped his brow, and continued, doggedly, in German. Tensions stretched across the room like elastic bands.

" You boarded the ski-lift—when ? " The Capitano grabbed his notes, delighted of an excuse not to meet the Baron's eyes.

" I can't tell you exactly. About a quarter past six, I suppose."

"I understand that you went up after Signor di Santi, and before the children and their nurse."

At the mention of Franco's name, Maria-Pia had stiffened slightly. But her voice was perfectly level as she answered, still in Italian, "That is correct."

"I want you," said Spezzi, a little surer of himself now, though still acutely aware of the absurdity of an interview conducted in two languages—"I want you to describe to me exactly how you remember Hauser looking when he came down past you."

Maria-Pia frowned. "I hardly noticed him at all," she said. "It was dark and snowing and very cold. I just remarked to myself that it was him—he was wearing those terrible boots. He was huddled up in his chair, which seemed perfectly natural under the circumstances."

"Did you know that Hauser possessed a gun?"

Maria-Pia looked scared. "A gun?" she said. "Yes . . . yes, I did."

At once, the Baron intervened. "Nonsense," he said. "How could my wife have known such a thing?"

Maria-Pia ignored him, and addressed Spezzi earnestly. "Everybody must have known," she said. "The other evening—I think it was Wednesday—he was sitting in the bar with his briefcase on the table. He pushed it to one side to make room for his drink, and a gun fell out of it on to the floor. I had a funny sort of feeling——" She stopped, and then said quickly, "I had a funny sort of feeling that he did it on purpose."

"Who else was in the bar?" Spezzi asked.

"Nearly everybody." Maria-Pia wrinkled her pretty nose in concentration. "Henry and Emmy weren't there," she said, "but I think everyone else was. I remember Mrs. Buckfast making some very acid remarks." She smiled.

"Were you surprised to see this gun?" Spezzi asked.

"Yes, I was. Very. I didn't know that people carried weapons about with them these days."

"This seems to be very much off the point," said the Baron, grimly. "Please get back to relevant questions."

Spezzi shuffled his papers. "To return to the events of yesterday, Baroness," he said. "Did you see Hauser at all earlier in the day?"

"I think I saw him after breakfast for a moment. But I was going off to ski, and I was in a hurry."

"I see." Spezzi paused. "Now, Baroness I have a few questions I must ask you concerning another person. I do not want to distress you in any way . . ."

Maria-Pia went from white to pale green, and gripped the arm of her chair. The Baron leant forward, tense. Spezzi went on, "It concerns Fraulein Gerda Braun."

Maria-Pia's hand, which had been picking at the cording of the arm-chair, relaxed like a dead bird. The Baron, however, remained tense.

"Gerda?" she said. There was real surprise in her voice. "What do you want to know about her?"

"Was she in the bar when Hauser dropped his gun?"

"No, of course not. She was putting the children to bed."

"What sort of a girl is she?" asked Spezzi, and it seemed to Henry that his voice trembled slightly.

"Charming." Maria-Pia spoke firmly. "Very quiet and reserved, and thoroughly efficient. The children love her, and yet they respect her—and it is difficult to fool children, you know."

"You would not say that she had a violent nature?"

"Violent?" Maria-Pia's voice grew more and more astonished. "Gerda?"

"After all," said Spezzi, carefully, "when you consider her background and her parents . . ."

"But she lived all her life on her father's farm in Bavaria," said Maria-Pia. "That is, until she went to Munich to take her training. Then she answered my advertisement and came to me, three years ago."

"You never met her parents."

" Yes, as a matter of fact, I did, once. Wait a moment"—
Maria-Pia paused, thoughtfully—" I believe she did tell me
that they were not her real parents : that they had adopted
her when she was tiny. I never thought about it."

" Who is she, then ? " The Baron rapped out the
question.

Bravely, Spezzi ignored it. " Thank you very much,
Baroness. It is not important. I just thought that——"

" If this girl has lied to us, we have a right to know," said
the Baron, coldly.

" No, no, Hermann." Maria-Pia spoke in German, for
the first time. " She hasn't lied to us—has she, Capitano ?
She told me that the Brauns were not her parents."

The Baron kept his eyes on Spezzi. " Who is she ? " he
asked again.

Spezzi was obviously uncomfortable, but he stood his
ground. " I assure you, Herr Baron, it is of no consequence
at all," he said.

The Baron glared at him. " I shall take steps to find out,"
he said. There was a short pause. " If you have nothing
further to ask concerning the crime, perhaps you would
leave us now. My wife is very tired."

Spezzi stood up. " Thank you for your co-operation,
Baroness . . . Herr Baron . . . I am very sorry I had to trouble
you."

He bowed briefly to both Maria-Pia and the Baron, and
made for the door, followed hastily by the shorthand writer.
Henry stood up slowly.

" Later on," he said, " I would welcome an opportunity
for a word with you, Baroness." For the last week he had
been calling her Maria-Pia, but it did not seem the moment
for familiarity.

Before the Baron could speak, she said eagerly, "Of
course, Henry. Whenever you like."

" Thank you," said Henry, gravely. He followed the
two Italians down the stairs.

Back in Rossati's office, Spezzi wiped his brow with a white silk handkerchief. Henry gave him a sympathetic grin, but the Capitano was in no mood to be consoled.

"The sooner we can arrest that girl and get it over," he muttered, miserably, "the happier I shall be." Then he sat down at the desk again, and sent for Franco.

Franco was pale, with deep circles of sleeplessness under his dark brown eyes. He told Spezzi in a quiet, unhappy voice that he was a sculptor, that he lived in Rome and was in Santa Chiara on holiday. He had been coming to the Bella Vista regularly for the last three years. He knew Hauser very slightly, he said. He had first met him at the house of an actor-friend in Rome three years ago, and it was, in fact, Hauser who had recommended the Bella Vista to him as a pleasant place for a skiing holiday. Since then he had met him at the hotel as a fellow-guest, but had never pursued the acquaintanceship further.

"Frankly, Capitano, he did not seem to me to be a very pleasant character," he said, but would not elaborate on this statement. He agreed that he had seen the gun fall out of Hauser's briefcase on Wednesday evening. "It struck me," he said, contemptuously, "that he did it on purpose to create a cheap effect."

Franco confirmed that he had preceded the Baroness up on the chair-lift the previous evening, but said that he had not noticed Hauser at all.

"I had my eyes shut," he said, briefly. "It was an uncomfortable ride, and I had other things to think of."

That concluded Franco's contribution to the evidence, and Henry, glancing at his watch, remarked that it was half-past twelve, and suggested a break for lunch. He had noticed Emmy coming up the path from the ski-lift, and so pointed out that the interrogation of the English could begin after lunch.

"Unless you want to see the Knipfers first," he added, to Spezzi.

"I will talk to them, of course," said the Capitano, "but

they seem to me to be unimportant. None of them were on the chair-lift at the time of the murder."

"On the other hand," said Henry, "I think they may be able to tell us quite a lot about Hauser. They spent a lot of time with him." And he went on to tell Spezzi about Frau Knipfer's outburst in the bar the previous evening.

Henry found Emmy in their bedroom, combing her hair.

"Your cable's gone off, safe and sound," she said. "You owe me the monstrous sum of five thousand lire. How did you get on this morning?"

Henry told her, briefly.

"I don't really believe it, do you?" she said slowly, when he had finished. "I can't see Gerda as homicidal."

"She's perfectly capable of killing," said Henry. "And she had both the motive and the opportunity. Don't forget that she was the last to get on to the lift, so there was nobody in the chair behind to see what she was doing. But all the same . . ." He paused.

"Your nose tells you . . ." Emmy teased him gently.

"No," said Henry. "I don't know enough about this case to bring the old nose into it yet. It's just that it seems out of character . . ." He paused, and then went on, "Oh, well, we shall see. Spezzi's made up his mind already—poor chap, he's obviously very taken with the girl, and that makes him all the more determined to do his duty ruthlessly. I do hope he's wrong."

"Let's go down to lunch," said Emmy.

Lunch was not a cheerful meal. Spezzi and his aide sat at Hauser's old table, casting the long shadow of the law over the whole room. The Knipfers ate silently and gloomily, as usual. Franco was back at a table by himself, and Henry was not surprised to see Gerda also sitting alone. The Baron's two children, who had been allowed to go out skiing with a private instructor that morning, had clattered noisily into the hall some minutes earlier, and been escorted firmly upstairs by Anna. Presumably they were having a family lunch with their parents in their private sitting-room —a procession of large trays had disappeared in that direction —while Gerda had been cast into the outer darkness of the dining-room. If she resented this, she did not show it. Not a flicker of emotion crossed her face.

The English party were already seated when Henry and Emmy came in. Emmy had felt serious qualms about taking their usual place at the communal table, in view of Henry's present embarrassing position, so she was delighted when Roger jumped to his feet and pulled out her chair for her. He seemed determined to do his best to atone for his rudeness of the night before.

" Here you are at last," he said. " We were beginning to give you up for lost. Come on, Henry—we've all ordered. How's the sleuthing ? "

" Dull," said Henry. They both sat down. " I warn you, it's your turn afterwards."

" Thank goodness for that," said Jimmy. " The strain was becoming unbearable. Are you going to drive us into corners by brilliantly ruthless cross-examination, until the guilty party breaks down and confesses ? "

" Heavens," said Henry, " I do hope not. No, all we're doing at the moment is working out a sort of time-table of everybody's movements yesterday. It's plodding, routine stuff, but it has to be done."

A silence laden with palpable disbelief followed this remark. Lunch arrived, and was eaten in a gloomy atmosphere of strain, broken only by Jimmy spilling his soup over the tablecloth. Henry came to the conclusion that young Passendell, for all his veneer of insouciance, was in fact in a bad state of nerves, and decided to put him out of his misery as swiftly as possible.

" Like to come first, Jimmy ? " he asked.

Jimmy looked sick, but he said, bravely enough, " O.K. Try anything once."

They adjourned to the office, where Spezzi and his aide were already waiting.

As it happened, the interview was uneventful, and added very little to what Henry already knew. Jimmy admitted his identity, declared that he had never seen or heard of Hauser before he arrived at the Bella Vista, and was emphatic that he had not set eyes on the murdered man between breakfast-time and the moment when he had noticed the huddled figure, dead or alive, going down on the lift.

"Dead or alive," he added, reflectively. "I wonder. Now that I come to think of it, I'd say probably dead—though of course it never occurred to me at the time. He looked sort of . . . limp. I thought he might be asleep."

"You were the first of the Bella Vista party to get on to the lift, weren't you?" said Henry.

"Was I? Yes, I suppose I was. I can't really remember."

"One more thing," said Henry. "Hauser had the room next to yours on the second floor. Did you ever see or hear anything suspicious going on there?"

Jimmy looked worried. "I don't quite know what you mean," he said.

"I mean conversation, or quarrelling, with anybody else in the hotel. I mean the gun, left about carelessly where anybody could see it."

"By Jove, yes, I did see the gun once," said Jimmy, eagerly. "That is, apart from when it fell out of his brief-case on Wednesday. When I came in from skiing one evening, Hauser's door was open, and the gun was lying on the table. It was acting as a sort of paperweight for some letters, or something." It must have been . . . yes, it was the day before he was—before he died."

"I see. Well, I think that's the lot. Thank you."

Jimmy had risen to go when Henry added, suddenly, "There's just one more thing. Whose idea was it—this holiday of yours at the Bella Vista?"

Jimmy looked a little uncomfortable. "It was Roger's, actually," he said. "He'd been here before, you see."

"It struck me as a little strange from the beginning," Henry added, "that you and Caro should come to such a tiny place, and travel by a cut-price second-class train. Forgive me for saying this, but I should have thought that St. Moritz would have been more your mark."

Jimmy grinned. "You're absolutely right," he said. "The journey was hell, wasn't it? But you see, poor old Roger isn't as well-oiled as the rest of us, and Caro was mad to go with him, so . . ."

"I see," said Henry. "Yes, I guessed it was something like that."

Caro was next on the list, and Henry did not enjoy interviewing her. She was in an obvious state of nerves, and looked as though she had been crying, and she evaded practically every question with, "I don't know," or "I can't remember." Henry, hating his job, led the questions round to the subject of Roger. After much hedging, Caro admitted that the holiday had been his idea.

"How long have you known him?" Henry asked, casually.

"I can't remember. Ages. Well, no . . . not ages, really. Six months. I don't know."

"Less than three years, in any case?"

"What do you mean? Why shouldn't I have known him three years?"

"Have you any idea why he suggested the Bella Vista for a holiday?"

"No. Yes. He'd been here before. Anyway, it was cheap."

"Yes," said Henry. "I imagine that had quite a lot to do with it, didn't it?"

"Well, what does it matter if it did? Roger can't help not being rich. Why does everyone pick on him?"

Henry took the plunge. "Did you know, Caro, that Roger had once been mixed up in a case of smuggling?"

Caro went as white as a sheet. "It's not true," she said. "I don't believe you. You've got no right to make accusations like that."

"I'm not making accusations," said Henry. "I'm asking you a question. Did you know?"

"No!" Caro almost shouted the word. "No, I didn't. And I still don't. You mustn't believe what people say."

Henry said, very gently, "Why are you so worried about him?"

"I'm not. I'm ... oh, you've got it all wrong. I'm not going to say any more. It's none of your business."

"What did you mean, in the bar yesterday, when you said that Hauser was a vile man?"

"I didn't mean it."

"But you said it. You must have had some reason."

"I just didn't like him."

"Is that all?"

"Of course it's all. I've got a right to dislike somebody, haven't I?"

"Without any reason?"

"Of course, if I want to. Why do you keep on about it?"

"I'm sorry," said Henry. "I'm only trying to get at the truth, you know."

"The truth ..." said Caro, and it was like a sigh. "Oh God, aren't we all ...?"

"Oh, help," thought Henry, "She's going to cry." Quickly, he said aloud, "All right. That's all for the moment. You'd better run along and have a cup of tea."

Caro nodded, dumbly, and walked out of the room with a great effort at composure.

"Very interesting," said Henry, to Spezzi. "Now we'll see what Mr. Staines has to say for himself."

"Yes," Spezzi smiled slowly. "That will be quite a revelation, I imagine."

Roger appeared completely at ease. Henry led him expertly and quickly through the events of the previous day—Hauser's announcement at breakfast, his own day's skiing to Immenfeld with Colonel Buckfast.

"That was the run that Giulio Vespi was killed on, wasn't it?" Henry asked.

Roger's face clouded. "Poor old Giulio," he said. "He was a good chap. But the run must have been bloody impossible when he tried it. It wasn't easy yesterday, but there's new snow now, and even though the *piste* is non-existent, it's clearly marked."

"You've been to the Bella Vista before, haven't you?"

"Last year. Last three weeks in January."

"So you know quite a few of the local people?"

"I wouldn't say that. Most of the ski instructors, and Rossati, of course . . . and the Buckfasts and Hauser were here for part of the time. I gather they're more or less permanent fixtures."

"Was that your only previous meeting with Hauser?"

"Of course. Where else could I have met him?"

Henry let this pass. "Did you like him?" he said.

To Henry's considerable surprise, Roger threw back his head and laughed aloud. "Oh, you coppers—you're unbelievable! 'Did I like him?' indeed, when you know perfectly well he was trying to blackmail me!"

"Blackmail you?" Henry's astonishment was perfectly genuine. "What about?"

"Don't let's be silly, old man," said Roger, easily. "You must have found the note by now. Where was it? In his wallet?"

Henry turned to Spezzi, and said in Italian, "Mr. Staines seems to think you might have found an incriminating note in Hauser's wallet. Did you?"

Spezzi's dismay and disappointment were quite pathetic. Shamefacedly, he fumbled in the breast pocket of his resplendent uniform, and produced a small piece of paper, torn from a diary, which he handed to Henry. On it was scrawled, in Italian. "*Lupo. The stores you are expecting are at the café. Collect them and load up to-night. R.S.*"

"Why didn't you show me this before?" said Henry, very sternly.

Spezzi looked profoundly unhappy. "I wished to take him by surprise," he said. "You are a friend of his, and . . ." An eloquent gesture completed the insinuation. "But now what happens? He mentions it himself before I can make my effect. I do not," added Spezzi gloomily, " understand the English."

Henry turned to Roger. " Well ? " he said. " What about it ? "

Roger was sitting back, relaxed, and watching the others with visible amusement. " I'm not worried about that," he said. " It's a clumsy forgery."

" That we shall see," snapped Spezzi.

" I don't know," Roger went on, " how Hauser found out about the *Nancy Maud*. We had a few chats together last year, and I suppose he must have got my address in London from the hotel register. Anyway, in October I got a letter from him. I couldn't have been more surprised."

He pulled out his wallet, and extracted a letter, which he passed to Henry. It was typewritten, on heavy and expensive writing paper.

> *Via Aurelia* 49
> *Roma*

> *October 4th*

> *Dear Mr. Staines,*
> *I wonder if you remember me ? I had the pleasure of meeting you at the Bella Vista hotel in Santa Chiara last January, and I was most impressed, during the talks which we had then, by your outstanding grasp of business matters and by your executive ability. Consequently, I thought of you at once when a most interesting business proposition arose recently—one which could be extremely lucrative if handled by the right man.*
> *I would very much like to discuss this matter personally with you, if you are interested. Since I am planning to visit the Bella Vista again during the month of January, I wonder whether you, too, would not consider spending your skiing holiday there ? In that way, we could talk privately and at our leisure about the scheme I have in mind.*
> *With my most distinguished salutations,*
> *Fritz Hauser*

Henry studied this remarkable document in silence : then he said : " So you came."

Roger grinned. " Of course I did, old boy. No harm in finding out what it was all about."

" You had no idea at all when you came here about the nature of this business proposition ? "

" Not the faintest."

" Didn't it strike you that the whole thing sounded extremely shady ? "

Roger said again, " There was no harm in finding out."

" All right, I'll accept that," said Henry. " Go on."

" Well, I came." There was a bitter note in Roger's voice now. " I came, and of course there was no business proposition whatsoever. Just a grubby attempt at blackmail. I knew the note wasn't genuine, of course—because I never wrote such a thing : the first time I set eyes on that little rat Donati was in the courtroom in Rome. But Hauser undoubtedly thought it was genuine. I presume Lupo wrote it himself, and sold it to Hauser."

" So what did you do ? "

" I laughed in his face," said Roger. " I told him that apart from the fact that I'm stony-broke, and the worst possible person to blackmail, the note was an obvious forgery, and he'd better go ahead and do his worst."

" Why didn't you report him to the authorities ? "

" My dear fellow, I'm on holiday," said Roger. " In any case, it would have meant raking up all the business of the *Nancy Maud*, and frankly, I want to forget it. No point in digging up old dirt."

" And what was Hauser's reaction when you laughed at him ? "

Roger, for the first time, seemed a little hesitant. " He wasn't pleased, as you can imagine," he said slowly. " He tried to bluster a bit, but at last it penetrated his thick skull that I wasn't in the least frightened of him. Then he changed his tune."

" You didn't by any chance," said Henry, " turn the tables on him and threaten him with prosecution ? "

There was a short silence. Roger lit a cigarette. At last he said, " You told me yesterday to stick to the truth, and I'm going to take your advice. It's understood, I hope, that this is in strict confidence."

" You know I can't promise you that," said Henry. " All I can say is that it won't be mentioned unless it becomes necessary evidence."

" O.K. Fair enough." Roger took a long pull at his cigarette. " All right, then. I did threaten to tell the police—I felt completely confident, and I intended to make him realise it. But he called my bluff. He invited me to prosecute him, and he also pointed out that—win or lose— Sir Charles Whittaker might have understandable objections to me as a son-in-law if such an unsavoury case were splurged across the newspapers. You see," he added, disarmingly, " I hope to marry Caro."

" And Hauser knew that ? "

" He was remarkably well-informed," said Roger, dryly. " Anyway, in the end we came to an agreement. I would not prosecute, and he would destroy the note. Even though it was a forgery, I didn't like the thought of a man like that running round with such a thing in his pocket. You see, unfortunately it was written on a page of an old diary of mine—I'd left it on board the *Nancy Maud* when she was stolen. The printing is fairly distinctive, as you can see, and I thought Hauser might be able to make more trouble for me if he was allowed to keep it."

Henry was looking very thoughtful. " When did you come to this agreement ? " he asked.

" The day before yesterday. We were having tea in the Olympia together. He took the note out of his wallet, and put a match to it. It burnt itself out in the ashtray. I thought that was the end of the matter."

" Then how did it happen that he still had the note when he was killed ? "

Roger said, angrily, " He must have tricked me. He held out the note for me to see, but when I put out my hand to take it, he snatched it away again, and it fell on the floor. I suppose that was when he switched it for a blank piece of paper. It wasn't until you so kindly dropped me a hint in the bar last night that I realised what must have happened."

To his annoyance, Henry felt his face redden. He hoped fervently that Spezzi's English was inadequate.

" I knew nothing about the note then," he said. " All I did was to advise you to tell the truth."

" Well, I have," said Roger. " Now you know."

" You realise," said Henry, " that we shall have to submit the note to graphologists, together with specimens of your handwriting ? "

Roger smiled. " Of course," he said. " Go ahead. I'm not worried."

" No," said Henry, thoughtfully. " I see you're not."

With perfect good humour, Roger handed over his passport, with its specimen signature, rewrote the words of the note without hesitation on a page of Spezzi's notebook, and turned out his pockets to find his packing list, written in the same flowing, flamboyant hand.

When he had gone, Henry gazed long and earnestly at the scrap of paper from Hauser's wallet, holding it alongside the note which Roger had just written. The handwriting was superficially similar, but even to Henry's inexpert eye the " blackmail " note looked like a palpable forgery. He said as much to Spezzi, who was unimpressed.

" He would obviously have tried to disguise his handwriting in Tangiers," said the Capitano. " We must leave it to the experts. Personally, I think the note is genuine."

" And what else, may I ask, did you find in Hauser's pockets ? " asked Henry, a trifle maliciously.

Spezzi's blue eyes were mirrors of injured innocence. " Nothing of any interest, my friend. Just what I told you." He paused. " And, if I may be so bold, how many more of the British witnesses have you been coaching in what to say at their interrogations ? "

He looked at Henry blandly, and then they both began to laugh.

" *Touché*," said Henry. " I'm sorry. But remember, I wouldn't have said a word to him if I'd known about the note."

" It should be a lesson to both of us," said Spezzi " But I trust there is no harm done. I will send these "—he indicated the notes, the packing-list and the passport— " to Rome to-night. Let us now see your gallant compatriot, the Colonel."

Colonel Buckfast seemed to be suffering from an exaggeratedly delicate sense of *de mortuis* which compelled him to approach the subject of Hauser's personality like a hippopotamus on tiptoe.

" Poor fellow," he muttered into his moustache. " Likeable chap in many ways. German, of course. Couldn't help that."

" As a matter of fact, he was Italian," said Henry.

" Italian, was he ? What terribly bad luck," said the Colonel, though whether he referred to Hauser's demise or his nationality was not clear.

Yes, he remembered him well from last year—and the year before, come to that.

" When we first arrived here," said Henry, " I got the impression that you didn't much care for him."

" Me ? " said the Colonel, reddening. " No, no. Nothing against him. Hardly knew the man."

" He never spoke to you about himself, or his profession ?"

" Good God, no." The Colonel sounded as though Henry had suggested some gross obscenity. " Why ever should he ? I tell you, I barely exchanged a word with him."

Colonel Buckfast brightened considerably when it came to describing the previous day's sport.

" First-class run," he said. " First class. No *piste*, of course. New snow—absolutely superb. We took it fairly slowly, and made Immenfeld by two o'clock—had a late lunch there, and then I tried a couple of the local runs while Staines went shopping. Then we took the train back, and met the rest of you in the Olympia."

"And what about your ride up on the ski-lift? Did you notice Hauser coming down?"

The Colonel cleared his throat. "It was extremely cold and uncomfortable, as you know," he said. "In fact, when the confounded thing broke down while we were waiting for it, it seemed the last straw. Inefficiency, that's all it is. Wouldn't be tolerated in Switzerland. But when you're dealing with Eyeties——" He suddenly became aware of Spezzi's concentrated stare, and broke off, abashed. "Anyway," he went on, with some haste, "When I did get on, I muffled myself up in my blanket, and frankly I lost all interest until I reached the top. Never even noticed the poor fellow coming down."

"You didn't hear a shot, I suppose?"

The Colonel shook his head. "Didn't hear a thing, apart from the bloody rattle—begging your pardon, Mrs. Tibbett, I forgot you were there—the rattle that the chair makes every time it passes a pylon. But if the gun had a silencer, and I presume it did, I don't suppose anyone would have heard it. The chairs are pretty widely spaced, you know. Ever tried to shout from one to the other?"

"I know," said Henry. "By the way, did you know Hauser had a gun?"

"I should think everybody in the place knew, the way he flashed it around," said the Colonel, tetchily. "Gave my wife quite a shock when he threw it on the floor in the bar the other evening. Very bad form, I thought, with ladies present."

"Threw it?"

"As good as. Did it on purpose—any fool could see that. My wife was really upset."

Reverting to the ride up the chair-lift, the Colonel gave it as the best of his recollection that he had come up behind

Jimmy and Roger, but before Caro, although he couldn't be sure. In any case, he reiterated, he would not have noticed any movement from the person in the chair in front : it was very dark, and—as he finally admitted—he had been half-asleep.

That concluded Colonel Buckfast's contribution to the evidence, and as it was by then five o'clock, Henry suggested a break for tea.

" Afterwards," said Spezzi, " I will have a word with these Knipfer people, and then I would welcome an opportunity to study these interviews and prepare a report."

" What about Mrs. Buckfast ? " asked Henry. " We haven't seen her yet."

" I hardly think she will have anything important to tell us," said Spezzi. " She was not on the chair-lift, and was in no way concerned. But by all means talk to her if you wish, and let me know if anything interesting emerges."

" I gather your money is still on Fraulein Gerda," said Henry.

Spezzi nodded slowly. " The plausible Mr. Staines will bear further investigation," he said, " but I do not fancy him as a murderer. No, it is the girl—so beautiful, so dangerous. She would stop at nothing, I am sure of it." And the gallant Capitano sighed deeply.

CHAPTER TEN

HERR KNIPFER strode purposefully into the office, clicked his heels and bowed to Emmy, Henry and Spezzi, and sat down with jerky precision. Before Spezzi could get a word out, he began, " I fear I shall not be able to assist you, Herr Kapitan. There is nothing I wish more than to see this crime solved, for Hauser was a friend of ours ; but as you know, I do not ski, and yesterday my wife and I left the hotel only to take a short walk. There is nothing I can tell you."

Spezzi said, quietly, " It is for me to decide, Herr Knipfer, whether you can help us or not."

For a moment, anger glinted in Knipfer's cold eyes. Then he said, " Ask your questions, then. You will see."

He admitted grudgingly that his name was Siegfried Knipfer, that he ran an import-export business in Hamburg, and was in Santa Chiara on holiday. He managed to impart this information in such a way as to make it clear that he considered the questions a gross impertinence.

" Herr Hauser seemed to be especially friendly with your daughter," Henry put in.

Knipfer turned to him with a smile of icy sarcasm.

" You are obviously a keen observer, Herr Tibbett," he said. " Nothing escapes you. Yes, Fritz Hauser was greatly taken with Trudi. In fact, I may as well tell you that he wished to marry her."

Spezzi's eyebrows shot up.

" Indeed ? " he said. " Did you approve ? "

Knipfer spoke carefully. " Naturally, I wished for time to consider his offer," he said. " After all, I knew very little about the man. I had never met him before. He seemed to be wealthy, which was satisfactory, but I am not a poor man. There would be no question of Trudi marrying for money. On the other hand, I would have to be assured that her husband was able to support her adequately. Personally, I was favourable towards the match. My daughter, alas, is no beauty, and such a chance may not occur again." He paused. "Unfortunately, my wife felt otherwise. For no particular reason, she took a dislike to Hauser. Women are apt to be sentimental in such matters. In fact "—he glanced uneasily at Henry—" in fact, she had protested against the engagement with some violence, and was inclined to become hysterical on the subject. For that reason, I am afraid that her first reaction to the news of Hauser's death was one of relief. I need hardly say that she now regrets this."

"I see," said Spezzi. "I would be interested to know whether you had, in fact, made any inquiries about Hauser and if so, with what results ? "

Knipfer regarded him with cold contempt. "One does not set detectives on a future son-in-law," he remarked. "We had arranged to visit Fritz in Rome during the spring. Meanwhile, I was content to take him at his face value."

"You liked him ? "

"Of course. Otherwise I would not have contemplated his proposal."

"To come to the events of yesterday," Spezzi went on. "Since you were in the hotel all day, perhaps you can tell us something of Hauser's movements."

Knipfer considered this. "We were having breakfast when he told the proprietor he was leaving," he said. "As a matter of fact, we knew it already. He had told us the previous night that he had to return to Rome."

"Did he say why ? "

"He said that the attraction of Trudi's company had already induced him to postpone his return, and that now he could no longer ignore the pressure of business."

"Did he specify the business ? "

"He did not. I imagine that it was of a financial nature. He was a doctor, as you must know—but I understand that his researches were merely a hobby. He made his money by deals on the Stock Exchange, and such transactions demand constant vigilance and attention."

" So you saw him at breakfast. What happened then ? "

" My wife and I went to sit on the terrace, as usual. Hauser joined us at about half-past ten—he said he had been packing. We had coffee together, and then he said he was going down to Santa Chiara for lunch, after he had made a telephone call. Shortly before twelve, he passed us on his way down to the lift. We bade him good-bye, but he said that he would see us again, as he had now decided to return to the hotel after lunch."

" And did you see him return ? "

" No. My wife and I went for a short walk after lunch, and then rested in our room. At six o'clock, Hauser knocked on our door to wish us good-bye."

" You are sure of the time ? "

" Yes. We were both asleep, and his knock woke us. I remarked to my wife that it was six already, and we should be getting dressed for dinner. Hauser repeated his invitation to us to visit him in Rome, and we promised to write. Then he left. He already had his hat and coat on, so I presume he went straight out to the ski-lift."

" One last question, Herr Knipfer." Spezzi twirled his pencil, in some embarrassment. " What were your daughter's feelings about this proposed marriage ? "

" Trudi ? " Knipfer smiled coldly. " Trudi was naturally flattered and pleased by his proposal. The question of whether or not it should be accepted was for me to decide."

Herr Knipfer was followed by his wife. She lowered her stout body gingerly on to the small chair, and clasped her hands together nervously. After confirming her husband's account of how they had spent the previous day, she turned suddenly to Henry.

" I have to apologise for my behaviour yesterday, when you told us Fritz Hauser was dead," she said. Her round blue eyes welled with unshed tears. " My husband must have told you of this talk of an engagement. I am a mother,

Herr Tibbett . . . you must understand and forgive me . . ."
Her voice quivered dangerously, and Henry murmured,
" Of course, of course . . ."

" I did not wish it," she went on. " He was too old for
my Trudi . . . an old man, Herr Tibbett . . . and he would
have taken her away from us to live in Rome. She is my
only child, my baby . . ."

Tears threatened again, so Henry said quickly, " And I
suppose she did not want to marry him ? "

Frau Knipfer seized on this. " Ach, you are so sympathetic. You see into a mother's heart . . . my poor little
girl . . ."

" And yet your husband was in favour of the marriage ? "

At this point, the tears became uncontrollable. " Men,"
sobbed Frau Knipfer, dabbing at her eyes with a miniscule
lace handkerchief. " How can men understand these
things ? Is it a disgrace to remain unmarried ? " This
last question she flung, passionately, at Emmy, who shook
her head and made soothing noises.

Frau Knipfer sniffed loudly, and went on more calmly,
" So when I heard that he was dead, I confess I did not
stop to pity the poor man. All I thought was ' Now my
Trudi is safe . . . now she can come back to Hamburg with
her mamma . . . ' "

Henry said, " Had you any other reason to dislike Hauser,
apart from the fact that he was too old for your daughter ? "

Frau Knipfer buried her face in her handkerchief again,
and shook her head vigorously. " No, no . . ." she cried.
" No reason at all. . . no reason at all . . . that is why I am so
ashamed to think what I said . . ."

Emmy had to help her out of the office, and upstairs to
her room, where she subsided on the bed in a welter of
emotion. By contrast, Trudi herself was perfectly calm.

Henry took a good look at the girl as she sat down, smooth-
ing her unbecoming dirndl skirt demurely over her plump
knees. He realised that he had never really noticed her face
before, so nebulous and characterless had she seemed. Now

he saw that there was a determined jawline under the rounded pink cheeks, and that the blue dolls' eyes—superficially so like her mother's—had, too, a touch of her father's cold determination.

In a low voice, Trudi answered Spezzi's questions. She had had a private skiing lesson in the morning, she said. She had lunched with her parents. After lunch, she had gone on to the terrace, where she sat eating chocolate.

" Did you see or speak to anyone ? " Spezzi asked.

" Frau Buckfast was there," said Trudi. " I offered her a piece of my chocolate. Then she went to sleep. Just before four o'clock, I saw Herr Hauser coming up the path from the ski-lift. I went indoors."

" Why ? "

" It was beginning to get cold."

" Did you speak to Herr Hauser ? "

" Yes. He stopped me in the hall. I said I thought he had already left the hotel, but he said his plans had changed. Then he . . . he insisted that I should take tea with him in the bar. He talked again about marriage."

" We are all deeply sympathetic, Fraulein Knipfer," said Spezzi, reddening slightly. " Until just now, nobody realised that you had lost your fiancé in such a tragic way. You must be extremely upset."

Trudi looked at him steadily. " Yes, I am," she said.

" Forgive me for treading on such delicate ground—but I take it that you were in love with Herr Hauser, and looked forward to marrying him."

" Of course," said Trudi. She looked straight at Spezzi, as if daring him to dispute this statement. Spezzi, considerably disconcerted, led the questioning back to safer ground.

" Please tell us what happened after tea ? "

" I said good-bye to Herr Hauser in the hall," said Trudi. " It must have been about twenty past four. Then I went up to my room. Later on, I saw him leaving the hotel. My room is on the top floor, over the front door. It was quite dark, but there is a light over the porch, and on the path.

I watched him walk down to the lift. It was snowing quite hard. I did not dream that I would never see him again."

Spezzi said, eagerly, " Did you happen to notice the time, Fraulein Knipfer ? "

" No," said Trudi. " I suppose it was soon after six, but I cannot be sure."

" Now, Fraulein—I am sorry to have to ask you, but can you tell us if Herr Hauser ever spoke to you about his business, or his life in Rome ? "

Trudi smiled slowly—a smile of secret amusement which Henry found rather frightening. " He spoke a lot about Rome," she said. " He told me of the life I would lead there. I know nothing about his business."

" He never mentioned to you that he had enemies ? "

" Enemies ? " Trudi smiled again. " My father says that a good business man can be judged by the number and quality of his enemies. I think Herr Hauser was a good business man."

Spezzi pounced on this. " So you knew that he had enemies ? Who were they ? "

The girl hesitated for a moment. Then she said, " I have no idea. You are reading too much into what I said. I was only giving you my impressions."

There was obviously no more to be got out of Trudi, for all Spezzi's probing questions. At last, dispirited, he dismissed her with a short homily on the foolishness of trying to conceal information of any sort from the hawk-like vigilance of the Italian police. Trudi smiled again, agreed, and departed, leaving Spezzi with the conviction that in some obscure and indefinable way he had been got at, scored off and generally made a fool of. Her secret laughter riled his proud spirit.

" The girl is a fool," he said. " She knows more than she will say, and she imagines that she has deceived us." He snorted sardonically, closed his notebook with a snap, and turned to his aide. " Martelli, go and tell the guests that the interrogations are finished for the time being. They may resume their normal skiing activites to-morrow, but remind them all that the Immenfeld run is definitely forbidden. And anyone planning to leave the hotel permanently must notify me at least twenty-four hours beforehand. When you have done that, type your reports and bring them to my room."

The young *carabiniere* rose gratefully from his hard chair, saluted smartly, and strode out into the hall with all the anticipatory relish of a junior official who has been entrusted briefly by his superiors with the pleasant task of harrying the common run of humanity.

Emmy got up, too, stretched her arms above her head, and lit a cigarette.

Henry turned to Spezzi. "What's your next move?" he asked.

"I shall study the transcripts of these interviews, prepare a time-table of events, and make a report," said the Capitano. "I would be grateful for translations of the English interviews as soon as possible."

"You shall have them by the morning," said Henry. "Are you planning to stay on at the Bella Vista?"

"I think not. Only for a day or two. Then I shall move to the village, and rely on you for reports of what goes on up here."

Henry nodded. "I was hoping you'd do that," he said. "The very fact that you're in uniform makes them all close up like clams at the sight of you. With me, they are more relaxed."

"Exactly," said Spezzi. He lit one of his dark and dangerous-looking cigarettes. "I need hardly tell you to keep an eye on Fraulein Braun."

"Indeed I shall," said Henry. "Incidentally, you don't mind if I do a bit of nosing around on my own, do you? I mean, talking to people, and so on."

"Anything you wish, my friend," said Spezzi, expansively. "Well, I shall leave you now, and——"

The sentence was never finished. It was cut off, as by a knife, by a surge of voices in the hall outside. Mrs. Buckfast's clarion-note predominated, rising above the others like the soloist in a 'cello concerto.

" I've never heard such nonsense," she boomed, menacingly. " I insist ! "

Martelli's voice, a thin piccolo-wail, piped in execrable English, " Signora, the Capitano he say no . . ."

" Rubbish," thundered Mrs. Buckfast. " Get out of my way, you silly little man."

" Rosamund, don't you think—" The Colonel's deep bass rumble was swept aside like a leaf in a storm.

" Let me into that office ! "

It is a debatable but purely academic question whether Horatius or Attila the Hun might have stood their ground in the face of such a challenge. Lesser men, of the calibre of Martelli and the Colonel, never had the ghost of a chance. Spezzi had barely time to stub out his cigarette and rise to his feet before the door burst open, revealing Mrs. Buckfast, a Hera in magenta velvet, flanked on either side by the awestruck, hovering faces of her husband and Martelli.

" Madam—" began Spezzi, grabbing at the flying coattails of dignity.

Mrs. Buckfast stepped into the room, and eyed him as a fighting bull might eye an incompetent matador.

" Since you did not see fit to call me, Capitano Spezzi," she said, " I have been obliged to force my way into your office." She paused, and snorted slightly. Then she advanced another step, and, with a great sense of drama, dropped her bombshell in a quiet, conversational tone of voice.

" I have come," said Rosamund Buckfast, " to confess."

In the ensuing uproar, only Mrs. Buckfast remained entirely calm, like a rock round which demented seas toss and whirl. The Colonel, bordering on apoplexy, shouted incessantly that his wife was obviously hysterical and did not know what she was saying : Spezzi screamed at Martelli to clear the room, invoked his Maker for the second time that day, and appealed for calm in a frenetic wail : even Henry found himself pleading urgently with Mrs. Buckfast to reconsider her statement, while Emmy contributed to the mêlée by going down on her hands and knees to retrieve the papers which had fluttered like doves from Spezzi's briefcase. The clamour naturally attracted the attention of everyone else in the hotel. Cups of tea and apéritifs were left untasted in the bar, potatoes languished unpeeled in the kitchen, as guests and staff alike swarmed to join the maelstrom in the hall.

In the end, it was Mrs. Buckfast herself who cleared the office of its unauthorised mob—the last to leave being the Colonel, who was dismissed with a single, peremptory, " Arthur ! ", and a sternly-pointed finger. Then she sat down with perfect composure, folded her hands in her lap, and waited.

Spezzi, pink with agitation and exertion, resumed his seat at the desk, and appealed to Henry. " Ask this mad-woman what she means," he pleaded. " She was nowhere near the ski-lift, and now she confesses. It is lunacy." And he mopped his brow energetically.

Henry, more shaken than he liked to admit, assumed his best Scotland Yard manner and said, " Do I understand, Mrs. Buckfast, that you wish to confess to the murder of Fritz Hauser ? "

Mrs. Buckfast looked at him pityingly. " Of course not," she said. " I should have thought that even you, Henry Tibbett, would have realised that I couldn't possibly have killed him."

Henry, feeling like a small boy rebuked by his Nanny, clutched the desk for support.

" Then perhaps you would explain just what you meant just now ? "

" With pleasure." Mrs. Buckfast looked around comfort-ably, sure of her audience. " Arthur," she said, " is an unsatisfactory husband in many ways."

There was an uneasy pause, broken only by Spezzi's muttered reiteration of the word "Mad . . . mad . . ."

"For instance," Mrs. Buckfast went on, conversationally, "his enthusiasms are quite incomprehensible to me. He refuses to learn bridge, which is a game I am very fond of : and then there is his passion for stamp collecting, which I do not share. But perhaps you didn't know about that ? "

"No," said Henry, feebly. "No, I didn't."

"But the worst of the lot," she went on, "has always been this insane love of skiing. Year after year, every leave, every holiday, he has insisted on skiing. Of course he tries to prevent me from coming with him. But after a regrettable incident in Paris some years ago—I won't bore you with the details, they are not edifying—as I say, after that I decided not to allow him to go abroad on his own again. So you see," she added, with great simplicity, "for a number of years I was very bored indeed."

Light was beginning to struggle fitfully through the mists in Henry's brain.

"You *were* bored," he repeated. "Until you came to Santa Chiara."

Rosamund Buckfast favoured him with a brief, congratulatory smile. "The first time we came here," she said, "I nearly died of sheer isolation and exasperation. I resolved never to come again, even though Arthur maintained that he had found what he was pleased to call his Shangri-La."

She stopped, and looked hopefully at Henry, as a schoolmistress might encourage a bright pupil to carry on the chain of reasoning for himself. Henry resolved not to disappoint her.

He said : "And then, sometime during your first visit here, you met Hauser."

Mrs. Buckfast nodded approvingly.

"You were both non-skiers," Henry went on, gaining confidence. "You spent a lot of time on the terrace together, talking. You confided your boredom to him, and he suggested a means of alleviating it. I imagine that at first it was put to you as a sort of harmless game."

Mrs. Buckfast beamed. "You are cleverer than you look," she said, kindly.

Spezzi emitted a low moan. "What is this—I don't understand what you are talking about," he complained.

"Smuggling," said Henry. "A harmless game. A nice little bit of extra pin-money. A breath of excitement in a very dull existence. At first, of course, it will have been perfectly innocuous merchandise. What did he start you on?"

"The first year, it was just a few bottles of brandy," said Mrs. Buckfast. "They were collected from my house by a Post Office messenger, who gave me an envelope with the payment, in cash. The year after that, it was watches. Hauser had the ingenious idea of hiding them inside the quilted lining of my knitting bag. I made over a hundred pounds on them. I don't deny that it was wrong," added Mrs. Buckfast, reasonably, "but I must be frank and admit that I enjoyed it."

"And what did you have to bring out from England?"

Mrs. Buckfast's face clouded. "That was the beginning of the trouble," she said. "I was told to bring over, un-opened, a package that would be delivered to me in London. It was a small canvas bag—it came by Post Office messenger, as usual. Now, I do like to know what I'm doing, especially when it's illegal. I ignored Hauser's orders, and opened the bag. I am not," she added unnecessarily, "a woman who is easily intimidated."

"And what was in the bag?"

"Diamonds." Mrs. Buckfast's voice was stern and disapproving. "I can tell you, I didn't like it. Brandy is one thing, but diamonds are another, as I told Hauser quite firmly when I got out here. I told him I had not bargained for anything of that sort, and that I would not go on with it. I might have known, of course, that the little brute had no scruples. He made it very clear that if I didn't do as he said,

he would inform the police of my activities. I couldn't risk
that, so there was nothing I could do about it."

"When was this?" Henry asked.

"Last year."

"And this year?"

"More diamonds to bring out of England. And for the
return journey"—she opened her capacious bag, and brought
out a small white package. "I have two dozen of these
upstairs," she said. "The same cargo that I had to take
home last year. I don't know what the pernicious stuff
is, as I am thankful to say I have no experience of such
things, but I imagine that it is probably cocaine."

She handed the package to Henry. "That was really
going too far," she went on. "I had already made up my
mind to go straight to the authorities in England as soon as I
got back, and make a clean breast of things. Had you not
concealed from us that you were a policeman"—and
she glared accusingly at Henry—"we might all have been
saved a lot of bother. However, be that as it may. Hauser
began to doubt my reliability. He was no fool. That was
why he threatened me."

"Threatened you?"

"The gun, the gun," said Mrs. Buckfast, impatiently.
"Wednesday evening, in the bar. That little performance
was for my benefit. I must admit it gave me quite a shock
for a moment. Poor Arthur—of course, he had no idea
why I was upset. Personally, I have no doubt that if Hauser
had lived, he would have attempted to kill me before we left.
He made such a point of announcing his departure to all and
sundry that I am convinced he never intended to go far
away. He was planning to sneak back and shoot me. Typical
of the man."

"Oh, come now, Mrs. Buckfast—" Henry began, but
she interrupted him.

"You didn't know him," she said, shortly. "I did."

"So you were very relieved when he was murdered?"

"I was delighted," she said, candidly, "and I should like

to congratulate whoever did it. Apart from getting Hauser out of the way, it has enabled me to talk this thing over with an English police officer, instead of a screaming bunch of Italians." She gazed witheringly at Spezzi. " I had resolved, you see, to go to the police first thing this morning—it seemed preferable to being murdered, though I must confess it was a choice of evils." She paused. " Well, that's that. Is this unbalanced little man going to arrest me ? "

Henry could not repress a smile. " I don't think that will be necessary, Mrs. Buckfast," he said. "The authorities will have to decide, naturally, what proceedings will be taken, but in view of the fact that you have come to us voluntarily and given us valuable information——"

Mrs. Buckfast nodded approvingly. "I felt sure you'd be sensible about it, being English," she said, magnanimously.

" Of course, we shall want a full statement from you, including any information you can give us about Hauser's associates in London."

" A pleasure, Mr. Tibbett. Whenever you like. For the moment, though, I really must go and explain things to my husband. I'm afraid Arthur may be very silly about the whole thing. Still, I suppose that's only to be expected. I will bring you the rest of the packages before dinner."

With that, she rose with dignity, and walked to the door. Henry made no effort to stop her, but merely said, " I suppose you realise that what you have just told us constitutes the strongest possible motive for you to murder Hauser yourself ? "

Rosamund Buckfast stopped in the doorway.

" Naturally, I am aware of that," she said, " but then, we've agreed that it would have been impossible, haven't we ? "

And she walked out into the hall, shutting the door carefully behind her.

CHAPTER ELEVEN

THE NEXT DAY was cloudless and sunny, and the prospect of skiing raised everybody's spirits. On the surface, life resumed its normal, carefree aspect—although the beginners' class found Pietro less merry than usual. He appeared gloomy and preoccupied, and refused to discuss the murder beyond remarking briefly that it was a calamity for the whole village.

"I suppose you realise, old chap, that you've got a class-ful of suspects. You'd better watch your step." Jimmy's irrepressible high spirits had returned, now that the ordeal of interrogation was over.

Pietro looked at him sombrely. "If I thought that the murderer of Fritz Hauser was in my class——" he began slowly. Then, thinking better of it, he did a scintillating jump-turn on his skis, and cried, "Right. To-day we start with something easy. Stem turns on the *piste*. After me!"

Henry had cried off skiing, and spent an hour closeted with Spezzi, after which he took the lift down to the village, where he caught a bus into Montelunga. At the post office he found, as he had hoped, a long cable from London awaiting him. This he perused thoughtfully over a cup of coffee at a sunny *trattoria*: and, after making some brief notes in his diary, he took a leaf out of Hauser's book and put a match to the cable, stirring it carefully until every vestige was reduced to ash. It was after midday when he got back to Santa Chiara.

His next objective was the *Generi Misti* run by Signora Vespi. He purchased a fresh supply of American cigarettes, and then said casually, in Italian, "Bad business, this death on the ski-lift."

"Terrible, *signore*, terrible." Signora Vespi heaved a series of seismatic sighs. "My poor husband is distracted. It was he who helped poor Fritz on to the ski-lift, you know.

138

And all yesterday the police were questioning him—my Mario, as innocent as a new-born babe. Is it just?" she demanded, passionately.

Henry agreed that it was monstrous, and added, "You knew Herr Hauser personally?"

Signora Vespi nodded vigorously. "But of course. He was born in the village. I remember him as a little boy . . ." Here Henry was treated to a flood of reminiscence about the young Hauser, his unusual brilliance and precocity, even as a child, and his subsequent, well-deserved success in the world. "So kind, so generous a man . . . so polite and sympathetic . . ." Of all the people Henry had spoken to so far, only Rosa Vespi seemed to have been genuinely fond of Hauser, and to regret his death.

"This has certainly been a tragic year for your family," he said. "First, your son——"

"Ah, Giulio . . . my poor Giulio . . . crazy for skiing, like all the Vespis. What can a woman do with such men, *signore*? When Mario hurt himself so badly, I said to him in the hospital—" She broke off to sell two picture postcards and a bar of chocolate to a stout German in purple *vorlagers*, and resumed as if nothing had intervened—"'Mario', I said, 'I am glad this has happened . . . yes, glad. For otherwise you would have killed yourself—just as your father did.' And so he would. All the Vespi's are the same. My Giulio was the best skier in the valley, but crazy . . . crazy . . ."

Taking a long shot, Henry said, "Giulio was very friendly with Fritz Hauser, wasn't he?"

"We all were." Signora Vespi sighed again. "When I think how he would come and share a simple meal with us, even when he was rich and famous . . . Why only—" Her attention was again distracted by a customer: this time an elegant French girl in search of sunglasses. She failed to make a sale, however—her selection being dismissed as hopelessly un-chic. Before the shop door had closed, she started again. "Poor dear Fritz. Many times, he used to say to me, 'Rosa, you should be proud of your sons. They have stayed in the valley, but they are cleverer than I.' It was not true, of course, but I loved him for it. And certainly Giulio was clever—very clever. You knew my Giulio, *signore* ? "

" Alas, no," said Henry. " I wish I had. I have heard so much about him."

" Ah, you are *molto simpatico*. Perhaps you would like to see Giulio's picture ? Come, I will show you. Maria ! "

In response to Signora Vespi's sudden scream, a pretty, fair-haired girl came clattering down the stairs, and into the shop from the door that led to the rest of the house.

" My daughter," said Rosa. " She will look after the shop for me."

Maria smiled shyly at Henry, as Signora Vespi ushered him into the inner room. Dutifully, he admired the out-standing good looks and obviously sterling qualities of the youth who gazed out so confidently from the black-draped shrine on the mantelpiece. Then he remarked appreciatively on the charm of the cluttered parlour, and ended up by enlarging on the splendour of the new radiogram.

" That was Giulio's," said Rosa Vespi, with sad pride. " He had it sent all the way from Milano. Yes, he was very clever—he earned much money from the tourists. The car, we gave to Pietro, for we are too old for such things. But the radio . . . it is magnificent, no ? And very valuable. Mario keeps it locked up. When he comes in, I will get him to open it and show you . . ."

She had her hand on the lid of the radiogram when a sharp voice from the doorway said, " Rosa ! "

Henry turned, and saw Mario. In his own home, the old man had a dignity and authority that Henry had not sus-pected. He looked drawn and worried, but he smiled wanly as he said, " Welcome to my home, *signore*. I hope my wife has not been boring you with her chatter." Turning to Rosa, he added, " The gentleman does not want to be bothered with radios at such a time. He wishes to talk about the murder, no ? "

"I did hope to have a word with you, Mario," said Henry. "I was going to suggest we might take a drink together."

"Rosa . . . vermouth . . . wine . . . quickly."

"No, no," Henry protested. "You must drink with me. I thought we might take a glass in the Bar Schmidt."

Mario looked at Henry sharply. "As you wish, *signore*. A great pleasure."

The Bar Schmidt was crowded with villagers taking their midday drinks. A rich aroma of garlic, black tobacco and stale vermouth hung like a pall over the shabby, wooden-walled bar-room, whose windows, Henry surmised, had not been opened since the previous summer, if then. In the medley of voices, Italian, German and the local mountain dialect, Ladino, were discernible in roughly equal proportions.

Mario was greeted by the other occupants of the bar with obvious friendliness not unmixed with curiosity—which turned to embarrassed respect when they saw Henry. Room was made for the newcomers on one of the well-worn benches, and Henry procured two glasses of sweet, dark vermouth from the bar.

When the appropriate "*Salute*" had been exchanged, and the glasses duly clinked together, Henry said: "I wanted a chat with you, Mario, because I felt sure you could help me to get an idea of what Fritz Hauser was really like. I understand from your wife that you knew him well, which is a piece of great good fortune. Tell me about him."

A sudden quiet had fallen over the bar, and Henry could feel every man there holding his breath, waiting for Mario's answer. The old man twisted his glass slowly in his gnarled fingers. Then he said, "I am afraid that all women talk too much, *signore*. Hauser came to see us once in a way—his father and mine were friends, and he visited us for old times' sake. My wife was very proud that he came, and now she likes to make out that we were great friends. It is not true."

Across the room, a group of men began talking in low voices, and one of them laughed and spat.

Henry said, " At least, you can tell me what sort of man he was."

Again the whole bar waited, uneasily, for the answer.

After some thought, Mario said, " He was a very clever man, and to us he was always polite and kind."

" And generous ? "

" Generous ? I do not understand."

" I thought," said Henry, " that since he was so rich, he might have given you some presents—you or your sons."

Mario shook his head firmly. " Never," he said. And added, "Hauser was not the kind of man to give things away."

Henry did not press the point. " I hope this affair will not be bad for the village—as far as the tourists are concerned, I mean," he said.

The atmosphere in the bar relaxed, like a sigh. Conversations sprang up, quietly at first, but soon gathering volume, and bursting into gesticulation.   Mario said : " The tourists will come more than ever, I expect. In any case they only want to ski, and a murder does not spoil the snow." He smiled, a little grimly. " An accident to the ski-lift, or a bad avalanche—those would be disasters to us. Not this."

" I'm glad to hear it," said Henry, cheerfully. " I suppose most of the village lives by tourism."

" Yes," said Mario, shortly.

" It must be a good living, in the season—especially for the ski instructors."

" Tourists are foolish with their money," said Mario. Then, unexpectedly taking the initiative, he added, " I know what you are thinking, Signor Tibbett. I heard my wife talking to you of radios and cars. You are asking yourself how an instructor can earn as much as Giulio did."

" Yes," said Henry. " I was."

Four men who were playing cards at the next table suddenly lost interest in their game : the barman, in the middle of serving a round of drinks, put the bottle of vermouth down quietly and strolled to a better vantage point behind the bar.

Mario said: "There have been many rich, stupid women —Americans. I did not like it, I was ashamed that my son should behave in such a manner. But what could I do? You know the Americans . . ."

The card players all grinned broadly, and one of them leant towards Henry, breathing a pungent whiff of garlic into his face, and rubbed his fingers together in the time-honoured Italian gesture that means "money". "Americans," he said, in a thick country accent. "We've all seen them—haven't we?"

A chorus of assent went up from the bar in general. Was it their fault if the Americans chose to spend like lunatics? If the women had more money than sense? Let them spend if they wished—it was good for the village . . .

"I know, I know," said Henry, smiling. Then he glanced at his watch, exclaimed at the lateness of the hour, and excused himself. As he went out into the snowy brightness of the street, he saw out of the corner of his eye that the card players—and several other men as well—had converged on Mario. All were smiling, and one of them thumped the old man encouragingly on the back.

"That should have stirred something up," Henry reflected, with satisfaction, as he walked towards the Olympia. He was also gratified to notice, as he passed the Vespi's house, the flutter of a lace curtain dropped hastily back into place over the parlour window.

The Olympia was almost empty. Behind the bar, Alfonzo, the white-coated barman, was polishing a glass lethargically. Henry perched on a stool and ordered a Campari to take away the taste of the sweet vermouth.

"Much excite in the village, this murder," said Alfonzo, conversationally. He spoke quite creditable English, and never missed an opportunity of airing it.

Henry nodded, abstractedly. Then he said, "Do you get many Americans here, Alfonzo?"

"Americans? One in some while. No, no Americans here."

"I don't mean now, this moment. I mean, during the season . . . last year . . . the year before . . ."

"Was a family Americano, three—four year past," said Alfonzo helpfully. But the subject clearly bored him, and he went on, "You know who shoot this Hauser, no? You are great policeman from London, everybody speak of it."

"I'm not a great policeman, and I have no idea who shot him," said Henry. "I'm sorry to disappoint you. Can I get some lunch here?"

"But of course, *signore*. Any table you wish."

"Thanks, Alfonzo." Henry put the money for his drink down on the bar, and climbed off his stool, saying, "If you remember any more Americans, you might let me know."

"*Si, si, signore*." Alfonzo was obviously puzzled, but prepared to humour the eccentric Englishman. As Henry walked over to a table, he called after him. "Was a lady from Cuba one year—ooh-la-la!" He laughed happily at the recollection.

"When was that?"

"I don't remember. My father tell me."

Supressing as unworthy and irrelevant a strong impulse to abandon his murder investigations in favour of finding out more about the legendary lady from Cuba, Henry sat down to an excellent lunch. After which he took the ski-lift back to the hotel.

Capitano Spezzi was in his room when Henry returned, wading doggedly through oceans of paper to compile his reports. He seemed glad of an excuse to stop work for a while, and welcomed Henry cordially, inviting him to partake of a villainous-looking cigarette. Henry declined politely, and lit his pipe.

"Well, what news have you for me?" Spezzi asked, stretching his long legs luxuriously, and blowing smoke through his nose.

"A cable from London with some background details of

the English contingent," said Henry. He glanced at his diary. "Roger Staines. Son of Mortimer Staines, the financier who crashed and shot himself five years ago. The son was brought up in great luxury and then left penniless at the age of twenty-eight—the *Nancy Maud* was just about the only thing of his father's that he managed to keep. He's thirty-three now—doesn't look it, I must say. Fine war record—joined the Navy in 1943, and made a name for himself carrying out lunatic escapades in small boats, mostly in the Med. D.S.O. and bar. Since his father's death, nobody knows quite how he's managed to exist. He apparently tried several jobs—selling Encyclopædias, ferrying yachts, and a short spell in an advertising agency. Didn't stick to any of them. However, he manages somehow to keep in with the smart, rich young set in London. I suppose," added Henry, " that he's in demand with society hostesses because he's a very personable bachelor, but none of them want him for a son-in-law for the simple fact that he's always chronically short of money."

" Yet he hopes to marry Miss Whittaker," Spezzi remarked.

" Apparently it's common gossip in London that he's determined to marry her," Henry said, " and the unkinder element takes it for granted that he's after her cash. Sir Charles has already protested vigorously, but Caro's mad about Roger, and the general opinion is that the old man is softening. Also, which is interesting, Staines has been spreading it around town that he's on to a good thing, and will shortly be in funds."

" Interesting indeed," Spezzi murmured.

" Yes," said Henry. " But if, as I imagine, Hauser was proposing to enroll him as a smuggler, I'd say that Roger Staines must be one of the few people who's really sorry that he's dead."

" Don't forget the blackmail, my friend," said Spezzi.

" That puzzles me," said Henry. " I can't see where it fits in. Unless, of course, Roger is actually telling the truth."

"Highly unlikely, in my opinion," said Spezzi, a trifle grimly. "Go on."

Henry consulted his diary again. "Colonel Arthur Buckfast, Royal Wessex Regiment, retired eight years ago. Member of the Army Ski Team from 1933 to '39. Hobbies, skiing and philately. Married in 1921, Rosamund Handford-Bell, daughter of the late General Sir Robert Handford-Bell. Since the Colonel's retirement, the Buckfasts have lived in a small house in Bayswater——"

"Where is this, please?" Spezzi asked.

"Just where you'd expect them to live," said Henry, with a grin. "Respectable residential quarter of London, neither very smart nor very expensive. Both the Buckfasts considered to be pillars of society. Just goes to show you never can tell."

"Indeed you can't," said Spezzi, rather sadly.

"Who's next? The Whittaker girl—we know about her. Jimmy Passendell, youngest son of Lord Raven, member of Lloyds, plenty of money and generally popular. A very old friend of the Whittakers. Incidentally, rumour has it that old Whittaker only agreed to this holiday on condition Jimmy came along to keep an eye on Caro." He closed his diary. "That's the lot. Nothing very sensational. Any news from Rome?"

"Not yet. I expect to hear to-morrow." Spezzi glanced quizzically at Henry. "Well, what's your opinion?"

"I've got what I think is a pretty good idea," said Henry, slowly. "But it'll need a lot more working out before I can prove anything, so I'll keep it to myself for the moment, if you don't mind. And you? Still got your money on Gerda?"

"I wish," said Spezzi, "that I could think of a good reason why it should not have been her. I . . . I pity the girl. But there it is."

"How do you suggest she got hold of the gun?" Henry asked. "You know, I have a hunch she meant it when she said she didn't know it existed."

"She could have taken it just as easily as anyone else,"

said Spezzi, mournfully. " Didn't Mr. Passendell tell us it was left out on the table for all to see the night before the murder ? "

" If Gerda—or anyone else—stole the gun that evening," said Henry, " doesn't it strike you as odd that Hauser was apparently quite unconcerned about it, and made no attempt to get it back ? "

" He had no right to carry a gun. He would not have dared to complain."

" Not to the police, of course. But I can't help feeling that——"

" You are sentimental, dear Enrico," said Spezzi. " You are trying to find loopholes for the girl. I sympathise, but I cannot let emotion rule me. I am a policeman."

" So am I," said Henry, slightly stung. " All right. Go ahead. Arrest her if you like. I'm sure the Baron would be delighted."

Spezzi looked stern. " I confidently expect to make an arrest within a day or two," he said.

" Well, bully for you," said Henry, in English. Then, in Italian, he added, " I'm off now. I want a few words with Signor Rossati."

He was not destined to have them until later, however. Hardly had he closed the door of Spezzi's bedroom behind him, than a door across the corridor opened a crack, and Maria-Pia peeped nervously out.

" Henry," she said, in an urgent whisper. " Henry, I must talk to you."

" A pleasure," said Henry. " Not skiing to-day ? "

Maria-Pia grabbed his hand, and pulled him into the sitting-room of her suite, quickly closing the door behind him. Henry was relieved to see that the Baron was not there.

" I am supposed to have a headache," she said, bitterly. " Actually, Hermann refuses to let me ski. He is keeping me here like a prisoner."

Henry could not think of any suitable reply to this

melodramatic statement, so he made a sympathetic noise, and waited for Maria-Pia to go on.

"I had to talk to you," she said. "I have been waiting all day for the chance. Hermann will be back soon—he has taken the children out for a walk. He is not afraid to leave me when he knows that Franco is out skiing."

She paused, and lit a cigarette with trembling fingers. "I am nearly crazy with worry," she said. "You see, Henry, I am in love with Franco."

"I had actually guessed as much," said Henry, kindly.

"Hermann suspected it," Maria-Pia went on. "There was no way we could meet. Then Franco found this place, and each winter for three years we have had a wonderful holiday together. It is all I live for. Do you think I am a terrible woman?" she added, looking at Henry shyly.

"Not terrible," said Henry. "A little foolhardy, perhaps. Never mind. Go on. What made you realise the Baron knew?"

"I overheard him talking to someone on the telephone, the morning I left Innsbruck. I had gone out shopping, but I forgot my purse, and had to go back. Hermann didn't hear me come in again. He was saying "—she repeated the words like a hated but well-learned lesson—"'I shall expect a full report on them both, with definite evidence.' And then the other person said something, and Hermann said, 'We have already discussed the question of payment. There is no more to be said.' I knew then that he was putting someone to spy on me. When you spoke to me in the train, I thought for a moment that it might be you. Forgive me."

"Not at all," said Henry. "I wondered at the time what you were so frightened about."

"So when I got here," Maria-Pia went on, "I tried to persuade Franco to go back to Rome, but he wouldn't. So I told him we must be very discreet. And so we were."

Henry could not repress a smile at this, and she answered it, saying quickly, "Oh, you English. You are discreet all the time, even after you're married. Anyhow," she went on, " a few days ago I found out who the spy was. It was Hauser."

" I see," said Henry, unsurprised. " How did you find out ? "

" Because he told me," she said, simply. " He showed me the evidence that he had—a signed statement from Rossati. He tried to sell it to me."

" Because your husband was not paying him enough. Very typical," Henry remarked. " Did you buy it ? "

" How could I ? " Maria-Pia was very close to tears. " I have no money of my own—none. Everything belongs to Hermann. He goes through every receipt, every cheque I cash. And Franco has no money. We were desperate. On the morning of . . . of the murder, I tried to plead with Hauser, to beg him not to ruin my life——"

" I know," said Henry. " I saw you. But why did you think that this would ruin your life ? I can't imagine that you are happy with your husband, and presumably he would use this evidence to get a divorce. Wouldn't you like that ? "

She gave him a tragic look. " You don't understand, Henry. My family is very old-fashioned—they would disown me. Franco and I would be penniless. Not that I would mind," she added hastily : but Henry could not imagine the pampered Maria-Pia relishing love in a cottage.

" And then there's Franco," she went on. " Hermann would claim huge damages, you can be sure. Franco would be ruined. But worst of all—what about the children ? Hermann would have them, and I know he'd never let me see them. I would die, I swear it . . . I would die . . ."

" You are in a mess, aren't you ? " said Henry, lightly. He was deliberately flippant, anxious to stave off the emotional outburst which was threatening. Maria-Pia seemed to realise this. She gave him a grateful little smile, and went on quickly.

" That man Hauser was a devil," she said. " He laughed at me. He said he would . . . oh, but what does that matter now ? The terrible thing now is that Hermann is trying to prove that Franco killed Hauser."

" Is he, indeed ? " said Henry, greatly intrigued. " As a matter of interest, did he ? "

Maria-Pia gave him a reproachful look. " Oh, Henry, you mustn't say things like that, even in fun. Franco wouldn't hurt a fly——"

" I wouldn't be absolutely sure of that," said Henry. " But I do see an objection. The fact that your husband arrived here on the evening Hauser was murdered leads one to suppose that Hauser had telephoned him earlier in the day and told him all he knew. In fact, we know that he made a call to Innsbruck during the morning. So if Franco did kill Hauser, it was a very stupid murder of revenge. The damage was already done."

" No, no, you don't understand," said Maria-Pia, with tragic urgency. " Hermann has told me everything. Hauser did telephone him in the morning, just as you said, and told him that he had the evidence. My husband agreed to drive up here in the afternoon, but he pointed out that it was a long way by car, and he might not arrive much before seven o'clock. Hauser said he would wait for Hermann at the hotel as long as he could, but that if it got too late he would leave the documents in an envelope with Rossati, who would meet Hermann at the Olympia when he arrived. Hauser said he could trust Rossati implicitly."

" Why didn't Hauser just send the evidence to your husband ? " Henry asked.

" I don't know, but I can guess," said Maria-Pia. " I don't think he intended to sue me for divorce—that would be too simple for a man like Hermann, and too kind. I think he wanted to catch us both together up here, and confront us with the evidence, and threaten to use it if we ever saw each other again. He wanted to play cat and mouse with both of us."

" And where is this precious evidence now ? " Henry asked. " I suppose Hermann has it."

"No," said Maria-Pia. "When Hermann got to Santa Chiara, he found the lift had been stopped because of Hauser's death. Then, after you and Emmy had left the Olympia, Rossati approached him and introduced himself. Hermann at once asked him for the envelope, and Rossati had to confess that he had lost it."

"Lost it?" said Henry, sharply. "When?"

"Hauser gave it to Rossati in the bar at five o'clock. Rossati had an appointment with the bank manager, so he came down at once on the lift. When he was through at the bank, he went to have a drink at the Bar Schmidt, and came over to the Olympia at about half-past six. It was then he discovered that the envelope had disappeared from his overcoat pocket. He swears it was stolen."

"But how on earth could Franco have taken it?"

"That's the terrible thing," said Maria-Pia. "When we had finished skiing, I took the children to the sports shop— I had promised them new sweaters. Franco didn't want to wait while we bought them, so he went off and had a drink at the Schmidt with some of the instructors. He admits he saw Rossati there, and spoke to him."

"Even so," said Henry, "how could he have known what was in the envelope?"

"If he'd seen it," said Maria-Pia, "addressed to Hermann in Hauser's writing, he'd have guessed at once. And anyway . . ." Maria-Pia stopped suddenly, in confusion.

"That evening," said Henry, "Franco came into the Olympia, and said something to you, and you said, 'How wonderful'. What did he say to you? Did he tell you he had got hold of the evidence and destroyed it?"

Maria-Pia was trembling. "No . . ." she whispered. "No . . ."

Henry looked at her sternly. "I wish you wouldn't lie," he said. "Of course, I can follow your train of thought perfectly. If Franco thought that Hermann already had the evidence, there would have been no point in his killing Hauser. But once he laid hands on that envelope, it becomes

a very different story. The evidence is out of the way—
but Hauser, alive, can produce it again. On the other hand,
with Hauser dead, it would be easy enough to persuade
Rossati to keep his mouth shut."

Maria-Pia began to cry, quietly. "Franco didn't steal
it," she said, in a choked voice.

"Look," said Henry. "I'm going to look on the worst
side, and assume Franco did get hold of the envelope. That
doesn't by any means prove that he killed Hauser. When is
he supposed to have taken the gun?"

Maria-Pia said, in a whisper, "You remember the night
before the murder? Everyone was dancing in the bar—
even Gerda. Only Franco and I left early. Anna has told
Hermann so. Hermann says that Franco could have taken
the gun from Hauser's room then."

"I'd forgotten that," said Henry slowly.

"But you see," said Maria-Pia, "I *know* that he didn't."

"How do you know?"

"Because," said the Baroness, blushing prettily, "he
was with me all night. But how can I tell Hermann that?"

"I see your difficulty," said Henry. "I presume that
you and Franco are now denying everything, and that
Rossati, whatever other damaging things he may say, is
keeping his own counsel about the contents of the envelope?"

Maria-Pia nodded, silently. It was at this moment that
Henry caught sight of the tall, gaunt figure of Baron von
Wurtburg, flanked rather incongruously on either side by
the diminutive ones of Hansi and Lotte, striding up the
path to the hotel.

"Well," he said, "from what you say, it certainly looks
as though Franco couldn't have killed Hauser: but the
only effective way to clear him is to find out who did, and
that's just what I'm trying to do. So whatever happens
don't use that convenient but embarrassing bit of evidence
—at least, not until I tell you that you must. Do you
understand?"

"Yes, Henry," said Maria-Pia.

CHAPTER TWELVE

ANNA INFORMED Henry that *il padrone* was in his private sitting-room, as usual at this hour of the day, and could not be disturbed except in a case of grave emergency. Finally, however, Henry managed to convince her that the matter was urgent, and, with some reluctance, she led him through the green baize door that separated the proprietor's suite from the rest of the hotel.

Rossati's sitting-room was plainly but comfortably furnished. Its two most striking features were a large, leather-covered desk, surmounted by a photograph of a strikingly beautiful dark girl whose face was vaguely familiar : and the proprietor himself, who was stretched full-length on a sofa, with Rome's leading daily newspaper spread over his face, sound asleep. He leapt up guiltily as Henry came in, and professed himself eager to assist in any possible way.

Henry started with deceptive triviality. He was interested, he said, to get a clear picture in his mind of Herr Hauser's last descent on the ski-lift.

" I imagine you must make the trip down very frequently, Signor Rossati," he said. " I understand you do not ski."

" No, no, never. When I came here, I was already too old to learn."

" Three years ago, wasn't it ? "

" That's right, *signore*."

" To get back to the ski-lift," said Henry. " How long would it take to walk down the path to the lift ? "

" Oh—two minutes, no more . . . perhaps a little longer if it is snowing badly."

" And in the dark ? "

" The path is well-lit, *signore*, as you know."

" Then you would position yourself and wait for the chair ? "

"Of course." Rossati looked puzzled, as well he might, for he had a suspicion that Henry knew all this as well as he did himself. But the latter persisted.

"Then the chair comes up behind you, you settle yourself in it, arrange the rug round your knees, lower the safety-arm—and by that time you are well on your way."

"But exactly," said Rossati. "In my own case, I never bother with the safety-arm—it is for novices only, you understand."

"Would you call Hauser a novice?"

"After all these years . . ." Rossati laughed. "Most certainly not."

Henry went on. "And, say, two minutes after boarding the chair, you are quite far away from the boarding platform?"

"But yes—you would have passed the first pylon."

"Thank you, Signor Rossati."

"A pleasure, Signor Tibbett. If there is anything else I can tell you——"

"Yes, there is," said Henry. "I'd like to know more about your relationship with Hauser. He must have thought a lot of you to entrust you with such a precious envelope to deliver to Baron von Wurtburg."

Rossati simpered. "Ah, you know about that? It is a great misfortune to me that it was stolen. I do not know what was in the envelope, of course, but it must have been important, for the Baron is angry—terribly angry. How could I know?"

Henry let this pass. "And I understand you think Signor di Santi took it?" he asked. . .

Rossati shrugged. "The Baron seems to think that Signor di Santi had a reason for wanting to get hold of the envelope," he said. "And he had the opportunity."

"I see," said Henry, dryly. Then he went on, "The Baroness is a valuable customer of yours, isn't she?"

"But of course, *signore* . . ."

"Then how is it," said Henry, "that Hauser was able to persuade you to sign a document which you knew would do her the greatest possible harm—and which, incidentally, would ensure that neither she nor her family ever came to your hotel again? A document which would damage the reputation of the Bella Vista immeasurably if it were made public?"

Rossati was sweating now, but he managed a smile as he said, "Ah, Signor Tibbett, you know all, I can see. It is useless to try to deceive you."

Henry said nothing. After a pause, Rossati went on, unhappily, "Herr Hauser told me it would be a criminal offence not to give evidence if I were required to do so——"

Henry cut in sharply, "Hauser was not a policeman, or even a lawyer. He had no power to make you sign anything. Certainly no power to make you spy on the Baroness. Unless . . ." Something suddenly clicked in Henry's mind, as if his card-index memory, working subconsciously, had abruptly turned up the name he needed. He looked at the photograph on the desk. "That," he said, "is a remarkably good picture of Sofia Caroni."

For a moment Rossati looked stunned. Then, embarrassingly, he began to sob loudly, his plump face disintegrating into a mask of despair. Manfully ignoring this, Henry went on relentlessly.

"I don't know your exact connection with her, but I've no doubt you will tell me in a minute, when you recover yourself. What is perfectly obvious is that Hauser had some hold over you—some evidence which would connect you with the Caroni case, and probably land you on a criminal charge. You left Rome hastily when the case came up. You, who had never skied in your life, bought an hotel up here in this remote spot, and you took pains to speak German, so that people would think you'd lived here all your life. Hauser traced you up here, and has been blackmailing you ever since. I don't suppose you enjoyed having your hotel used as a headquarters for dope smuggling, did you?"

Rossati's sobs had subsided now, and he sat with his head in his hands, a picture of silent misery.

"I think," said Henry, more kindly, "that the time has come to tell me all about it."

There was a silence. Then, without lifting his head, Rossati began to speak.

"Sofia," he said, in a trembling voice. "Poor Sofia. She was my daughter." He hesitated, then went on. "She changed her name to go on the stage, you see. Her mother died when Sofia was only ten. We had very little money ... times were hard for us. You cannot blame me for being pleased when Count Brandozi began to take an interest in her. At first, I thought he would marry her ... I swear it."

"As I remember," said Henry, "he was already married, with seven children. However, we'll skip that. Sofia became a pleasant source of income. Then these new friends of hers introduced her to dope, among other things. Am I right?"

Rossati nodded, dumbly.

"They probably used you as a go-between to get the stuff for them," Henry went on, improvising wildly. To his considerable surprise, Rossati nodded again. "Where did you get it? From Hauser?"

Rossati lifted his tear-stained face. "No, no," he cried. "I had no idea that he had anything to do with it. I collected it from a chemist. I had to sign a receipt each time. Then my poor Sofia died and——"

"Was found dead," Henry supplemented, "in the Count's country cottage after a particularly nasty orgy. And the scandal broke. What happened then?"

"Hauser was her doctor," Rossati whispered. "He came to see me, and was deeply sympathetic. It was he who suggested I should come here, away from it all. He even lent me money to buy the hotel. Then, one day, he turned up here—with all the receipts I had ever given to the chemist. He had only to take them to the police, and——"

"So from then on," said Henry, "he used this hotel any

way he liked. You were worried the other day when Capitano Spezzi asked you about Hauser's bill—because of course he had no bill. On the contrary, I imagine he took money from you every time he came here."

"Everything." Even in his misery, Rossati managed to be indignant at the injustice of it. "Every penny of profit, he took. He left me just enough to run the hotel, so that there would be guests——"

"How many of the guests are genuine, and how many are Hauser's nominees?" Henry asked.

"I don't know, *signore*. I swear I don't," cried Rossati. "The first year Signor di Santi came here, he told me Hauser had recommended the hotel to him. And last year Hauser made me write to Signor Staines, offering him reduced terms. That's all I know. He told me nothing—not even about the smuggling, though I guessed it." Rossati looked at Henry pathetically. "What will happen to me now, *signore*?" he quavered. "The police . . . will the police. . . ?"

"I have no idea what action the Italian police will take," said Henry. "The Caroni case is closed, and it's possible that if you help us now——"

"Anything, Signor Tibbett, anything . . . Ah, what happiness," sighed Rossati, "if I could run my hotel as I wish . . . without fear . . . and keep the profits," he added, on a more practical note.

"Now," said Henry. "About that envelope. Which contained your own signed statement. You honestly think that Signor di Santi stole it?

Rossati seemed to come to a great decision. "Signor Tibbett," he said, not without a certain dignity, " from now on I will tell you the truth."

"That'll be a nice change," said Henry. "Well?"

"The Baroness and Signor di Santi," said Rossati, " they are nice people. And good customers. When I saw poor Signor di Santi in the Bar Schmidt, I could only think of what Hauser had done to me, and how I hated him. And I was ashamed that he had made me spy on them. I grew brave. Hauser had left—I was prepared to deny everything. I . . . I gave Signor di Santi the envelope."

"A generous, if misguided, impulse," said Henry, "which may well land him on a murder charge."

"How could I know that?" moaned Rossati. "I did it for the best. I wanted to help him."

"And now you're trying to help him by accusing him of stealing it?"

Rossati mumbled unhappily something about a murder changing everything.

"There are more graceful ways of saving your own skin than by slandering other people," Henry pointed out. "How do I know you didn't kill Hauser yourself? You had plenty of reason to."

This produced a storm of protest, a wailing of alibis.

"All right, all right," said Henry at last, damming the flood of eloquence. "We'll just put you down on the list as yet another person who was delighted to see Hauser dead. If you think of anything else you've lied to us about, you might let me know."

He walked quickly out of Rossati's room, and into the hall, where he met Emmy, who had just returned from skiing.

"Darling," she said, "you look green. What's been happening?"

"Nothing," said Henry. "Just a particularly nasty half-hour. I loathe," he added, "demolishing people."

Emmy gave his hand a quick squeeze. "I know you do," she said. "Come and buy me a drink."

It was only some time later that Henry realised, gratefully, that she had not asked who had been demolished, or why.

In the bar, Henry observed with interest the effect that the murder, and its subsequent repercussions, were having on the guests at the Bella Vista.

Mrs. Buckfast, he was amused to see, had not changed one

whit after her dramatic confession. She swept majestically into the bar, nodded a brief " Good evening," to Henry and Emmy, ordered a small sherry, sent it back because it was too dry, and upbraided Anna because an extra pillow which she had demanded had not yet made its appearance : in short, she was absolutely her normal self. The Colonel, on the other hand, had clearly been shattered to his very foundations by the revelation of his wife's misdemeanours. He looked ten years older, and appeared to be trying to avoid meeting anyone's eye. When he saw Henry, he turned first purple and then white, and, during his wife's altercation with Anna, he shuffled shame-facedly over to the bar where Henry and Emmy were sitting.

" Good evening, Colonel Buckfast. Good day's skiing ? " asked Emmy, in a friendly voice.

The unhappy Colonel cleared his throat, and was understood to mumble that he hadn't been out that day.

" Oh, what a shame," said Emmy. " The snow was heavenly."

Colonel Buckfast hummed and hawed and cleared his throat again. Finally, he managed to say, " Owe you an apology, Tibbett . . . business of my wife . . . don't know what to say . . . shameful . . ."

" It's very easy to understand how it happened," said Henry. " I'm sure Mrs. Buckfast didn't mean any harm. And it does her great credit that she came to us with the whole story."

" No excuse . . ." muttered the Colonel. " Disgraceful, the whole thing . . . disgraceful . . ." He paused, and then went on, more embarrassed than ever. " Will . . . em . . . that is . . . will the police . . . do you think ? No right to ask you, of course . . . no right at all . . ."

" I can't say what will happen," said Henry, with genuine sympathy, " But I promise you I'll do all I can to see that the affair is forgotten."

" By God, Tibbett . . ." said the Colonel, deeply moved. He attempted to find further words to express his gratitude, failed, and was recalled by a peremptory "Arthur !" from his unrepentant spouse. He smiled feebly.

"Wife . . ." he explained. "Wants me . . . needs support . . . time like this . . . poor little woman . . . damned decent of you, Tibbett . . ."

"Arthur, your rum grog's getting cold," said Mrs. Buckfast, ringingly.

"Ah, yes . . . grog . . . excuse me . . ." The Colonel shambled back to his table.

Roger and Caro were the next to come down. Caro had changed into a pair of brilliant red trousers and a green sweater, which only served to enhance the pallor of her face and the dark circles under her eyes. Roger had his arm round her shoulders, and he gave her a little hug and a reassuring smile as they came in. Caro made straight for the far end of the bar, but Roger restrained her, and steered her firmly over to Henry and Emmy.

"'Evening," he said. "Lovely day it's been. Perfect snow." Then, seeing the Buckfasts, he called over to them. "Hope you're feeling better, Colonel. We missed you on the slopes."

The Colonel said something unintelligible into his moustache, and Mrs. Buckfast answered firmly, "Arthur will be quite all right by to-morrow, Mr. Staines. Just one of his silly headaches."

"The poor old chap looks really ill," Roger said to Emmy, *sotto voce*. "What's up with him ?"

"I expect he's been overdoing it," said Emmy, quickly. "After all, he's not as young as he was."

"Pity," said Roger. "He must have been a superb skier in his day. Well, now, what are we all drinking ? Henry ? Emmy ? Caro ?"

Henry and Emmy protested that their glasses were full, and Caro said, "Nothing. I don't know. Oh, all right, a brandy."

"Bear up, darling," said Roger cheerfully, and added, to

Henry, "This child is feeling the strain. Have you been bullying her?"

"Oh, Roger, don't—" Caro began, and then stopped.

"Me?" said Henry. "What an idea. I never bully people."

"Only your poor wife," said Emmy. "I was up all night writing out his beastly reports." She grinned at Caro, who smiled faintly.

"By the way," Roger went on, with rather too-elaborate casualness, "any news from the handwriting experts in Rome?"

"Not yet," said Henry.

"I hope they're enjoying themselves with that little lot," said Roger, brightly. "From now on, I have no secrets from the Italian police. In the archives of Rome, carefully filed, you will find an exact account of how many pairs of underpants, gents' natty socks, brothel-creepers——"

"Roger!" Caro interrupted him. "What do you mean?"

"Only that the local gendarmerie have confiscated my packing list as vital evidence," said Roger. "I thought I told you."

"Oh, no . . . no, they can't have . . ." Caro had turned from white to green, and suddenly swayed forward on her stool, clutching at the bar for support.

Instantly, Roger had his arm round her, and Emmy said anxiously, "Caro, are you all right?"

"Yes . . . I'm sorry . . . I'm O.K. now." Caro gave herself a little shake, sat up straight, and said, "Make that a double brandy, Roger. I feel reckless to-night."

"Anything you say, ma'am," said Roger. His voice was light, but Henry noticed that he watched Caro with intent and worried care. At this moment, Jimmy came into the bar. He hesitated a moment when he saw Roger and Caro, and then walked over to Henry.

"I wonder," he said, with unusual seriousness, "if I could have a word with you."

"Of course," said Henry. "Here or elsewhere?"

"Elsewhere, if you don't mind. It's . . . it's rather private."

"Secrets, secrets," said Roger, reprovingly. "Or are you thinking of confessing, by any chance?"

Jimmy gave him a brief look, full of dislike, and said to Henry, "Do you mind coming up to my room for a minute?"

"Of course not." Henry slid down off his stool. "Look after the old lady for me, will you?" he said to Roger. "I'll be back."

Jimmy led the way, silently, across the hall and up the stairs to his room. He closed the door carefully, and then said: "I'm sorry to bother you like this, but I'm terribly worried about Caro. You see, I feel responsible for her."

"She certainly seems to be in a state of nerves," Henry agreed. "Any idea why?"

"Not really, but I can guess." Jimmy looked unusually grim. "It's all Roger's fault."

"I understand," said Henry, "that Roger hopes to marry Caro."

Jimmy nodded, sombrely. "She's a wild one," he said, slowly. "Wild, and stubborn as hell. I've known her since she was knee-high to a grasshopper, and she's always been the same. Her parents don't like Roger but she's absolutely determined to marry him, whatever any of us say. She won't hear a word against him."

"Yes, I had heard that," said Henry.

"A few months ago," Jimmy went on, "Roger started boasting all over the place that he'd found a way of getting rich quick. Caro was delighted, but I didn't like the sound of it, and neither did her father and mother. So we decided that I should have a serious talk with Roger, and see if I could find out what he was up to."

"And did you get anything out of him?" Henry asked.

"Not much. He put on a great act about loving Caro desperately and wanting to do well for her sake. I pumped him all I could about this money he was going to make, but all he would say was that it was a hush-hush deal with a Continental firm, and that he was going to arrange the final details while we were here on holiday. Which is why," Jimmy went on, " I'm absolutely certain that Roger was mixed up in some way with Hauser. And now, Caro's obviously nearly out of her mind with worry about something or other, and she won't tell me about it, and . . ." He paused, and then, with a palpable effort, blurted out, " The fact is, I'm simply terrified that Roger may have killed Hauser, and got Caro involved in some way. I suppose that's the last thing one should say to the police, but you're a reasonable chap, and . . ." His voice trailed off, uncertainly.

Henry looked at Jimmy's worried young face, and felt very sorry for him indeed. " I'm glad you told me all this," he said, " and I do sympathise. I'll tell you one thing. I think it's highly unlikely that either Roger or Caro had anything to do with Hauser's death. Mind you, I can't promise. I'm only giving you my opinion on the facts so far. But there is another thing——"

" I knew there'd be a bloody big ' but '."

" I don't know myself how big it is," said Henry. " You're certainly right when you suppose that Roger was involved with Hauser."

" I knew it," said Jimmy. " The fool."

" However, let's look on the bright side," Henry went on, with a trifle more confidence than he felt. " Now that Roger has seen the sort of mess that these things can lead to, I'm prepared to bet that he'll come to his senses. If you ask me, he really is in love with Caro, and once all this business is over, I suggest that you try to be rather more sympathetic to both of them. I'm sorry," he added, diffidently, " to lecture you like a Dutch uncle, but it's very difficult for someone like you, who has all the security in the world behind you, to appreciate the point of view of somebody like Roger, who is desperately trying to keep up appearances on very little money. Do you see what I mean ? "

Jimmy nodded gravely.

"The impression I get," said Henry, "is that both those two have decided that the whole world is against them—and that's a very dangerous way to feel. So if you really want to help Caro, the best thing you can do is to be on her side . . . and Roger's."

Jimmy stubbed out a cigarette, slowly. "All right," he said. "I'll try. So long as you're sure Roger is in the clear."

Henry looked as uncomfortable as he felt. "I can't be sure of anything yet," he said, "but I've given you my opinion. In any case, whatever happens, I'm damn sure Caro will stand by him. I like that girl."

After dinner, Henry said to Emmy, "Let's talk—I want to clear the rubbish out of my mind."

So they went up to their room, settled themselves comfortably on the bed, and lit cigarettes. First of all, Henry outlined to Emmy all that had happened during the day. She listened intently, occasionally putting a question, but never a comment. When he had finished, she said, "I can't ever remember a case with so many motives. Hauser must have been just about the most hated man in Europe."

"Hardly surprising, when you consider his chosen profession," said Henry. "Now, tell me what you think about it all."

"Well," said Emmy, slowly. "Since you said you thought Gerda was capable of murder, I've been watching her a lot, and I think you're probably right. But I don't see when she could have taken the gun. Although of course—has it occurred to you that we're all just assuming that Hauser was shot with his own gun? Couldn't there have been another?"

"There could, of course," said Henry, "but it's very unlikely. We know Hauser had a gun of that calibre, and it has undoubtedly disappeared."

"When could Gerda have taken it?"

"Don't forget that she didn't come down to the bar until

later than the rest of us, the night before the murder," said Henry. "Roger went up and fetched her, if you remember. She could have taken it then. Or there's another possibility. Hauser's luggage was sitting in the Olympia from midday onwards on the day he was killed. The gun could just as easily have been stolen from there."

"When ?" Emmy demanded. "Everybody except you and Hauser were either out skiing or up at the hotel all day."

"What colour were Hauser's suitcases ?" Henry asked, suddenly.

Emmy frowned. "A sort of lightish brown leather," she said.

"How do you know ?" said Henry.

"Because . . . gosh, I hadn't thought of it till this minute. Of course. I saw them stacked up in the passage at the Olympia when I went to spend a penny. And I wasn't the only one, was I ?"

"You weren't," said Henry. "Caro went to the cloak-room before you arrived, and so did Roger and the Colonel. Gerda, if you remember, went straight through to hang up her anorak before she even sat down at the table. The only people who didn't leave the restaurant were Jimmy, Franco, Maria-Pia, the children and myself."

"So Gerda could easily have taken the gun," said Emmy, thoughtfully. "Then what makes you think that she's innocent ? "

"My nose—" Henry began, and then he laughed. "I mean, it's just that it doesn't seem in character for Gerda to leave anything to chance. And, as Spezzi has it worked out, the whole thing would have been a series of coincidences. Of course, if it transpires that in some way Gerda knew exactly what Hauser's movements were going to be—then it would be a very different matter."

"Supposing," said Emmy, slowly, "supposing that the gun was taken for another reason altogether—to shoot somebody else. And then the murderer saw Hauser coming down on the lift, and couldn't resist the opportunity ? "

"I'd thought of that," said Henry. "It's an uncomfortable idea, because if it's so, then the murderer must be planning to strike again, at his original victim. But I really don't believe it. Who else would anybody want to murder?"

"Well . . . perhaps Franco had decided to kill the Baron."

"Pull yourself together, darling," said Henry, kindly. "Think. For a start, Franco didn't know the Baron was coming up here—though I'll admit he might have guessed it: but he's about the only person who had no chance at all of taking the gun. Maria-Pia's evidence clears him for the night before the murder, and he never left the table while we were at the Olympia."

"Why couldn't he have nipped upstairs and taken the gun while Maria-Pia was talking to Hauser after breakfast?"

"Because he was in the kitchen, collecting his packed lunch," said Henry. "I've checked with Anna."

"Of course," said Emmy, "it could have been a conspiracy. Maria-Pia may know very well that he took the gun the night before."

"Do you really believe that?" Henry said. "In any case, I personally am sure—whatever Spezzi may think—that the gun was in Hauser's possession when he packed. Otherwise he'd have raised hell with Rossati."

"Rossati hated him, remember," said Emmy. "Perhaps he knew the gun was missing, and hasn't told you."

"By the time I left him to-day, he was telling the truth," said Henry, sombrely.

"Suppose he took it himself? No, that's no good, because he couldn't possibly have done the shooting. Oh dear," said Emmy, unhappily, "it seems to be narrowing down to Gerda, Roger, Jimmy or the Colonel. I don't like it at all."

"What's your opinion of Roger?" Henry asked suddenly. Emmy hesitated. "I can't help liking him," she said.

"Meaning that you feel you shouldn't?"

"He's fairly unscrupulous," said Emmy, "and not entirely honest—but I think he's got standards of his own that may not be quite conventional, but are pretty rigid, all the same. I can imagine him killing in hot blood—but not deliberately planning a murder."

"And what about the Knipfers?"

"Horrid," said Emmy, promptly. "The girl might be all right on her own, but she hasn't a chance with parents like that. But anyway, they're out of the running, aren't they?"

"It would seem so," said Henry, "but there's no doubt the girl knows more than she will admit—and I've a hunch I know what it is."

"I don't suppose you're going to tell me," said Emmy resignedly.

"No, I'm not," said Henry. "Not yet."

CHAPTER THIRTEEN

AT HALF-PAST eight the next morning, there was a knock on Henry's door, and Spezzi came in, armed with a bulging briefcase.

"I plan to leave the hotel to-day," he said, "so I have brought you copies of my reports, and the time-table I have worked out. I trust you will find them helpful."

The young *carabiniere* loomed up in the doorway, and told Spezzi he was wanted: so the Capitano handed Henry a sheaf of papers and excused himself. Henry said to Emmy, "You'd better go down and get on with your breakfast. I want to study these."

"I'll stay here with you. I've got a good book."

Henry read quickly through the neatly-typed interview reports, and glanced at Spezzi's personal exposition of the case—in which the Capitano reached the conclusion that Fraulein Gerda Braun was the guilty party, although positive proof was still lacking. Then he gave himself up to earnest contemplation of the time-table.

9.00 a.m.	Hauser calls Rossati to the dining-room and announces his intention of leaving by the last train. Overheard by all the guests except the Baroness.
9.15	The Baroness speaks to Hauser in the bar.
9.20	Hauser pays his bill in Rossati's office.
9.30-10.00	The skiers depart. Mrs. Buckfast and the Knipfers go onto the terrace. Hauser goes up to pack.
10.30	Beppi goes to Hauser's room, speaks to him, collects the luggage and takes it to the lift.
10.35	Hauser speaks to the Knipfers on the terrace.
11.00 (approx.)	Hauser makes a phone call to Innsbruck.

11.35	Hauser takes the lift down to the village.
12.10 p.m. (approx.)	Mario sends the luggage down on the lift.
12.30	Miss Whittaker and Mr. Passendell return for lunch.
12.35	Carlo takes Hauser's luggage to the Olympia.
2.30	The skiers depart again. The Knipfers go for a walk. Mrs. Buckfast and Fraulein Knipfer sit on the terrace.
3.30 (approx.)	Fraulein Knipfer sees Hauser coming up the path from the ski-lift to the hotel.
3.45	Hauser and Fraulein Knipfer take tea in the bar.
4.30	Fraulein Knipfer goes up to her room. Beppi sees Mrs. Buckfast talking to Hauser in the bar. Miss Whittaker and Mr. Passendell arrive at the Olympia for tea.
4.45	Mrs. Tibbett arrives at the Olympia.
5.00	Staines and Col. Buckfast arrive at the Olympia. (*N.B.* A train from Immenfeld gets in to Santa Chiara at 4.55). Rossati speaks to Hauser in the bar, then takes the lift down to the village.
5.20	The Baroness, Fraulein Gerda and the children arrive at the Olympia.
5.30	Signor di Santi arrives at the Olympia.
6.05	The party at the Olympia pay their bills and leave.
6.10	Hauser leaves the hotel, seen by Beppi and Fraulein Knipfer.
6.15 (at the latest)	The party from the Olympia board the lift. Mr. Passendell first, then the other English, the Baroness, di Santi, the children and Gerda.
6.16	Hauser gets on to the lift at the top.
6.17	The lift breaks down.
6.19	The lift starts again.

6.43   Hauser arrives at the bottom of the lift, shot dead. Gerda, the last of the skiers, arrives at the top.

6.44   The lift is stopped.

Henry studied this document with intense concentration for some time, and then he said, " I owe Spezzi an apology."

Emmy put her book down. " Why ? " she said.

" Because I teased him about his passion for fixing accurate times." Henry passed the time-table to Emmy. " Take a good look at that," he said.

Emmy read it several times, and then said, " I can't see that it tells us anything we didn't know before."

" It doesn't," said Henry. " It just makes the whole thing clear, that's all. It's given me a vital bit of evidence I need to clinch my theory."

Emmy read the time-table again. " I don't see anything remarkable in it," she said at last.

" Don't you ? " said Henry. " Well, there is. Spezzi's time-table, plus a little logical deduction, plus a remark made by one of the witnesses—and the case is virtually solved. All I have to do now is to tie the threads together."

" I'm not even going to ask you to explain," said Emmy, with a rueful grin, " because I know you won't. But you might at least tell me which witness it was that made this chance remark."

" With pleasure," said Henry. " It was Colonel Buckfast."

After breakfast, Emmy hurried off to join her ski class—the others skiers had already left. Henry had decided to go down to the village, and he was in his room putting his anorak on, when the door burst open, and Spezzi charged into the room, deeply agitated.

" Enrico, I must talk to you," he cried. He mopped his brow. " I have just been with the Baron."

" Bad luck," said Henry, sympathetically. " I suppose he wants you to arrest Franco di Santi."

" How did you know ? "

" Because I had a talk with the Baroness last night," said Henry. " At her request," he added, hastily.

Spezzi sat down on the bed and nodded gloomily. " He's got Rossati in there," he said, " and they've both made complete statements to me about this divorce evidence—did the Baroness tell you ? "

Henry nodded.

" The Baroness is having hysterics," Spezzi went on, miserably, " Rossati's in a state of jitters, and prepared to swear to anything. The Baron is as cold as ice, and absolutely determined. What am I to do ? "

He made a despairing gesture.

" I'd arrest Franco, if I were you," said Henry, helpfully.

Spezzi groaned. " *Mamma mia*, is that all you can say ? And what do I do then ? There's a case against him, I admit—but it's not proved, by any means. If he's convicted, the Baroness will never forgive me, and if he's not, the Baron will be after my blood. Anyway, I believe the boy is innocent. I wish I'd never heard of this wretched case. And all you can say is, ' I'd arrest him if I were you.' *O, Dio, Dio, Dio.*"

" I meant it," said Henry. " For several reasons. If by any chance di Santi *is* guilty, there's no point in delaying any longer. If he's not, the fact that an arrest has been made may encourage the real murderer to get careless, and make a mistake. Anyhow," he added, " with the Baron in his present mood, I should think Franco would be safer in prison than out of it."

" You really think that ? " asked Spezzi, incredulously.

" Yes," said Henry, " I do."

By lunch-time, the Albergo Bella Vista was buzzing with excitement, and rumour ran riot. On his return from skiing, Franco—very pale but calm—had been escorted out of the hotel by Spezzi and his aide. From the head of the stairs, the Baron watched the grim little procession leave the hotel with an expression of satisfaction that was not pleasant to see : then he turned on his heel and walked into his suite, slamming the door behind him. From her window, Trudi Knipfer saw Franco being led away : there was an expression of perplexity on her face. The English peeped from behind half-closed doors, and shivered with a mixture of pity and relief. Rossati went into the kitchen and began bullying his staff.

When the prisoner and his escort were well away, Henry went down to the bar. Everyone in the hotel seemed to be there, with the exception of the von Wurtburgs and Gerda, and conversation spluttered and erupted excitedly. There was a dramatic silence, however, as Henry came in. Everybody turned to stare, and he felt like a freak at a side-show. He walked over to the bar, and ordered a Campari-soda. The talk started again, more quietly and furtively, and then Henry was aware of someone standing just behind him.

" So it was poor old Franco all the time, was it ? " Roger was standing at Henry's shoulder, smiling with a sort of heady abandon. " Who'd have thought it ? Well, I suppose the rest of us can breathe again now."

" So it would appear," said Henry.

" Well, I don't want to sound heartless," remarked Jimmy, who had come over to the bar with Caro, and was now knocking back brandy at a considerable rate, " but thank God it wasn't one of us. At least we know where we stand now." He turned to Caro, who was morosely sipping lemonade. " Look, Caro," he said, " now that this business is all over, I was wondering if you and Roger would like to——"

" All over ? " said Caro. She put her glass down carefully on the bar, and looked Jimmy straight in the eyes. " As far as I'm concerned, it hasn't begun yet."

And with that, she walked out of the bar. Roger immediately put down his drink, and went after her. Their voices came indistinctly from the hall outside—Roger's soothing, Caro's protesting.

" I give up," said Jimmy to Henry. " I've been leaning

over backwards to be nice, like you said, and that's all the thanks I get for it. What on earth is the matter with the girl now?"

"I don't know," said Henry. "But I mean to find out."

After lunch, Henry took the lift down and had a long talk with Carlo, taking him again over his recollections of the evening of Hauser's death. The news of Franco's arrest had spread like wildfire through the village, and Carlo was now inclined to remember a sinister look on di Santi's face as he boarded the lift, and a suspicious bulge in his pocket. Henry listened with polite scepticism, and then returned to the hotel.

Mrs. Buckfast was sitting alone on the terrace, and Henry went over to her and pulled up a chair.

"So the case is solved, Mr. Tibbett," she remarked, her knitting needles clicking busily. "I must congratulate you."

"Not me," said Henry. "All the work was done by the Italian police."

Mrs. Buckfast sniffed unbelievingly.

"My side of it," Henry went on, "is to find out all I can about the English end of the dope-ring. I'd be very interested to hear just what Hauser said to you in the bar, on the afternoon he was killed."

Mrs. Buckfast looked a little rattled. "He gave me last-minute instructions about disposing of the stuff," she said.

"What were they?'

"The usual thing. A messenger would call at my house. I told him quite frankly that I disapproved of the whole thing."

"And what did he say to that?"

"He threatened me, of course." Mrs. Buckfast smiled grimly. "He made a lot of veiled remarks about it being very dangerous to make mistakes, as other people had found to their cost. That was when I finally decided to go to the police."

"I see," said Henry, thoughtfully.

A little later, Emmy came in from skiing : when she had changed, they both went down to the bar.

It was very quiet. A desultory conversation in German drifted over from the Knipfers' table ; the Buckfasts sat and stared at each other as if neither was pleased at the prospect of the other's countenance. Then there were brisk footsteps in the hall, and Gerda came in. For the first time, her iron composure seemed ruffled. Her face was flushed, and her eyes burned with anger. She walked straight up to Henry and said loudly, " You coward ! You miserable, snivelling coward ! "

Henry looked at her with interest. " I don't quite understand what you mean, Fraulein Braun," he said.

Gerda's eyes blazed. " Oh, yes, you do," she said. " I've been out skiing all day, so I've only just heard. You've arrested Franco di Santi."

" Not I," said Henry. " Capitano Spezzi has arrested him."

" Capitano Spezzi . . ." Gerda's voice shook. " Capitano Spezzi thought that I was guilty . . . I knew that and I respected him for it—it was an honest opinion. I respected it, and I thought he was a fine man—but he's as bad as you are. As bad and as spineless ! "

" Really, Fraulein—" Henry began, but she cut him short. " It's no good looking at me like that. I know very well why you arrested Franco. *He* made you do it."

" You're referring to Baron von Wurtburg, I suppose," said Henry.

To his surprise, Gerda's eyes filled with tears. " He's a brute and a bully," she said. " He won't even let me see her—or the children. He's as bad as Hauser. I wish he was dead, too."

She drew herself up very straight. " Anyway," she went on, " he's not going to have the satisfaction of seeing an innocent man condemned for murder. You'd better telephone Santa Chiara now, Herr Tibbett, and tell them to let Franco go. Because I want to tell you that I——"

Henry stood up suddenly, with a maladroit movement that knocked Emmy's drink off the bar. The glass shattered on the floor, and the bright red vermouth spattered Gerda's white shirt, like blood. Before the German girl had time to recover herself, Henry was apologising profusely, and Emmy was mopping the shirt with her handkerchief. Gerda stood perfectly still, trembling a little.

" I want to tell you—" she began again, but Henry said quickly, " Fraulein, I'm terribly afraid that stuff will stain. We must do something about it. Emmy, dear, haven't you got some patent cleaning lotion upstairs ? Perhaps if you took Gerda up——"

" Yes," said Emmy. " Come along with me."

" Go with my wife," said Henry, firmly, to Gerda.

Emmy grabbed Gerda's arm, and led her, protesting, out of the bar.

Henry finished his drink, and then went upstairs.

He met Emmy and Gerda coming out of the latter's room. Gerda had changed her shirt, and looked calmer, though still angry.

" She keeps trying to tell me something," said Emmy, " but I pretended I couldn't understand any German. You'd better talk to her."

" I certainly had," said Henry. And to Gerda he said, in German, " Now, Fraulein, I understand there's something you want to tell me. I suggest we go to my room. My wife will come too," he added, hastily.

Gerda gave him a brief, unamused look. " Very well," she said.

As soon as the door had closed behind them, Henry said, " First of all, I'd like to say something to you. I don't know what it is you want to tell me, but I do assure you that quixotic gestures are unnecessary. If you've got any useful information that will help us to identify the murderer, let's have it. Otherwise—please trust me."

" Franco didn't do it." said Gerda.

" That's very possible," said Henry. " And if he didn't,

he won't be in prison long, you can depend on that. I promise you faithfully that no innocent person will suffer." He paused. " Well, have you anything sensible to tell me ? "

Gerda gave him a long, appraising look. At last she said, " No."

" Good," said Henry, cheerfully. " I'm sorry about your shirt. And by the way—Captain Spezzi isn't as foolish as you think, Fraulein. He is a very intelligent and estimable young man."

A ghost of a smile flickered across Gerda's face, and Emmy thought, " Good heavens, the girl is quite beautiful. She should smile more often."

At the door, Gerda suddenly stopped. She turned to face Henry again, and she said, " There is one thing I think I should tell you."

" What is that, Fraulein ? "

" I . . . I hoped it would not be necessary," she said, " but now . . ." She paused. " It's about Herr Staines."

" Well ? "

" The night before the murder," said Gerda, slowly, " he came up to fetch me, and asked me to come down and join the dancing."

" I remember," said Henry.

" I had been into the children's room to make sure they were asleep," Gerda went on, " and I met him in the corridor."

" Yes ? " said Henry.

With some reluctance, Gerda said, " He was coming out of Hauser's bedroom."

" Was he ? " said Henry. " Does he know that you saw him ? "

" I don't think so," said Gerda. " I waited until he was out in the corridor before I came out of the children's room. He looked . . . he looked very worried and rather grim. I am sorry I did not tell you before."

Henry sat up late that night, smoking and thinking,

going over in detail all the pieces of the intricate jigsaw of evidence which were beginning to fall into place with a relentless inevitability, forming a coherent pattern in which so few pieces were now missing. Once, before she went to sleep, Emmy said, "You know now don't you?" and Henry said, without pride, "Yes, I'm afraid I do."

The result of this nocturnal brooding was, of course, that they both overslept, and did not get down to breakfast until nearly half-past nine. Emmy bolted her food and rushed off to join her class ("I shall get fired if I'm late again," she said, agitatedly). Henry fell for the temptation of yet another delicious roll and cherry jam. He came out of the dining-room to find a spirited altercation going on in the hall between Spezzi, who had just come up on the ski-lift, and the Baron.

"The man is arrested, the case is closed, and my wife and I will leave to-day," the Baron was saying, in a voice that would have frozen oil.

"But Herr Baron . . . I deeply regret . . . it is not possible. There are formalities of evidence——"

"My evidence can be taken in Innsbruck," said the Baron. "We, too, have a police force, Herr Kapitan."

Henry was about to go to Spezzi's assistance, when Maria-Pia saved him the trouble. She appeared at the head of the stairs, as white as a sheet, and said in a small voice, "What is all this, Hermann? You want us to leave?"

The Baron, irritated by this diversion, said shortly, "Yes. We leave for Innsbruck to-day. You, I and the children. I have already discharged Gerda."

Maria-Pia closed her enormous brown eyes for a moment, then opened them wide and said stridently, "I won't go!"

"Now, now, my dear—please don't make a scene." The Baron, embarrassed, strode over to the foot of the stairs. "It is far better that we go."

"I won't!" Maria-Pia's voice was almost a scream. She clung desperately to the banisters, as if she expected to be dragged away to Innsbruck then and there, by force.

"I won't! You can't make me! Henry, don't let him! Don't let him!"

The Baron wheeled round to face Henry. Like a ferocious animal at bay, he glared in turn at his three adversaries. Then he said, "My wife is naturally distraught by all these terrible events. You can see that it is for her good that I intend to take her home immediately."

"If you will forgive me for saying so, Herr Baron," said Henry, "I think that your wife is ill, and should not undertake the journey. Quite apart from the fact that the police require your presence here——"

Maria-Pia suddenly began to laugh, hysterically. "Ill!" she cried. "Ill!" The words were wrenched out between great choking breaths that could have been sobs or laughter. "Ill! Oh, my God——"

Then she was suddenly silent, and stood swaying for a moment, her slender body bending like a sapling in the wind, before she pitched forward and fell head-first down the stairs. There was a dull thud and a sharp crack as she hit the bottom step, and lay still.

Pandemonium broke loose at once. Spezzi ran to telephone for a doctor, Rossati screamed, and Henry had to fight his way through a knot of waitresses to get to Maria-Pia's side. Before he had a chance to look at her, a quiet voice said, "Out of my way, please!" and the Baron gathered his wife's frail, limp body into his arms with a curious gentleness, and carried her upstairs. For once, he made no protest when Henry followed.

Henry smoothed the rumpled bedclothes, and the Baron laid Maria-Pia down with delicate care. Then he said, in a low, anxious voice, quite unlike his normal brusque tone, "She's not . . . not badly hurt, is she?"

"I'm not a doctor," said Henry. "But I know a bit about it. Let me look at her."

The Baron, as if unable to bear the tension, turned away from the bed and walked over to the window. Henry bent over the motionless body. As he did so, Maria-Pia opened her eyes, flutteringly: and, to Henry's astonishment, immediately closed one of them again in what was most undoubtedly a wink.

"Henry," she whispered.

"How do you feel?" Henry asked, feeling exceptionally foolish himself.

"I knocked myself out, didn't I?" she went on, barely audibly. "My leg hurts. Have I broken anything?"

"I don't know," said Henry. "The doctor will be here soon."

"I bet I have," murmured Maria-Pia, with immense satisfaction. Then a spasm of pain crossed her face. "Get the doctor soon, Henry."

"He won't be long. Just lie still," said Henry. He gave her a big grin, then straightened, and said, "She'll be all right, Herr Baron, but she's had slight concussion and she may have broken her leg. She'll obviously need complete rest for a few days."

The Baron, who had been standing quite still with his back to Henry, did not move. He said, "Please come out on to the balcony, Herr Tibbett. I wish to talk to you."

Henry followed him out into the sunshine. The Baron carefully closed the door that led to the bedroom, and then said, "I believe that Franco di Santi is guilty."

Henry said nothing. In a voice which was almost pleading, the Baron went on, "I have to protect my wife from such a man, Herr Tibbett. From a murderer."

"You're making a very big assumption there," said Henry. "Nothing has been proved against him."

"There is no doubt," said the Baron, shortly. And he added, in a voice that was little more than a whisper, "There cannot be any doubt . . ."

There was a pause, and then Henry said, tentatively, "Of course, I sympathise with your point of view, Herr Baron. I understand that there was talk of a divorce——"

The Baron wheeled round to face Henry, and there was a sort of anguish in his cold eyes. "Never!" he cried.

"Never! I would never divorce my wife." Surprisingly, he added, "I love her."

"I know you do," said Henry.

"This man Hauser—" Every word the Baron spoke seemed to be wrenched from him with a painful effort. "It was he who told me. I did not believe him. I would have given my life not to believe him. But I had to know. I had to find the truth. Do you understand that?"

"Yes," said Henry, slowly. "I understand that."

"Do you imagine I enjoyed setting a dirty spy on my wife? Can't you see that when he telephoned me, I hated him, as I have never hated a man before? More than I hated di Santi, even. I find it ironic that one of my enemies should kill the other. It is like a judgment on them both."

"Supposing," said Henry, "that Franco di Santi is proved to be innocent. What will you do then?"

The Baron turned away, and leant on the pale woodwork of the balcony. His gaze seemed fascinated by the steep, snowy slopes below. "That is my affair, Herr Tibbett," he said, very quietly. "Whatever happens, I shall see to it that Maria-Pia is happy."

There was a long silence, then the Baron straightened, and said in his usual, clipped voice, "So the Baroness is not seriously hurt. That is very welcome news. I do not think I need trouble you further."

He turned away in a clear gesture of dismissal. Henry stepped quietly back into the sunny bedroom, and walked quickly past the small, motionless figure on the bed, and out into the cool, pine-scented corridor.

CHAPTER FOURTEEN

THERE WERE TIMES, Henry reflected, when he hated his profession, and this was one of them. He looked forward with deep unhappiness to the tasks he had set himself for the day—the final checking, the last moves that would close the net of evidence on someone who had been driven by desperation to a desperate act.

He decided to cheer himself up by skiing down to the village on his own.

Half-way down, he came upon his own class, who were making gallant if not very successful efforts to master the stem cristiania turn. Pietro waved cheerily, and Henry came to a wobbling halt beside Caro, who was waiting for her turn. The class had been augmented by three new arrivals—an Italian couple and a young German—so that Pietro was busily yelling instructions and advice in three languages.

" This is hellishly difficult," said Caro. " I'll never get it, I'm sure. Are you going to join us ? "

" Welcome back, Enrico," cried Pietro, bounding up the slope with incredible ease, lifting his skis like a *Schuhplattler* dancer. " You come for the stem cristiania, eh ? Just in time."

" I'm afraid not," said Henry. " I've got to go to the village. I had a ridiculous idea that it would be quicker on skis than on the lift."

" Aha, the brave one, skiing all alone," Pietro laughed, attractively. " No more ski school for you, eh ? To-day Run One, to-morrow Run Three, the day after—the Gully, perhaps ? "

" It's all very well for you to laugh," said Henry. " How the devil d'you do that ? " he added, as Pietro, with a lightning movement, dug a stick into the snow and jumped round it, feet parallel, to face the other way.

"Easy—so!" Pietro obligingly repeated the performance on one foot, to the applause of the class.

"Have you done the Gully yet this season, Pietro?" Jimmy asked. They had all looked with awe at this formidable run, which was little more than a crevasse which ran like a white streak down the mountain-side, not far from the ski-lift.

"No—is still forbidden. Not safe yet. But I do it soon —you will see. Very soon now I do it. Zim!" Pietro made a flashing movement of his hand from shoulder to knee. "Just like that. Steep like a wall. *Benissimo!*"

"Horrible!" said Jimmy. "Don't ever dare take us there."

"Next week, perhaps," said Pietro, mischievously. "When you have learn well the stem cristiania. Now, Mister Jimmy. Bend ze knees—and hoop-la!"

Henry left them to it, and proceeded cautiously on his way. Apart from about a dozen falls, and a hair-raising encounter with a horse-drawn sledge laden with logs, he reached the bottom in good order, and felt very pleased with himself. He took off his skis, left them at the bottom of the lift, and went into the Olympia.

Apart from a few mid-morning coffee-drinkers, the café was empty. Alfonzo greeted him warmly.

"Coffee? Of course, *signore.* Straight at once."

The Espresso machine hissed, spluttered and disgorged a cup of delicious, steaming coffee. Deftly, in what appeared to be a single movement, Alfonzo assembled the cup, a tiny jug of cream and a packet of sugar on a small tray, and placed it with a flourish on the bar. "So, the murder is solved, *signore?* Poor Signor di Santi—everyone very sorry. What for did he do it?"

"Now, now," said Henry, reprovingly. "You know very well I can't talk about the case. Anyway, it has yet to be proved that he did do it."

"Ah, the English, so correct always." Alfonzo beamed. "The other day, you ask me about Americanos, no? I am silly. I have forgot. · Many Americanos here—last year, year before—ladies, you understand, all alone, very rich. Much money for the ski instructors. I am silly to forgot."

"Thanks, Alfonzo," said Henry, smiling. "Now tell me something else. You knew Herr Hauser well by sight, didn't you ? "

"The dead one ? But of course. Many times he come in here."

"Did he," Henry asked, "have lunch here the day he was killed ? "

"No, no, *signore*. His luggage was here—I took it myself from Carlo. But he never came in all day, I am certain." Alfonzo leant over the bar, confidentially. "The American ladies," he said, "much like Giulio—Mario's boy, the one who die. Give him much money."

"I'm sure they did," said Henry.

"Everybody know this," said Alfonzo, slightly on the defensive.

"Everybody knows it now, anyway," said Henry. "So long, Alfonzo. Be seeing you."

Henry's next port of call was the little bus station in the centre of the village. Both bus and railway time-tables were displayed in the small wooden waiting-room, and Henry studied them earnestly. He learnt that there was a bus to Montelunga at ten minutes to twelve, and one to Immenfeld at noon. A train departed for Immenfeld at half-past eleven and returned, headed for Montelunga, at twelve-twenty : after this, you had to wait until half-past two for transport in either direction—as in all civilised countries, the two-hour lunch interval was sacrosanct.

Although not relishing the prospect of four more cups of coffee in quick succession, Henry doggedly went on with his self-appointed task. He visited every café in the village, and in each he asked the same question and got the same answer. Hauser had not lunched there on the day of his death.

Bloated with coffee, and feeling more and more depressed,

Henry then made his way to Signora Vespi's shop. There were no other customers, and it was only too easy to encourage the proprietress to talk. After dealing thoroughly with the shock to her nervous system occasioned by Franco's arrest, the impossibility of making a livelihood with salami at its present price, and the excellence of the weather, Signora Vespi paused for breath, and Henry said : " By the way, Signora, you never told me that Herr Hauser came here for lunch on the day he was killed."

The fine flow of Rosa's rhetoric dried up, as if a tap had been turned off. She looked very disconcerted.

" I . . . that is, *signore* . . . he did not . . ."

" Oh, yes, he did," said Henry. " Why didn't you tell me ? "

" I didn't think . . . Mario said . . ."

" After all," said Henry, " there wasn't anything unusual about it, was there ? You told me he often came here."

" *Si, signore* . . . that is, only sometimes . . ."

" Can you remember what he talked about that day ? " Henry asked. " It might be important."

" Nothing, *signore* . . . he only came to say good-bye. We had a little lunch, and then I came back to the shop and the men talked. I don't know what about—I didn't hear them."

" When you say ' the men,' you mean Mario, Pietro and Hauser ? "

" *Si, signore,*"

" Perhaps they talked about Giulio," Henry suggested.

" Yes, yes, about Giulio," cried Rosa, eagerly. " Herr Hauser was so sympathetic . . . it must have been about poor Giulio that they talked."

" I see," said Henry. " Thank you signora. You have helped me a lot."

He went out again into the blinding sunshine, and walked slowly up to the ski-lift. There was a queue, and Carlo was busy. Henry stood and watched the skiers taking their chairs : from time to time he glanced at his watch. Then he turned and walked down to the ski school office.

The man at the desk was only too eager to talk. This terrible murder, and now the arrest—such goings-on for a quiet little village . . .

"As a matter of fact," said Henry, "it's another death I'm interested in at the moment. Giulio Vespi's."

"Ah, the poor boy. Our best instructor. And yet one must admit that it was his own fault. Rosa tells me that Mario did all he could to prevent his son from attempting the run—there were angry words about it, but it was no good. Nobody could stop Giulio doing as he wished."

"Tell me what happened," said Henry. "When did he start the run, and when was he missed?"

The man considered. "He set off after lunch," he said. "It was on a Sunday, you see, so there was no ski school. He planned to return by the train at five o'clock. When he didn't arrive, his family grew worried, for that is the only train on a Sunday. So they went to look for him."

"His family?" said Henry, sharply. "Not a search party?"

"Later, the search party went out. But they are all crazy, the Vespis. It was young Pietro who found him first—he went off on that same run after five in the evening. Admittedly, he has done much skiing by night, but even so it was lunacy. He was lucky not to be killed also."

"How did Pietro find him?"

"He followed Giulio's ski tracks, and stopped on the edge of the crevasse where his brother had fallen. He saw the body on the rocks below. Of course, if Giulio had fallen into deep snow, we might not have found him for many months—but as it was, Pietro saw him, and skied on into Immenfeld to give the alarm. Then the search party went out. It was all we could do to prevent Mario going with them."

"I see," said Henry, thoughtfully. "Thank you."

"A pleasure, *signore*."

Unhappily, Henry went back to the Olympia—now crowded with returned skiers—and ordered a solitary lunch, most of which he did not eat. As he was ordering his coffee, he was surprised to see Colonel Buckfast, Roger and Gerda come in together. The Colonel had recovered most of his usual buoyancy after a good morning's sport. He came over to Henry's table.

"Been out this morning?" he inquired. Henry had realised by this time that to the Colonel " out " invariably meant " out on skis," so he said, " Yes. Nothing in your class, I'm afraid. Just a gentle Run One. I see you took Fraulein Gerda with you," he added.

"We didn't exactly take her," said the Colonel, lowering his voice tactfully. "Met her on the Alpe Rosa, skiing all alone, poor girl. Sorry for her, y'know. Asked her to join us."

"I'm glad you did," said Henry. "She seems to be a very lonely person."

"Good skier," said the Colonel. "I can't say much to her, of course. No German. But young Staines was prattling away quite a bit. Well, lunch now. Mustn't waste the good weather."

The three skiers ate their lunch quickly, and left the café just before two o'clock. Soon afterwards, Henry followed them. He was already in the ski-lift queue when he remembered that Emmy had warned him that they were out of toothpaste, and so he went down to the chemist's at the far end of the village to get it. When he came back, the queue had lengthened considerably, and it was half-past two before he had collected his skis and begun the ride up to the Bella Vista.

It was a glorious afternoon. The sun sparkled, highlighting the smooth white *piste* of Run One, and throwing into sharp relief the stray tracks made by solitary skiers in the virgin snow: it struck warmly on the pink peaks high above Henry's head as he sailed up between the pine trees, and threw up a diamond shimmer from the snow banked on the platforms of the pylons as they slid away one after the other beneath his dangling feet. The whole landscape exuded a reckless joy, which only served to deepen Henry's melancholy. There was only one thing to hope for now, and by all the laws of men and gods he had no right to hope for it.

At the top, he slid off his chair, slung his skis on his shoulder, and was beginning to walk up to the hotel, when Mario stopped him.

" Signor Tibbett ! "

" Yes, Mario ? " Henry looked at the old man with compassion : he, too, seemed depressed and worried.

" Signor Tibbett—I cannot leave the lift now, but there is something I must say to you. Something very important. Can I see you at the hotel this evening ? "

" Of course, Mario. Come up as soon as the lift stops."

" Thank you, Signor Tibbett. I will be there."

The next chair arrived, and Mario limped quickly back to work. Henry walked slowly up the path.

Signor Rossati was in his office, writing letters. In answer to Henry's query, he said that Fraulein Knipfer had gone out for her ski lesson—her parents were on the terrace. The Baron, also, was out. Yes, the doctor had been, but he had no idea of his diagnosis. Anna had reported the Baroness as being cheerful, and sitting up in bed for lunch.

Henry went upstairs, but instead of going into his own room, he climbed to the top floor, and opened the door of the room occupied by Trudi Knipfer. It corresponded to the Baron's sitting-room, but, being two stories higher, had a sloping ceiling and no balcony. It was immaculately tidy. The dressing-table boasted nothing but a photograph of Herr Knipfer, in a tooled leather frame, a hard hairbrush and a comb : beside the bed was a small travelling clock : otherwise there were no visible signs of occupancy, apart from a checked sponge-bag hanging up beside the washbasin. Henry took a quick look round, his face thoughtful. Then he went over to the window.

The view from here was even finer than that from the

lower rooms. Santa Chiara looked even smaller and more toy-like, and the mountain peaks behind the village glowed against the dark blue sky. Looking down, Henry saw the Baron's balcony below him. Lower still, two pairs of sturdily-shod feet propped comfortably on footstools were all that could be seen of the Knipfers, *père et mère*, as they took the sun on the terrace. The path to the ski-lift wound its way in a graceful curve below, a ribbon of darkness over-shadowed by its steep banks of snow : and beyond it, Henry could see Mario going about his business at the head of the lift.

Henry turned back into the room, and, feeling like a thief, opened the dressing-table drawers. They yielded nothing more than neatly-ranged piles of clothes and handkerchiefs, and a large number of hairpins. He was considerably interested to remark that one of the small drawers beside the mirror was locked.

After a final, appraising glance at Herr Knipfer's un-prepossessing features in their leather frame, Henry stepped quietly out into the corridor, and went down to the first floor. He knocked on Maria-Pia's door.

" Who is it ? " she called.

" Henry. May I come in ? "

" Of course, Henry."

The Baroness, looking pale but enchanting in a fluffy pink and white négligée, was propped up on a plethora of pillows, reading a fashion magazine. At the end of the bed the blankets were turned back, to reveal a small, honey-coloured foot protruding from a large white plaster cast.

" You see, Henry," said Maria-Pia, proudly, " I did break it."

" You're a terror," said Henry. " How do you feel ? "

" I'm fine now," she said. " Have you seen Franco ? "

" Not this morning. But don't worry about him. He's in good hands."

Maria-Pia giggled. " Hermann is furious," she said.

"I'm not surprised," said Henry, severely. "You gave us all a very nasty fright. Did you have to go as far as all that?"

"Henry." She gave him a reproachful look. "How *could* I leave Santa Chiara with poor Franco incarcerated down there? If I do have to . . . to give my evidence . . . I must be here with you to support me. Once we got back to Innsbruck, Hermann would find some way of stopping me talking to the police."

"I had thought that your powers of verbal persuasion——"

"With Hermann? That just shows how little you know him. Anyway, I did feel faint," she added, defensively.

Henry grinned. "It was a magnificent performance," he said. "You had me fooled. But you might easily have broken your neck, you know."

Maria-Pia suddenly grew grave, and her eyes filled with tears. "It might have been better if I had," she said.

"Now, now, none of that."

"Henry—Franco didn't do it, did he? Promise me he didn't . . ."

"I'm not going to promise you anything. But if I'm right in what I think, it'll be all over by to-night."

"And after that . . . what will happen to me afterwards? Henry, you must help me. You said you would."

"My dear girl," said Henry, helplessly, "your private life is something you've got to work out for yourself. Other people can't solve that kind of problem for you."

"But Henry——"

"And do remember," Henry went on, "that although I agree Hermann is a difficult character, he really is devoted to you, in his own way. Don't hurt him more than you can help."

"Hurt him?" Maria-Pia laughed, sharply. "Nothing could ever hurt him."

"You can," said Henry. "You hurt him first of all by marrying him, and you've been carrying on the good work ever since, until he's become quite desperate. Don't think," he added hastily, as the tears welled in her eyes, "that I'm not sympathetic. It's a hell of a position for you. But things may be . . . difficult . . . for Hermann. Try to remember that the agony hasn't been all on one side."

Maria-Pia sniffed. "'You don't have to live with him,'" she said. "It's all very well for you to talk."

"I know," said Henry. He stood up, and took her hand, which was lying like a delicate golden leaf on the white coverlet. "You're a very brave girl. Keep it up."

With that, he left her, and went downstairs.

In the hall, he was surprised to see Spezzi in Rossati's office. He had a paper in his hand, and was poring over a large book which lay open on the desk. As Henry approached, he shut the book—which Henry could now see was the hotel register—and picked it up. He nodded curtly to Rossati, and came out into the hall, his pleasant face very grave.

"An extraordinary development has occurred," he said to Henry. "Where can we talk?"

"Come up to my room."

When the door had closed behind them, Spezzi said, "I heard from Rome at lunch-time."

"About Hauser?"

"Oh, that. Yes, a lot of stuff—only confirming what we'd already guessed. Among other things, they found in his apartment sufficient evidence to connect Rossati with the Caroni case."

Henry nodded. "I knew about that," he said. "I hadn't had time to tell you."

Spezzi gave him a surprised look, but went on. "No, the really sensational thing is about Roger Staines."

"Oh," said Henry. "What's the verdict?" He felt a cold fear.

"The note is a forgery," said Spezzi, shortly.

Henry was conscious of a distinct sensation of relief. "I'm glad to hear it," he said. "What's bothering you, then?"

Instead of answering Spezzi handed Henry Roger's packing list, which had been sent to Rome. "This," he said.

Henry looked at it. "Two pairs of ski trousers," he read, "four sweaters, four pairs of underpants—" He looked up. "Nothing very shattering there, surely?"

"Turn it over," said Spezzi.

On the back of the paper, hastily scribbled in a different hand, was written, "*Cocktails, Thursday, Lady Floyd,* 181 *Hyde Park Grove. Don't forget.*"

"Well?" said Henry, blankly.

"The person who wrote that," said Spezzi, with more than a touch of drama, "also wrote the forged note."

Sharply, Henry said, "Who was it? Do you know?"

Spezzi opened the hotel register, laid it on the bed, and put the packing list down on the open page beside one of the entries. There was no doubt about it: the widely looped, exuberant handwriting was unmistakable. The person who had scribbled on the back of Roger's packing-list had also written, in the register: "*Caroline Whittaker, British subject, London.*"

Henry looked at the register and the grubby piece of paper in silence for a long time. Then he said, "Oh, my God. How silly can people get?"

"But what does it mean?" Spezzi had turned away, and was pacing the room, deep in concentration. Almost to himself, he said, "Where is the sense in it? That Miss Caroline should forge such a note—it would be ridiculous if it were not obviously true. And all the time we imagined that she was in love with him . . ."

"Well, there's nothing we can do about it for the moment," said Henry. "She's out skiing. I'll question her as soon as she comes in—and Staines, too. I just hope she'll have the sense to tell me the truth, but I rather doubt it. At least it explains why she's been like a cat on hot bricks all this week. As soon as she heard you'd sent the packing list to Rome, she must have known that somebody would very likely have the wit to turn it over and look at the writing on the back. And there's another odd thing." And he told Spezzi Gerda's information about Roger's visit to Hauser's room.

"I wouldn't pay too much attention to that," said Spezzi, briefly. "The girl is guilty herself, so she will naturally lie to cast suspicion on others."

"You still think that?" said Henry. "I wonder. In any case, I think and hope that the whole thing will be cleared up once and for all to-night."

"To-night? When you question Miss Caroline, you mean?"

"No," said Henry. "When Mario comes to see me after the ski-lift has stopped. He has something to tell me."

"Mario?" said Spezzi, surprised. "What can he tell you?"

"The name of the murderer," said Henry.

The next two hours dragged unbearably.

At five o'clock, Henry heard voices in the hall, and went downstairs to find the English class arriving back from their skiing. Pietro was with them. While the others went to put their skis away in the shed, Pietro went into Rossati's office. He came out a moment later, looking sulky and cross.

"These Austrians," he said to Henry. "They make me sick."

"What's the matter?" Henry asked.

"I come all the way up here to see the Baroness—I have known her for several years, I was once her instructor. When I hear she have accident, I come up—I bring her a present." He produced from his anorak pocket a small box of Perugina chocolates, exquisitely wrapped in white and gold paper. "And now Rossati tells me her husband is out, and has left orders that nobody may see her. She is not dying—no? Why may she not see her friends?"

"She has a broken leg, and she—she's suffering from shock," said Henry, pacifically. "Perhaps it's just as well that she shouldn't have visitors. But it's very kind of you.

Shall I take the chocolates to her ? I am a favoured visitor, you see—being a policeman, they can't very well keep me out."

Pietro smiled. "Thank you, Enrico," he said. "And—give her all my good wishes . . . the good wishes of the village. We know this is a sad time for her."

"I'll do that," said Henry. He pocketed the chocolates, as Jimmy and Caro came in from the ski-store.

"Paid your sick-bed respects already, Pietro ? " Jimmy asked, gaily. "That was quick. Hello, Henry, old trout. How did the lone run go ? "

"I am not allowed to see the Baroness," said Pietro, shortly. "Her husband has forbidden it."

"Can't say I blame him," said Jimmy. "If I had a wife, I certainly wouldn't let you into her bedroom. Too risky altogether. Come and have a drink or some tea or something."

Jimmy bore Pietro off into the bar. Caro, who had been standing just behind them, stayed where she was and looked at Henry.

"I'm afraid I must have a talk to you, Caro," he said.

"I see," said Caro. "Very well." There was no surprise in her voice.

"Let's go in here," said Henry. He opened the door that led into what was described as the Residents' Sitting Room, though nobody had ever been known to sit there. It was a small room, dismally over-furnished with large, dark arm-chairs and deplorable *art nouveau* tables in pale, shiny wood. Henry switched on the light—for the dusk was deepening fast—and shut the door.

"Sit down," he said.

"I'd rather not, thank you," said Caro, in a small voice.

"Please yourself." Henry sat down in one of the arm-chairs and lit a cigarette. He offered one to Caro, but she shook her head negatively.

"You know," said Henry, after a moment, "I wish to goodness you'd tell me all about it. It's far better for you to make a clean breast of everything than have us find out bit by bit. And we shall, you know."

Caro said nothing.

"This business of the note that Roger was supposed to have written in Tangiers," Henry went on. "The police in Rome have identified it as being in your handwriting."

"What note? I don't know what you're talking about," said Caro.

Henry took Roger's packing list out of his pocket, turned it over, and held it out to Caro.

"Did you write this?"

"I can't remember."

"Oh dear, you are making things difficult," said Henry, with a sigh. "At least, you will agree that you signed your own name in the hotel register?"

Grudgingly, Caro said, "Yes."

"Then," said Henry, "you also wrote this"—he tapped the packing list—"and you also tried—not very successfully —to forge Roger's writing on a note that was found in Hauser's wallet."

Caro looked at him squarely. "Prove it," she said.

"Look, Caro," said Henry, despairingly, "I'm honestly not out for your blood—or Roger's either, for that matter. But forgery is a very serious matter indeed, and if you won't give me any sort of an explanation . . ."

He paused. Caro, who was standing behind one of the big armchairs, lowered her short-cropped blonde head and began picking nervously at the chocolate-brown moquette upholstery: but still she said nothing.

"My God," said Henry, with more than a touch of anger, "I've a good mind to hand you over to Spezzi and let you stew in your own juice."

Caro raised her head, and her blue eyes were tragic. "Please, Henry," she said. "I *can't* tell you anything. I simply can't."

"You can tell me one thing," said Henry, more kindly. "Are you still in love with Roger?"

" Of course."

" You haven't by any mad chance decided that you prefer Pietro Vespi, have you ? "

" Of course I haven't."

" In that case," said Henry, " if you won't tell me the truth I can only assume that you're either mad or bad. By the way," he added, " what was Roger doing in Hauser's room the night before the murder ? "

Caro looked terrified. " I don't know," she said.

" But you knew he was there ? "

" No, I didn't. You're putting words into my mouth ! "

There was a silence. " Well, I'm sorry, Caro," said Henry, at length, " but there's nothing whatsoever I can do for you if you go on like this. Spezzi and his boys will take over from now on, and the best advice I can give you is to get a good lawyer, quick. You're going to need one."

" I can look after myself," said Caro.

" That, my child, is exactly what you obviously can't do. Hell," said Henry, reasonably, " even Roger had the sense to tell the truth when he was questioned."

" Did he ? " said Caro, with a trace of impudence. " Did he tell you he'd been in Hauser's room ? "

" That's none of your business," said Henry. " Go on then. Off with you. I'm bored with this. If you come to your senses, let me know."

For a moment, Caro hesitated, and Henry thought that she was going to say something : but she changed her mind, turned quickly and ran out of the room and up the stairs.

Jimmy was in the hall with Pietro.

" What's up with Caro now ? " Jimmy asked, as he watched her retreating figure.

" Loss of memory," said Henry, shortly. He was tired and upset, and his interview with Caro had done nothing to add to his peace of mind.

" Miss Caro is not well ? " Pietro asked, with concern.

" She's all right," said Henry. " Just a little upset."

"I know this." Pietro's face was troubled. "When she first come here, she ski so good, she is gay. But since this murder—" He made a despairing gesture. "I worry," he said. "I do not understand."

"She's all right," said Henry, again. And Jimmy said, "D'you really have to go, Pietro? Stay and have another drink."

Pietro looked at his watch. "No, no," he said. "Is nearly half-past five, see? I have—how you say it—a date in the village." He smiled flashingly.

"It's jolly dark," said Jimmy. "The moon's not up yet. Mind how you go."

"No need to worry for me," said Pietro, easily. "I do this run many times in the dark—not so fast as in daytime, or is not safe. But you come and see me start—you will see I am O.K."

"All right," said Jimmy. "Come on, Henry—do you good to get some fresh air."

So the three men walked down to the start of Run One, and Henry and Jimmy waved Pietro on his way to the village. As they turned away, after the speeding figure had been lost to sight among the trees, Henry glanced over to the ski-lift. It was deserted now, although the chairs still clanked round on their endless belt. He could see Mario, walking up and down outside his hut, and blowing on his fingers to warm them, for the evening air was sharp with frost. "I wonder," he thought to himself. "I wonder . . . oh, well, I shall know soon . . ."

Henry found Emmy in their bedroom, padding about in bare feet searching for her stockings, which she swore she had left hanging over the back of the chair.

"Hello, darling," she said. "Anything new?"

She grew very grave when Henry told her about Caro. "The silly child," she said.

"It's all very well to dismiss it as silliness," said Henry sombrely. "It may be a lot worse than that."

Emmy stopped her searching, and said, "Caro? Oh,

surely not, Henry. She's such a nice creature. Oh, hell, what *has* Anna done with my stockings?"

Eventually they came to light under one of Henry's shirts, by which time he had discovered that his back-stud was missing. At length, however, they both succeeded in changing into their *après ski* regalia. As Emmy sat brushing her thick, dark hair with decisive strokes, Henry straightened his tie, and said, "Well, I'm ready. I suppose I'd better go and find Spezzi, if he's still here, and report on my utter lack of success with Caro. What time is it?"

"Five-past six," said Emmy, looking at her watch.

"Mario won't be here for well over an hour, then," said Henry. "I'd better see Spezzi and get it over."

"Mario?"

"He's coming up to see me when the lift stops. And I think and hope that it'll be the end of the case. You see, he——"

Henry got no further. There was a brusque knock on the door, and Spezzi burst in without waiting for an answer.

"Enrico!" he cried. "You must come at once. Something terrible has happened!"

Henry felt an icy hand close on his heart. "What?" he said.

"It's Mario . . . poor old Mario. He's dead—shot on the ski-lift, just like Hauser!"

CHAPTER FIFTEEN

For a moment, Henry looked completely stunned.

"It's not possible," he said, half to himself.

"Alas, it is possible. It has happened." Spezzi sat down on the bed. "This afternoon, when you said that Mario knew the name of the murderer, I confess that I did not believe you. Now it is only too clear that you were right. He knew—and he paid for his knowledge with his life."

Henry pulled himself together with an effort. "Tell me all you know about it, quickly," he said. "Then we'll go down."

"I know very little," said Spezzi. "Carlo telephoned the news from the village. He was very shocked—could hardly speak. He kept saying over and over again that it was just like Herr Hauser."

"When did he ring?"

"This minute. I came straight up to you. He has stopped the lift and called the doctor. Meanwhile, he waits for instructions from us."

"Right." Henry spoke briskly now, and turned thankfully to the prospect of action. Only thus could he beat off the nightmare that was beginning to close in. "Has everybody from the hotel arrived up yet?"

"I don't know."

"We'll go and see. Emmy, will you check up on Gerda, and then try the Baron's suite to make sure he's back? You'd better have a look for Trudi Knipfer, too."

"Of course," said Emmy, and went quickly out of the room.

There was no need to search for Roger and Colonel Buckfast. They were in the hall, and Henry and Spezzi could hear their voices as they came out into the corridor.

"Never known it happen before," the Colonel was saying. "Hope the fellow's not ill."

"He's been looking pretty ghastly lately, I must say," said Roger.

Henry came down the stairs. "Who are you talking about?" he asked.

"Mario," said Roger.

"Most extraordinary thing," said the Colonel. "I thought at the time it was him—pretty dark, of course, couldn't see very well. But I said to myself on the lift— I said, 'By Jove, that looks like old Mario going down.' And sure enough, when we got to the top, he wasn't there. Never known such a thing."

"We're afraid he must be ill," said Roger.

"I'm afraid I've got bad news for you," said Henry. "Mario is dead. He was shot."

"Oh, God." Roger had gone deathly pale, and the Colonel took an uncertain step towards Henry, and then put out his hand and grasped the banister for support. He looked as if he might easily be sick.

"Shot?" he repeated, stupidly. "Shot?"

"On the ski-lift, I presume," said Roger, in a voice of thin ice.

"I don't know yet," said Henry, "but it sounds like it."

"Charming, I must say." Roger turned to Colonel Buckfast. "How do you like the feeling of being a prime suspect in a case of double murder, Colonel?"

"A . . . a what . . . ?"

"Don't you realise that you and Gerda and I were the only people who were going up on the lift on both occasions?" said Roger. "Stands to reason, doesn't it? One of us is the culprit."

The Colonel seemed to be fighting for breath. "I don't know how you can speak so flippantly, Staines," he said at last. "In any case, the Baron was on the lift, too. He went up about five minutes before we did."

"Ah, but he wasn't even in Santa Chiara when Hauser

was killed," Roger pointed out, maliciously. " No, it's one
of us, I'm afraid. Who are you putting your money on—
Gerda or me ? Or are you going to confess ? "

" My dear Staines——" began the Colonel, outraged, but
Henry interrupted him crisply.

" So Gerda came up with you, did she ? And the Baron
was already on the lift. That means that everyone is back
at the hotel." He broke off for a quick consultation in
Italian with Spezzi, and then went on, " I am going down
to the village now. Capitano Spezzi will stay up here, and
he agrees with me that an immediate search must be made
for the gun. He has no warrant, of course, and you are
quite at liberty to refuse, but I very much hope you will
co-operate with us. There have been two deaths already,
and we can't risk a third."

Both men professed themselves only too willing to be
searched. Rossati was called, and agreed tearfully to the
hotel being combed for the missing weapon. Henry called
Emmy, and suggested to Spezzi that she should search the
women—a proposition which Spezzi accepted gratefully.
Henry left it to Spezzi and Rossati between them to break
the bad news to the Baron, and made his way down to the
ski-lift.

He spent some minutes in Mario's hut—silent now
except for the insistent ticking of the clock. Then he
examined carefully the platform outside the hut, where the
chairs now hung still—sinister shapes casting long, spidery
shadows across the snow under the lamplight. He studied
with particular care the book in which Mario had logged the
breakdowns of the lift, but found nothing more sensational
than the fact that a fuse had blown and been repaired shortly
after three o'clock that afternoon.

Finally, he picked up the telephone which connected
Mario's cabin to Carlo's, and wound the old-fashioned handle
which rang the bell in the lower hut. Carlo's voice answered
at once.

"Tibbett here," said Henry. "Start the lift, will you, Carlo? I'm coming down."

It was an eerie ride. Henry watched the procession of empty chairs as they slid upwards beside him, and, with a completely illogical stab of fear, half-expected to see one of them occupied . . . occupied by a shadowy figure who held a gun, pointed steadily at the victim for whom there was no escape, borne relentlessly onwards as he was by the mechanism of the lift, closer and closer to his death.

Impatiently dismissing this childish fancy, Henry shut his eyes and gave himself up to intensive concentration. But the problem whirled like a roundabout in his mind, one face after another rising up, mocking him : and all the time the same thought thundered in his brain, like an angry sea. " I must have been wrong . . . I must have been wrong . . ."

The scene at the bottom of the lift was bitterly reminiscent of the evening of Hauser's death—except that to-night it was not snowing. Mario lay where he had fallen in the snow—a pathetic, shapeless bundle of old clothes that had lately been a man. Carlo stood beside his friend's body, like a dog keeping watch over his dead master, and Henry saw the tears on his lean, wrinkled face.

Several young *carabinieri* had been deputed to keep the local population away from the ski-lift : but whereas in the case of Hauser's death this job had been carried out in the face of much voluble curiosity on the part of the crowd, countered by good-natured banter from the police, this time the villagers stood in silence, and only occasionally, when one of them edged too far forward, did a *carabiniere* put out a gently restraining hand. This death was not for them a thrill of scandal, or a feast for idle, inquisitive speculation : it was a death in the village, a death in the family.

The doctor—a small, dark, cheerful character in horn-rimmed spectacles—greeted Henry warmly. " I haven't examined him yet," he said, " except to make sure that he's dead. No doubt about that, I'm afraid, poor old fellow. The photographers have got their pictures, so if you'd like

to take a look at him, we can get him off to the mortuary,
and I can get on with the job."

"Thank you," said Henry. "I won't be long."

Carlo stood aside silently as Henry bent over the body.
Mario's face looked very tranquil. He might have been
sleeping in the snow, but for an ugly red stain that had
spread over his grubby white shirt. Henry straightened.

"Tell me what happened," he said to Carlo. "You
tried to help him off the chair——?"

"It is terrible, *signore* . . . terrible. I had spoken to him
on the telephone not long before——"

"When ?"

"I cannot be sure of the time," said Carlo, miserably.
"About half-past five, I suppose, or a little later. I told
him that the last of the Bella Vista people had just got on to
the lift, and that I didn't think we would have any more
customers this evening. He . . . he had not been well, *signore*,
and . . ."

"Go on," said Henry, encouragingly.

"I didn't mean any harm," said Carlo, contritely, "but
I did not see why he should wait about up there in the cold
for another hour and a half. I . . . I suggested that when
Mr. Staines reached the top—he was the last on the lift, you
see—Mario might come down."

"Is he allowed to do that ?" Henry asked.

Carlo shuffled his feet, awkwardly. "It is against the
rules, I know, *signore* . . . but Mario is an old man, and
my son, who works the Alpe Rosa lift, was already home.
We live nearby. If anyone had come who wanted help
at the top, my son would have gone up ahead to help them
off."

"Supposing a fuse blew at the top ?"

"I would have telephoned to Beppi at the Bella Vista,"
said Carlo. "He understands the lift. He has taken Mario's
place before."

"This was a fairly usual arrangement, was it ?" Henry
asked.

" No, no, *signore* . . . only once or twice, when Mario was not well. In any case, he refused to come down."

" What did he say ? "

" He said he had an appointment at the Bella Vista when the lift stopped. He said it was most important."

" I see. What happened then ? "

" I asked him how he was going to get back to the village, and he said he would ski. I told him he was crazy, for I knew he was not well and he certainly should not ski in the dark. But he laughed, and said, ' Perhaps they will start the lift specially for me after what I tell them.' Then he rang off."

" What did you do then ? "

" I waited here," said Carlo. " My son brought me a cup of coffee, and I had a word with Pietro—he came down on skis soon after. That was at a quarter to six—I know, because Pietro called out to me to tell him the time from my clock. He had an appointment, he said, and feared to be late. I suppose it was about a quarter of an hour later that I saw Mario coming down on the lift. First, I was pleased that he had changed his mind and taken my advice. Then I thought —the Bella Vista guests cannot have reached the top before Mario started down. He must have felt very ill to leave the lift with skiers still on it, and to miss his important engagement. As he came closer, I saw that he was limp . . . as if he had fainted, perhaps. And the safety arm was down, which was strange. So I came quickly to help him, and . . ." Carlo's voice broke. " Just like Herr Hauser," he said, with difficulty. " Just like Herr Hauser . . ."

" You tried to help him . . ." Henry prompted, gently.

" I took his arm, and he fell—so. And then I saw that my friend Mario was dead . . ." Carlo turned away, deeply moved.

" Thank you, Carlo," said Henry. Then he turned back to Mario, and, moving him very gently, he extracted the meagre contents of the old man's pockets. He made a little pile of the pathetic relics—five hundred lire, mostly in small change : a battered pocket-knife : a big, old-fashioned door key and a smaller, newer key : a stub of pencil : a very dirty handkerchief : and five black cigarettes in a purple packet. Whatever Mario had been intending to tell Henry, he had apparently had no intention of supporting it with any tangible evidence.

Henry tied these belongings up carefully in his own hand-kerchief, and said to the doctor, " All right. You can take him away now. I'm going up to the hotel again. You might telephone me when you've had a look at him."

" Certainly, *signore*."

The stretcher-bearers were just moving forward when the ranks of villagers suddenly parted—silently and by common consent—and a tall figure stepped into the circle of lamp-light.

" Where is my father ? " said Pietro. Under the harsh light, his fine face seemed to be carved out of granite, white and stern, and scored with deep shadows. Henry laid a hand on the young man's arm.

" *Caro Pietro*," he said. " What can I say ? "

Pietro was gazing down at his father's body. " They told me in the Bar Schmidt," he said. " I went straight to my mother. Now she has sent me to bring him home."

Henry and the doctor exchanged quick glances. Then Henry said, " I'm afraid that's not possible, Pietro."

Pietro's eyes flashed. " Not possible ? Hasn't my mother suffered enough already, without——? "

" Your father was murdered," said Henry. " Later you can take him home, but first the doctor must examine him. It is absolutely necessary if we are to discover who killed him."

Pietro did not answer, but stepped forward and went down on his knees beside Mario's body. He lowered his head, as if in prayer, and in the dead silence the church clock began to strike seven, like a funeral bell. At last, Pietro looked up, and his face was grim. " Very well, Enrico," he said. " I accept your ruling." He glanced down at his father's still face for a moment, and added, softly, "There are debts which must be settled."

Then, abruptly, he got to his feet and strode away through the crowd, which parted silently to let him pass.

The Bella Vista was wrapped in an ominous silence when Henry got back. All the residents—with the exception of the von Wurtburgs—were in the bar. They had split into small groups, talking in hushed and nervous voices. Roger and Caro were at the most distant table in the corner, conversing earnestly. Jimmy was at the bar, and the Buckfasts sat silently at their usual table. Near the door, the three Knipfers were carrying on a low-pitched conversation in German with Gerda. Spezzi and Emmy were nowhere to be seen.

Henry went upstairs, and found Emmy in Gerda's room, going through the contents of the chest of drawers.

" I hate doing this," she said. " There's nothing here, of course. Spezzi even made me search Trudi Knipfer, and after this I've got to go through her room, even though she came up to the hotel ages ago, even before Jimmy and Caro."

Gerda's room revealed nothing of interest, apart from a small snapshot, carefully-framed, which showed a strikingly handsome, blond man and a pretty, plump, dark woman dressed in the fashion of twenty-five years ago : the woman was holding on her knee a small dark girl of three or four, who was laughing uproariously. There was also a larger portrait of the man—a carefully-retouched study of the kind which actors of the 'thirties liked to send to their fans. It was inscribed, " *To my darling wife, with all my love— Gottfried. May,* 1936."

Henry glanced at the photographs, sighed, and said, " No, there's nothing here. Let's have a look at Trudi's room."

Fraulein Knipfer's room was as bleak and bereft of interest as it had been when Henry had examined it earlier in the day. Now, however, he did not feel that he could let the locked drawer pass, and he told Emmy to go and fetch Trudi.

"Fraulein Knipfer," Henry said, politely, "I am sorry to trouble you, but as you know we have to search everybody's rooms, for there is a gun missing. I wonder if you would give me the key to this drawer?"

"No," said Trudi. "I won't." She looked at Henry with mingled contempt and dislike.

"I really would advise it, Fraulein," said Henry. "You see, if you refuse, we can but put the worst possible construction on it. I shall have to put a police guard on this room to-night, and Capitano Spezzi will return in the morning with a warrant, and break the drawer open. I am sure you would not want that."

"The gun is not in there," said Trudi. "Merely something private of mine. It can't be important."

"I'm sorry, Fraulein. I will have to insist."

Trudi hesitated for a moment, and then said, coldly, "You cannot have searched the room very thoroughly, or you would have found the key."

Brushing roughly past Henry, she went over to the washbasin, and fumbled in her sponge-bag to produce a small key. "There!" she said. She almost threw the key at Henry, and went quickly out, slamming the door.

Henry unlocked the drawer. Inside was a small diary. He sat down on the bed to read it.

There was nothing very remarkable about most of the entries. They recorded a rather dreary life in Hamburg, apparently dominated by the personality of "Papa". The family's arrival at the Bella Vista was duly noted, and then came a brief entry which read. "*To-night Papa told me I must marry F. H.*" After this, "F. H." cropped up in each day's entry, generally accompanied by some scathing comment. On the day before Hauser's death, Trudi had written, "*To-day I told Papa I could not go through with this marriage. He was insistent. Of course I cannot disobey him. I must think of some way out.*" For the day of the murder, there was a single, short, entry. "*F. H. was killed to-day. I feel a wonderful sense of relief, and I know what I must do now.*"

Henry stood up, and put the diary in his pocket. "I'll have to show this to Spezzi," he said. "Let's go down."

They found the Capitano and his adjutant in the hall, and all four of them went into Rossati's office, which had been commandeered once more.

"We have searched everywhere—everywhere," Spezzi said. "Nothing to be found. And, after all, the murderer did not have much time to dispose of the gun. Rossati was in the bar, and Anna in the kitchen. Rossati saw the Baron come in and go straight upstairs, and then a few minutes later, all three skiers came in from the ski store."

"You've looked there, of course."

"I've taken it apart," said Spezzi, with a wry smile. "Anyway, they were all three in there together, which would have made it difficult for the murderer to find an elaborate hiding-place. According to Rossati, Gerda went straight upstairs, and the two men stayed in the hall, where we found them."

"Well, I'm sorry you've had such a lot of fruitless work." said Henry. "But it had to be done. Emmy and I did find something that may be important."

He gave Spezzi the diary, and the latter read it with intense concentration. When he came to the entry on the day of Hauser's death, he gave a low whistle. "Very interesting, Enrico," he said. "Or it would be, if there was the remotest possibility that Fraulein Knipfer could have committed either of the murders. Unfortunately, there isn't."

"I find it interesting all the same," said Henry. "Well, now, to get back to the gun. I didn't really expect that you would find it here. My guess is that this time it really was thrown from the ski-lift. Thank God it isn't snowing. How soon can your men get out to look for it?"

"I'll send a party out to-night, if you like," said Spezzi, doubtfully, "but there's only a half-moon, and I very much doubt if they'd find it in the dark."

He walked over to the window, opened it and looked out.

"It's clouding over," he said, "but I don't think it will snow to-night. I'll tell you what we'll do. There's a fair amount of light under the ski-lift itself, especially near the pylons. I'll send some men out to search there. Of course, if the murderer threw the gun into one of the ravines—and I must say that's what I would have done in the circumstances—then we won't find it to-night : nor if it was thrown clear of the lift and into the trees, but that would have meant quite a big movement, which would probably have been noticed by the person in the chair behind."

"Unless the murderer came up last." Henry pointed out.

"True. But I fear that is not the case." Spezzi sighed. "Anyway, we'll take a look."

"It's very good of you," said Henry. "I do think it's important."

CHAPTER SIXTEEN

Spezzi had only just finished telephoning to the village to organise the search-party, when there was a knock on the door, and Roger came in. He looked at Henry sheepishly, like a schoolboy facing an awkward few minutes with his headmaster.

"I wonder if I can have a word with you, Henry," he said, diffidently. "There's . . . there's something I want to tell you."

Henry gave him a severe look. "I'm extremely glad to hear it," he said. "I was just going to send for you."

"I rather meant . . . that is, could I see you privately?" Roger glanced apologetically at Spezzi.

"No," said Henry, firmly. "This is an official interview, and Emmy will be taking it down in shorthand."

Roger looked extremely unhappy, but he sat down, and said, with as good a grace as he could muster, "Oh, all right. If you insist."

There was a long pause. Then Henry said, "Well, are you going to make a statement, or am I going to question you?"

"It's about this business of Hauser," said Roger, at length. "This second murder has put me in a hell of a tricky position, and the only way out that I can see is to make a clean breast of things."

"About time, too," said Henry, grimly.

"I told you before that Hauser had no business proposition for me," Roger went on. "I'm afraid that wasn't true. He wanted me to smuggle stuff out of here for him, and—well, to be honest, I agreed. It seemed to me like a pretty good way of raising the wind, and I'm somewhat embarrassed financially just now. I should have told you all this before, of course, but . . . well, I'm sure you can appreciate why I didn't."

"You're not telling me anything I didn't know," said Henry. "By the way, what did you do with Hauser's second letter? I suppose you burnt it."

"How did you know about that?" asked Roger, incredulously.

"It was obvious," said Henry, "that there must have been a second letter—unless he telephoned you in London. Apart from anything else, no date was mentioned in the letter you showed me. Just a vague reference to 'the month of January'. Hauser didn't as a rule stay here for more than two weeks at a time, so he was bound to have fixed a definite date for meeting you. In fact, the whole letter was as phony as a tin half-crown. You discussed all this with him here last year, didn't you?"

Roger gave Henry the ghost of a grin. "All right," he said. "You're too clever by half. Yes, he did mention it first last year, and I indicated that I might be interested. I wasn't surprised to get his letter—it just confirmed the tentative arrangement we'd made. I wrote back saying I was on, and he wrote again fixing January 25th for our rendezvous."

"January 25th?" said Henry. "That's to-day."

"He told me," said Roger, "that he would be leaving the Bella Vista on the twelfth—four days before we arrived, in fact—and coming back on the twenty-fourth. I was very surprised to find him here, as you can imagine, but he simply said that his plans had changed at the last moment. But he said not to worry, he would go back to Rome to collect my . . . my cargo, as it were, and bring it up sometime during our second week here. In fact, he was on his way to fetch it when he was killed. So you see . . . I admit I haven't behaved like a plaster saint, but you must admit that I had a very strong motive for keeping Hauser alive."

"And what about your story of blackmail?"

Roger laughed, nervously. "Oh, that," he said. "That wasn't anything, really. Hauser was a pretty nasty little character, as you doubtless know, and he tried to use that note to make me accept less than my fair share of the loot, and as a sort of insurance that I wouldn't rat on him. But even he had to admit it was a forgery when he compared it to my real handwriting."

" So the account you gave us of Hauser burning the note was also a complete lie ? "

" I'm terribly afraid so." Roger smiled disarmingly, and with a highly plausible air of candour, he added, " You see, I knew you'd find the note, but I was naïve enough to hope that you wouldn't connect it with me. As soon as you mentioned the *Nancy Maud* in the bar that evening, I realised that you'd put two and two together, and I reckoned I'd better think up a story to explain why I didn't report Hauser's blackmailing efforts to the police straight away. I didn't intend all the other business to come to light, you understand."

" I understand only too well," said Henry, dryly. " If I may say so, your fabrication was a little over-ingenious, and left a lot of loopholes. However, we haven't come yet to the really curious part of the story. Caro must have told you that the police in Rome have identified the forgery as being in her handwriting."

Roger flushed angrily, and more than a trace of belligerence showed in his voice, as he said, " Yes, she has. And I think it's despicable, the way you've been frightening the poor kid with talk of lawyers and prosecutions. You must know as well as I do that these so-called handwriting experts are two-a-penny, and for every one that says she wrote it, I bet I can produce two to say she didn't. It's not by any means conclusive evidence, and as it's patently obvious to the most meagre intelligence that the girl had neither the motive nor the opportunity to——"

" I should save your righteous indignation, if I were you," said Henry. " You might instead give me your opinion as to why Caro has been in a state of nervous terror ever since Hauser died."

" That's my fault, I'm afraid," said Roger. " I never

intended Caro to know anything about my nefarious dealings with Hauser, but as bad luck would have it, she overheard us talking the very first day we got here. She didn't hear much, but enough to make her suspicious. To cut a long story short, she nagged and nagged at me until finally I told her the truth, like a fool. Then, of course, she got hysterical and tried to put the kybosh on the whole idea. To hear the way she carried on, you'd have thought I was planning a . . . planning to steal the Crown Jewels, or something. She threatened to tell her father if I didn't promise to have no more to do with Hauser."

"So," said Henry, "you told her you'd dearly love to back out, but you couldn't, because Hauser was black-mailing you."

Roger had the grace to look ashamed of himself. "What else could I do?" he said. "That was why she had her knife into poor old Fritz to such a marked extent."

"And what," said Henry, "were you doing in Hauser's room the night before he was killed?"

"By God, you know everything, don't you?" said Roger, admiringly. "As a matter of fact, that was a perfectly innocent visit. I went in to pick up a book he'd promised to lend me."

"What book?"

"*Cara Teresa*, by Renato Lucano," said Roger promptly. "It's marvellously sordid, and it hasn't been published in England yet. I read Italian pretty fluently, you see. The book's in my room now, if you want to see it."

Henry looked inquiringly at Spezzi, who nodded, and said, "Yes, the book is there."

"Did you see the gun?" Henry asked Roger.

"Yes. It was on the table."

Henry looked at Roger quizzically. The young man's face was a picture of honest ingenuousness, and he said, "Actually, I'm immensely relieved to have got all that off my chest. As it turns out, I'm damn glad I didn't get mixed up with Hauser and his smuggling."

"Talking of smuggling," said Henry, "what was your cargo supposed to consist of?"

"Watches," said Roger, without hesitation.

"You're sure of that?"

"Of course I'm sure. The arrangement was that I came out here twice a year on holiday—summer and winter. Hauser said I must always come with a party, on the cheap train—it was good cover, he said. I was to take back a fairly big consignment each time. Then I was going to bring stuff out of England, too, but we hadn't got around to discussing that. There wouldn't have been a fortune in it, of course, but it would have made me a nice steady little bit."

"You can count yourself extremely lucky that Hauser didn't live long enough to get you involved," said Henry, grimly. "It wouldn't have been watches for long, you know. And there'd have been no going back. I sincerely hope you've learnt your lesson."

"You can say that again," said Roger, ruefully. "Strictly legal activities for Staines from now on."

"And now that you've made your confession," Henry proceeded, with a slight edge of irony, "let's talk about the second murder. I'd like as detailed as possible an account of your movements to-day."

"You know most of them," said Roger. "I went out with old Buckfast in the morning, and we did Run Three and the Alpe Rosa, where we collected Gerda. We lunched at the Olympia, as you know, and came up in the lift as soon as it started, to have another shot at Run Three before it got too crowded." He paused, and then went on. "I may as well tell you straight out that all three of us knew that Mario was coming to see you to-night."

"You did?" Henry was surprised. "How?"

"Well, we came up on the lift just behind Pietro, who was coming to collect his class, and while we were putting our skis on at the top, I heard him talking to Mario. He must have been worried about the old man—I must say, I thought myself that he looked pretty ghastly. Anyway, I heard Pietro say, ' You're a stubborn old fool, father. Why don't you just go home quietly ? ' and Mario said, ' I've already told you I'm seeing Signor Tibbett to-night, and nothing's going to stop me.' Of course," Roger went on, sombrely, " I was the only one who understood what they were saying—at least, I don't think Gerda speaks Italian. Certainly the Colonel doesn't. But like an idiot I repeated it to them."

" What did they say ? "

" Nothing much." Roger frowned. " We'd agreed to make a race of it down Run Three, and Buckfast started fussing about not having got the right goggles. He insisted on going off to the hotel to get them—thereby holding us up to such an extent that the bloody run was jampacked with people by the time we took off, and the whole thing was ruined. However . . . where was I ? Oh yes. Mario. Well, Gerda and I speculated a bit about what Mario wanted with you, and then the Colonel came back, and we set off : but, as I said, the *piste* was like Piccadilly Circus at rush-hour, so after one run we legged it over to the Alpe Rosa again. We packed in at about a quarter to five, and went to the Olympia for tea. The Baron was there, too, incidentally."

" Did you speak to him ? "

" Not really. He's an unsociable sort of cove. Just nodded in a markedly chilly manner when we came in. He left several minutes before we did. When we got to the lift, Carlo told us we were the last, as the Baron had just gone up."

" What time was that ? "

" I don't honestly know," said Roger. " Just before half-past five, I suppose. We didn't stay long over tea."

" You were the last to go up on the lift, I understand."

" Yes. Gerda went first, then the Colonel, then me."

" And you saw Mario coming down ? "

" Yes—at least, as I said, I didn't know it was him. It never occurred to me until we found he wasn't at the top."

" How far up were you when you passed him ? "

Roger considered. "Something over half-way, I think," he said. "Difficult to be sure."

"Now," said Henry, "think hard, because this is important. Did you see anything drop from the ski-lift—as if one of the people in front of you had thrown, or dropped——"

"The gun ?" Roger smiled faintly. "No," he said. "I've been considering that possibility myself. Mind you, I can't swear to anything, but I'm pretty darn sure I would have noticed it."

That seemed to be all that Roger could tell them, so Henry sent him off to join the others, who had already started dinner. He suggested that he and Emmy, with Spezzi and his aide, should have their meal brought to them in the office, so that he could translate the gist of Roger's interview to Spezzi while they ate. They had nearly finished their main course when the telephone rang, and Henry answered it.

It was the doctor from Santa Chiara. "Preliminary report, Inspector," he said, cheerfully. "Death caused by .32 bullet in the heart—wound almost identical with Hauser's, though I would say that the range this time was slightly shorter—though of course one can't fix it to within inches. Death instantaneous, and within an hour of my examination. With your permission, I'll send the two bullets off for testing straight away. It should be simple to establish whether they came from the same gun."

Henry had only just put the receiver back into place when the phone shrilled again. This time it was for Spezzi, who answered it with his mouth full of cheese. He listened for a moment, then swallowed hastily, said, "Hold on !" and turned to Henry, his eyes sparkling with excitement.

"Enrico !" he cried, "They have found the gun !"

"Thank God," said Henry, piously. "Where ?"

There was another brief conversation, and then Spezzi put his hand over the mouthpiece of the phone, and said, "Under the ski-lift—at the foot of a pylon, about three-quarters of the way down. They want to know what to do with it."

"Take down all its details—number, make and so on," said Henry, "and let us have them over the phone. Then send the gun straight away for testing with the bullets, and for fingerprinting."

Spezzi relayed these instructions, with many more of his own about care in handling the weapon for fear of spoiling any prints. Then he rang off, and said, triumphantly, "Now we are getting somewhere! This time the murderer has been careless!"

"There's one thing that occurs to me," said Emmy. "If both bullets were fired from the same gun, that surely lets poor Franco out."

"Yes," said Spezzi, with undisguised relief, when Henry had translated this for him. "I expect to be able to release him to-morrow. It was certainly fortunate for the young man, as it turned out, that he was safely in prison to-day. Even the Baron can hardly maintain that he could have killed Mario : and the Baroness will be grateful, I hope, that his innocence is proved. So all will be happy. Yes," he went on, lighting a cigarette, "the case narrows down at last. It is clear that we have only three suspects now— the Colonel, young Staines, and Fraulein Gerda. From what you have told me, I should say that it is most unlikely that Staines killed Hauser. The Colonel had no motive, and is a thoroughly upright character. Which leaves us with Fraulein Gerda, as I have said all along."

"None of that is proof," said Henry, "and psychologically speaking——"

Spezzi waved an airy hand. "Your trouble, my dear Enrico," he said, with what Henry considered insufferable smugness, "is that you look for complications where none exist. You say, 'This person *could* have committed the crime, but it is not in their character to do so.' What sort of reasoning is that ? And then you are sentimental. You wish to exonerate the girl because she is beautiful and tragic.

But I tell you, when it comes to murder, there is no predicting what people will do. I am straightforward. I look for the obvious explanation, the logical explanation, and you sneer, but you will see that I am right. In this case, I wish with all my heart that I could be wrong, for Fraulein Gerda is . . ." He stopped, sighed, and then said, " But we have to face facts."

" That," said Henry, " is exactly what I'm trying to do. *All* the facts," he added, " not just the convenient ones."

" I do not understand."

But Henry, who had been touched on the raw of his pride both by Spezzi's self-satisfaction and by the allegation of sentimentality (which he knew only too well to contain a grain of truth), became stubbornly silent, and devoted himself to the demolition of a tangerine.

After dinner, they bearded the Baron in his suite. The latter, already nettled by the ignominy of being searched, was unhelpful in the extreme.

He had driven to Montelunga after lunch, he said, on private business which was no concern of Spezzi's. He had returned at half-past four and taken tea at the Olympia. Shortly before half-past five, he had taken the ski-lift up to the hotel. He had noticed somebody coming down when he was about two-thirds of the way up. Of course he had not speculated as to who it might be. Some peasant, he presumed. The matter did not interest him in the least. He had also been extremely irritated to find no attendant at the top, and had made up his mind to report the matter to the authorities. He hoped sincerely that it would not happen again : but he supposed that laxness of discipline was only to be expected from the Italians.

Rattled, Spezzi asked if the Baron had seen Gerda, Roger and the Colonel in the Olympia. Coldly, the Baron replied that he had. No, he had not spoken to them : he could hardly be expected to carry on a social conversation with a domestic servant whom he had recently dismissed. If the

English visitors liked to keep such company, that was entirely their affair.

So far, the Baron had run exactly true to form. But at the end of the interview, he made a surprising remark.

"I presume," he said, with no amelioration of his bitter expression, "that you will now see fit to release di Santi."

Spezzi hedged, murmuring something about positive identification of the bullets. The Baron smiled, without humour.

"I am, I hope, a just man," he said. "I acknowledge that it was largely on my instigation that the young man was arrested, and clearly I was mistaken. You will do me a favour by setting him free at the earliest possible moment."

With that, the interview terminated, and Henry and Spezzi turned with relief to the more congenial business of interrogating Colonel Buckfast.

Roger's words in the hall had evidently made a deep impression on the Colonel. He was as nervous as a cat, and started off by demanding the presence of his own lawyer and the British Consul.

"My dear Colonel," said Henry, "nobody is accusing you of anything. We're only trying to get a clear picture of what happened."

"My position ... delicate ... extremely delicate," said the Colonel, redly. "Extremely. I know my rights as a citizen."

Henry sighed. "So do I," he said. "But it really would be a whole lot simpler if you'd just confirm a few facts that Staines has given us."

"What has he been saying?" demanded the Colonel, sharply.

So Henry read him Roger's account of the day's skiing, and grudgingly the Colonel admitted that it was accurate. When Henry reached the bit about the goggles, Colonel Buckfast grew more voluble.

"Staines was quite shirty about being held up," he said,

" but it's extremely unwise to take risks with the eyes. Snow blindness. Not as uncommon as people think. Always impressed on us in The Team."

" The sun had got brighter, had it ? " Henry asked.

The Colonel gave him a pitying look. " It is apt to at midday," he said, with elephantine sarcasm. " I have goggles with interchangeable eye-pieces—you know the things. Last time I wore them, it was snowing, so the yellow eye-piece was in place. Stupidly left the green one in my room. Didn't take me more than five minutes. The fuss young Staines made, you'd have thought I'd committed a crime." He realised too late the unfortunate implication of this turn of phrase, and reddened. " That is to say——"

" I know what you mean," said Henry, smiling. " The young are apt to be impatient."

The Colonel could not fix the time of the party's ascent on the lift any more accurately than Roger had done, but he stuck to his earlier statement that he had recognised Mario in the down-going chair, when he himself was nearing the top, and that he thought the old man looked ill.

" What made you think that ? " Henry asked.

But the Colonel could not find words to explain his impression. Mario had been looking seedy for several days, he said. They had all remarked it.

" You knew he was planning to come and see me ? " Henry asked.

" So Staines said. I didn't pay much attention. I thought we'd heard the last of the murder with di Santi's arrest."

After affirming that he had most certainly not seen anything falling from the ski-lift—and then admitting that he had had his eyes closed for most of the ride—the Colonel withdrew, a study in profoundly rattled dignity.

Spezzi said, " And now—we will see the Fraulein."

Henry never forgot the interview that followed. Gerda and Spezzi faced each other across the polished expanse of the desk in an atmosphere charged with pent-up emotion. Spezzi, determined to fulfil his duty in spite of his personal feelings, was harsher than Henry had ever seen him. Gerda, quiet and calm, wore a look of anguish which wrung Henry's heart. "If only they could have met under different circumstances . . ." he reflected. As it was, the tension seemed to Henry to make the encounter a grim and tragic equivalent of a hard-fought final on the Centre Court at Wimbledon.

Spezzi tried every tactic he knew, working from the suave springing of unexpected questions, through quiet menace to eventual bullying and shouting. Gerda parried every attack like a tennis player who wears down a more volatile opponent with steadily consistent drives from the back-line. Again and again it was Spezzi who was caught out of position as he tried, metaphorically, to storm the net. The final score was set and match to the German girl. Spezzi, however, didn't know when he was beaten, and continued to slam down aces.

"It may interest you to know," he barked, "that we have found the gun ! "

"I am very glad," said Gerda.

"You took it from Hauser's briefcase at the Olympia ! " thundered Spezzi. "Admit it ! "

Gerda flinched as if she had been hit, but she said, quietly, "I am very sorry, Capitano. I did not. I did not know the gun existed."

"You went to the cloakroom that day ! Don't attempt to deny it ! "

"I am not denying it. I went to hang up my anorak."

"And you hid the gun in the pocket."

"No."

"You waited until you saw Hauser coming down——"

"Forgive me, Capitano, but I must point out that I thought Hauser had left the hotel many hours earlier."

"So ! You were interested in his movements ! "

"Not specially. But he said at breakfast time that he was going to the village for lunch and did not expect to return to the hotel."

" But when you saw his luggage in the Olympia, you knew he had not left Santa Chiara ! "

" Of course. He had said he was leaving by the last train."

" It's no use trying to bluff me," cried Spezzi. " You killed Mario because he knew you were Hauser's murderer and he was going to tell the Inspector ! "

" How could he have known such a thing, Capitano ? "

" He saw you with the gun ! " Spezzi shouted. " He found where you had hidden it ! "

" Oh ? And where had I hidden it ? "

" How do I know, now Mario is dead ? " screamed the exasperated Capitano. " But you knew that he knew that you knew——" He paused for breath, and to untangle his phrasing.

" How strange, then," said Gerda, " that Mario did not tell you sooner."

And so it went on. When Spezzi had finally exhausted himself, he reluctantly dismissed the girl, with a curt warning that she had no hope of concealing her crime, and that it would be better for her to confess. The door closed quietly behind her, and Spezzi mopped his brow. Then he shot a suspicious look at Henry, and said, " Oh, she's clever, all right—and a cool one, too. Don't think I have made the mistake of underestimating her."

Henry said nothing.

Goaded, the unfortunate Spezzi burst out, " Very well, if she didn't do it, who did ? God knows, I would like more than anything to see her proved innocent. But do you help me ? Yesterday you thought you had solved the case, but we don't hear any more about that now, I notice. It's easy to criticise ! Where's your solution ? "

" I'll tell you soon enough," said Henry. The sight of Spezzi's distress had made him considerably ashamed of his previous childish irritation. " Just because we work by different methods," he went on, " there's no reason why we shouldn't both come to the same conclusion in the end. I am sure that we will do so."

" As far as I am concerned, the case is clear," said Spezzi. " I only wish I had arrested the girl at once, as I wanted to. Then poor Mario would still be alive now." He stood up. " I do not think we can do any more to-night," he said.

" Are you going to work out a time-table for this murder ?" Henry asked.

" Of course," said Spezzi, with a touch of hauteur.

" Please let me have a copy," said Henry. " It was most valuable last time."

Spezzi, not absolutely certain whether to take this as a compliment or an insult, contented himself with saying, " Of course," once again.

Before the Capitano left the room, Henry said, " By the way—this is only a suggestion, but if I were you, I wouldn't confine everybody to the hotel to-morrow. It doesn't really serve any useful purpose, and it makes them all thoroughly irritable. In my opinion, the only way we'll get proof in this case is to give the murderer plenty of rope."

" I had already come to that conclusion," said Spezzi, stiffly.

When the Capitano and the *carabinieri* had gone, Emmy said, " Phew ! Poor Gerda ! He's really got it in for her."

" Yes," said Henry absently. He scratched the back of his neck. " You know, Emmy, my nose tells me we're approaching this case from the wrong end altogether. I've been as stupid as anyone, I fully admit—because I allowed myself to be side-tracked, instead of sticking to my original line of thought. But when you face the facts—as Spezzi so penetratingly advised—you get a different perspective altogether . . . altogether . . . do you see what I mean ? "

" No," said Emmy, " but I'll take your word for it."

She felt a rising excitement. This was the first time on this case that Henry had talked about " my nose " with complete unselfconsciousness—it was an expression that came out spontaneously when he was deep in thought and really on the track of something. In the early stages of an investigation, when he was groping uncertainly, he would occasionally use the same phrase—but in inverted commas, as it were, and with an apologetic smile. This time it was the real thing.

Upstairs, as they got ready for bed, Henry was silent and thoughtful, moving about the room like a man in a dream. Emmy went to the window, and opened it.

" It's a heavy sort of night," she said. " Lots of cloud and no moon to be seen. It's rather weird. Even the ski-lift lights look cold and spooky—and there's a great dark shadow where one of them has gone out, as if the lift had broken its back . . ." She shivered, and turned away from the window.

Henry had not been listening. He was sitting on the bed with his sandy head in his hands, and all he said was, " There's something that I've missed . . . there must be . . . there must be . . ."

CHAPTER SEVENTEEN

THE NEXT MORNING dawned drab and overcast. As Spezzi had predicted, no snow had fallen overnight, but the sky was heavy with it, and it could only be a matter of a few hours before the great, grey-bellied clouds discharged their freight, curtaining the landscape in cold, misty whiteness.

Henry woke early, and roused Emmy. "Will you do something for me, darling?" he said.

"What is it?" she asked, sleepily.

"Get up now, take the lift down as soon as it starts, and catch the 9.40 train to Immenfeld."

"To Immenfeld?" Emmy sat up in bed, tousled and surprised. "Whatever for?"

"I want you to try and find out what Roger was doing there on the day of Hauser's murder."

"Roger? But he skied there with the Colonel, and——"

"And the Colonel said," Henry put in, "that after lunch he had done some of the local runs while Roger went shopping. There are mighty few Englishmen in Immenfeld, and with any luck they'll remember him. I want to know what he did, what he bought, and who he spoke to. And also if there's any significant amount of time not accounted for."

"O.K." Emmy got out of bed and stretched. "I can't see the sense of it, but anything you say."

So she and Henry breakfasted early and she went off to the ski-lift, having arranged to rendezvous with Henry in the Olympia at half-past twelve.

Meanwhile, Henry climbed to the top floor of the hotel, and knocked at Trudi Knipfer's door.

"Come in," she called. She was standing in front of the mirror in her ski-clothes, twisting her thick fair hair into ugly plaits. She looked very disconcerted when she saw Henry.

" Oh, it's you. May I have my diary back, please ? "

" Not quite yet, I'm afraid," said Henry. " The Italian police have it."

" They have no right to keep it," said Trudi, coldly. " I shall speak to the Captain about it." There was a pause, and then she said, " Well ? What do you want ? "

" Just a word with you before you go skiing, if you don't mind, Fraulein," said Henry.

" Go ahead," said Trudi. She went on doing her hair.

" You must have heard," said Henry, " about Mario's murder yesterday."

" They told me he was dead," said Trudi, without expression.

" The two deaths are undoubtedly connected—Mario's and Hauser's," Henry went on.

" Of course," said Trudi, shortly, her voice distorted by the fact that her mouth was full of hairpins. These she now proceeded to jab viciously into place one by one.

" You don't sound as though you were surprised to hear of Mario's death," said Henry.

Trudi's eyes met his steadily in the mirror. " Were you ? " she asked.

" Very," said Henry. " You see, he had arranged to come and see me last night."

" So Gerda told us," said Trudi. " Still, I suppose he is allowed to change his mind. He probably lost his nerve."

" What do you mean by that ? "

" Well," said the girl, " I understand that he had already started to go down on the ski-lift when he . . . when he died. So presumably he had decided not to come and see you after all."

There was a pause. " Fraulein Knipfer," Henry said, very gravely, " I believe that you know who killed Fritz Hauser."

Trudi turned round and faced him. "Do you know?" she demanded.

"Yes," said Henry, "I think I do."

"Then you need no help from me or anyone else."

"Would you say," Henry persisted, "that the same person was responsible for both deaths?"

"That's obvious, isn't it?" said Trudi. "And now, perhaps you will excuse me. I must have breakfast, or I shall be late for my lesson."

At the door she paused, and then said, "You will forgive me, Herr Tibbett—but I am surprised that, with a detective of your brilliance working on it, the case is not closed by now." With which calculated insult she walked out of the room.

Henry went slowly and thoughtfully downstairs, and sought out Rossati, who was in his office.

"I'd like to know, Signor Rossati," he said, "just what you were doing between a quarter-past five and a quarter to six yesterday evening?"

"Me?" Rossati looked scared stiff. "It is no secret, Signor Tibbett. I was in here, writing some letters. The door was open, and everybody must have seen me."

"Who do you mean by everybody?"

"Signor Jimmy and the two young ladies. And the Knipfers."

"Where were they?"

"In the bar, having tea," said Rossati. "The three Knipfers went in first—soon after a quarter-past five, I should think. Then, at about half-past, Signor Jimmy came down with the two young ladies. They, too, went into the bar."

"Thank you," said Henry.

He then went in search of Anna, who confirmed that she had served tea to the Knipfers and the English party: and finally, he had a word with Herr Knipfer, who was with his wife on the terrace.

"Of course it is so," said the German, stiffly. "All six of us were in the bar."

"Did anybody leave the room?" Henry asked.

"Certainly not. We were all still there when Captain Spezzi came and insisted that we should be searched."

"And that," thought Henry, "seems to be that."

He went up to his room to fetch his anorak, and noticed on the dressing-table the box of chocolates which Pietro had brought for Maria-Pia. In the excitement of the previous evening, he had forgotten all about them.

He picked up the chocolates, went down to the first-floor, and knocked on Maria-Pia's door.

"See, Henry," she greeted him, proudly, "I am up."

Sure enough, she was out of bed, sitting in an armchair by the window, with her ungainly, plaster-coated leg emerging incongruously from the frills of a lemon-yellow peignoir.

"I am glad you have come to see me," she said. "Hermann has gone out for a walk, and the children are skiing, and now that the snow is falling I feel very sad and lonely."

Henry looked out of the window. Sure enough, the snow was coming down in fine, misty flakes, and the landscape looked grey and uninviting.

"I've brought something to cheer you up," he said. "A present." And he gave her the chocolates.

"Oh, Henry—you shouldn't have——"

"They're not from me, I'm ashamed to say," said Henry. "They're from Pietro. With the good wishes and sympathy of the entire village. He wanted to see you himself yesterday, but he wasn't allowed up."

"Oh, poor Pietro." Maria-Pia looked up, stricken. "Henry, I am a terrible, brutal woman. I have been so busy feeling thankful that Franco is safe. . ." She looked up at him anxiously. "He is safe now, isn't he, Henry? Why hasn't he been released?"

"I think he soon will be," said Henry.

"Thank God," said Maria-Pia, simply. "But it is no

excuse for me. I've hardly stopped to think about poor Mario . . . or about Rosa and Maria and Pietro. And now he sends me a present, and it puts me to shame. It should be the other way round. He is the one who needs sympathy now."

"Yes," said Henry. He pulled up a chair, and sat down beside her. "They seem to be a very tragic family. First Giulio, and now Mario. It seems like the cruellest sort of bad luck. But I've often noticed how misfortune seems to run in some families, for no apparent reason."

"There may be a reason in this case," said Maria-Pia.

"What do you mean ?"

"There's a wild streak in all the Vespis," said Maria-Pia. "Not Rosa, of course—she's like Mother Earth. But the men have always been crazy. Mario's father was killed in the mountains, you know. It's a local legend. Apparently some foolish rich Englishman bet him he wouldn't climb the Alpe Rosa in pitch darkness. There was quite a big sum of money involved—big for him, that is—and nothing would stop him. He got to the top, and left his ice-axe there to prove it : and then he fell. He was still alive when they found him, and all he cared about was that he had won the bet. 'Stop snivelling,' he said to Mario, who was about fifteen then, 'and go and get the money.' When Mario came back with the Englishman's cheque, his father said, 'Tell him I prefer golden sovereigns.' And then he died. Mario has often told me the story. They say in the village that no Vespi ever dies in his bed. I suppose Mario's father did—but hardly in the orthodox way."

"I wonder what happened to that money ?" said Henry.

"Oh, it wouldn't amount to much these days," said Maria-Pia. "I think it was about a hundred pounds. If I know Mario, he'd keep it like a miser for years, and then give it to his sons. I dare say Giulio had most of it."

"Giulio seems to have been a remarkably rich young man, one way and another," said Henry. "Where did it all come from, do you think ?"

"Oh, well . . ." Maria-Pia spread her hands in a wide gesture. "You know how it is in these villages. All the young instructors——" She broke off suddenly. "Here comes Hermann," she said.

Henry looked out of the window, and saw the Baron coming up the path through the whirling snow.

"You'd better go now," said Maria-Pia. "Give Pietro my love and my thanks and my sympathy . . . and give him this, too . . ."

There was a big bowl of red roses on a table at her elbow. She pulled one out, and handed it to Henry. "Hermann bought them for me in Montelunga yesterday," she said. "Heaven knows what they cost. I wish I could send them all to Rosa and Pietro, but I dare not. So just take one. And tell them I will pray for them."

"I'll do that," said Henry, moved. It was easy to see why people loved Maria-Pia. "Good-bye for now. I'll come and see you again soon."

"Oh, please do. And if you see Franco——"

"I'll give him a suitable message," said Henry, gravely. He left the room, and only just in time, for the Baron was already in the hall when he came downstairs. Henry put the rose hastily into his pocket, feeling like a character in a French farce, and went off to fetch his skis.

He skied slowly through the scurrying snow, which was now falling fast, making visibility difficult : and, once down, made straight for the Olympia, feeling certain that Emmy would have been waiting for some time. When he got there, however, he was amazed to see that the clock over the bar alleged that it was no more than a quarter to twelve—in fact, his descent had taken less than an hour. So he left his skis on the rack outside the café and made his way to the Vespi's house. The shop was shut and all the shutters closed, and a group of cold, miserable reporters hung about outside in the driving snow, cursing their luck. Henry's arrival at least gave the poor creatures something to do, and he was immediately mobbed. With difficulty, he pushed his way through the crowd, shaking off the importunate pleas for a statement, and knocked at the door of the shop.

At first, there was dead silence. Henry took a pace back from the door and looked up, just in time to see a small, pale face peeping out from behind the lace curtains of an upstairs window. Shortly after this, there was a scuffle of footsteps and the sound of bolts being drawn, and the door opened a crack to reveal the owner of the face—Maria, Rosa's young daughter.

" What is it ? " she whispered.

" I'm very sorry to have to disturb you," said Henry, " but I'm afraid I must see your mother."

" Come in," said Maria. She opened the door another inch, just enough to let Henry slip inside, and then slammed it again in the tantalised face of the press.

The shop was as dark as a tomb. Henry stood still, accustoming his eyes to the gloom, while Maria shot the heavy bolts back into place. Then he followed her, picking his way between the barrels of *pasta* and lentils, behind the counter and into the parlour. Here, too, the shutters were closed, but the two candles on the mantelpiece gave a guttering light, so that Giulio's photographed face flickered in and out of sight, like a worn film in a badly-equipped cinema. The effect was to give it a disturbing sort of life, and Henry had a sudden feeling that the young man was watching him intently : but the expression on the handsome face was as enigmatic as ever, revealing no secrets.

" I will tell Mama," Maria whispered, and ran upstairs.

With a heavy heart, Henry took from his pocket the knotted handkerchief which contained Mario's meagre possessions, and also the rose—now slightly the worse for wear— which Maria-Pia had given him. A moment later there was a slow, heavy footfall on the stairs, and Rosa Vespi came in. Henry was shocked at the change in her. The round, merry face was white and drawn, and the twinkling black eyes looked, in the dim light, like shadowy caverns of despair.

In a voice that was startlingly harsh after Maria's whispering, Rosa said, "What do you want now? Why can't you leave us in peace?"

"I beg you to forgive me, *signora*," said Henry, "and to accept my deepest sympathy. I have come to bring you this. It is from Baroness von Wurtburg. She asked me to say that she was praying for you."

"The Baroness is very kind," said Rosa, without expression. She took the rose and laid it on the mantelpiece.

"Also," said Henry, "I wished to return these to you." He laid his handkerchief on the table, and unknotted it, revealing the pathetic contents.

Rosa looked briefly at the little pile on the table. "So they have decided not to rob him after all, have they? We must be thankful." Her voice was very bitter.

"There was never any intention of robbing him, *signora*," said Henry, gently. "We only hoped that among Mario's possessions we might find a clue to his murderer."

"What does it matter now?" said Rosa, in a voice without hope. She sat down, heavily. "He's dead, isn't he? What's the difference who killed him?"

Henry did not answer, but brought the two keys over to Rosa, holding them so that she could see them in the uncertain light.

"Signora Vespi," he said, "do you recognise these keys?"

Rosa looked at them dully. "Of course," she said. "That is the key of the shop, and the other is the key of the radio."

"The radio?"

"Try it, if you wish," she said. "Mario was proud of the radio. He liked to carry the key with him."

Henry walked over to the radiogram, fitted the small key into the lock, and turned it anti-clockwise. Nothing happened. Then he turned it clockwise: the key turned easily, but when he tried to lift the lid, it would not move.

"The radio was not locked," he said. "I thought Mario kept it locked."

"It's possible it was not locked," said Rosa, without interest. "Pietro also had a key."

Henry unlocked the lid of the cabinet again, and opened it. The metalwork of the arm and soundhead glinted in the candlelight. He shut the lid again, and put the two keys back with the rest of Mario's possessions. Then he came and sat down in a chair, facing Rosa.

"*Signora*," he said, "I am afraid I must ask you some questions. I know how distressing it must be for you, but I am sure you are as eager as we are to find the culprit."

Listlessly, Rosa said again, "What does it matter now?" But at least she did not refuse point-blank to answer, so Henry, encouraged, went on.

"First of all, do you know if Mario had any enemies?"

"Enemies?" Rosa raised her head slowly, and looked at Henry. "Everybody loved Mario. Everybody—the whole village. You know that, *signore*."

"Yes," said Henry. "I do. But the police think that your husband was killed because he knew the name of Herr Hauser's murderer—and he was coming to tell it to me last night. Now—did he give you any hint of who the guilty person might be?"

Rosa began to weep, quietly. "He was strange, the last days," she said. "But he told me nothing. He was ill with worry—especially after Signor di Santi was arrested. And yesterday he said to me, 'I know what I must do now, Rosa . . .'"

With a slight shock, Henry recognised the phrase that he had read in Trudi Knipfer's diary. "*I know what I must do now . . .*" He said, "But he never mentioned any name?"

"No, no, *signore*, never." Rosa was talking more fluently now, as if it were a relief to put her anguish into words. "But yesterday . . . yesterday after lunch, he talked for a long time to Pietro, in here. I was in the kitchen, and I heard their voices. Then he came out to me, and that was when he said it. 'I know what I must do now, Rosa,' he said. 'I must see Signor Tibbett to-night. Do not wait dinner for me.' Then he kissed me, and he went out, and I never saw him again until . . ." Her voice broke in a sob.

Henry persisted, gently, " So it was something that Pietro said to him that decided him ? Did you ask Pietro what they had talked about ? "

Rosa nodded. " Of course," she said, in a steadier voice. " I came straight in here from the kitchen. Pietro was standing by the radio, looking out of the window. I could see that he was upset. He said that Mario had talked a lot about Herr Hauser, and asked him of things that had happened on the day of the murder : and he said, ' It is because you told Papa of Signor Tibbett's visit here this morning that he has this crazy idea '—I had told Mario at lunch, you see, that you had been to see me. ' If Papa does know anything,' Pietro said, ' it is dangerous for him to go to the police.' And I said, ' Pietro, you must stop him. If he knows bad things, he must forget them and say nothing, or he will not be safe.' And Pietro did try to stop him, *signore* —but it was too late."

" Yes," said Henry, sadly, " it was too late."

" Pietro," Rosa repeated, and there were tears in her voice. " Mad Pietro . . . mad Mario . . . mad Giulio . . . soon I will be all alone . . ."

" Come now, *signora*," said Henry, soothingly. " You have had great tragedies, but Pietro is still——"

" He is mad, *signore*, mad—like the others." Rosa looked up at him. " You heard what he did ? "

" No," said Henry.

" This morning—" said Rosa—" this morning, with his father lying dead . . . I heard him going downstairs early— much earlier than usual. I came after him, and begged him not to go, but he said he must. It was a bet, he said. I pleaded with him, but he said his father would have wished it, and his grandfather, too. I could not stop him, and so he did it."

" Did what ? " Henry asked.

" The Gully, *signore*." Rosa's voice was very low now.

"It was Carlo and the other instructors—they bet Pietro
he would not go down the Gully this morning, before ski
school. Last night, they came here and told him the bet
was cancelled—I heard them. But Pietro would not have
it. 'A bet is a bet,' he said. That is what Mario's father
said, and he died."

"But Pietro did not die," said Henry.

"It will be the same with him as with all the Vespis,"
said Rosa wearily. "They do not die in their beds."

Henry was glad to get out of the tragic oppressiveness of
Rosa's parlour into the snowy brightness of the street. The
snow was falling lightly now, and the mist had dispersed.
He walked through the village to the Olympia, and met
Emmy in the doorway.

"Nice timing," she remarked cheerfully. "I'm ravenous.
Let's have some food."

"You look like a dog with two tails," said Henry. "Did
you find out something interesting?"

"I'll tell you when I've ordered my lunch," said Emmy,
tantalisingly.

They found themselves a corner table, and ordered
tagliatelli verdi, a speciality of the restaurant, washed down
by a bottle of *Soave*. When the waiter had departed for the
kitchen, Henry said, "Come on, now. Tell me."

"Considering I only had about two hours," said Emmy,
not without a certain smugness, "I think I did jolly well."

"But what——?"

"Wait for it," said Emmy. "Let me tell it my own
way."

"All right, but get on with it."

"Well," she said, "I started off by asking at the station
about restaurants, and there is only one decent one. So I
went along there, and by great good luck the waitress
remembered them—partly because they were in late for
lunch, and partly because Roger asked her where the ski
shops were. She thinks they left the restaurant at about
three."

"That would be right," said Henry. "The Colonel said they were in Immenfeld by two."

"There are two ski shops," said Emmy, "so I tried them both. The first one is almost next door to the restaurant, so I guessed he'd have gone there. They remembered him, too. They said he inquired about some ski sticks, but didn't buy anything."

"Did you check on the time with them?"

"Of course," said Emmy. "They thought it was soon after three."

"Good," said Henry. "What did you do then?"

"After that—" Emmy went on, but she was interrupted by the arrival of the steaming dish of green *pasta*. When they had helped themselves liberally to the delicious ribbons of *tagliatelli* and butter, Emmy took up her story again, with her mouth full.

"After that," she said, "I tried all the shops in the main street. It didn't take terribly long, because it's only a small place. There are the usual assortment of food shops and ski shops and general tourist places, like there are here."

She paused to eat some more, and then resumed. "I found that he went into the other ski shop, too—to have his skis waxed. He said he had forgotten to bring his own wax. They were very vague about the time—in the middle of the afternoon, they said."

"Well, say that took him until about half-past three, or a little after. It still leaves nearly an hour before the train back."

Emmy went on. "He may have bought some cigarettes—the woman was very vague, but she thought she remembered an Englishman in a blue anorak. But there was another shop he definitely *did* go into, and he bought something there, and I bet you can't guess what it was."

"All right, I'll buy it," said Henry. "Go on."

"Well, there's a sort of mixed stationers and household shop, with newspapers and cards and souvenirs and a few books—you know, like the one near the church here."

Henry nodded.

" And," Emmy went on, " he went in there, and he spent a lot of time looking at cards and books and things, and in the end he bought a book, and the girl remembered what it was."

" Don't tell me," said Henry.

" Yes," said Emmy, triumphantly, " it was *Cara Teresa*, by Renato Lucano ! "

After lunch, Henry said, " I'm going down to the ski school now. I want to see Pietro."

" Anything you'd like me to do ? " Emmy asked.

" Go skiing," said Henry. " I'll see you back at the hotel for tea."

At the office of the ski school, however, he had a disappointment. The weather conditions had been so bad in the morning that Pietro had decided to abandon the class at half-past eleven. He had returned with his pupils to the Bella Vista for an early lunch, with the idea that if the snow and mist cleared they would set off at two o'clock and tackle a long run. A call to the Bella Vista proved that this had, in fact, happened.

Henry inquired if Roger was there, but was told that he and Gerda had both left early in the morning, taking packed lunches with them.

Frustrated, Henry went down the village street to the Police Station. Here he found Spezzi, considerably elated by the report on the gun, which had just come in.

" It's Hauser's, no doubt about it," he said. " They have traced the purchase from the number. And both bullets were fired from it. No fingerprints, of course. One can't really expect any. Everybody wears gloves in the snow."

" Well, I'm glad that's cleared up," said Henry. And he went on to report on his interview with Rosa Vespi.

Spezzi was immensely interested. " You did better than I did," he confessed, a little ruefully. " I called there early this morning, when poor Mario's body had only just been brought from the mortuary. What with that, and the fact that Rosa was in a state about some escapade of Pietro's, you can imagine that I got nothing but hysterics. I was planning to return this afternoon, but you have done the job for me." He paused. "So it was something that Pietro said that made him certain, was it? Have you seen Pietro?"

"I've tried," said Henry, "but I can't get him until this evening. Shall we talk to him together when he gets back?"

"With pleasure," said Spezzi. He rang the ski school office, and left a message for Pietro to report to the Police Station as soon as he got in.

Henry then went on to relate Emmy's discovery in Immenfeld, which impressed Spezzi considerably. "Very nice work," he commented. "It was an inspiration on your part to think of that. This book is an important piece of evidence."

"Perhaps," Henry said. "Actually, it was something else that my wife found out that interested me more."

Spezzi looked at him sharply. "I am concerned with the book," he said. "This Mr. Staines of yours—always lies, and more lies. Soon we shall find out the truth. And yet for all that, I am sure it is the girl who is guilty. It must be."

"Have you made your time-table yet?" Henry asked, anxious to change the subject.

"It is just completed." Spezzi indicated a pile of type-written sheets on the desk. "Wait. I will add the information you have just given me."

He took out his fountain pen, and wrote quickly on the top copy of the time-table. "Were you able to get accurate times from Signora Vespi?" he asked, as he wrote.

"I'm afraid I didn't even try," said Henry. "But when you remember that Mario always goes up on the lift at a quarter to two, you should be able to guess them."

After a minute or so, Spezzi handed the sheet of paper over to Henry, who read it carefully.

9—9.30 a.m. The skiers leave the Bella Vista. Passendell

	and Miss Whittaker practise on Run One with Pietro. Staines and Col. Buckfast on Run Three.
10.30 (approx)	Staines and Buckfast go to the Alpe Rosa, where they join up with Fraulein Gerda.
12.30 p.m.	Pietro's class returns to the Bella Vista for lunch. Mario stops the lift, and begins to ski down.
12.45 (approx)	Mario arrives home for lunch.
12.55	Staines, Buckfast and Gerda arrive at the Olympia.
1.15—1.40	During this time, Rosa hears Mario and Pietro talking.
1.40	Mario tells Rosa he is going to see Inspector Tibbett, and leaves the house.
1.45	Mario takes the lift up. Rosa talks to Pietro.
1.59	Staines, Buckfast and Gerda leave the Olympia.
2.00	Pietro takes the lift up, followed by the other three.
2.25	They reach the top. Pietro speaks to Mario, overheard by Staines, who tells the others.
2.30	Inspector Tibbett gets on to the lift at the bottom. Buckfast goes back to the hotel for his goggles.
2.40	The skiers set off down Run Three.
2.55	Inspector Tibbett reaches the top of the lift. Mario asks him for an appointment later on.
3.00 (approx)	The three skiers go to the Alpe Rosa.
4.30	Baron von Wurtburg returns from Montelunga by car, and goes to the Olympia. (*N.B.* No times available for the Baron's descent on the lift and departure for Montelunga, but since he lunched

	at the hotel he may be judged to have left soon after 2 o'clock).
4.35 (approx)	Pietro, Passendell and Miss Whittaker take the lift to the Bella Vista.
4.50 (approx)	Staines, Gerda and the Colonel arrive at the Olympia.
5.00	Pietro and his class arrive at the Bella Vista.
5.20	The Baron leaves the Olympia.
5.25	The other three leave the Olympia. The Baron starts up on the lift.
5.30	Gerda boards the lift, followed by the Colonel and Staines. Pietro leaves the Bella Vista to ski to the village.
5.32	Carlo telephones Mario.
5.38	Mario boards the lift. Carlo's son brings him coffee.
5.45	Pietro arrives in Santa Chiara, and talks to Carlo.
5.50	The Baron reaches the top of the lift.
5.55	The other skiers reach the top.
6.03	Mario arrives at the bottom of the lift, shot dead.

After ten minutes or so spent in silent perusal of this document, Henry looked up and grinned at Spezzi. " You and your time-tables," he said.

" What do you mean ? "

" The first one made the murderer crystal clear," said Henry. " But this one makes the second murder absolutely impossible."

" Impossible ? "

" Work it out for yourself," said Henry. " On the face of it, none of the people mentioned on that piece of paper could possibly have killed Mario. And nobody else was anywhere near the scene of the crime. Have you considered that it might have been suicide ? "

"You are joking, my friend," said Spezzi, with a little laugh that could not quite conceal his agitation.

"Yes, I am," said Henry, very seriously. "I wish I wasn't."

"But this talk of the second murder being impossible——"

"Everybody concerned," said Henry, "has a perfect alibi—on the face of it. Since Mario was evidently killed, there must be a flaw in one of those alibis, but I'm blowed if I can see it."

"But the people on the lift——"

"Look at the time-table," said Henry. "Your men found the gun under a pylon more than half-way down. If you'll look at the times on your chart, you'll see that none of the four people going up could possibly have passed Mario until they were well over half-way up. So how could anyone have thrown the gun away *before* they shot the old man?"

Spezzi looked again at the time-table, and then said, "We haven't got definite proof that it was at five-thirty they got on the lift."

"You came and told me of Mario's death at five-past six," said Henry. "By the time we got down to the hall, say a minute later, the Baron and Gerda were already upstairs, and Roger and the Colonel were in the hall. They had all walked up from the lift, and put their skis away. In order to meet Mario before they reached the half-way mark, they'd have had to get on to the lift at 5.40 at the earliest, which means they wouldn't even have arrived at the top by five-past six."

Spezzi brooded gloomily. "What about all the others?" he asked.

"Jimmy and Caro were together at the hotel," said Henry. "So were the three Knipfers—I've checked with Anna: they were all having tea in the bar. Pietro was nearly at the bottom of Run One when Mario got on to the lift. Rossati was writing letters in his office—he saw the people in the bar, and they saw him."

"Mrs. Buckfast isn't accounted for," said Spezzi, suddenly.

"I know," said Henry, "but she was certainly in the hotel. I'll check up on her. But the whole point is that I'm absolutely certain I've solved this case, in spite of the fact that the second murder has me baffled. The first is clear enough."

"The first is clear?" Spezzi was astounded. "What do you mean?"

"I'll tell you," said Henry. "Have you got a copy of your original time-table and the interview reports? Right. Now, if you study it, you'll see that this is what must have happened . . ."

CHAPTER EIGHTEEN

It was nearly two hours later that Spezzi finally got up from his desk, lit a cigarette, and said, " Yes. Yes, of course, it is all clear now. I should have seen it for myself. But what are we to do ? And Mario . . . how was Mario killed ? "

" That's what I've been asking myself all day," said Henry. " As for what we should do—I said to you yesterday that I thought our only hope was to give the murderer plenty of rope. We've done that, and I think we can go still further. I suggest you release di Santi, remove all restrictions—except, of course, that nobody must leave Santa Chiara—and wait for developments."

" Perhaps when we talk to Pietro—? " Spezzi suggested hopefully.

" I very much doubt if we shall learn anything that we don't already know," said Henry.

" If only we could have got positive proof of the first murder . . ." said Spezzi, sombrely.

" If only," said Henry. " But now that Mario is dead, I suppose we never shall—not positive proof. But you do agree with my conclusions ? "

Spezzi nodded. " I have no choice," he said.

" There's another thing I'd like to do, with your permission," Henry added. He outlined his plan briefly, and Spezzi said, " Of course, Enrico. Anything you like."

" Other than that," said Henry, " I don't see what we can do but wait—and take the precautions I've suggested."

" You are right," said Spezzi. " But to find how the second murder was achieved—that is the problem. I wonder if we shall ever solve it ? "

" I wonder," said Henry.

A few minutes later, there was a knock on the door, and a young *carabiniere* came in, escorting a very frightened-looking Pietro. His face relaxed a little when he saw Henry.

"What is this, Enrico?" he asked. "They tell me at the ski school that I am wanted here——"

"I'm sorry we had to bring you here," said Henry, "but we couldn't get hold of you before. It's just that we want to ask you some questions, so that we may find out who killed your father."

Pietro looked relieved, and at Spezzi's invitation accepted a cigarette and sat down.

"Will you put the questions, Capitano, or shall I?" asked Henry.

"You, please," said Spezzi. "But in Italian," he added, with a smile.

The shorthand writer was sent for, and while they waited, Henry studied Pietro's face. His father's death had left its mark on the young man. He seemed older and sterner than before, and his expression had a definitiveness, a strength of purpose, that lent him new distinction.

When all was ready, Henry began, "I saw your mother this morning, Pietro. I gathered from her that it was a conversation that your father had with you at lunch-time yesterday that finally decided him to come and see me. Naturally, we are interested to know what was said."

Pietro frowned. "It is quite true, what my mother told you," he said. "But I have been over and over it in my mind. I cannot imagine what information I gave him."

"Tell us what was said."

"I cannot remember every word," said Pietro, "but he asked me all about our tea-party at the Olympia on the day Hauser was shot. He wanted to know what people had said, and when they came and went. He asked me about Rossati and the Baron, too—when they arrived and what they did."

"He knew that Hauser carried a gun in his briefcase?"

"Yes. We all knew that. Fritz had showed it to us, for fun."

"Did he ask you any other questions?"

" No. It was all about that evening."

" Nothing else ? "

" No, that was all."

" And you have no idea which bit of information was useful to him ? "

" None. He thought for a time after I had finished, and then he said, ' Yes, it is all clear now. I will see Signor Tibbett to-night, and tell him who killed Fritz.' "

" And you tried to dissuade him. Why ? "

Pietro shrugged. " Whoever had killed Hauser could kill again," he said. " I did not want my father mixing himself up in such an affair. ' Leave it to the police,' I said. ' Whether you are right or wrong, everyone will know you have given information, and you may put yourself in danger.' "

" You didn't trust us to protect him ? " said Henry.

Pietro looked at him. " You could not protect him," he said. " He was murdered. And yet," he added, softly, " I am tortured because in the end it was my fault."

" Your fault ? "

" Yes," said Pietro, and his face was very grave. " I was foolish. Mama begged me to stop Father from going to see you, and that is what I tried to do when I got to the top of the lift. But I was overheard—and so he was killed. If I could avenge myself on the murderer—" He stopped.

" How do you know you were overheard ? "

" I had not seen that Signor Roger was just behind me. When I turned away from my father, he was there. He must have heard, and he speaks Italian very well. Mind you," added Pietro hastily, " I am not accusing him. He will undoubtedly have repeated what he heard to all the others."

Henry pondered this for a moment, and then said, " There is another conversation I am interested in. The one you and your father had with Hauser on the day of the first murder."

Pietro looked startled. " That ? That was nothing."

" I should like to know what was said," Henry persisted.

Pietro thought for a moment, and then said, " Fritz Hauser was very fond of my brother Giulio. He had come to give us his sympathy on Giulio's death. We talked of my brother."

" I see," said Henry. " By the way, I understand that you were the first to find Giulio. Can you tell us about it ? "

Pietro looked very surprised, but he made a little gesture, and said, " What is there to tell ? I followed his ski tracks —it was just light enough to see them. They led me to the edge of the ravine, and then I saw him."

" What had caused him to fall, do you think ? "

" Nobody will ever know for certain," Pietro answered, " but I have a good idea. It is a very treacherous slope, that one, with hidden crevasses which are not visible as one comes down. When the run is opened, the *piste* is clearly marked, but when Giulio went there was no *piste* to follow. He went too near the edge of a ravine. When he saw his danger, he must have tried to turn—but there was a tree-stump with spreading roots just hidden by the snow. He must have hit the stump, which knocked one ski off, and before he could regain his balance . . . It is easily done."

" So you saw him. Did you climb down to him ? "

Pietro gave a tiny, rueful smile. " You have been talking to the men in the search party, I can see," he said. " Yes, I did climb down. I could not leave him there without . . ." He broke off, and then continued. " He was already dead, poor Giulio. So I went on to Immenfeld and called the search party. When they arrived with their lights, they could see I had been down the ravine before them, but they promised they would tell no one. On account of my mother, you see. It was a rash thing to do, and it would have distressed her greatly—she worries over such things. It was always the same—for my father, my brother and me. We liked to be adventurous, but my mother must never know."

" Pietro," said Henry, suddenly. " Was Giulio smuggling contraband into Austria for Fritz Hauser when he died ? "

A look of real fear came into Pietro's eyes. " No, no," he said. " No, he would never have done that."

" He always had plenty of money, I understand."

" He was a popular instructor, Enrico."

" More popular than any of the others—than you ? "

" Oh, yes. He was a marvel. And so handsome. All those Americans——"

" Look here," said Henry, " I know very well there weren't any Americans. Giulio got his money from somewhere, and you must have known about it."

" No, no, Enrico. You are quite wrong."

" We'll see," said Henry, grimly. " All right, you can go now."

When Henry got back to the hotel, he found a grave-faced Rossati waiting for him in the hall.

" Alas, Signor Tibbett, I fear I have bad news . . ."

Henry's heart sank. " What ? " he said.

" Poor Signora Tibbett . . . it is so sad . . . so sad . . ."

" Emmy ! " Henry went cold. " What's the matter with her ? "

" An accident, I fear, *signore*—they said it was an accident——"

Without waiting to hear any more, Henry took the stairs two at a time and ran down the corridor as if a thousand fiends were after him. So great was his relief when he saw Emmy lying on the bed, calmly reading a book, that he laughed aloud.

" So you think it's funny, do you ? " she said, in a pained voice. " I can assure you it's damn painful."

" I'm sorry, darling. I was laughing at myself, because I was in such a blue funk about you. I thought it might have been . . . something worse."

" Didn't Rossati tell you what happened ? "

" I didn't give him a chance." Henry went over to the bed, and kissed his wife with some warmth. Then he said, " Now tell me about it."

"Oh, it was so silly," she said. "We were doing Run Three, and it's not easy with the new snow. Anyway, I took a corner too fast, and came a cropper and twisted my blasted ankle." She raised her right leg, displaying an ankle of more-than-usual diameter, swathed in bandages. "And to make matters worse," she went on, "one of my skis came off and did the run in record time on its own, with about ten Frenchmen in hot pursuit. And I sat down with a resounding thump on the sharp edge of the other ski and both my sticks. My bottom is just like those platforms on the ski-lift pylons —completely corrugated—and it's even sorer than my ankle."

"Poor old love," said Henry, sympathetically. "How did you get back to the hotel?"

"The blood wagon," said Emmy, not without a certain pride.

"The what?"

"That's what they call the sledge that brings you down when you're hurt," she explained. "I must say it was marvellously well-organised. I was wrapped up in blankets and strapped down—I felt just like an Egyptian mummy. And then they whisked me down the mountain head-first at a fantastic speed. It was terribly exciting."

"It sounds horrible," said Henry.

"It's not, honestly," said Emmy. "They're so competent, these people, you don't feel a bit frightened. We went straight to the doctor, who's an angel, and he fixed me up and drove me back to the ski-lift in his car. Beppi met me at the top, and carried me up here as though I was a small overnight bag. He's fantastically strong, that man."

"What did the doctor say?" asked Henry. "Is it bad?"

"Oh, it's nothing at all. Just a sprain. But I can't ski again this year, which is maddening."

"What damn bad luck, darling. Will you have to stay in bed?"

"Good Lord, no," said Emmy, cheerfully. "I'm coming

down to dinner. I can hop beautifully with my ski-sticks."

The news of Emmy's misfortune spread quickly through the hotel. Soon the room was crowded with well-wishers. Jimmy brought a bottle of brandy and a pack of cards to cheer the invalid, and it soon transpired that both he and Caro were keen on bridge. Henry regretfully excused himself from making up the four, saying that he still had work to do, but he remembered Mrs. Buckfast's remark during her sensational interview with Spezzi, and suggested that they should enlist her. Leaving the four of them contentedly engrossed in the playing of a highly problematical small slam which Jimmy had recklessly called (" Only ten points, partner, but I thought we'd have a bash," he remarked gaily to an unamused Mrs. Buckfast as he laid down his hand), Henry went in search of Roger.

He found the latter in his room, changing.

" Sit down, old man," said Roger hospitably. " Sorry to hear about Emmy. How is she ? "

" She's fine, thank you," said Henry. And then he said, " I'm afraid this isn't a social call, Roger. You've got some explaining to do, and you'd better do it fast."

" Oh." Roger stopped abruptly in the middle of tying his tie, and turned to face Henry. " It's like that, is it ? Well, what do you want explained ? "

" This, among other things," said Henry. He picked up the paper-covered copy of *Cara Teresa*, which was lying on the bedside table.

" I've told you about that."

" It won't do, I'm afraid. We know that you bought this in Immenfeld. Unfortunately for you, the girl in the shop remembered you."

There was a pause. Then Roger said, " I see. Been checking up pretty thoroughly, haven't you ? "

" This is a case of murder," said Henry. " Everything has to be checked." After a short silence, he went on, " And there's another thing. I think I ought to warn you that Caro is liable to be arrested any moment on a charge of forging, without your knowledge or consent, a document designed to incriminate you. You put up a very good bluff on her behalf yesterday, but I'm afraid Spezzi's going to call it. I ought not to tell you this, I suppose, but I happen to know he's planning to arrest her to-morrow morning. So if there's anything you can tell us which might help her——"

Roger had gone very white. He looked at Henry for a moment, and then he said, " All right. You win. I'll tell you the truth."

" That's the third time you've said that," said Henry, pleasantly. " You can't expect me to be over-impressed."

" But this really is the truth," said Roger, with a trace of desperation. " You can't possibly accuse Caro of writing that note without my knowledge or consent, because I asked her to do it."

" I appreciate your chivalrous instincts," said Henry, " but surely you don't expect Spezzi to believe a story like that ? "

" It's true, I tell you," said Roger. " We were playing a silly sort of game one evening, trying to imitate each other's handwriting. I tore a page out of my diary for her to write on, and when she asked what she should put, for some crazy reason I suggested those words. Subconscious, I suppose. The *Nancy Maud* affair had been on my mind. And then Hauser got hold of the paper."

Henry shook his head. " That," he said, " holds about as much water as a broken sieve. Why those words ? How did Hauser get hold of it ? Why did you tell us he tried to blackmail you as soon as you arrived ? You'd better think again. You'll never get Caro out of trouble with a cock and bull story like that."

Roger glared at him, but said nothing. Henry went on, " Perhaps it would be easier if I told you what really happened. Then you can correct me if I'm wrong."

There was another silence. Roger's face had darkened, and he looked dangerous. Henry continued, pleasantly, " I told you once before, Roger, that your trouble was over-ingenuity. You can't be content with a simple plan, or even with a simple lie. You've got a good, quick brain which might be extremely useful if you'd direct it towards something worthwhile. As it is, you do nothing but think up tortuous schemes which generally fall down under the sheer weight of their own intricacy."

"I don't know what you mean," said Roger, thickly.

"I'll explain," said Henry. "The note which Hauser had was genuine, of course. He was much too careful an operator to use a forgery. Whatever the court in Rome may have decided, I could tell the moment I met you that you're exactly the type of man who would revel in a bit of relatively harmless smuggling, especially if it involved sailing a small boat. At the same time, I think you were telling the truth when you said that Donati stole the *Nancy Maud*."

Roger opened his mouth to say something, thought better of it, and closed it again.

"You had intended, of course, to make the trip yourself, and you engaged Donati and the other boy as crew, because the loading and unloading were more than you could cope with single-handed. You wrote a note to Donati on a page torn out of your diary—by the way, you get the same diary every year, don't you ?"

Reluctantly, Roger said, "My bookie sends me one every Christmas."

"But," Henry went on, "Donati double-crossed you. Not only did he sail ahead of time, hoping to sell the cargo and keep the profits himself, but he also hung on to your note to safeguard himself against your taking any action."

"Then why didn't he produce it in court ?" Roger burst out. Henry guessed that this was a point which had been bothering Roger considerably.

"Because," he said, with a smile, "he hadn't got it by then. Hauser took it from him before the trial. Hauser was his real boss, and you were being deliberately lured into the net. You see, Hauser liked to have his subordinates absolutely under his thumb. And he realised that although you'd jump at the chance of running watches and cigarettes, you might very likely draw the line at dope."

" Dope ? " said Roger. He looked really shaken now.

" Of course," said Henry. " That was his real business. Here, then, we have you—in the clear as far as the *Nancy Maud* case is concerned, but keen as mustard to have another go. So Hauser got you out here last year, with Rossati's help.

Roger nodded, hopelessly. " Rossati sent me a prospectus of the hotel," he said, " with a letter saying that in order to encourage English skiers, they were prepared to offer special rates. The prices he quoted were so ridiculously low, that as I was hard up and keen on skiing . . ." He paused. " But why did Hauser wait so long after the *Nancy Maud* case before he contacted me ? "

" Two reasons," said Henry. " One was to let the publicity of the case die down, and the other was that he thought he had a satisfactory operator here. Then, last year, he began to have his doubts. So he got on to you. The next bit you told us, pretty truthfully. Everything was fixed up. You were delighted. You were instructed to come out again this year, bringing a thoroughly respectable English party as cover. It must have been a nasty blow to you when Hauser produced that note."

Henry looked hopefully at Roger for confirmation, but the latter maintained a moody silence. So Henry went on, " Now most people in your position would have been content to steal the note, and leave it at that. But your superingenious brain thought up a better scheme. You decided to turn the tables on Hauser. So you persuaded Caro to forge a copy of the note on a page of your current diary, and you switched it for the original. In fact, you did what you accused Hauser of doing—but the other way round. Then you challenged him to a showdown. Nothing would have pleased you more than to see that note sent to the police. It was a palpable forgery, and Hauser would have been in the cart. Of course, you did take the risk of Jimmy's writing being identified, but I agree it was a remote possibility. It was extremely bad luck that you forgot she had written on the back of your packing list. Am I boring you?"

"Go on," said Roger.

"Well," said Henry, "you came unstuck because you underestimated Hauser. He was far too clever for you. He spotted the forgery, and a chance remark of Caro's in the bar about pencil and paper games enabled him to put two and two together. It was a pretty safe bet that Caro had done it for you, anyway. So Hauser now had you even more firmly where he wanted you. At that famous tea-party that you told us about, I imagine he threatened to take both the forged note and a sample of Caro's handwriting to the police. After all, he could get hold of the hotel register easily enough. When Gerda saw you coming out of Hauser's room, I imagine you must have been making a last, frantic search to find the forged note and destroy it. You didn't find the note ... but the gun was lying on the table."

"I didn't take it!" Roger shouted. "I didn't take the gun!"

"Perhaps not—not then. But it could very well have given you the idea. And the next day, when you saw Hauser's briefcase at the Olympia——"

"It's not true!" cried Roger, frantically. "All right, I'll admit everything else—but I didn't take the gun! I didn't kill him!"

"But you will agree, won't you," said Henry, softly, "that far from having no motive to do so, you had the strongest possible one. The only one, I think, that could drive a man like you to violence. Caro's safety."

"Oh, God." Roger sat down heavily on the bed. "I tell you I didn't." After a pause, he added, "What do you want me to do now?"

"I want a signed statement from you," said Henry, briskly, "admitting ... all that you are prepared to admit. Anything else, we can add later."

"But . . . Caro ?" Roger's distress was very obvious. "What will happen to Caro ?"

"You told me," said Henry, carefully, "that you were playing a game when you asked her to write the note, and that she didn't know what it was for. If you put that in your statement, it should clear her of any blame. Of course, such a statement will have obvious disadvantages from your point of view, but——"

"I'll write it now." Roger stood up, suddenly quiet and determined. "And this time, it really will be the truth."

"I do hope so," said Henry, none too optimistically.

He left Roger writing frantically, and went down to the bar.

In the hall, he was waylaid by Gerda. She was dressed in slim black trousers and a white cotton shirt, which made her look as monochrome as a photograph.

"Herr Tibbett," she said, "I want to ask for your help."

"What can I do for you ?"

"I am in a very difficult position," said Gerda, quietly. "I know very well that Capitano Spezzi thinks I am a murderess. That is not true. But, Herr Tibbett, I must leave the Bella Vista. The Baron has discharged me, as you know, with one week's notice. It is not possible for me to stay on in the hotel with no job. I cannot pay. I must return to Germany and find other employment. But the Capitano will not let me go."

"You have asked him ?"

"I telephoned him to-day. He positively refuses."

"I see." Henry looked thoughtful. "Yes, it is difficult for you. I'll tell you what I'll do. I'll have a word with the Baron. It seems to me that he must in all justice agree to pay your hotel bill while you are forced to stay here."

Gerda gave an impatient little sigh. "That is not the point, Herr Tibbett. I must find another job. I have to get away from here."

"I'm very sorry," said Henry, "but I don't see what else

I can do for you. I agree with Capitano Spezzi that until the case is closed we cannot allow anybody to leave, especially if they wish to go to another country."

Gerda looked at him steadily. " So you will not help me," she said. " Very well. I shall have to make the best arrangements I can."

Abruptly, she turned on her heel, and walked quickly across the hall and up the stairs.

The only occupants of the bar were the Knipfers, who were drinking beer in one corner, and Colonel Buckfast, who sat at the bar sipping a whisky and soda. He welcomed Henry warmly.

" Beginning to feel like an exile in here," he confided. " Wife playing cards with your wife, I believe . . . sorry about the accident . . . not serious, I hope ? "

Henry assured him that Emmy was on the road to recovery, and the Colonel mumbled his satisfaction at the news, and then cleared his throat loudly. Finally he said, " No hard feelings about . . . British Consul and so forth . . . have to protect oneself, y'know. . . have a drink."

" Thanks," said Henry. " I'll have a Martini, please—straight, no gin."

" Outlandish, these Eyetie drinks," remarked the Colonel. " Martini, Anna ! Can't abide 'em myself. And as for the whisky . . . genuine Scotch made in Naples, if you ask me."

There was a lull in the conversation while Anna brought Henry's drink, and then the Colonel went on, " Heard about young Pietro ? "

" What about him ? "

" The Gully. First thing this morning. Amazing effort. Saw the tracks when I did my first run—before the snow started. Wouldn't have believed it otherwise. Take off my hat to him. Amazing effort. Could have used him in The Team."

Having bestowed on Pietro the highest praise he knew, the Colonel returned to his whisky.

" He did it for a bet, I understand," said Henry.

"Yes. Carlo was telling me. He and the other lads all turned out to see it. Talk of the village."

"Have you ever done the Gully yourself?" Henry asked.

"Not for years," said the Colonel. "Frankly, it's too fast a run for my taste. Anno domini, I suppose. Speed's all very fine, but can become an obsession. Want to watch it."

"I've got a long way to go before I need worry about that," said Henry smiling.

"Young Staines now," the Colonel went on. "Mad on speed. Insists on making every run a race. Claims he can do Run One in seven minutes. Don't believe it. Times himself with a stopwatch, you know," he added, lowering his voice: one would have thought that he was accusing Roger of some nameless perversion.

"What's your best time?" Henry asked.

"For Run One? All depends on conditions. Ten or eleven minutes, I suppose, going really fast. Much slower in bad visibility, of course—over twenty minutes, probably."

"It takes me an hour in ideal conditions," said Henry, ruefully.

"No need to be depressed," said the Colonel, kindly. "First season, after all. Have to start slowly. You'll improve." He looked at Henry critically. "Solid legs," he added, cryptically.

"Thank you," said Henry, rightly interpreting this as a compliment.

A little while later, Roger and Caro came in, and intimated their desire to talk to Henry. The three of them sat down at a table, and Roger handed over several pages of closely-packed handwriting.

"There you are," he said. "All signed and sealed. I've shown it to Caro."

"Thank you," said Henry. He glanced briefly at the sheets of writing, and then pocketed them. "Well," he said to Caro, "why couldn't you have told me all this sooner, you silly girl? You've nothing more to worry about now."

"No, I suppose I haven't. But Roger has."

"The great thing to remember," said Henry, rather pontifically, "is always to tell the truth, especially in a murder case. I hope that neither of you will be so stupid again."

"But Henry," said Caro, "what will Roger——?"

Henry held up his hand. "No more of that to-night," he said. "The office is closed, and official business over. I suggest we all have a drink."

CHAPTER NINETEEN

THE NEXT TWO days—Friday and Saturday—seemed to last for ever. Henry spent some time with Spezzi, discussing their plan of campaign. Outwardly, all was serene, and the Italian press made a few scathing comments on the lack of progress made by the police.

On the Friday, Franco di Santi was released from prison. He did not return to the Bella Vista, but, as he was forbidden to leave Santa Chiara, took a room at a small *pension* in the village. He kept very much to himself, and skied alone.

Henry rejoined the class on Friday afternoon, and found that they had all got considerably ahead of him—all now accomplishing an occasional good stem cristiania turn. He remarked on this fact to Caro, as the two of them stood alone together at the top of a slope, waiting for their turn to practise. Caro did not answer him directly, but said instead, " Henry, I'm worried about that statement of Roger's."

" I know you are," said Henry.

" You see," she said, " it isn't strictly true. I——"

" I know that, too," said Henry, and set off down the hill at speed before she could reply.

On Friday evening, Henry fulfilled his promise to Spezzi, and questioned Mrs. Buckfast about where she had been at the time of Mario's murder. She replied coldly that she had been on the terrace, as Henry knew very well, until half-past four, when it got cold. She had then gone up to her room and written postcards.

Henry had another talk with Rossati, who maintained that he had had the hall under constant observation from five-fifteen onwards. " Nobody used the front door," he said. " I would have seen them. And Signora Buckfast did not come downstairs until much later on."

" I presume you could also see the door to the ski store,"

257

said Henry. " Is there any other way out of the hotel ? "

" Only through the kitchen," said Rossati, " and Beppi and the cook were in there."

The weather improved steadily, and became idyllic. On Saturday, the Gully was declared open—but only the most intrepid skiers took advantage of this fact. Henry saw a few of the instructors coming down, and marvelled at the incredible speed with which they covered the distance, their ski-tracks streaming out behind them like the vapour-trails of aircraft. On Saturday afternoon, Spezzi lifted his embargo on the Immenfeld run. The ski school, however, issued a warning that the run should not be attempted, as they had had no time to mark the *piste*, and the last section was still dangerous. Another event that day—notable in a small way —was Henry's first successful stem cristiania turn.

In spite of this triumph, however, he found sleep difficult that night. He was satisfied with the response that his tactics were arousing, but it worried him deeply to be so near the brink of a complete solution, and yet to be in the dark. Not as to the identity of the murderer—he was sure that he knew that now—but as to the method. Round and round in his mind went the kaleidoscope of facts and impressions which he felt sure held the key to the mystery . . . snatches of conversation : Spezzi's time-tables : Spezzi himself, with his patronising smile : Rossati's servile unctuousness and Pietro's thin-drawn features : Roger's plausible candour and Caro's tears : the Colonel's bluff heartiness and his wife's impassive bad temper : Maria-Pia, touching in her simple, amoral sincerity : the Baron, with his harsh, wounded sense of justice : Jimmy, apparently so worried and so innocent : the Knipfers—the mother's face blurred in an untidy flurry of tears, the father grim and unbending : Trudi, with her secret diary and her secret thoughts, keeping her own counsel : Rosa Vespi in her grief : and the unknown, Giulio . . .

At half-past two, Henry got up and had a long drink of water. Then he said to himself, " Go to sleep. You've done all you can. To-morrow . . . we'll see what happens to-morrow . . ."

He got back into bed, and inadvertently kicked Emmy, who murmured complainingly in her sleep. Poor Emmy . . . bad luck hurting herself like that . . . dear Emmy. . . . He drifted off into an uneasy sleep.

Henry woke with a start to find Emmy sitting up, reading, and sunshine streaming in through the window.

"You've surfaced at last, have you?" said Emmy. "You were sleeping so soundly I hadn't the heart to wake you."

"What's the time?" said Henry.

"Nearly ten o'clock."

"Good God!" Henry sat up. "Why did you let me sleep so late?"

"Does it matter?" said Emmy, lazily. "It's Sunday."

"It certainly does matter. I've got things to do." Henry jumped out of bed, kicking away the downy coverlet, and Emmy said, "Here, have a care. Remember my wounds."

Henry suddenly stood stock-still, an unimpressive, sandy-haired figure in blue-and-white striped pyjamas. Then he clapped a hand to his head.

"Got it!" he shouted.

"Got what?" asked Emmy, disconcerted.

"You told me! You—you adorable, clever angel! You told me, and I never saw it . . . I never even noticed. Wait a minute. Let me think." He began pacing the room. "Yes. Yes, it's possible. It's just possible." He stopped abruptly. "Tell me something."

He asked Emmy a question, and very surprised, she answered, "Yes, I suppose so. That morning. But what has that got to do with it?"

"I've got to get dressed!" Henry shouted. He flew round the room like a whirlwind, assembling pants, ski trousers, shirt, sweater and socks with the speed of a croupier raking in counters. His ski boots seemed to take an hour to put on, but at last he was ready.

"Henry," said Emmy, helplessly, "I don't understand. You must tell me——"

"Later," he said. "Can't stop now."

He ran downstairs, and out to the ski-lift. There, he commandeered the telephone, and rang Carlo. He asked him two questions—and received the answers he expected. Then he hurried back to the hotel, and nearly knocked Mrs. Buckfast flat on her face in the hall.

"In a hurry, Mr. Tibbett?" she asked, coldly.

"Yes," said Henry. "Where is everybody?"

"Out skiing, I presume," said Mrs. Buckfast with a sniff. "Sunday is the same as any other day up here. Except that there's no ski school, of course."

She passed majestically on her way to the terrace, and at that moment Jimmy came in, with snow on his trousers and a healthy flush on his cheeks.

"Hello, lazybones," he said. "Why aren't you out there? I left before nine, and had a splendid time doing Run One, and now I reckon I've earned a rum grog."

"Where's everyone else?" Henry demanded.

"Caro's not up yet, and I haven't seen the Knipfers, but everyone else has gone off unhappily to Immenfeld."

"What do you mean by that?"

"It was really rather funny," said Jimmy. "Roger and Gerda and the Colonel all said at breakfast that they were taking a morning off. But when I came up on the lift just now, I saw them. They'd all skulked in their rooms, I suppose, until they thought that everyone else was well away, and then crept out, obviously hoping to do some lone skiing—and there they all were, all starting off for Immenfeld at the same time. And Pietro had arrived up, too, and was going on the same run. The Colonel did a sort of double-take, as though he'd seen the others for the first time, and said, ' Well, well. Changed your minds, did you? So we're all going to Immenfeld. We'd better join up.' "

"And did they?" asked Henry, sharply.

"Pietro told them the *piste* was dangerous after the new

snow," said Jimmy, " and wasn't supposed to be open. He said he was going officially to try out the run, and they shouldn't come : but they were all adamant, so eventually they went off together. It was a hoot."

" It's anything but a hoot," said Henry. " It's deadly serious."

" Good heavens, how very sensational," said Jimmy. " What do you mean ? "

" I mean murder," said Henry, grimly. " How long ago did they leave ? "

" Oh, just this minute."

" Well, someone will have to go after them, and pretty damn quick," said Henry. " Oh my God—there's nobody left in the hotel who can ski ! "

" Beppi," said Jimmy. " Beppi skis."

Henry barged unceremoniously into Rossati's office, to be met with the bland and unhelpful information that it was Beppi's Sunday off, and he had gone to see his family in Montelunga. Jimmy, who was still inclined to take the matter light-heartedly, began making feather-brained suggestions, but Henry checked him with such vehemence that he stood tongue-tied and ashamed. Desperately, Henry said to Rossati," There *must* be someone who can ski. I tell you, there's a murderer in that party, and the others are in terrible danger. I very much doubt if they will reach Immenfeld alive."

A tall, thin shadow fell across the desk, and Henry looked up to see the Baron standing in the doorway.

" I came to request my bill," he said, " but I could not help overhearing. You need a skier ? "

" Desperately," said Henry.

Without emotion, the Baron said, " I will go."

" But you haven't any skis—and this is a dangerous run which you don't know——"

The Baron looked at Henry coldly. " Naturally, I have my skis," he said. " So far I have not used them. And you may be interested to know that I was champion of Austria twelve years ago. I know the Immenfeld run well. Tell me what I must do."

As the Baron put on his skis, Henry explained the situation as concisely as he could. "There's no time to explain fully," he ended, rather helplessly. "You'll just have to take my word for it."

The Baron did not raise a single query. "I see," he said, in his clipped, unpleasant voice. "And Spezzi is at Immenfeld. I suggest you join him there. Take the chair-lift up, and climb as far as you can, if I have not already reached the village." He turned to Jimmy. "There is no time to lose," he said, "will you be so kind as to say good-bye to my wife for me?"

"Of course," said Jimmy. It was almost a whisper.

"They have about ten minutes' start," said the Baron. "A party cannot travel as fast as a lone skier, and I shall accomplish the climbs in better time than they do. I shall certainly overtake them. I hope it will be in time."

He gave Henry a stiff little bow. "I shall see you in Immenfeld, Inspector," he said. And with that he was gone.

Afterwards, when the story of the epic run to Immenfeld was told and re-told, it never occurred to anybody to give Henry credit for the considerable courage and resource which were required for a skier of his standard to accomplish Run One to Santa Chiara in fourteen minutes. And yet, in its way, it was a remarkable feat. Henry knew very well that the ten minutes he could save by skiing down might be crucial: there was no other way. He telephoned to the Police Station at Santa Chiara, instructed them to have their fastest car and their best driver waiting at the bottom of the ski-run, and also gave a message to be delivered post-haste to Capitano Spezzi, if the latter could be located in Immenfeld by telephone. Then he put his skis on.

Henry could never remember, afterwards, any clear details of that hectic run. A blurred recollection remained of terrifying, uncontrolled speed; of hurtling frantically down precipitous slopes ; of the startled faces of other skiers as this seeming lunatic shot past them with ski-sticks flailing inexpertly. He fell frequently : scrambled up and was off again without taking time to catch his breath. Muttering to himself the rules he had been taught—" Lean out . . . weight on the bottom foot . . . knees bent "—he cut a corner by attacking a long, icy side-slip as steep as a wall : accomplished half of it, fell, and slithered the rest agonisingly on his seat. After what seemed an eternity, he saw the last, easy run-out opening up ahead of him : he took it like the wind, and fell, clumsily, for the last time at the edge of the road, right beside the waiting police car. When he got to his feet, he found that he was shaking like a leaf from head to toe, and his knees felt as though they had turned to water. It was all he could do to get his skis off. The young police driver clipped the skis and sticks on to the roof-rack of the car beside his own, and they were off.

On the way, Henry got a rough picture of the layout of the Immenfeld run from the driver. From the Bella Vista, the run started with a wide, steep, bumpy snowfield—very fast, but not unduly difficult for a good skier. This ended at the bottom of a small, high-set valley, whence it was necessary to climb to the top of the next ridge. A very difficult side-slip followed, and then a comparatively easy, open slope which soon led down into the trees. Here there were some treacherous wood-paths—narrow and steep, with hairpin bends. After that, another climb to the top of the ridge that marked the Austrian border, and the last section of the run began. At first, the going was steep and open, but it was at the point where the trees began again that the real danger-spots of the run lay. Several deep, rocky chasms split the mountain-side, and it was essential to follow the marked *piste* to avoid them, as they were invisible until one was upon them. It was one of these ravines which had claimed Giulio, among other victims. The slope was so steep that it was easy to lose control, and for that reason the run was forbidden to skiers in all but the most favourable conditions.

This dangerous section lasted for about two kilometres. After that, the trees grew more densely, and the paths, though precipitous and tricky to negotiate, were clearly defined and easy to follow. There was an alternative, more direct and steeper footpath by which one could walk up through the woods. Finally, the run emerged on to the spacious, simple nursery slopes of Immenfeld, which were served by a chair-lift which ran up from the village as far as the tree line.

As the driver explained all this to Henry, the car careered dangerously over the snowy roads, the chains on its back tyres clattering and jangling as they bit into the slippery surface. The frontier post had been warned, and the long red-and-white striped poles swung up silently to let the car through. The final stretch was down a narrow, unfenced mountain-track, with dizzy U-bends winding lower and lower towards the village of Immenfeld. Henry closed his eyes as the car skidded suicidally round a hairpin bend—and opened them to see the driver smiling happily.

" Lovely road, isn't it ? " said the young *carabinierie*, and meant it.

" It's rather narrow," said Henry, faintly.

" They're going to widen it soon, I'm told."

" I'm delighted to hear it."

" For the bus, you understand, It's fine as it is for private cars and lorries, but the bus has to take the corners carefully."

Henry digested this piece of information in silence. He did not refer to the width of the road again.

It was exactly thirty-five minutes after leaving the Bella Vista that the car pulled up in a spray of snow outside the Police Station at Immenfeld. An Austrian policeman was waiting at the door.

" We contacted Capitano Spezzi a few minutes ago," he said. " He has gone to the ski-lift."

Another two minutes, and Henry, Spezzi and the driver were at the head of the ski-lift queue—much to the irritation of the sportsmen of Immenfeld. Never had a chair-lift seemed to move so slowly, but in fact it was only ten minutes later that they reached the top, slung their skis on their shoulders, and started the long climb up through the woods.

The driver had described the footpath as steep. Henry reflected bitterly that "vertical" would have been an apter word. Here and there, rudimentary steps had been hacked out to make progress easier, but these were icy and treacherous, even for a man in ski boots. Henry prided himself on keeping in good physical condition—he played squash regularly all the year round, swam, and kept his hand in at cricket : but beside these mountain-bred Italians he felt like an obese octogenarian. Gasping for breath, he struggled despairingly to keep up with them, his skis growing heavier by the moment and cutting cruelly into his shoulders. The whole world narrowed itself down into that twisting, back-breaking path, into the next step, and then the next. On and on, up and up, Henry plodded and scrambled, every muscle crying out for relief, his breath coming in noisy gulps, his throat dry and his legs leaden. It was at the moment when he felt he could go no further without a rest that the trees suddenly began to thin out, and Spezzi, who was leading, stopped and called out, " There they are ! "

Henry panted up to join the other two, and they stood for a moment, hidden in the shadow of the trees, looking upwards. Through the sparse, dark columns of the firs, the gleaming expanse of snow soared up dazzlingly to the ridge, high above. And on the slope were four tiny figures. It was too far away to see which was which : they looked like black ants on the mountain-side, and it flashed across Henry's mind that Pietro must have decided not to wear his usual red anorak. The four skiers were coming down at speed, their skis cutting crisp, weaving tracks in the virgin snow.

" Put your skis on," said Spezzi, sharply. " No use trying to climb without them in soft snow. You have skins ? " he added, to Henry.

" No."

"We'll have to go ahead then. Keep up as best you can."

Feverishly, Henry fumbled to get his skis on. Before he had secured the first one, Spezzi and the *carabinieri* had started off up the slope, climbing with amazing rapidity as the bristles of coarse fur on the underside of their skis gripped the snow. Henry snapped down the clip that tightened the binding of his second ski, and went after them.

High above, the four skiers swooped downwards like birds in flight, turning gracefully one after the other, and sending up gossamer snow-sprays in their wake. Then Henry saw that the leading skier was gesticulating to the others with a flourish of ski-sticks—it looked like a warning of suddenly-perceived danger. Abruptly, all four turned sharply to the left, and gathered speed. At the same instant, a fifth figure appeared on the ridge. It stood poised for a moment, and then took off, gracefully as a diver, traversing the mountain in a series of swift turns. Little by little, the pursuer gained ground on the other four. All were very much closer now, and faintly Henry heard a shout, repeated over and over again.

"*Achtung*! Stop! Stop!"

Suddenly, completely without warning, the leading skier swung into a tight right-handed turn.

"*Achtung*!"

The other three heard at last, turned at high speed, and came to a halt in three simultaneous fountains of flying snow. But the leading skier only gathered speed. Now it was a chase between the first and the last—the hunter and the hunted: and at that moment Spezzi and the *carabinieri* came out of the shelter of the trees and into the open. The leading skier saw them, and turned like lightning. His pursuer turned, too. Henry, struggling to make progress up the slope, heard a voice, a thin scream on the wind.

"I can do it!"

Henry stopped climbing and stood stock-still, just in the shadow of the trees, and watched, with a terrible fascination. Little by little, foot by foot, the pursuer seemed to be gaining ground on his quarry. Then the slim, black figure of the leading skier accelerated, as though propelled by some superhuman force of desperation, and the distance between the two widened again. One after the other they streaked their zig-zag course down the white mountain— tracing out a grim pattern of death and despair with the precision and beauty of ballet dancers, playing the last act of an evil drama against the incongruous backdrop of diamond-bright snow and dazzling sunshine. Only the mountain peaks, implacable and relentless as avenging Furies, matched the high and terrible spirit of a race in which the stakes were life itself.

Slowly, inexorably, the hunter gained on his quarry again. When the two were almost abreast, the leading figure suddenly, without warning, did a spectacular jump-turn, changing direction completely and heading for the shelter of the dense forest far away from the *piste* that led to Immenfeld. His pursuer, caught by surpise, attempted to follow, was thrown off balance, and fell. For a moment, there was nothing to be seen but a helpless flailing of ski-sticks, while the exultant quarry sped on towards the trees. Then the second skier was on his feet again—but it seemed that his chances of overtaking had gone for ever.

It was then that Henry and the other watchers saw something that was to haunt all of them for the rest of their lives. For suddenly, the pursuer was no longer zig-zagging down the mountain in a series of turns, following the other's tracks : instead, the crouched, black figure was coming straight down the precipitous slope like a thunderbolt, a human body aimed like a bullet from a gun. There was a sickening, splintering crash at the moment of collision. Then both were down in the snow—skis, sticks and bodies inextricably tangled. They seemed to be struggling together, as they rolled helplessly down the mountain-side : and then, without warning, they both disappeared.

Spezzi had stopped, and Henry panted up to come abreast

of him. Curtly, Spezzi said to the *carabinieri*, " Tell the others to stay where they are." For the other three skiers, who had watched the chase, motionless, were now starting to move slowly down the mountain.

" Come," said Spezzi to Henry. He led the way over the snow to the spot where the skiers had vanished. As Henry followed, some way behind, he saw that Spezzi was standing quite still, looking down.

" Take care," said the Capitano.

Henry took a tentative step forward, and then froze with horror as he saw that what had appeared to be merely a rolling ridge in the snow was in fact the lip of a deep crevasse that opened at his very feet.

" The Baron ? " he said.

" I fear so," said Spezzi.

Henry stepped cautiously forward to stand beside Spezzi, and looked down. On the snowy floor of the ravine, fifty feet below them, lay two bodies, still and broken. The tall, thin figure of the Baron was spread-eagled face downwards: beside him, on his back, his body twisted grotesquely but his face miraculously unharmed, lay Pietro Vespi.

A shadow fell across the snow beside Spezzi, and Henry looked up to see that Gerda was standing there. Spezzi turned to her, and for once did not seem to resent the fact that his orders had been disobeyed. In a quiet voice, the Capitano said, " Fraulein, can you ever forgive me for what I thought of you ? "

Gerda did not answer, and Henry saw that she was crying.

" Fraulein—" began the Capitano, but Gerda said, very softly, " I am all right, Herr Capitano. They are happy tears."

Henry turned away, and began to ski slowly down the mountain towards Immenfeld.

CHAPTER TWENTY

IT WAS A sombre, chastened group of people who greeted Henry when he eventually got back from Immenfeld that evening. There was no sign of the Knipfers, and Gerda was with Maria-Pia : but everyone else was in the bar, talking in hushed and shocked voices. Emmy was naturally bombarded with questions, to which all she could do was to answer, truthfully, " I don't know any more than you do, except that Henry knew the truth about Pietro this morning. You'll have to wait until he gets back."

" I can't believe it," Roger had said, over and over again. " Pietro, of all people. And to think that he tried to kill us . . ."

" No doubt about it," assented the Colonel, gruffly. " Told us we were going off the *piste*, and that if we kept to the left there was a straight *schuss* down to the tree-path."

" And of course we believed him," Roger added. " We'd only done the run once before, after all, and in quite different conditions. We were going flat out—we'd never have stopped in time. As it was, we were on the edge of the ravine when the Baron shouted . . ."

" And to think of all the things we said about the Baron," put in Jimmy. " I feel like a heel . . ."

" But Pietro . . ." said Caro, in helpless bewilderment. " Emmy, how *could* it have been Pietro . . . ? "

And so the discussion went on, endlessly and in circles. When Henry walked in, there was a dead silence. They were all shocked to see how deadly tired he looked, and how old. He went over to the table where they were all sitting, kissed Emmy, and pulled up a chair.

" I'd like a whisky," he said.

All the men leapt to their feet, and Jimmy beat Roger to the bar by one second. Henry drank, gratefully, and then said, " I suppose you want an explanation. I think you deserve one." He glanced round the table, and then said, " Where's Gerda ? "

Emmy told him, and he nodded. Then he said, " It's a complicated story to tell, but it's very simple really. I suppose you'd like me to start at the beginning."

There was a chorus of assent, and Henry went on : " The key to the whole thing, of course, was the character and career of Fritz Hauser. I dare say you all know by now that the major part of his income came from peddling dope."

They all nodded, and Mrs. Buckfast blushed richly, probably for the first and last time in her life.

" Hauser," Henry continued, " had an easy and prosperous life in Berlin and then in Rome. He was a qualified doctor, and he used his practice as a cover for his real business of selling cocaine to disreputable characters with more money than sense. It was only when his connection with the Caroni case made it too hot for him to continue that he decided to take up smuggling. He was born and brought up in this valley, and he knew very well how perfectly it was situated for smuggling by ski in the winter and by climbers in summer. His first move was to get complete control of this hotel by installing as manager a man who was in his power. This became his headquarters. At first, I think, he only envisaged the possibility of running dope over the Austrian border—he had plenty of ready customers, for he had once practised in Vienna. The genuine holiday-makers were here merely as necessary camouflage. Afterwards, he also got the idea of using some of them to transport the stuff to England for him. But that's something we needn't go into now : fortunately, that end of the operation didn't succeed too well."

Avoiding the embarrassed eyes of Roger and Mrs. Buckfast, he went on quickly. " For the Austrian operation, he needed the services of a first-class skier and climber and he knew from his early recollections of Santa Chiara that the Vespi family was likely to be able to supply one with all the skill, nerve and unscrupulousness he needed. He must have been delighted to find that both the boys, Giulio and Pietro, had inherited from their grandfather not only a reckless physical courage, but also a passion for money which he could easily exploit. This obsession with wealth had skipped a generation, for there was no sign of it in Mario. Anyhow, Hauser chose Giulio—the elder and the more brilliant skier. From the first, I felt certain that Giulio's death was a vitally important feature in this drama. Of course, everyone in the village knew how he made his money, although I don't for a moment suppose that they knew just what an unsavoury trade he was in. Smuggling in these parts is generally regarded as a sport rather than a crime."

"But what made you suspect all this in the beginning?" Jimmy put in. "After all, anyone can have a skiing accident."

"There was a small, nagging inconsistency about the account of his death that worried me," said Henry. He looked at Roger. "I think you know what I mean."

Roger nodded. "The ski-sticks," he said.

"Exactly," said Henry. "One ski was knocked off when Giulio fell, and it obviously careered off by itself and was buried in a snowbank. That's perfectly understandable. But we were also told that Giulio's sticks were never found. Now, apart from the fact that the leather loop round the wrist makes it difficult to lose a ski-stick, it's elementary that anybody who took a fall like that would hang on to his sticks for dear life. No, the sticks must have gone over the brink of the ravine with Giulio. Which means that they were found, by someone. As soon as I heard that Pietro had been the first person to discover his brother's body I knew that he must have found the sticks and hidden them."

"But why on earth should he have done that?" asked Caro.

"That's exactly what I asked myself. The answer is very simple. Ski-sticks are hollow, and you can get an extremely valuable cargo of cocaine into each one. It was an ingenious and foolproof method. Giulio would ski down into Immenfeld, go to one of the ski shops and exchange his sticks for another pair, similarly constructed with a screwtop opening under the leather handle. He was paid, and returned to Santa Chiara for his next consignment."

"Did you get the man in the ski shop?" Roger asked.

"Yes," said Henry, shortly. "Your inquiries were extremely useful. They told me which shop to go to."

"It was that little rat-faced fellow, wasn't it?" said Roger. "He looked scared as hell when I started asking if he ever took orders for specially-made sticks. But I don't see how I helped."

"Emmy made inquiries at both shops," said Henry. "One of them admitted quite openly that you'd been asking about ski-sticks. But rat-face told her you'd gone in to have your skis waxed. That sounded pretty silly to me. I know you always keep your wax in your anorak pocket—and even if you'd forgotten yours, Colonel Buckfast would have had some. What was your idea, by the way? A little free-lance detection?"

Roger looked uncomfortable. "I was in a pretty tricky spot, as you know," he said. "I thought if I could get evidence on Hauser . . ." He stopped, and then said, "I didn't think there was any harm in it."

"But tell us about Pietro," Caro persisted.

"Pietro," said Henry, "was considerably more ruthless than Giulio, and he was also insanely jealous of his brother's money. I would like to think that he climbed down into the ravine in a genuine attempt to help Giulio—but when he saw the broken sticks, and what they contained, everything became clear to him. He took the sticks, as I said, and hid them. He knew that he had a valuable consignment of cocaine in his possession—and he was determined to get the full market price for it. His only trouble was that he did not know how to dispose of it. Giulio had had the sense to keep the details of his expeditions a dead secret. So Pietro resolved to approach Hauser, and get himself taken on as Giulio's successor. In fact, I doubt if he had to bother. My guess is that Hauser came to him with that very proposition. Of course, it was Giulio's death that made Hauser change his plans and stay on in Santa Chiara. He wanted to organise another courier before he left, and Pietro was the obvious person."

" Then why in heaven's name did Pietro kill him ? " the Colonel rasped out.

" And how ? " added Jimmy. " Pietro was with us in the Olympia that evening, and he stayed on there after we left."

" And what about the gun ? " added Caro.

Henry looked at them sadly. " You've got it all wrong," he said. " Pietro didn't kill Fritz Hauser."

" You mean . . . somebody else . . ." Roger began, and then stopped. There was an uneasy silence.

Henry said, " The one thing about Hauser's murder that struck me most forcibly was the fantastic element of chance that would have been involved if anybody on the ski-lift had shot him. Goodness knows, enough of you had motives—and that clouded the issue. I needn't go into details, but at least five of the people on the lift that evening must have been delighted to see Hauser dead. The fact remains, however, that none of you could possibly have known that he would be coming down as you went up. As Gerda so rightly pointed out, the obvious assumption was that he had left the hotel much earlier. The only people in the hotel who definitely knew he would be going down at that hour were the Knipfers, Rossati and Mrs. Buckfast."

" Are you trying to suggest—? " began Mrs. Buckfast, outraged.

Henry held up his hand. " I said, the only people in the hotel. There were two others. The Baron and Mario."

" How did they know ? " Jimmy demanded.

" The Baron had arranged to meet Hauser here at the hotel if he could get to Santa Chiara in time—he was driving up from Innsbruck. Hauser had agreed to postpone his departure until the last possible moment."

" I see," said Jimmy. " And Mario ? "

"Hauser lunched with the Vespis on the day he was killed," said Henry. "He also chatted to Mario in the morning about his plans. It is reasonable to assume that he knew when Hauser would be using the lift."

"But none of those people could have done it," said Jimmy, with a worried frown. "The Baron had only just arrived in the village. The Knipfers were all in the hotel and so was Mrs. Buckfast——"

"The first conclusion that I came to," said Henry, "was that Hauser was not shot on the ski-lift. It followed that he was already dead when he was put into his chair. There was another small piece of evidence that confirmed my point of view. Gerda mentioned that Hauser was swaying in his chair, but that the safety-arm prevented him from falling out. But, according to Rossati, Hauser was so used to the ski-lift that he never used the safety-arm. Obviously it had been put in position to keep his body securely in the chair."

"You mean, then, that he was shot before he left the hotel?" said Caro, in a voice full of horror.

"I considered that possibility," said Henry, "but it wouldn't do. Hauser was seen leaving the hotel both by Fraulein Knipfer and Beppi, the porter. It was too much to suspect them of being in league. No, Hauser was shot at the top of the ski-lift."

In an awe-struck voice, Jimmy said, "Then it must have been Mario . . ."

"Yes," said Henry. "I made up my mind very early on that Mario must be the murderer. All I needed was some conclusive proof, and also a clear idea of the motive."

"Good God," said the Colonel, in a hushed whisper. "Mario . . ."

"But look here," said Roger, "Mario was an old man, and he limped quite badly. You mean to say that he shot Hauser, and then lugged his body to the lift and put it on to a moving chair——?"

"But the chair wasn't moving," said Henry. "If you

remember, the lift broke down. And it was that fact that gave me the proof I needed."

"I don't understand," said Jimmy.

Henry pulled a piece of paper from his pocket. "This," he said, "is a time-table of exactly what happened that evening, which Capitano Spezzi compiled. Taken together with something that Colonel Buckfast said in evidence, it proves conclusively that Mario was lying."

"Something I said?" repeated the Colonel, reddening.

"Yes," said Henry. "You told us that the lift broke down while you were waiting for it."

"That's right," said Jimmy. "I could have told you that. It happened just after we'd bought our tickets."

Henry consulted the paper. "It was five-past six when we all left the Olympia," he said. "Even allowing ten minutes—which is too generous—to get to the ski-lift, Jimmy would have been ready to board it at a quarter past six. Now, if there's a queue, and every chair is taken, six people get on to that lift every minute—I've timed it. Gerda had arrived at the top and was walking up to the hotel before I stopped the lift at a quarter to seven—which means that she must have been in her chair by seventeen minutes past six, and she was the last person to go up. You, Colonel Buckfast, must have been in your chair at six-sixteen. And yet Mario insisted that the breakdown did not occur until seventeen minutes past, and entered the time most carefully in the log book which he kept in his cabin. Allowing for the fact that even electric clocks may vary slightly, I cannot believe that it took you from five-past six to seventeen minutes past to get from the Olympia to the ski-lift."

"The lift broke down just as we reached it," said Caro. "We all had to wait until it started again. It must have stopped just after ten-past."

"Exactly," said Henry. "Which made Mario's timing seven minutes out—which is a long time. Just to make sure, I asked Carlo about it—and although he didn't, unfortunately, log the time of the breakdown, he remembers that it was, in fact, before a quarter past that it happened. There was another odd thing, too. Hauser was seen to leave the hotel at ten-past six. But even allowing for the breakdown, he didn't get on to the lift till sixteen minutes past. It certainly doesn't take six minutes to walk down that path."

"Then what really happened?" demanded the Colonel.

"This," said Henry. "Mario saw Hauser walking down the path at about eleven minutes past. He pulled the fuse himself—he could not risk anyone coming up for the next couple of minutes—and shot Hauser as he reached the platform. Then he put the body on to the chair, and re-started the lift."

"But the gun—how did he get the gun?" asked Jimmy.

"Nothing could have been easier," said Henry. "I always felt sure that Hauser would have shown some concern if the gun had been missing when he packed that morning. It's true that one of our party could have broken into the briefcase at the Olympia, but it would have been an extremely risky business—the lock was quite a solid one, and people were coming and going down that passage all the time. Also, there was my original objection that nobody could have counted on seeing Hauser again. But consider what an opportunity Mario had. Hauser's luggage was lying unattended in his cabin for nearly three hours during the morning. He had all the time he wanted to break open the case and extract the gun before he sent the luggage down."

"I still don't see how you could be absolutely sure," said Jimmy.

"I didn't need to have positive proof," said Henry. "You see, I had worked all this out before I realised that there had been an eye-witness to the murder."

"An eye-witness? But that's impossible," Caro objected. "Everybody was either at the hotel or in the Olympia, and you can't see the ski-lift platform from the hotel, because of the curve in the path."

"Oh, yes, you can," said Henry. "From one bedroom. The top-floor room over the front door. It's high enough to see over the snow-banks of the path."

"Trudi Knipfer's room," said Roger.

"Exactly," said Henry. "She told us she had seen Hauser walking down to the lift. In fact, she saw more than that. She saw the murder. And she made up her mind what she must do about it, which was to keep her mouth shut. She had good reason for disliking Hauser, and she was determined not to give Mario away. I don't think she would have let Franco suffer for the murder—but she wasn't going to say anything until the last possible moment. She is a young woman of considerable character."

"What I don't see," said Jimmy, "is why on earth Mario should have killed Hauser. After all, if his family was making so much money . . ."

"Mario was a good man," said Henry, surprisingly. "He idolised his sons, and according to his own rights, he acted justly. I admit that some of this is guesswork on my part, and with Mario and Pietro both dead I suppose we shall never know exactly what happened. For a start, it's reasonable to assume that Mario blamed Hauser for Giulio's death. It's a nice point whether he was right or not. Certainly, Hauser had involved Giulio in the dope-ring—but my guess is that it was sheer greed for more money that made him set out on that lunatic run. Snow conditions were bad this year, and he couldn't wait until they improved to get his hands on some more cash. I also think that it was only on the day of Giulio's death that Mario discovered just what sort of contraband his son was smuggling. We know that they had a quarrel, and Mario did his utmost to prevent Giulio from attempting the run. The last straw came when Mario discovered that Pietro was being enlisted to take Giulio's place. He determined to put a stop to it at all costs, and the simplest and most direct way he could think of was to kill Fritz Hauser. He took the gun, probably intending to kill Hauser at lunch-time. But when he heard that Hauser was proposing to return to the hotel in the afternoon, he changed his plan."

"What on earth did Trudi Knipfer think when Mario was killed?" Jimmy asked.

Henry sighed. "She thought, of course, that Mario had committed suicide—and she was pretty scathing with me because I hadn't come to the same conclusion. Actually, it's just what I would have thought myself, if it hadn't been for . . ." Henry paused. "In fact," he said, "it was what I had been hoping for. I had no desire at all to arrest the old man. I suppose it was very wrong of me, but I went around the village that morning making it as clear as I could that I suspected Mario. I knew he would hear of it in the Bar Schmidt at lunchtime—and from his wife—and I thought it would give him a way out. As it happened, he chose the more honourable way."

"What do you mean?" asked the Colonel.

"He was very distressed at Franco's arrest," said Henry. "Everybody remarked how ill he was looking, and it's no wonder. So when I came up on the lift after lunch that day, he asked me if he could come and see me in the evening. He was, of course, intending to make a full confession. The thing that finally decided him to do it was a talk with Pietro. We've been told a lot of lies about what was said. The real gist of the conversation, I am sure, was a final appeal from Mario to Pietro to abandon the idea of dope-running, and a flat refusal on Pietro's part. So Mario played his trump card—he told Pietro he was going to confess to the murder, and, incidentally, to tell us the whole story of Giulio and Pietro and the dope-running."

Henry paused, and rubbed the back of his head with his hand. "I don't think Pietro was wholly wicked," he said. "I don't think he would have killed his father just for financial gain. But the Vespis are a law unto themselves, and it may well have seemed to Pietro that it was more merciful to save his father from the agony of trial and sentence. I don't know. In any case, that was probably his excuse to himself for what he did. By now it had become an obsession with him to get hold of the money which was so nearly in his pocket. He had a further consignment of cocaine from Hauser—we found it in his anorak pocket. To Pietro, the money he could get for the cocaine meant escape from the valley, which he hated. It meant escape to make his fortune —you know that he had wild, impracticable dreams of going to America and getting rich. Santa Chiara wasn't big enough for him. Two things stood between him and his crazy ambition. One was the fact that the Immenfeld run was closed by the police : the other was his father's threat to confess. So he decided to kill Mario."

" It's horrible," said Caro. She shuddered.

" How did Pietro get hold of the gun?" Roger asked.

" Mario had kept the gun locked up since Hauser's death," said Henry. " He carried only two keys in his pocket. One was the key to his front door, and the other was the key of the radiogram which Giulio had bought. That is where the gun must have been hidden. But Mario had forgotten that Pietro also had a key to the radiogram. After Mario had left the house on the day he was killed, Rosa found Pietro standing beside the gramophone. He must have just unlocked it, and taken the gun out. It was still unlocked when I saw it the next day."

" But Henry," said Jimmy, " this is all very well, but Pietro couldn't possibly have killed Mario. You and I both saw him off on his way down to the village, and he must have been more than half-way down when Mario was killed. Do you mean he shot him from below the ski-lift ? "

" No," said Henry. " That was the most baffling part of the whole case. When Mario was killed, I had a moment of terrible doubt. I thought I had been wrong about the whole thing. Then I went over the facts of the first murder again, and I decided that I couldn't possibly be mistaken. It *had* to be Mario. That being so, who would want to kill the old man—except his son? Pietro was the only person who had any reason to take drastic measures to prevent Mario from making his confession. And yet, on the face of it, the thing was impossible. He started off from here at half-past five, and arrived at Carlo's hut soon after a quarter to six. A perfectly reasonable time for the run, considering that it was dark."

"There's no way he could have shot Mario," said the Colonel, flatly. "That was good going, even for a first-class skier."

"That was my problem," said Henry, "and I couldn't solve it. So Capitano Spezzi and I decided to give Pietro all the scope we could, and try to trap him. The Immenfeld run was declared open on Saturday. We knew Pietro would make his getaway attempt on Sunday—the only day he would not be missed until the evening, since there is no ski school. We had no real hope of charging him with the murder. And then—this morning—I suddenly realised how he could have done it. It was something that Emmy said."

"The most ridiculous thing," said Emmy. "It was a remark I made about my bottom."

"Your what ? " said the Colonel, turning scarlet.

"My bottom," said Emmy. "After I had my accident. I told Henry that I'd sat down hard on the edge of my ski, and my bottom was as corrugated as one of the pylon platforms.

"I fail to see what interest that can have for the rest of us," said Mrs. Buckfast, coldly.

Henry grinned. "I'd better go back a bit further," he said. "Pietro's plan was highly ingenious. It was designed to give him a complete alibi. The crux of the scheme was a stupid bet that Pietro had taken with some of the other instructors to attempt the Gully early yesterday morning."

"He did it, too," said the Colonel. "I saw his tracks."

"And what has Emmy's bottom got to do with all this ? " Caro demanded.

"Emmy," said Henry, "went down on the lift at nine o'clock on the morning after Mario's murder—before it started to snow. Now just think. Did any of you know that the pylon platforms were made of corrugated iron?"

There was a thoughtful silence. Then Jimmy said, "I've never seen them when they weren't covered in snow."

"Precisely," said Henry. "The snow began about ten o'clock that morning. But at nine o'clock, Emmy saw one of those platforms swept clear of snow. She must have noticed it subconsciously as she came down."

"It was about the third pylon from the top," said Emmy. "I didn't really think about it. I just registered it as odd that the one platform should have been swept."

"But why was it swept?" The Colonel was utterly bewildered. "I don't see what you're driving at."

"It had to be swept," said Henry, "to remove the evidence of footprints on it."

Everybody looked blank, so Henry went on. "This is what Pietro did. He set off from here down Run One, having taken pains that Jimmy and I should see him off, and he drew our attention particularly to the time. As you know, Run One crosses under the lift at the third pylon. Pietro skied as far as that, like the wind—it would take him about a minute. Then he stopped, took off his skis, and climbed the ladder on to the platform. He used the fire broom on the pylon to sweep the snow off, so that his footprints wouldn't show, and he also smashed the bulb in the pylon light—Emmy pointed that out to me, too, and I was too dumb to realise what it meant. Then he hopped a chair— it's difficult, but possible to do from the platform—and rode up to the top again, taking his skis with him, of course. There he shot Mario, put his body on to a chair, and left the gun on his father's lap, knowing that it would either fall off half-way down or else still be there as evidence of suicide when Mario reached the bottom. All that would take him about ten minutes. That gave him five minutes to get back to Carlo's hut."

"Impossible," said the Colonel.

"Not," said Henry, "if he went by the Gully."

There was an incredulous silence. "You mean he did the Gully in the dark?" asked the Colonel at last, in an awe-struck voice.

"Yes," said Henry. "In the dark. It was an extraordinary feat, but then Pietro was an extraordinary skier. He got to the bottom, and established his alibi by talking to Carlo. All that remained in the way of evidence were his ski-tracks in the Gully. Pietro got up early the next morning, and when he found that it hadn't snowed, he climbed just a little way up the mountain, out of sight of the village. Carlo was one of the men who had taken the bet, and I checked with him this morning. Pietro had arranged to make the attempt at a quarter to nine : but when the lads turned up, they found Pietro just completing the run, and they accepted the evidence of his ski tracks as proof that he had done it. He told them that he had had to start earlier in order to get out of the house before his mother woke up, and they believed him without question. Everybody knew Rosa Vespi's feelings about Pietro making the attempt."

"The Gully . . . in the dark," the Colonel repeated, wonderingly.

"It was a counsel of desperation," said Henry. "I can't help admitting that it was extremely bad luck that he didn't get away with it. If the snow had fallen an hour earlier—if Emmy hadn't noticed the pattern on the pylon platform . . . but there it is. Like a fool, however, I didn't put two and two together until this morning, and to make matters worse, I overslept. You can imagine my feelings when I heard that three other people had set off with Pietro to Immenfeld."

He looked at Roger and the Colonel, and smiled. "Unfort-unately," he said, "all your minds worked in the same way. The Immenfeld run was open again, and all four of you—I include Gerda and Pietro—had reasons for wanting to do it alone, and reckoned you could sneak out unobserved if you went later than the other skiers. As far as you two were concerned," he added, "I imagine you were just trying to avoid each other's company. The Colonel wanted to take things slowly, and Roger wanted to race. Neither of you wished to say openly that you were bored with each other, and it had become an accepted thing that you should ski together. Am I right?"

The Colonel went deep purple, and murmured something unintelligible about not being as young as he was. Roger looked at his feet, and said, "Yes, you're quite right. I'm sorry, sir," he added, to the Colonel. "You see, I'm trying to work my speed up. I thought I might try to get into a team of some sort one day."

"Quite right, too," said the Colonel. "Apologise. Must have been an old bore for you to ski with." They beamed at each other.

"As for Gerda," Henry went on, "she, too, had reasons of her own for wanting to get away from Santa Chiara—personal reasons. I think that it is likely that she . . . well, it doesn't matter now. The fact remains that you all turned up at the start of the run at the same time, and so did Pietro. He could hardly refuse to go with you, though to do him credit, he did try to prevent you from going. But you can see how embarrassing your presence was to him. This wasn't just a routine smuggling run. With Hauser dead, that little racket would have dried up anyway. No, Pietro was planning to disappear—permanently. He had a murder on his hands and a small fortune in illicit dope in his pockets—and he was on his way to stage his own death."

"Good heavens," said the Colonel.

"It was to have been a repetition of Giulio's, of course," said Henry, "with a broken ski or so as evidence—but no body. That wouldn't be over-surprising. Sometimes the victims are buried in snow, and the bodies aren't found until the spring."

"How do you know all this?" asked Roger. He sounded very shaken indeed.

"From your friend at the ski shop in Immenfeld," said Henry. "It didn't take much persuasion to make him tell us the whole story. Pietro had arranged the plan with him by telephone. Pietro would stage the accident on the dangerous slope—then walk down into the trees, where rat-face was to be waiting with the money for the dope, and a nice set of false papers. He had his finger in a lot of nasty rackets, that chap. Of course, it wouldn't have worked out like that. Capitano Spezzi had a very efficient reception committee waiting in Immenfeld. And then I heard that all four of you had set off together. Pietro was in a desperate position, and I guessed he wouldn't abandon his plan at that stage. There was only one answer—a tragic accident involving all four of you, with only three bodies to be found. Not a very nice thought."

"So if the Baron hadn't caught up with them in time . . ." Caro's voice quavered, and she grasped Roger's hand.

"The Baron," said Henry, slowly, "was a very brave man indeed. He not only saved three lives to-day. He deliberately sacrificed his own."

"So that Pietro wouldn't escape . . ." said Jimmy.

Henry looked down. "I think that was the reason," he said.

EPILOGUE

It was four days later. Henry and Maria-Pia were sitting in the sunshine on the balcony of her suite. Below them, they could see the children, Hansi and Lotte, pelting each other with snowballs under the benevolent eye of Emmy, who was sunning herself on a bench outside the hotel, and pretending to read a magazine.

"So," said Maria-Pia, "you leave this afternoon. And so do we. You go back to your life in London, and I . . ." She stopped, and gazed at the children playing below.

"What will you do ?" Henry asked gently.

"I asked you to solve my problems for me," said Maria-Pia, slowly. "That was a foolish thing to do. Nobody can solve problems for other people."

"I know," said Henry.

"I have been very wicked," said Maria-Pia, simply, "and this terrible thing has happened to me because I deserved it. I was not worthy of happiness, and now I have lost the chance of it for ever. That is just."

There was a moment of silence, and then Henry said, "Your husband was a remarkable man, Maria-Pia. I told you once that he loved you to distraction. I would go further. I think he loved you more than life."

"What do you mean ?"

"Just this," said Henry. "He knew that Immenfeld was crowded with policemen—Pietro could not have escaped. Hermann did what I asked him to—and did it magnificently —in warning the three others of their danger. What he did after that was . . . was his own affair."

Maria-Pia didn't answer, but her eyes filled with tears.

"Nobody would expect you to get over it quickly," Henry went on, "but in time I think you will be happy again. I think that is what Hermann wanted."

There was a long pause, and then Maria-Pia said, "You know that I am taking Rosa and Maria Vespi back to Innsbruck with me?"

"Yes," said Henry. "I think it's a wonderful thing you are doing. Wonderful and typical."

Maria-Pia gave him a sad little smile. "I had to find someone to look after the children now that I have lost Gerda," she said. "I shall train Maria myself. She will make a good Nanny. And Rosa is going to be my house-keeper."

Henry smiled. "Gerda is out skiing with the gallant Capitano again, I presume?" he said.

"Yes," said Maria-Pia. "She has taken a job at the Olympia, you know." She smiled again, and there was something of her old sparkle in her voice as she said, "I think it's very suitable. I'm sure they'll be very happy."

"I hope so," said Henry. "Poor old Spezzi. He must have suffered the tortures of the damned when he thought Gerda was guilty. I'm not surprised she tried to run away."

"She was really trying to slip over the border into Austria and do a bunk, was she?" said Maria-Pia, inelegantly.

"I'm certain she was," said Henry, "though of course I haven't given her a hint that such a thing had occurred to me. It was pretty grim for her. She'd lost her job, and the man she was in love with thought she was a double murder-ess. At one time, when Franco was arrested, she was so desperate that she tried to put an end to everything by con-fessing to the murder herself. Fortunately, I nipped that in the bud."

"Thank goodness you did," said Maria-Pia. "That would have been really awful."

"She wanted to do it for your sake," said Henry. "She's very fond of you, you know."

Maria-Pia opened her big brown eyes very wide. "Good-ness," she said, "I'd no idea ..."

"We all are," said Henry. He took her hand for a moment, and suddenly kissed it. Then, rather red in the face, he walked quickly out of the room and down the stairs.

In the hall, he met Trudi Knipfer. Unsmilingly, she said, " I have been meaning to talk to you, Herr Tibbett. I owe you an apology."

Henry grinned. " Officially, Fraulein," he said, " I am naturally very angry with you for withholding vital evidence."

Trudi looked him in the eyes. " Would you have given the old man away ? " she demanded. " Would you—if you'd hated Fritz Hauser as much as I did ? "

" That's a very difficult question to answer," said Henry. " I'll ask you one, instead. Why were you still prepared to marry him, if you felt like that ? "

" My father wished it," said Trudi, shortly.

" Why ? " asked Henry.

Trudi hesitated for a moment. " He thought—" she began, but a brusque voice interrupted from the terrace.

" Trudi ! My pipe is in my room ! "

" Yes, Papa," said Trudi. And she was gone.

" And that," thought Henry, " is a small mystery which will never be solved. Oh, well . . ."

He went into the bar. Roger was sitting there alone, drinking coffee.

" Nice to see a friendly face," he remarked to Henry. " All the others are packing."

" I came," said Henry, " to give you this. I thought you might want it."

He pulled Roger's statement out of his pocket.

" I should burn it, if I were you," he added. " I don't think you or Caro will want to be reminded of it again. Officially, of course, I know nothing about it and never did."

He left the paper on the table, and walked out quickly before Roger could say a word.

Outside in the sunshine, Emmy put down her magazine and said, " Everything packed and ready ? "

"All done," said Henry. He sat down on the bench beside her. "How does the ankle feel to-day?"

"Oh, much better," she said. "I can't put any weight on it yet, though. Even if we were staying on here, I don't suppose I could ski again inside a month. But next year . . ."

Henry looked at her, his eyebrows raised. "You want to come again next year? After all that's happened?"

"Of course I do. We'll take our holiday in January, and have a glorious fortnight's skiing with no murders, and I'll be doing parallel cristianias—you'll see." She suddenly gave him an anxious look, and added, in a different tone, "You do want to come again, don't you? I mean—you do like skiing?"

"I hate it," said Henry, cheerfully, "but I know very well I'll be back next year and the year after and every year for as long as we can afford it. It's as bad as a dose of Hauser's cocaine."

They sat in silence for a few minutes, gazing out over the sunlit beauty of the valley. Then Henry was recalled to reality by a voice at his elbow.

"Signor Tibbett."

He turned, to see Rossati standing there. In the proprietor's hand was a large piece of paper.

"Signor Tibbett," he said, "It has been a pleasure and an honour to have you at my little hotel. I trust that all these unpleasant events will not turn you against the Bella Vista, for I should be so happy if you came again next year. Next year you will see changes. I am going to redecorate the bar, and I shall engage a little band for dancing." His eyes grew dreamy. "I shall refurnish the residents' sitting-room," he went on, "and all the bedrooms. I shall install two more bathrooms and hold tea-dances every Thursday. I shall engage a chef and have charcoal grill in the dining-room. My hotel will be the finest in all Italy . . . my very own hotel . . . Signor Tibbett "—his voice trembled with the ecstasy of the moment—" Signor Tibbett, may I present you with your bill?"